Unlucky Star

Pamela Jameson

ISBN: 1-4140-2391-X (e-book)
ISBN: 1-4140-2390-1 (Paperback)

Library of Congress Control Number: 2003098152

This book is printed on acid free paper.

Printed in the United States of America
Bloomington, IN

Cover photo & art copyright 2003 www.clipart.com

1stBooks - rev. 01/22/04

For Kaiulani

"Conceive how this must tell upon the nerves in the islands where the number of dead already so far exceeds that of the living, and the dead multiply and the living dwindle at so swift a rate. Conceive how the remnant huddles about the embers of the fire of life; even as old Red Indians, deserted on the march and in the snow, the kindly tribe all gone, the last flame expiring, and the night around populous with wolves."

Robert Louis Stevenson
"In The South Seas"

Chapter One

Mama Nui, also known as Princess Ruth, clapped her hands together at the sight of the new baby princess, Kaiulani, cradled in her nurse's arms.

"Thank heaven it's a girl!" she cried out in Hawaiian, the only language she would ever speak in public. "A Princess, a real Princess!" she kissed the infant's cheeks.

"Girls manage much better, don't they, sweetheart," she cooed to the baby. "And they're more sensible, too," Mama Nui proclaimed to the room at large.

"Nonsense!" Princess Likelike growled, tired and worn out from her long labor the day before and feeling stifled by the sultry mid-October afternoon. "A boy would do just as well."

"And girls are smarter, too, you know! It's almost always true!" Mama Nui sang out as she lifted the newborn high in the air. "Everyone wait and see! I am giving this angel her own estate, her very own, and she will do so well for herself, you'll all see!" Resting her cheek against the top of Kaiulani's warm head she inhaled the sweet, delicious smell. "Yes, baby." Tiny fingers fluttered over her massive face. "You will be a comfort to us all."

"Heaven knows we need it," Likelike's sister, Princess Liliuokalani, sighed.

"Oh, why don't you just speak English, Ruth?!" Likelike complained, thinking how unfair it was that she had to put up with the dowager's bossy moods and frequent flashes of temper. Just because she was rich - well, what of it? She also happened to be one of the most pushy and loudest women around. And, at more than six feet and close to 400 pounds, she took up more space than anyone Likelike had ever known.

"Never," Mama Nui said pleasantly, her bass voice rumbling out like thunder. "Why should I? Let them speak Hawaiian. Who was here first? And what do you think those *haoles* mean to me? Less than nothing, that's what."

She spoke confidentially to the baby. "They are very rude, to begin with, and they move much too fast, all hunched and bundled up together like little rabbits." She looked over at the new mother. "You know it is true," she said sternly. "They rush around all the damn time, going nowhere at all, making noise and trouble while they do it."

One of the ladies in attendance laughed at the notion.

"And their so-called 'singing' - pah! It sounds just like little birds being slaughtered. Oh, yes, it does!" Mama Nui handed the baby back to her nurse, then cried out abruptly in a shrill, painfully accurate imitation of a bad church choir.

"Oooo, oooo!" She flapped her huge arms about like wings. "Like little *o-o* birds being plucked for their feathers!"

"Be careful," the nurse, Nahini, giggled. "You will give somebody ideas about how to make capes out of the *haoles*, now."

Princess Ruth shot her a glance that silenced her at once. The huge woman shrugged her shoulders, then rolled them slowly, one at a time, like individual hills. "Those *haoles* have no real music in them. Only fits and starts of squeaking, scurrying all over like little mice."

Likelike, who had been listening with disapproval, was suddenly struck by a vision of her husband, Archibald Cleghorn, with his thin build, fine bones and frequently pursed-up mouth. He did look at times like a rabbit or a mouse. Except, of course, when he was angry. In spite of herself, she laughed.

Mama Nui grinned at Likelike. A generous smile lit up her ravaged old face and pushed her nose even flatter against her cheeks so that she looked like she could see in all directions at once, to infinity. She patted Likelike's hand and indicated the wriggling baby.

"Your lovely daughter agrees with me. See, she is trying to dance the hula, to honor her Hawaiian ancestors."

They laughed together at Kaiulani's wild writhing. Mama Nui touched the child's forehead and she at once calmed down. Then, in the odd way that babies can have of suddenly appearing to focus, Kaiulani seemed to look right into the eyes of her towering godmother. Then the baby's face exploded into a bright smile and Mama Nui returned the grin.

* * * * * * * * * * * * * * * * * * * *

The architecture that clustered along the dirt roads of Old Honolulu was a hodgepodge of styles and designs. Traditional Hawaiian shacks nestled beside stiff little wooden frame houses and sprawled out next to grim Puritanical churches, complete with sharp spires that duplicated almost exactly their prototypes back in New England. Picket fences, some already ragged and splintered, stood rigid in straight little lines or trailed at length over dusty hills and around makeshift storefronts.

The Bishop & Company Bank was a heavy stone building with at least a dozen, Gothic-style, triple frame windows on each side, and two more thrown in for good measure above the front door. A short cement sidewalk went up to the entrance, then reached across both walkways to exactly the length of the building and not one centimeter more. The grass thatched huts looked shabby and vulnerable next to the new, one and two frame wooden buildings, although many of these were already weathered and washed out from baking in the relentless sun.

Some of the older thatched houses had been weirdly "improved" with jarring additions such as irregular glass windows which seemed totally out of place and looked like strange, staring eyes. A few of the huts had spindly porches, patched together with palm trees to serve as awkward, improvised pillars. There was a powerful sense of uneasy contrast and combination, as if the rich family of the groom and the poorer family of the bride had arrived for the wedding all at wrong and different times and now everyone had to figure out their own places to stay.

* * * * * * * * * * * * * * * * * * * *

On the ride back home with Emelia, her companion, Princess Ruth Keelikolani looked out the window of the carriage and shook her head when she saw an elderly Hawaiian couple out on their tiny *lanai* working to repair an ancient fishing net. The man and woman, frail but handsome, their skin dark as burnished copper, worked methodically, rhythmically, in the unhurried manner of the Hawaiians.

"Ah, Emelia," Ruth said to the petite, half-French, half-Hawaiian woman beside her. "This used to be a very fine place, this Honolulu. You can't imagine how fine." She shifted her great weight over to one side. Emelia tucked small, bright yellow pillows back into place around the Princess' massive form.

"Did you know my great-grandfather was king of Hawaii when Captain Cook landed?" Princess Ruth smiled for an instant, then scowled.

"Pah! Captain Crook is more like it! My first husband died of the smallpox brought over by those so-called 'civilized' *haoles*. She crooned her husband's name softly, with great tenderness. "Leleiokolu. Only 22. Oh, how we loved each other then, back when Hawaii was beautiful."

"They killed my babies." Her voice turned hard. "With their dysentery and their damned measles."

"One, two, three." She held up fingers and shook her head. "Don't tell me about their 'improvements,'" she warned. "Progress? Pah. All from those stupid *haoles'* diseases, four in a row I lost, and each one taking my heart every time."

The old Princess sang low and plaintively in Hawaiian. "*Ua ohi pakahi ia aku nei e ka po.*" "The night has taken them one by one." Ruth wiped away tears as Emelia patted her hand.

"We think we can bear only so much sorrow, Emelia. Then more sorrow comes. Our hearts were made to love and break, and then to love and break again."

"So, Captain Crook 'discovered' our islands, did he? From what I've heard he couldn't discover the nose in front of his face. Oh, look, Emelia!" Ruth leaned dangerously over to one side of the carriage to wave to a group of native dancers who stood holding out *leis*. "It's the *hula* dancers we met last Sunday in the park!"

"*Mahalo's*" and "*Aloha Nui's*" flew back and forth as the cluster of men and women wearing traditional *tapa* skirts surrounded the carriage.

Leis landed in Ruth and Emelia's laps and the scents of ginger and jasmine warmed the air. "Ah," Mama Nui exclaimed with pleasure. "Emelia, please remember to invite them to our next party."

Ruth called out good-bys as they drove on. "The king will be proud to see such devoted performers." She looked sidelong at her companion. "And I shall have the great satisfaction of seeing the *haoles* not know where to look when our dancers undulate in sacred prayer."

At last Emelia laughed.

"Well, perhaps you can tell me," - Ruth was indignant, - "Why on earth these *haoles* are so absolutely shameless as they steal our land and profits from us, yet become silent and ashamed at the sight of a little *aloha*, at the slightest glimpse of a healthy, beautiful body?"

Emelia shrugged and plumped up another pillow.

"I bet it is not like that in France, eh? Only the Americans and the English are so crabby, looking all the time like they just swallowed something sour. I will never speak English, though I can, of course, and perfectly well, too, never worry. It is so—ugly - unmusical—so breathless. It makes them look like they have not relieved themselves in days."

"*Oui, c'est vrai*," Emelia agreed, patting Mama Nui's broad arm. "Like someone has tied them up in knots; their little mouths, especially."

"I am giving to Princess Kaiulani, my godchild, the Ainahau estate, Emelia. 'Land of cool breezes,' the *haoles* are calling it now; probably because they can't pronounce 'Ainahau.' That ridiculous father of hers will try to turn it into one of those horrible, English-style gardens, all clipped and trimmed and pruned." Ruth scoffed. "And her flighty Mama will no doubt insist on having an endless number of those dreadful "teas" and "socials," as she calls them, with far too many *haoles* for my taste. Foolish and stubborn, that young woman. A terrible combination, those two."

The old Princess' eyes lit up like the flames of Pele's wrath. "But this Kaiulani - oh, she will be something else! She is very clever, Emelia, I could tell that right away. A real fighter, too! She will do everything in her power to restore Hawaii to the Hawaiians! Kaiulani will be the finest queen Hawaii has ever known!"

The carriage lurched to a halt and Emelia began to stuff the small pillows into a large, embroidered bag.

"You'll see," Ruth said. "They'll all see. Kaiulani will inspire us all. I feel it in my bones, Emelia. She will not fail."

Princess Ruth shifted her cumbersome bulk in an effort to rise, then groaned and sank back again to rest. She fanned herself with a tiny lace fan she kept tied to her wrist.

"Don't get me wrong. Her father is not entirely without feeling, even though he is a *haole*. Do you know, Emelia, one of those business friends of his, of Cleghorn's, tried to tell me that I needed 'advice!?' 'For your land dealings,' he said! That Theo Davies, it was, the tall red head. I need advice!? Doesn't he know I just sold 10,500 acres on Kauai for $27,000?! At least he must know I am the wealthiest woman in these islands! Archie tells him everything, I've heard; so I know he must know that." She considered for a moment. "Do you think this Davies wants to buy something from me?"

Emelia shrugged.

"I pretended I couldn't understand him, which really isn't that far from the truth. Trying to understand a haole is like trying to dance with the moon."

* * * * * * * * * * * * * * * * * * *

When Princess Victoria Lunalilo Kaiulani was born they say that rainbows shimmered briefly but brilliantly throughout all the Islands of Hawaii. Her godfather, King David Kalakaua, ordered a royal gun salute and five hundred banyan trees were planted in her honor. The bells of Hawaii rang out for days to welcome her.

Vast changes had taken place in Hawaii in the hundred years before Kaiulani's birth, from the time the Westerners came to rip open the insular world of the Islands. Most of these changes began in 1778 when Captain Cook and his crew, the bulk of them diseased and murderous convicts shipping out to sea to avoid long sentences in jail, landed on Kauai off the far Waimea shores.

Because the Hawaiian Islands are farther away from any body of land than anywhere else in the world, when the Hawaiians had visitors, it was a very exciting event, especially for the visitors. The native people were inclined to take such things in stride, with their easy-going attitude of "wait and see." "*Mai ho'a'ano aku o loa'a I ka niho,*" they liked to say. "Do not stir up the water which is tranquil."

Long before Captain Cook and his rough crew arrived, several nations had marked Hawaii as their own. France, Russia, England, Spain, Germany and Japan had all staked claims. Each had planted first their anchors and then their flags, at least once or twice. They dug their banners into Hawaii's soft, sandy beaches, the brash colors looking harsh and out-of-place until they began to fade in the tropical sun. And the self-proclaimed 'conquerors' made long, tedious speeches about how their kings or queens or emperors were now the official, mighty and rightful rulers of the land.

The foreigners were quite full of themselves, as they had come from such a long way away and were not used to such mild weather and so much sun. Most of them entertained the notion that the Hawaiians thought they were gods. This was all because of their big, unwieldy ships; their pale, washed-out skin; and their sharp iron knives, which cut so much better and faster than wood. Among themselves, the Hawaiians felt sorry for the fish-bellied people with their pinched, blinking eyes and cracked, dry lips. But they were a kind race and did not let on to the mild revulsion they felt at the visitors' unpleasant odors, which were something like *tapa* cloth left out in many rains, or pig meat too long in the sun. They watched their visitors' frantic activities with polite attention, for a while, but soon slipped away from these overwrought, noisy people to swim again or fish or make love in the sun.

Eventually, the visitors became homesick and left; or went crazy with "rock fever;" or died. The handful that stayed began to slow down and relax into "island-style." They learned to give themselves over to the nature and beauty all around them and became, in time, if not really Hawaiian, then half or a quarter Hawaiian, maybe; and were often the parents of half-Hawaiian offspring. Some even remained to raise their children and love their common-law, native wives.

The Hawaiians' name for these newcomers was "*ha'oles*" which meant "without breath." The foreigners were called this because they spoke and breathed in a tight, gasping way, like fish dying on the shore, and they seemed to be incapable of making most of the gentle, flute like sounds of the language. The Hawaiians tried to encourage them, and to think of ways to reassure these perpetually anxious people. They hoped to make life more comfortable for their worried new friends, who often could not swim or even speak without engaging in a constant struggle with both the water and the air.

After some of these Westerners came to stay, many changes took place in Hawaii in a very short time. The ancient system of *kapu*, - or *tapu*, or tabu, or taboo, - was destroyed soon after the Westerners arrived. The foreigners believed this was a great success that was all of their own doing. They never understood that the *kapu* really had been broken because the Chiefess Kaahumanu had always liked bananas.

This was one of the many stories that Mama Nui loved to tell, and she told it often when Kaiulani was a small child.

* * * * * * * * * * * * * * * * * * * *

The Story of the Great Queen Kaahumanu

Queen Kaahumanu, one of the many beautiful and strong women of Hawaii, was the favorite wife of the five wives of King Kamehameha II. She was also the first female lawmaker to officially rule with her husband. Kaahumana could nullify any of the king's acts, just as he could hers. She was so respected by her people that, after the king's death, she was elevated to the high position of Kuhina-Nui, joint ruler of all the land, with full power of veto, exactly like the king.

All this was before the Westerners came and told the Hawaiians that they should be ashamed of being ruled by a woman. The English, in particular, conveniently ignoring the fact of their own queens, were strident in encouraging the people to "throw off the yoke of female tyranny." So, soon after the haoles came, the office of Kuhina-Nui was abolished.

Queen Kaahumanu weighed about three hundred and fifty pounds and stood six feet, three inches tall. The beautiful people then were toned, tanned and large because they spent hours every day climbing, swimming and running. The most sought-after women were six feet or more, and weighed between three and four hundred pounds. They boated, surfed, fished and practically lived in the water, and were almost as strong as the men.

Kaahumanu, who was just as fierce, independent and strong willed as her husband, had several love affairs. Frustrated that he did not have her all to himself, the king declared her body kapu. And, although Kaahumanu was very sad when a chieftain lover she had cared for paid for their nights of joy with his life, she continued to love whom she would. She had a deep and abiding affection for her husband, as did he for her, but she refused to be false to her own nature. The Queen never bore any children, royal or otherwise, but she did manage to control her husband's sons, as she had their father before them, for years after the great king had passed.

When her beloved husband died, the Queen in her terrible grief took up his spear and enfolded herself in his warrior's cloak, placing his yellow-feathered helmet on her head. She liked the way these things fit her. So, when Kaahumanu went to greet young Liholiho, the king's son who was heir to the throne, the new widow was dressed for full battle and honors.

A quiet, respectful young man, Liholiho observed his impressive stepmother in silence. She called him "O Divine One", just as she should, when she told him of his father's wish for her to rule as the Vice-King, or Kuhina-Nui, and for Liholiho and his retainers to accept her. Since Liholiho was really not too sure about what he had to do to be in charge, the new, fledgling King was actually grateful and happy to have an insider to turn to. Secretly, in fact, he did not mind being told what to do.

Now, Liholiho's mama, Queen Keopuolani, was another powerful woman, also of a very good size. And it happened that Queen Keopuolani had an abiding fondness for pork, which the kapu had forbidden women to eat. By an odd coincidence, Queen Kaahumanu liked pork, too. Both women, as it turned out, shared a taste for bananas, which were also forbidden to them by law. Neither had ever cared much for coconuts, so the kapu on those was no problem.

The penalty for breaking kapu was severe punishment or even death. Neither Kaahumanu nor Keopuolani had any wish to die; they only wanted to eat what they liked, when and where they liked it. The queens soon became good friends and, in sharing their secrets as *close friends do, discovered their common, thwarted desires. They agreed that the kapu that kept women from eating with men was entirely unreasonable. On top of everything else, it meant the extra work of using two separate sets of dishes for every occasion at all times. So they talked together some more about what they knew of Liholiho, son of one, co-ruler of the other.*

One day, in a most offhand manner, Kaahumanu casually but slowly ate a banana in the presence of her stepson, the king, when it was only the two of them, alone. Although Liholiho may have been terribly shocked by her action, he was first of all a civil young man and tactfully chose to ignore this offense. After all, his mother was a queen, too, and she had brought him up to be courteous and polite to his elders an, to women. A few weeks later his own mother just happened to be lunching on Liholiho's favorite foods, pineapple and poi, when her son the king came to see her. She sweetly invited the king to sit with her and partake. He was cordial, of course, but refused and did not stay long at his mother's that day.

One week later Kaahumanu and Keopuolani were sharing a queenly feast when Liholiho happened to stroll by. The women waved, he smiled and waved back, and then he realized with breathless surprise that his younger brother, a boy of ten, was seated at the queens' table, his mouth quite full of mashed bananas. Liholiho tactfully looked away. A few days after that, he happened upon them again all eating together. Queen Keopuolani delicately wiped a bit of taro from her mouth and smiled tenderly at her son.

"Oh, my," Keopuolani said loudly to her friend, Kaahumanu, licking her fingers again, "Never have I tasted such delicious poi!" Liholiho sighed a little as he watched Keopuolani feed a choice morsel of pork to Kaahumanu, who opened her mouth wide like a bird. Liholiho's stomach growled and abruptly he turned away, feeling unexpectedly cross.

Several days of meals and snacks followed in this fashion. Liholiho remained aloof, while the Queens smiled and cooed at him and remained quite steady on their course.

Then came a large public celebration in honor of an excellent catch of squid. Liholiho, who was unaccustomed to drinking, had already indulged in several cups of awa brew before he wandered over to the women's area where his mother and stepmother sat laughing and eating. The king, a little unsteady, laughed along with them, and then absent-mindedly began to pick at their food. Before he knew it he was nibbling away at treats, and his mother had even fed him a little bite of banana.

A shocked sound, like bees buzzing or lava hissing, spread throughout the crowd. A deep silence fell, but the king was so busy eating that he didn't notice at first. Then the silence shook him out of his trance. Liholiho slowly turned to face the people who stared at him with wide-open eyes. Then, with a sheepish look, the king held up a slice of pineapple in one hand and a piece of roast pork in the other. Impulsively, joyfully, he stuffed them into his mouth. A gasp rose from the crowd. Then, one man stood and another and another, all raising their cups to salute their king. One brave husband boldly stepped out from the men's enclave to sit down with the women, right next to his wife. He kissed her full on the lips and then began to eat. Soon, others followed his lead.

Later that evening, when Liholiho came to from his hangover, he realized that something important had changed, though he couldn't remember exactly what, or how it had happened. The Hawaiians, however, remembered. It was as if the people had been waiting a long time for the right moment to come so they could tear down the kapus. That very same night several of the men, full of awa and courage, burned down one of the heiahus, the ancient places where the gods had been worshipped. For many nights after that, heiahus were destroyed, again and again. The kapus would never be the same.

* * * * * * * * * * * * * * * * * * *

During the time of Queen Kaahumanu, missionaries had been arriving in droves to preach the magic of their "god in a box," for that is how the Hawaiians perceived the great mystery of the haoles' black book, the Bible.

The Queen at first refused to look at, never mind talk to, the scrawny, impudent people who always seemed angry or ashamed. Later, when she discovered how they could blush, the bright blood turning their pale faces rosy and making them draw in their breath like little fishes, she thrilled in finding ways to "color them up." Her favorite method was to visit them at their houses just after she had taken a long swim, wearing her own bronze skin and nothing else, and watch with delight as their eyes flickered all around like crazy birds unable to land.

One of the missionary's wives, who was smarter than most of the rest and had a lovely, soothing voice, began to read stories to the Queen about the god in a box. So charmed was Kaahumanu by this voice which flowed like an easy river that she listened, first for hours and then for days. After some time of being cajoled by these loving, soft sounds, Kaahumanu agreed to cover her ample body with clothes. She wore clothes when she married the handsome king of Kauai, and then wore them again just a few weeks later when she married his handsome son. Soon after that, she sent one of her soldiers to rule Kauai and paraded both of her handsome husbands in a carriage as they rode together to go to church, all of them wearing clothes.

* * * * * * * * * * * * * * * * * * * *

Mama Nui never tired of telling Kaiulani these stories about the history of Hawaii and the people who had come before her. She told her about Kinau, the brave woman who had helped enforce the laws that Hawaii hadn't needed until the Westerners came.

* * * * * * * * * * * * * * * * * * * *

The Story of Kamamalu, the Last Kuhina-Nui

Kinau, another wife of King Kamehahameha, succeeded Kaahumanu as Kuhina-Nui. Like Kaahumanu before her, Kinau, too, had learned to read and write. She tried hard to protect her people from the drunkenness, robbery, murder and sorrow that followed in the path of those truly evil spirits from the west, - brandy, whiskey and rum.

A champion of education, Kinau made it mandatory for children to go to school and encouraged adults to learn as well. There were many arguments between her and the new, very young king, Kauikeouli, who had foreign advisers that constantly whispered in his ears to tell him that the power of the monarch had been compromised by the Kuhina-Nui's meddling. Kauikeouli decided he had no time for an old woman from another age. So he created a council of chiefs, thereby dividing the monarchy's power again and again, making Hawaii weaker each time.

Kinau's infant daughter, Victoria Kamamalu, was the next and last Kuhina-Nui. While Kamamalu was coming of age, Kinau's half sister served in her stead. Out of a desire to make everything equal, this sister had opened Hawaii to other religions. So the earliest missionaries reluctantly had to make room for the Mormons and the Catholics and others.

Kamamalu, who was beautiful, mysterious and sad, grew up very lonely. She was smart and hard working, but the judgment of her heart was not wise. She fell in love with a married auctioneer, an Englishman named Monsarrat. The king, who did not approve, forced Kamamalu to sign papers banishing her love from the Islands forever. Soon after that, she died of a broken heart at the tender age of twenty-eight.

* * * * * * * * * * * * * * * * * * *

Another event that changed Hawaii forever was the Great *Mahele*, the dividing up of the land. This was another story that Mama Nui told Kaiulani over and over again.

* * * * * * * * * * * * * * * * * * *

The Story of the Great Mahele

Before the Westerners came, bringing their rules and laws of ownership and possession, the land was there to support the community. The people were there to do and care for each other, as relatives or lovers or by gifts of "hanai," the common practice of adopting children or even parents. Hanai was a tradition that worked very well, like most of the Hawaiians' systems of sharing. In those days, children could have many parents; they were often given over as infants to the care of others, freely and with aloha.

Soon after the Westerners landed the chiefs were forced to levy high taxes on their people, so that they could buy the new western goods that began to flood into their country. Before this, the people had paid the chiefs in trade, or with the fruits of their labor, like pigs, poi, potatoes, fish, hogs and squash. The women contributed the fine tapa cloth and baskets that they alone were allowed to weave. But by 1850 the pressure had increased on the chiefs and the people, too, as they all were taught again and again, (in an orderly fashion, of course), that they needed to own and buy more and more to be happy.

So the chiefs decreed that all of the taxes must be paid only in silver or gold. But the kanakas, the common people of the country, had no money; they had no silver, they had no gold. They had only their pigs and poi and squash, and even these were beginning to go fast as they tried to feed the rapidly increasing population of Westerners.

And so the young kanaka women began to come to the cities, to Lahina and Honolulu, to trade their bodies to the foreigners for printed cloths and coins. Accustomed to giving their affections freely and of their own will, the women saw nothing wrong in this exchange. But when the missionaries and the missionaries' wives explained to them that they had committed evil sins, they saw themselves through others eyes and were ashamed. They also were frightened, for they still had no money to pay taxes and back home in the country their families were still starving and begging for their help.

In 1848, The Great Mahele divided the Hawaiians and their land for the first time. And, by this time, the king and the chiefs were all under great pressure from the foreign powers who now "owned" the majority of the businesses and most of the land in Hawaii; at least according to themselves and their own systems. These foreigners wanted badly for the king to recognize them, to make them legitimate and official. This was not so much for them selves, they explained, but mostly so that the western powers would be able to respect the Hawaiians; and in this way the common people of Hawaii would be protected from the threat of chiefly tyranny.

By now, the chiefs were desperate to find a way to pay back all the money that the foreigners said they owed them for "improving" and "rescuing" their own lands. Therefore, shaking his head in dismay, the king divided up the world that had been Hawaii into hundreds of small pieces. Unlike the starfish, however, which regenerates itself when it is wounded, Hawaii never came back together again.

And the Hawaiian people died out at an appalling rate. Only now there was no place to bury them that did not cost money, or have to be given to them out of the Westerners' great 'charity'; or else leased to them; at a good rate, of course. Progress and civilization were truly underway in this once primitive land. So why, then, did the people long for the former days of 'tyranny' by the chiefs ands chiefesses, when the land nurtured them, and they could die and be buried for free? When there were more living Hawaiians than Hawaiian ghosts?

* * * * * * * * * * * * * * * * * * *

These were the stories Mama Nui told Kaiulani, again and again.

And while the Hawaiian people became ghosts the sugar industry increased by 10,000%. And many of the missionaries from America, Britain and France built tidy empires of their own.

Four-fifths of the Hawaiian population was destroyed in less than a hundred years, struck down by the foreigners' gifts of influenza, cholera, venereal disease and leprosy. In the 100 years before Kaiulani was born, the native Hawaiian population went from four million to 40,000 left. This number was insufficient, of course, for the tremendous new needs for labor, so workers were brought in from China, Portugal and Japan. And the viruses, which had been killing the Hawaiians, mutated into even more exotic and complicated strains.

The Westerners had many explanations for the uncanny demise of the Hawaiians. They blamed "*awa*," the mild herbal intoxicant drink, for the terrible dissipation of the people, conveniently forgetting about the whiskey and other lethal foreign spirits they had brought over on the boat with them, which they often paid as wages to the people for working on their own land. "Pagan" religion was blamed, too. Many of the missionary settlers were sure that all these "reckless barbarians" needed was a strong dose of Christianity, or Catholicism, or their other imported salvations which, oddly, the people had already had in a variety of devastating forms. Some said that the

Hawaiians routinely practiced infanticide, or that the "tribes" had killed each other off in endless wars.

By 1850, it was all made official. The commoners were given the "right" to own land, and the foreigners the right to buy it, although in reality they already had. In no time at all most of the country had been packaged and parceled, everything legal and in foreign hands. Before the Westerners there had been no concept of privately owned land. In fact, nothing not made by the human hand could ever be owned or even set apart for exclusive use, because everything belonged in common to all.

Into this tumultuous world, on October 16, 1875, Princess Kaiulani was born. Her father, Archibald Cleghorn, a Scotsman, came from a long line of gardeners and merchants. He had taken over a dry cleaning business from his dying father and soon opened branches in Molokai, Maui and the Big Island. A champion of civic affairs, Archibald Cleghorn was a thirty-five year old bachelor, with three half-Hawaiian daughters out of wedlock, when he married Princess Miriam Likelike, who was nineteen years old.

Like her sister, Liliuokalani, and their brothers, Kalakaua and Leleiohuku, Likelike was an *ali'i*, or royalty, descended from the "Four Sacred Ones." Everyone in the family was musical, so there was an ongoing variety of singing clubs and competitions for who could play or write or sing the best new song. After David Kalakaua became king, Archibald Cleghorn was appointed to several government posts, and eventually served as Governor of Oahu.

Five years after her parents married, Kaiulani, their only child, was born. From her father she received her patrician nose and a keen sense of justice, developed through a strong taste for politics and power learned at her father's knee. From her mother she inherited a love of music, an inclination to melancholy and her obsidian-dark eyes, curly, dark hair and tender rosebud mouth.

17

Chapter Two

The morning of Kaiulani's Christening was cool by Hawaiian standards; the temperature hovered between 74 and 76 degrees. The modest, one story house of Archibald and Likelike Cleghorn, on Emma Street, bustled in anticipation of the first official visit to honor the new, royal child.

"Why must there be such a fuss?!?" Likelike flicked imaginary dust away from her bustle and her batted at her low-cut bodice. For the twentieth time she shifted the pendant on her bracelet and tugged at the choker-style necklace made of delicate feathers that encircled her throat.

"He's only my brother, after all! It's not as if he's never been here before!"

"Now, Miriam." Her husband, a slim, wiry man, towered above her. His bushy eyebrows, mutton-chop beard and thin mustache were all salt and pepper gray. "We don't need to be so nervous," he tried to soothe her. "It's just that it's his first official visit before the Christening. It won't last long, and he is, after all, her godfather, you know." Archibald Cleghorn was seventeen years older than his wife.

"Yes, yes, yes, I know! What I don't know is why everyone has to come over here first! This house is too small for any company at all, and we don't seem to be able to keep decent servants for even one minute -!"

Archibald Cleghorn folded his bony fingers over his wife's pretty, plump hands. "You look lovely, my darling, as always, and everything will be fine." "Come on, now," his tone was cajoling,

"Come out on the *lanai* for a moment. See how my roses have bloomed in this weather."

Likelike's face softened as he caressed her. "Oh, Archie. Sometimes I think you care more about your gardens than about me. And the baby," she added, as an afterthought.

He twined his arm around her small waist.

"Still," she said, "let's see what kind of a mess they've made of the decorations."

A profusion of golden flowers greeted them as they stepped out into the mid-morning sun. *Kahilis*, the tall, fans reserved for royalty, which were made from the bright yellow feathers of the *o'o* bird, leaned on the porch rails, ready for the servants' hands. A ukulele and several guitars stood close by for the casual, spontaneous entertainment that was the hallmark of Likelike's musical family; and for which both her brother and sister, King David Kalakaua and Princess Liliuokalani, were especially renowned. The air of Honolulu smelled as it usually did, of multitudes of flowers - gardenia, jasmine, oleander, ginger, carnations. Likelike allowed herself a sigh.

"Well, I'll look at it as just another party. Only far too small to be any good." She glanced mischievously up at her spouse. "Since no one who is any fun is coming to this party, only some old politicians and my relatives." She picked at the pearl buttons on her white kid gloves. "Of course, it's at the wrong time, too. No important party is ever in the morning; only dull, business teas and birthday *luas* for children..."

"Which, in fact, this is, my dear," Archie cheerfully reminded her.

"Oh. Yes, I suppose it is. Where is that nurse, anyway? I have to make sure the baby is presentable. Why must I always do everything," she grumbled softly as she hurried away.

* * * * * * * * * * * * * * * * * * *

The Old Wooden Palace on King and Richard Streets was a one-story house made of coral and wood. Governor Kekuanaoa had it built as a gift for Princess Victoria Kamamalu so she would have a place to spend her summers away from the Chief's Children's School.

When King Kalakaua took it over to use as a palace he wanted to name it St. Alexander's, after the area. But his privy council had convinced him to call it *Io-lani*, instead. Iolani meant hawk, or Bird of Heaven, and was the most sacred name in the Hawaiian language.

The morning of Kaiulani's christening Kalakaua, along with his queen, Kapiolani, and his sister, Princess Liliuokalani, were putting the final touches on their ensembles.

David Kalakaua had soulful dark eyes and a proud, elegant stance. Muscular and robust, he moved with the easy, careless grace of an accomplished dancer, which he was. The rich, warm resonance of his voice reflected his passion for music and song. Tight, glistening black curls framed his leonine head and smaller ringlets curled down his cheeks and over his sensual, full mouth in a neatly trimmed mustache.

"Which do you think, my dear," he asked his wife of thirty years as the valet held up against his broad chest two sashes, one after the other, intricately woven of gold braid. "The yellow or the blue?"

Queen Kapiolani narrowed her eyes to consider the choices. "Oh, I don't know." She turned to her sister-in-law, a handsome woman who observed the proceedings with a critical eye. "Liliu, what do you say?"

"Well," Liliuokalani said in her measured tones, "I think the yellow, as the welcoming of a new princess is certainly an occasion of state worthy of the royal colors."

Kalakaua took his sister's hand in his own. "Lili, Lili, Lili. Always the proper one." He turned smiling back to his wife. "Do you know, when we were children, she would always tell me what to do?" Liliu began to protest but the king only laughed. "Always, about everything, all of the time."

Kapiolani smiled at the two, so similar in features and manner. "Well, some things never change."

Liliu adjusted the yellow sash on her brother's chest. "Only then he called me 'Lydia' and told me he wanted to marry me, and I had to tell him again and again it was not the Christian thing to do."

"Christian! Pah!" Kalakaua shook his head. "I am only—and will be, forever, - Hawaiian, through and through. I am a *kahuna,* a royal priest and I dedicate myself to my country and my people, who are my life. The Royal Genealogical Society of noble descendants and the great *Kumulipo*, chant of creation, will preserve our history and hold us together by -"

"I know, I know." Liliuokalani brushed the braid back into place on his sash. "- by the *Olona* cord, *kaula hipu'u*, on which all the *kahunas* preserved our history before words were ever written."

"Yes," the king said eagerly, 'and -'"

His sister held a finger to his lips. "You know that I love Hawaii just as much as you do." She touched the Anglican cross that at all times hung around her neck. "We only have a difference in styles; that is all."

"Of course, my dear sister. As we are not the same person, we will naturally have different ways of doing and behaving."

Liliu shot him a piercing look, even as a twinkle lit up her fiery eyes. "Well," she said lightly, "At least it's a good thing we don't fight as we used to. When we were children, of course."

"Of course," the king agreed. He smoothed his jacket over his strong shoulders and observed himself in the mirror, satisfied.

Kapiolani shifted a medal back into place on his chest.

"My sister and I may have our little quarrels - "Kalakaua smiled at Liliuokalani, "- as all sisters and brothers do, - but we are of one mind in our desire to restore Hawaii and the Hawaiians -"

Liliuokalani finished. "'- to their rightful position of power and pride.' I helped write that speech, remember?"

"Yes, yes," Kalakaua laughed. "And many other songs and speeches besides that one."

Kapiolani extended her delicate, peacock feather fan out toward her husband. "We really must go now or we'll never get there before Ruth. You know how she hates it if everyone is not there when she makes her entrance."

* * * * * * * * * * * * * * * * * * *

In another part of town the High Chiefess Princess Ruth, known to all as Mama Nui, frowned at her mirror. Several attendants fussed over her costume, a low cut, off-the-shoulder evening gown of dark blue silk that swaddled her enormous bulk like a midnight sea. Mama Nui moved with the peculiar, delicate grace that very large people sometimes have. An ornate bracelet of seed pearls and garnets circled her wrist, and an exquisite necklace, a century and a half old, carved out of ivory and bone and decorated with human hair, rested against her ample bosom. A brilliant spray of fuchsia flowers ornamented her thick gray and black curls, piled high in an elaborate arrangement on top of her head. Her oddly wide, flat nose, splayed out across her face, was rumored to be the souvenir of a fight that got out of control with a passionate but abusive first husband; though there were those who said it was actually the result of a bout with some childhood disease.

"What do you think, Emelia?" she asked the companion who was never far from her side.

"Never mind," she continued without waiting for an answer, "you don't need to say it. I should have more color in the flowers; I can see that now. Tell Tipi to bring me a few of those orchids from the verandah; that will make a nice touch. Better make it three or four -" She studied her reflection again. - "Let's say five, just in case."

Emelia deftly navigated her mistress down the stairs and into a custom designed carriage. The horses whinnied as Mama Nui adjusted her great bulk against the golden yellow, velvet pillows that traveled with her wherever she went. Six large orchids trembled now at the top and sides of her coiffure. Packages wrapped in brightly painted tapa cloths sat beside her on the seat. Emelia settled in, looking like a doll next to her mistress.

"Hurry, please!" Mama Nui called out to the driver with a bear-like growl. "We don't want to keep our Princess waiting!"

When they arrived at the house on Emma Street, Mama Nui took her time descending from the carriage while Emelia braced her up on one side and a strapping coachman, Ruth's height but less than half her size, steadied her on the other. They walked together down the short lane of palm trees that lead up to the house and then stopped at the small *lanai*, which was overflowing with flowers. As Mama Nui ascended the few stairs one at a time, they groaned and creaked dangerously but held.

Likelike flashed into the doorway to greet them, darting about like a fish in shallow waters. "Ruth, darling! We're so glad you could come!"

"Well," Mama Nui brushed masses of yellow flowers away from her skirt. "You might have made a little more room on your porch, then." Ignoring Likelike's pout, she patted the young mother's cheek in an offhand way. "Never mind, never mind. I would walk through shark pools to see my baby again."

Mama Nui reached deep into the neckline of her dress and extracted a small black silk bag. She opened it with one hand and sprinkled a tiny amount of coarse, silvery powder over the threshold, murmuring a few words in Hawaiian so old that Likelike could not make out the meaning.

"A blessing on our Princess," Ruth explained as she took in Likelike's frown. "Wealth, long life and happiness."

"I knew that," Likelike countered.

Ruth sailed past her, making sounds like a small steamship in her eagerness to get inside.

"Where is she?" she boomed. "Where is that baby?"

The small living room was crowded. Archibald Cleghorn held his daughter while King Kalakaua made funny faces at her. Kaiulani would occasionally squirm when her godfather tickled her face with his mutton chop whiskers.

"Very good, Archie! Very good!" The King stood stately and solid next to his skinny brother-in-law.

Cleghorn blushed a light pink down to the roots of his gray and sandy-colored hair. "Well, uh, I, eh, - well, it's not so—it's not - unusual, you know!" he objected.

"Ah, unfortunately," the King sighed as he held a hand across his own chest. "Here in Hawaii, it is." When the King gently brushed a finger against the baby's downy cheek, Kaiulani gripped it in her tiny fist and he laughed with delight. "Good hold, good strength!" He turned sideways to catch Cleghorn's eye.

"Babies are too rare in Hawaii these days. That is why I always say to our people that self-preservation is their first and greatest duty. All our other acts are in vain, I tell them, unless we can increase the race." Kaiulani tossed fitfully as she pulled at and released his finger. "Unless we can stay the wasting hand that is destroying our people -"

Mama Nui managed to push in between the two men, the vast materials of her dress billowing out like sails. "Yes, David, darling, we know all about it. 'Increase the race; *Hoolu lahui.*'" She scooped the baby out of her father's arms. Her enormous size invariably had a narcotic effect on children and animals. Kaiulani snuggled into her arms and fell asleep.

"Well," Ruth said. "I personally intend to do my part for my country and my race by giving this baby her very own estate." "Of course," she said airily to Cleghorn. "You and Likelike may live there, too." She cooed at the child asleep in her arms. "Ainahau, sweetheart, my baby; all for you. Where so many chiefs and chiefesses before you have lived. Manoa Valley's breeze will wake you in the morning and put you to sleep again at night. The perfect setting for my precious jewel."

"And a fine location for gardening, too, by the by," she said to Cleghorn. "Hawaiian style, of course."

* * * * * * * * * * * * * * * * * * * *

On Christmas Day, 1875, Princess Victoria Kaiulani, two months old and snugly wrapped in the arms of her nurse, Nahini, was carried into St. Andrew's Episcopal Church. Dawn had come early that day, shading the sky with watercolor hues of lavender and rose that reflected in the ocean's waves. The air was as soft as a kiss. Hawaii was gorgeous that morning and stayed that way all day long.

The Hawaiians had come from all of the Islands, some from as far away as Kauai and Nihau, to see their Princess christened. Inside, outside and for blocks around the grounds of the church they stood to catch even a glimpse of the baby *ali'i*. White gardenias, the symbol of innocence and purity, decorated the old church, spilling out even over the font. Many of the people carried jasmine flowers, pale yellow and richly fragrant, to signify hope and to honor the child.

Kaiulani's dark curls shined against the white cashmere baptismal gown, bordered in golden yellow satin and embroidered with ivory and pink silk.

Outside the gates of St. Andrew's Captain Henri Berger spoke briskly to the Royal Hawaiian band, resplendent in their navy and white suits.

"Please, please, if you please!" Berger sported a handlebar mustache and a jaunty cap that was always tilted to one side. He tapped his baton on the makeshift stand.

"Silence now, please!" The bandleader cleared his throat. "Composed by *moi* to celebrate the christening of our *chere Princesse.*" The German and French accents struggling for dominance in his voice made him sound a little like a barker in a music hall. When he raised his arms with a discreet flourish, forty-five musicians drew in their breath to play.

"*Ze* Kaiulani March!"

The band struck up the lilting tune that people had been humming all over Honolulu since the baby's arrival. A pair of haole businessmen strolled by. They wore dark suits with ornate and garish brocade vests. The smaller one had an angular face while the other looked flushed and overheated, as if he regularly drank too much.

"Look at all those *kanakas*," the larger man whistled. "I had no idea there were that many left!"

"What the hell's a 'Kaiulani?'" the sharp-faced man asked his companion.

"New baby princess. Half colored, half white."

"Didn't know they could <u>have</u> babies anymore!" The other snorted derisively.

"Most of 'em can't," the heavy man said. He lit up a cigar, taking his time, and slowly exhaled as he paused for effect. "Must have been the white half -" he suggestively jabbed the cigar at his partner to emphasize the joke - "did all the work!"

The thin man laughed and shook his head in appreciation as they walked away. "Just like everything else around here!"

Inside St. Andrews Church, Bishop Willis, a florid man with a long, pinched nose, went on and on, his fruity, overly-modulated tones reverberating throughout the packed church. In the front pew, seated near the baby and the bishop, were the godparents. King Kalakaua beamed at him while Mama Nui affected the scowl she always had when there were *haoles* around. She alternated gazing lovingly on her goddaughter with glaring fiercely at the disconcerted Bishop. Behind them sat the baby's mother, Princess Likelike, looking at 23 quite like a child herself. Beside her was Princess Liliuokalani.

All members of the family wore accents of the royal yellow, a warm, dark gold. In the other seats, which were reserved for the *ali'i* and their consorts, were Kalakaua's queen, the serene and lovely Julia

Kapiolani; John Dominis, Princess Liliuokalani's husband; and Archibald Cleghorn, who was slightly taller than John Dominis but shared with him an anxious, troubled demeanor. The English man and the Scot looked insubstantial and out of place next to the robust weight of the Hawaiians.

On Queen Kapiolani's right, tucked in close beside her, were the royal couple's adopted sons, Kaiulani's cousins. Jonah Kalanianole, nicknamed "Kuhio," the older of the two at twelve years, shifted restlessly in his seat. His brother, seven- year old David Kawananakoa, or "Koa," was a handsome, solemn boy who listened attentively as Willis' monotonous sermon droned on.

"Her name, which means 'The Royal Sacred One' in Hawaiian, reminds us of our duty to be faithful and true to the honor and nobility of royal ways. Of our obligation to treat fairly and impartially the lowest and poorest among us, as well as those who are among the most high and wealthy."

"Our most special thanks on this blessed day," Bishop Willis turned to smile in a placating way down at Mama Nui, who glowered at him even more. "To Princess Ruth Keelikolani who has so generously presented to Princess Kaiulani, at this the beginning of her tender, new life, the lovely estate of Ainahau, known as the land of cool breezes, ten beautiful acres of prime land in lovely Waikiki—"

Keeping her face still and strategically placing a fan to hide her mouth, Princess Liliuokalani leaned in to her sister and whispered in a dry tone, "Perhaps we could get one of those cool breezes in here sometime before we die."

Her younger sister stifled a giggle. Liliuokalani resumed with the same deadpan expression, "He speaks of cool breezes but is full of hot air."

"He does like to hear himself talk." Likelike nudged her sister, then fanned herself with a program. "It's so stuffy in here!" she hissed.

Liliuokalani barely moved her lips, tickling her sister's ear. "He's cheap, this Bishop. Didn't want to spend the money for more windows. He owns this church, you know."

On the women's right, Cleghorn twitched in his seat and shot them a disapproving look. Likelike smiled at him sweetly as she continued whispering to her sister. "You know what they say about the missionaries -"

Liliuokalani's eyes sparkled. "They came to do good -"

Delighted, Likelike spoke out loud in her eagerness to deliver the punch line. "- and did well!"

Cleghorn glared at them sternly and even Bishop Willis cleared his throat and paused. When he began again his attention was directed exclusively to the king.

"In the hopes and fondest desire that all our races and peoples may come together in harmony and good will -"

Kalakaua had pulled out his pocket watch from a very long and noisy chain. The King looked pointedly at the time and then delicately gestured at the bishop to wrap it up.

At a brisker pace and louder the clergyman continued, "Your family and people are gathered here today to wish you well in this world -"

Kalakaua made another hurrying gesture at the clergyman, surreptitiously holding up his watch. The Bishop, nonplussed, grabbed for his notes from under the podium.

"Uh, eh - So, I now, then, christen you, in the name of our Lord -"

Awkwardly, he sprinkled water on the patient baby. "Princess Victoria -"

Willis began to stumble badly over the words - "Kawekiu Lunalilo Kalaninuiahilapalapa—"

The Bishop gave a sigh of relief as he finished pronouncing the final name—"Kaiulani."

Everyone began clapping vigorously at once, causing the startled clergyman to take an abrupt bow, like an actor on stage.

Princess Ruth could bear it no longer. Struggling to her feet with the assistance of Emelia, she scooped the baby out of the arms of the protesting nurse and held her high for the people to see as she thundered out a blessing in Hawaiian.

The people responded in kind and the church rang out with cries of *"Ho'omaikai'i! Ho'omaikai'i Nui!"*

Mama Nui cradled the baby in her generous arms as the crowd began to stream out into the sunlight. Koa appeared at her elbow, having somehow managed to push through the crowd to reach her.

"Mama Nui?"

She looked down at the small boy. "Yes, baby?" Her deep, rolling voice was soft as velvet when she felt like it.

"May I kiss Kaiulani, please?"

"Of course you may, darling!" She lowered the baby to his level and he respectfully bussed her cheek.

"See how he loves her!" Mama Nui boomed out. "See how he loves his cousin!" She smiled down into his face. "You must always look after her, Koa."

Koa nodded at the huge, elderly princess holding the tiny new one snuggled safe in her arms. "I will always take care of her, Mama Nui," he said. "Always. I promise."

Outside the church Mama Nui handed the baby over to the king. He, too, held the child high to show her off to the Hawaiians, his imposing presence contrasting strongly with the bundle in his arms.

"May this child grow up to be a shining example of the words of the Great Kamehahameha!"

"Hoolu lahui!" The king shouted out. "The law of the land is preserved in righteousness!"

The people answered him with cheers.

* * * * * * * * * * * * * * * * * * * *

The christening celebration that night took place at the Old Wooden Palace. The dark walls were carved with countless scenes of the creation of the land, the lives of the ancestors, the pagan gods and their rites and other ancient ritual symbols. The rooms were decorated with the same royal, golden-yellow color that had been in the church that day. A strong scent of sandalwood permeated everywhere and was especially powerful where the walls were most intricately carved. The worn and rickety wooden floorboards creaked and complained at every movement.

By the time the servants had finished clearing away the last course in the main dining room, it was after nine o'clock. Champagne and wine continued to flow freely as they began to set up for dessert.

The King and Queen sat together at the head of the longest table. Around them were the royal family and their spouses, along with several politicians, both *haole* and Hawaiian, and a few businessmen, mostly American and English, with their wives. At the far end of the smallest table a token missionary from one of the more liberal sects huddled with his mousy wife.

Sanford Ballard Dole, the pineapple and sugar magnate, sat beside Lorrin Andrews Thurston, an up-and-coming young lawyer. Although both were missionary's sons, in their styles they were like night and day.

Thurston, the younger by fifteen years, was brash and outspoken, inclined to pick fights. His table manners were abominable, his voice always unpleasantly loud; and to all but Dole he spoke with obvious disdain. The man beside him was lean, austerely handsome, invariably polite and reserved. Although he had been born and raised in Hawaii, Dole affected a New England manner to his core. Genial and perpetually alert, Sanford Dole was, above all else, the perfect gentleman. He never raised his voice and was a constant foil and tonic to Thurston's belligerent aggression. They were a decidedly odd pair. The ambitious young lawyer hung on every word of the cool, older man who would become one of Hawaii's best-known politicians.

Close by them sat Theo K. Davies, an English landowner and staunch friend of the Hawaii for the Hawaiians movement. Davies was an avid supporter of Kalakaua's programs to return the land to its old customs and restore its wealth to the people who had been residents for so many generations. Curiously, although he was a fair and reasonable man, Davies found no contradiction in continuing to profit handsomely from his many business interests in Hawaii. At least, as he explained it to himself, while the country was still in transition.

Dole leaned over toward the king and spoke soothingly, as if talking to an overly tired child.

"A treaty of reciprocity with the United States would allow our Hawaiian sugar to continue to enter America without any custom duties at all, your highness."

Dole paused for an instant to wave away a server's offer of more champagne. "The boon to our economy would be immeasurable."

Kalakaua held his glass out for the server to fill. "Yes, Mr. Dole," he responded congenially. "And most especially for those foreigners who have holdings here in the Islands. But so few of our Hawaiians own anything at all anymore - not their land, nor their homes; not even a grass shack."

Thurston, who could not hold his liquor and was much the worse for several glasses of champagne, murmured sarcastically under his breath. "'Consider the lilies of the field; they toil not.'"

Princess Liliuokalani, who was seated quite near Thurston, turned sharply toward him. "I beg your pardon, sir?"

Dole attempted to smooth over the gaffe as best he could, offering the Princess a sweet from a silver dish. "A quote from the Bible, madam," he proffered along with the candy.

Liliuokalani riveted her penetrating gaze on the older man, and spoke in even tones that matched his own. "I know it very well, Mr. Dole. I was raised on the Bible. 'They toil not, neither do they spin.' A not, perhaps, entirely inaccurate description of the gentle nature of the Hawaiian people, who are both peaceful and loving -" Her eyes returned to Thurston - "unless they are provoked."

Theo Davies nodded and patted Liliuokalani's hand. "I have never known a race as fine and generous as the Hawaiians!"

"And that calls for another toast!" Kalakaua held up his empty glass.

As the server came around with champagne again, Dole indicated tersely that he would accept only a drop. Escalating into a sullen mood, Thurston refused on principle. Observing the two of them, Kalakaua began to laugh.

"You missionaries' sons are so careful about your pleasures - not too much of this, just a little of that. No cards, no dancing, no drinking beyond precisely a certain point. Where do you find your pleasure in life?"

"In righting that which is wrong and in setting things straight!" Thurston's surly intensity combined with his inebriated condition gave his face a twisted look.

Kalakaua laughed again. "Oh, my! Well, you will have quite a job of that here in Hawaii. We must toast to that, then. To 'setting things straight.'"

Dole and Thurston reluctantly raised their glasses to join in. Thurston's glass had been filled with water, which he clumsily sloshed onto the tablecloth.

Queen Kapiolani leaned in close to her husband and spoke in a low tone. The King at once rose to his feet and held his glass high.

"My lovely Queen," he said as she smiled at him, "Kapiolani and I have two fine adopted sons—*hanai* sons - whom we love very dearly. But otherwise, sadly, we have no children of our own. So it is with special pleasure that I propose a toast to my royal goddaughter, the Princess Kaiulani! Our Nation's Hope! May she grow up to rule both wisely and well!"

Everyone toasted to her health and fortune. Then Thurston moved unsteadily onto his feet, oblivious to Dole's warning stare.

"Another toast!" His words were on the edge of slurring. "A saying from our late, great American president, Mr. Abraham Lincoln." Again he spilled a considerable amount of water onto the already damp cloth. "'Let us have faith that right makes might, and in that faith let us dare to do our duty.'" Thurston stopped, pleased with himself for getting all the words out and lurching to the side as he spoke again. "'As we understand it.'" There was a tepid, polite response.

"And yet one more." Princess Liliuokalani rose, her tone pleasant but steely. She addressed Thurston but her cool smile also took in Dole. "From the Greek philosopher, Herodotus, who is occasionally read even by some of our simple people."

Liliu turned to look at her brother as she quoted. "'The king's might is greater than human, and his arm is very long.'"

Kalakaua nodded, basking in his sister's tribute.

Suddenly, Likelike fairly leaped up from her seat. "Oh, do come on, everyone! It's so stuffy in here!" She clapped her dainty hands together. "Everyone to the dance floor!" The tension of the moment was broken and the grateful crowd piled out of the room.

* * * * * * * * * * * * * * * * * * *

Later that night Archibald Cleghorn, flushed from the heat of dancing and champagne, leaned for a moment on his brother-in-law's arm. "So, what about these *'kahunas'* I keep hearing so much about from my wife? Are they part of your plan for a 'simpler life'?" He tucked his head in close to Kalakaua's large face. "Priests, would you say, or witch doctors, maybe?"

"Neither, I'd say." Kalakaua smiled indulgently at his tipsy relative and winked in confidence at Liliuokalani. "Maybe they are a little bit like the missionaries, only much better educated, of course -"

"And without the real estate holdings," Theo Davies added dryly.

Everyone but Kalakaua laughed. Thoughtful and musing, the King continued on in a dreamy voice. "More like the holy men of the American Indian tribes. The Sioux, the Cheyenne, the Cherokee -"

Liliu patted his hand. "You were always enchanted by those American tribes. Even as a child." Turning to Archie she said, "Their priests, so to speak, I believe are referred to as 'shamans' there. They are the wisest men of the tribe, those most learned in the arts of healing and all forms of religious rituals and planting ceremonies for securing the blessings of the ancestors and the good will of the natural forces..."

Archibald Cleghorn interrupted her, impatient. "Yes, well, that's all very well and good, but don't you think that sort of thing promotes a certain kind of primitive behavior? A somewhat backward way of seeing things -?"

"Not at all, my friend." Kalakaua shook his head. "On the contrary. The *kahunas'* art allows people to look deeper into 'things' - themselves, their world and others around them. To see below the shallow surface of material reality and beyond the fleeting nature of our small lives. Into a fuller universe, one which encompasses that which has gone before us and that which is yet to come."

A commotion on the dance floor interrupted him. The dancing had stopped abruptly and Queen Kapiolani and Princess Likelike were calling for quiet.

A gnarled, old man came into the room at a snail's pace, humming softly to himself as he kept time with a small gourd drum. Draped in a white robe, he wore a *lei* of shiny green, fragrant *maile* leaves around his neck. On either side of him were two escorts or assistants who wore ginger flower and jasmine garlands. One carried a calabash of holy water, which he sprinkled on the ground in front of and behind the path of the old *kahuna*. The other blew rhythmically at intervals into a conch shell horn, evoking a lonely sound. From the opposite side of the room Mama Nui, carrying Kaiulani, and Emelia and the nurse, Nahini, walked toward the three men.

When they came together in the center of the room Nahini dropped a cloak woven of vivid red and yellow feathers onto the floor. The old man sat down on the robe and Mama Nui handed him the baby.

The low, droning hum and the mournful note of the conch shell became softer as Kapiolani spoke. "A traditional blessing for the long life and happiness of the Princess."

Cleghorn, who stood beside his wife, tugged at her sleeve. "Really, Miriam! Couldn't this have been done at some other, less visible time?"

Eyes glowing, Likelike silenced him with a look.

The Queen placed a tiny, yellow-feathered *lei* around the baby's neck and took Likelike's hand in her own. Then they joined hands to complete a circle with Mama Nui and the ancient *kahuna*.

Likelike began to chant, almost as if in a trance, alternating her words with the old man's eerie singing. "Innumerable are the stars. The large stars. The small ones."

Mama Nui's powerful baritone took over. "The red stars of Pele. Infinite space."

Kapiolani's sweet tremolo chimed in. "Let that which is unknown become known. Let that which is unknowable be left alone."

When the *kahuna* suddenly stopped chanting, the space around their small circle seemed to expand, growing closer and brighter. The man with the calabash handed him something and the old man stretched up with it and seemed to become larger and taller.

Above the baby's head he held a carved wooden hawk, the symbol of Hawaiian royalty since the beginning of time. The bird's strong wings were spread wide in a movement of full flight. The hawk seemed to be reaching out for the little girl as if trying to protect her from any harm.

In a clear, strong voice the *kahuna* called out his blessing and, for a moment, it seemed as if the bird had come to life and cried out, finding its voice in the gnarled, elderly body that reached out and over Kaiulani like enfolding wings.

* * * * * * * * * * * * * * * * * * *

An hour later Liliuokalani, Kalakaua and Theo Davies stood off to one side of the dance floor as the seemingly tireless Likelike spun around again and again with one partner after another. Behind the trio the kahili bearers stood, holding on to the ivory and tortoise shell handles of their tall yellow standards, occasionally fanning a light breeze in the direction of the royal family and their friends.

"They don't call him 'The Merry Monarch' for nothing," Liliu told Theo as she patted her brother's hand. A shadow of worry crossed over her face. "But sometimes I fear he is too easy going for his own good."

Kalakaua returned her grasp and smiled. "Not a bit different than when we were children! Always she wants to tell me what to do!"

"And yet," Theo said to them, "Anyone can tell that you have the same goal in your desire to restore Hawaii to the Hawaiians."

"Perhaps," Kalakaua said wistfully, "the new *Ka Hale Naua* Society will prove a good tool for renewing some of our traditions."

"Music and dance," Liliu joined in.

"Science, literature, art," Kalakaua's voice was full of longing. "All have begun to fade out in our quest for material things, in all of our busy-ness, as we are overcome by the need for politics and government. What is it that Dole always says about 'Negotiation'?"

"And 'Manifest Destiny,' too." Theo added without apparent sarcasm.

"I suppose, yes; that, too, whatever it means." Kalakaua was bemused. "More of that missionaries' sons' language. At times I am quite sure it is they who hold the stronger superstitions, with all their talk about 'Fate' and 'Things that are meant to be'…"

"In the past," Theo ventured, "it seems there was more time to simply live…"

"Or perhaps to live simply," Liliuokalani returned.

Chapter Three

Kaiulani was one week away from her third birthday when the Cleghorn family moved to the estate that Mama Nui had given to her when she was born. Archibald Cleghorn could be a perfectionist when it came to attention to detail and he had required a great deal of time to refurbish the houses, build sheds and set up the ponds and landscaping to his exact specifications before they could move in.

Ainahau had, for centuries, been the residence of Oahu's Highest Chiefs and Chiefesses. Royalty had met there with royalty, and entertained governors, captains, lords and ladies from all the other Islands and even other lands. Nearby Manoa Valley sent over the mild, balmy breezes that kept the land constantly ventilated and temperate, so that it was a nearly ideal environment for gardening, as well as a haven and sanctuary for a wide range of animals and birds.

The main house at Ainahau fronted on the ocean. The estate's ten acres were covered with an abundance of vines, shrubs and tropical trees, including the five hundred banyan trees that had been imported and planted to honor Kaiulani's birth. The young Princess' own banyan tree, the very first one to arrive on the islands, had been planted by her own father, dead center in front of the main house. Already lush at thirty years old when Cleghorn had it brought over from India, this majestic parent of all the Hawaiian banyans spread its foliage over a vast area to weave a web of shadow and light over everything it covered. To both sides of this banyan were unusual, solitary trees, also the first of their kind in Hawaii. On one side a Chinese "soap tree", light rose in color and useful for making lotions and cleansers, unfolded its thick, waxy fronds like strange, succulent tongues. The brilliant, blood red, spiny flowers of the red India tree, on the other side of the banyan, were shaped like tiger's claws and they spiked the air with a sharp, pungent perfume.

Archibald Cleghorn's immense talent for cultivation was in evidence everywhere. Mango and teak trees flourished beside rare varieties of fragrant spice and coconut trees. Mingled scents of cinnamon, camphor and cypress warmed the air while the large, showy flowers of the hibiscus peeked out from under and around date palms heavy with fruit. This profusion of bowers and beasts at Ainahau combined to create such a wild yet radiant harmony that visitors, especially those from far away, would catch their breath at the sensuous, natural luxury. They would often speak of the "paradise" that was Hawaii.

Kaiulani's pet turtle, Jehoshaphat, a giant the size of a small pony, ambled around the property like a benign, ancient lord. Sometimes he slept peacefully at the edge of one of the many lily ponds; other times he strolled incuriously along the pathways through the rambling grounds that seemed to go on forever.

The peacocks and their lively mistress were the main attraction at Ainahau. Kaiulani fed the birds by hand, and her "*pikakae*" followed her around like adoring, oversized puppies. To the Hawaiians Kaiulani became their "Princess of the Peacocks." The Chinese jasmine flowers she delighted in, and later wore as her only perfume, were called "*pikake*" in her honor.

For hours the small child and her slim Scottish father would sit under the branches of Kaiulani's banyan, shading them selves from the sun as he read to her, or walking about together, attending to the grounds. Archibald Cleghorn would talk to her about politics in Honolulu and on the other Islands, or discourse on the figures of note that came through Ainahau on personal and public visits. Attentively she listened as her father held forth about money, power, business patterns and ethical behavior. One of his favorite topics was the question of "character" and he returned to it often as he struggled to make sense of the upheaval in their world.

"So, my Kaiulani. My little tiger."

She smiled sweetly at him. "Yes, Papa?"

"Nothing, daughter. I just like to say your name."

Her father made a stiff, funny little bow, like a waiter or an old servant, with one hand held in front of him and the other behind. "You are my Princess of the Peacocks."

"Silly Papa," she scolded him fondly.

They worked in companionable silence, side by side, pulling up weeds and patting the rich, damp earth back into place.

A half hour later Miss Barnes, a sharp faced woman from England with a thin upper lip and clipped, shrill speech, appeared on the *lanai* and called for Kaiulani and her father to come in to lunch. Sighing, they straightened up from the loamy earth and began to dust the dirt off their clothes.

Kaiulani's current governess and nanny was very strict about meal times. "Your mother will not be in for lunch today, Kaiulani," Miss Barnes announced. "Therefore we shall eat in the small dining room," she declared with great personal satisfaction, for she hated having to clean up the larger room after meals. "Come quickly. *Vite, vite!*" she trilled out in her own unique, jarring version of a French accent.

* * * * * * * * * * * * * * * * * *

In another room in the main house Likelike and Liliuokalani were getting ready to go to an afternoon party at the Fornanders, their neighbors the next island over. Likelike had been on intimate terms with the family ever since her long ago, brief engagement to their eldest son, John Fornander, a dashing young man with a slow, easy smile.

Liliuokalani, on the other hand, barely knew them, having spent the bulk of her childhood away from home, raised at the strict High Chief's school, where she was intensely involved with a plethora of rules, all of them strictly enforced by the stern, devout Christian teachers.

Liliuokalani, or "Lydia," as she had been baptized, had learned to think quickly and be slow to anger at the *haoles'* school where there were only a handful of other *ali'i* children besides her self. Drilled in weighty codes of competition and infused with a staunch morality, Liliu had been taught that 'Doing wrong to the people' was the greatest sin that the *ali'i* could ever commit; coming in a close second was 'inhospitality.' Early on she had determined to be irreproachable in her manners and behavior.

She and her sister could be strongly divided, at times, over issues of behavior. Likelike, who was high-spirited and hot tempered, would clash with her older sister over what was 'moral' and 'right', to the point of violent disagreement. They had very different ideas about what was 'stuffy' or, worse still, 'unnatural.' At this moment, however, it was the usually calm Liliu who was about to lose patience with her younger sister's inability to make a decision about what to wear.

"Oh, perhaps it should be the yellow silk, after all," Likelike mused, holding up a frilly, beribboned dress as she gazed at her small frame in the mirror for the fourth or fifth time.

Liliu, who was soberly clad, impatiently tapped her finger on the sandalwood vanity dresser, which was littered with scarves, jewelry and gloves.

"You will look fine, my dear, no matter what you wear. But if you do not make up your mind soon there will be no point in going at all; at least not for the horseback riding."

Likelike became still more agitated, and quickly turned away to avoid her sister's eyes. "Oh, all right, all right, then, the lavender lawn dress." She lifted a flowered gown from a pile on the bed and slipped it on. "What do you think; the coral earrings or the black pearls?"

"I'm sure I don't know," her sister coolly intoned, "why this is such a major task for you. It's not as if we'll be meeting anyone important; and your husband is staying at home."

Likelike laughed in a light, silvery tone, but was careful to stay turned away from her sister's sharp gaze.

"Well, no, of course not. I suppose I am just being silly. You go on downstairs, now, Lily, and have a little tea. I'll be down in just a moment."

Her sister looked at her skeptically. Gently, Likelike pushed Liliu out of the room as she murmured, "Oh, I promise. I do. Just ten more minutes, that's all."

The older sister continued to stare at the younger as she began to close the bedroom door.

"Well, all right, then, no more than fifteen!" Likelike said.

* * * * * * * * * * * * * * * * * *

The Fornanders' party was a subdued, melancholy affair. Instead of the happy reunion of two family clans it was a tentative meeting of the few survivors after the untimely deaths of too many, both young and old, from disease and despair.

John Thomas Fornander, four years older than Likelike, had recently returned from completing a college education in England. Raised in the islands, he had been brown and strong from the Hawaiian sun, muscular from years of swimming and riding. Now he was pale and thin after his four years in England. His voice held a new, foreign sound, and he said "raw-ther" and "ought" with a distinct, upper class British reserve. His family was gathered around him, anxious to welcome him and show him off but at the same time hesitant and shy in the presence of the handsome, pallid stranger who had once played in their midst as a lively, laughing young man.

The royal sisters arrived in an exquisite tortoise shell covered carriage that looked like something out of a fairy tale. When Likelike, attended by a servant, stepped down from the coach, John Fornander's face lit up and he rushed over to greet her.

"Likelike! I can hardly believe it!" He took her hand. "Is it really you? How wonderful to see you!"

"After so many years," Likelike demurely replied, but her eyes were shining like diamonds.

"I've thought of you all the time, nevertheless," John protested as he firmly placed her at his side.

"But you must have been so terribly busy, what with all those English people and society. Oh, do tell me all about it!" Likelike clapped her hands like a child.

Embarrassed by this overt display of affection, Liliu turned sharply to their hostess. "I am so sorry we are a little late. I hope we have not missed the riding? You know how my sister loves to ride."

Mrs. Fornander smiled a little. "Of course, of course."

Much later that afternoon, near dusk, Liliuokalani, angry and annoyed, decided to go out to look for her sister who had been gone, as had John Thomas, for more than three hours.

"I cannot imagine where they are," she said a little curtly to the sedate woman who was showing her still more pictures of friends and relatives from the past, all gone, lost to illness or time. "Perhaps I shall look for them. Would you be so kind as to saddle me a horse?"

"Of course, of course," said the sad Mrs. Fornander.

Liliuokalani's fury continued to build as she rode around the estate in search of her errant sister and the man who, she realized now, was Likelike's former beau.

"Why must she always be so flighty?" Liliu fumed. "Never considering the consequences, always after whatever excitement she can find in the moment. Not one thought in her head about tomorrow, or the future. And she's a mother now, too. Doesn't she bother to consider -"

Liliu caught her horse up short at the sight of the couple in the glen just below her.

In the overhanging shade of a *kukui* candlenut tree Likelike raised her hand to tenderly brush something away from John's face. Shaking his head in despair, he gently drew her to him and rested her head against his shoulder. Their tears began to fall as they delicately folded themselves into each other's arms and held fast.

Something in their embrace was so tentative and fragile and, at the same time, so final, that Liliuokalani held her breath. A hard, tight knot began to ache deep in the base of her throat. Slowly, silently, she turned away from them and began to make her way back to the house.

The haunting notes of a song began to shape themselves in her mind as she rode. Like a voice repeating over and over she heard them. "Farewell. Farewell to thee. Farewell." And then, "Aloha, aloha," again and again, like the poignant, mourning cry of a bird who has lost its mate.

Liliuokalani started to work on a lyric that same night. It would become *"Aloha Oe,"* the most well known of all her songs. But she never spoke to her sister about what she had seen that afternoon in the shadows of the glen.

Chapter Four

The Reverend Sereno Bishop had been planning his lecture for months. On several occasions he had conferred about the speech with Sanford Dole, who had helped him, perhaps, a little. This meant, unfortunately, that Lorrin Thurston, that uncouth rabble-rouser, had also been involved in most of their meetings. Dole had made some presumptuous and rather too extensive suggestions, Bishop thought, about shaping the talk to come across as more socially aware and less directly, overtly concerned with economics. But afterwards, Bishop had considered his advice carefully and for some time. He had, at last, renamed the lecture, "Why Are the Hawaiians Dying Out?" His former title, "How to Do Business in Hawaii," would not, he could see now, do.

The audience would be quite an impressive collection of businessmen, most of them hailing from American and English big cities, a few of them religious and every one of them extremely interested in all the many prospects for industry and growth in Hawaii.

It was with great reluctance that the Reverend Bishop had ultimately decided not to use the lines from a current and very popular poem that began, "Westward the course of empire takes its way." A pity. It would have been such a delicate way of suggesting the element of fate inherent in the Hawaiians' demise without ever having to actually use the phrase "Manifest Destiny" at all. He had, however, scoffed at Dole's repeated suggestions that there might be anything untoward or inappropriate about his opening statements, in which he had made very clever use of Mr. Charles Darwin's fashionable concept of "survival of the fittest." True, it was not strictly in keeping with religious tenants, but, then, so few things really were these days.

And the Reverend stood by his statements! The western immigrants were, in fact, "thrifty" and "capable;" he had seen it demonstrated again and again. And the natives were "inefficient and improvident." It was true and he saw nothing at all wrong with being frank about the truth. Dole could give his own damn lecture, if he was so inclined.

At last it was the evening of November 18, 1880. The hall of the Honolulu Social Science Association was a sea of faces, mostly men of business and social stature, but with even a few women mixed into the audience for good measure. Primarily respectable types, these women, the Reverend observed, although here and there he did notice some rather more colorful and lively characters. Relatives, he hoped; perhaps sisters or nieces? At any rate, it was none of his concern. He was happy to see the room so full.

Clearing his throat, Bishop tapped lightly on the podium for silence. He began with the usual introductory remarks about how Hawaii was "The Cross Roads of the Pacific," a near paradise with its fertile ground, accessibility and close to perfect climate. A ripple of response ran through the house when some of the audience recognized the Darwin quote about "survival of the fittest." Bishop also noted several nods of approval when he stressed how there was no real competitive struggle for survival in Hawaii. And yet, he countered, and yet, how could it be that the migrating races thrived and multiplied, their children bigger and stronger than the parents, while the diminishing Hawaiian population died off easily, leaving few or no offspring? (He had struck the phrase "dying off like flies" from an earlier draft, realizing it might be open to misinterpretation.)

In the next section he went on at some length about the perplexing fact that the "disabilities," whatever they were, of the Hawaiian species seemed to have sprung up, curiously, with the onset of contact with the white race. Why, even the Chinamen and the Japanese, the "cognate race" that had been brought in for recent growing labor needs—

Here, the Reverend paused to smile benignly at a woman in the front row who was giggling. The feathers on her oversized hat, -

well, it appeared, really, to be all or most of an entire bird, - the feathers and wings bobbled about in time with her laughter.

Why, he began again, with redoubled sincerity, even the Chinese and Japanese, inferior in strength, stature and general overall soundness, - even they survived and propagated, while the poor Hawaiians were fast approaching the possibility of extinction! How could this be? It was time to examine the particulars. To discover from whence the weakness of the native Polynesian peoples sprang. What deadly malady, he asked, has been steadily killing off this race for five—he paused for emphasis - yes, <u>five</u> generations?

An assistant scurried up to the podium and turned the first page of the lecture sheets. His services had not really been necessary, but Bishop liked the idea, implying as it did a certain dignified, almost liturgical touch. On a sudden inspiration Bishop motioned him to turn back again to the title page. The Reverend looked slowly, deliberately, out over the first five rows of the audience. This gave him the appearance, he knew from long experimentation, of seeming to send his piercing gaze out over all present. He tapped at the first word of his title as he asked his audience in a booming voice, again, "<u>Why</u>!? Why, indeed?!"

"Again," he paused. "We must ask—why." Murmurs of approval greeted his question. A few of the gentlemen even brought out pens and paper to take notes.

Bishop's first point was, as usual, Unchastity. The Hawaiian female, he explained confidentially, was strangely like the males of other races in her aggressive solicitation of sexual pleasure. Chastity, believe it or not, had formerly held no place in Hawaiian domestic life. The reality had been that a woman "who withheld herself was considered to be sour and ungracious." As he had expected, the audience gasped.

"And yet," he continued, his voice hoarse with righteous indignation, "any woman was free to enjoy her husband's affection while invading his rights of personal property by giving her self, sexually, at whim, to others! Like brute animals, these people had lived wildly, without any sense of evil or sin. Sexual diseases were unknown; and this primitive, aboriginal race thrived in its ignorance and promiscuity. It was not until the white man imported diseases that these child-like innocents were made to pay the piper!"

Dole had said to take that out, the part about the piper, but Bishop liked the sound of it too well.

"Pay the piper, indeed!" he repeated. "Multitudes had died right away and the rest were left enfeebled and poisoned. Their survivors were also impaired and easily fell victim to deaths by colds and consumption and every kind of disease after that, both native and imported! Worse still, their sexual passions were inflamed, with syphilis itself acting as a ferment, and their lives became even more debased than before!"

"There was also, of course," he said in a more muted tone, "that lewd, lascivious *hula-hula* dance, which the Hawaiians actually claimed was sacred! They even performed it in public, in the streets! Man and woman alike, without shame!"

He stopped to wipe his sweating brow. Men in the audience loosened their collars and ties. Some of the women, the more proper seeming types, stared down at their hands; while some of the others, the, well, more colorful ones, - smirked. Bishop looked sternly at them all before he began again.

"Infants," Bishop explained in a grieving tone, "were often born diseased or even dead; or else they succumbed to the carelessness of hostile conditions and incompetent care. Miscarriages and sterility had made the conditions even worse so that, by now, a Hawaiian family with two children to boast of was considered lucky and large. The few healthy women who remained refused to give up their vices of swimming, running and riding; so spontaneous abortion, too, contributed as well to their demise."

Exhausted by the weightiness of his topic, he waved limply for the assistant to turn the page. "DRUNKENNESS" was writ large and bold at the top, so the Reverend related sadly how the Hawaiian had been an "apt disciple" of the products of the foreigners' stills; like all savages, he simply did not know when to stop.

With a brisk motion the Reverend himself turned the next page and read out, "OPPRESSION BY THE CHIEFS." His main, exciting points already made, Bishop moved quickly through the part about how the chiefs had levied heavy demands for so long, taking larger and larger portions of the people's wealth and labors. He went on to explain how infectious epidemics, such as malaria, leprosy, small pox, measles and tuberculosis, to name a few, had also unfortunately arrived with the foreigners to further deplete the native race.

Moving in for the final stretch he touched on the behavior of the sinister local sorcerers, the so-called "medicine men *kahunas*." He spoke of the culture's negative system of belief that served only to render the already debilitated Hawaiians "weaker still in their minds." Broken down by melancholy as well as by disease they were further demoralized by their repulsive idolatry of that obscene *hula-hula* dance and the sinfulness of their vicious pagan carvings and bestial animal gods.

He could see the crowd growing restless so he plunged back briefly into Unchastity to rouse them again and soon after ended with his standard warning that licentiousness and sorcery had to be "hunted down and exterminated like the venomous reptiles that they are." This, and only this, he warned, might help to stop the poisoning of the Hawaiian peoples.

To rousing applause the Reverend Sereno Bishop bowed modestly and walked down from the podium. He was immediately thronged by people who were eager, as he had known they would be, for names, information and advice on how to proceed. Most of them he would send to Dole or even, in a pinch, to Thurston. Flushed with excitement and pleasure, he was truly grateful for his calling to help save the Hawaiian race. The Lord had blessed him with another good, no, really, an excellent night.

* * * * * * * * * * * * * * * * * * *

Sanford Ballard Dole had been born in Honolulu, and was raised primarily by his Hawaiian nursemaid. His missionary parents had their hands full running and supervising the Punahou School for the many missionaries' children. Dole's Hawaiian nanny, called Kiele after the gardenia flower perfume she wore, had filled young Sanford's mind with the tales and superstitions of her native culture, which his parents routinely tried to beat out of him, when they could find the time.

An intelligent and precocious child, little Sanford had determined early on to avoid the unpleasant dilemma of "Spare the rod and spoil the child" by having no offspring of his own. He would, instead, he decided, work in government, so that he himself could help make decisions about what was fair; set up the rules; and assess and act upon the best interests for the greater good of the community. In this way, he would be able to discover again and again, each and every time, what it was that would keep him in the strongest, most secure position of unassailable power and authority for the rest of his life. And that was what he had done.

At forty-three years old, Sanford Dole had made for himself one of the most renowned indoor gardens in all of Honolulu. His greenhouse trapped the light and sun in thousands of tight, close pockets.

Dole inhaled the humid, musty air with the immense satisfaction of one who knows he has done a superior job. He lightly dusted off his garden smock and then strolled around to take in with pleasure the results of his hard work. He stopped in front of a bevy of bizarre, miniature trees, all potted in small wooden baskets. Bending down over one of them, he eyed it critically, then grabbed up a pair of razor-sharp shears and began to trim precise, careful snips off its branches. Only when he was done did he bother to address his companion, Lorrin Thurston, who had watched him work, fidgeting by his side.

"I've invited you to my home, Thurston, because I believe you have -." He leaned forward to clip off the end of another diminutive branch. "- Potential." Dole returned to his usual ramrod straight posture and pointed his scissors directly at Thurston's heart. "But if you sincerely wish to have an effect on the situation in Hawaii, you must go into politics, Thurston. Reform politics. An entire party of missionaries, and their supporters, who will uphold the moral good for all. Live and breathe it, Thurston. Everyday. Are you prepared to do that?"

Without waiting for an answer, Dole yanked Thurston's hand away from a vine of flowers that the younger man had absent-mindedly begun to tear apart. Stripping off his gardening gloves, Dole kept his eyes fixed on the lawyer's embarrassed face.

"Write for the newspapers, Thurston. The Hawaiian Gazette. Write for anything. Lecture. Reach the American populace whenever and wherever you can. Inform them about the delicate, important question of Hawaiian control. Run for the Legislature. Become a representative, an independent candidate of the Opposition Party. I will do everything in my power - and it is not inconsiderable - to support you."

A peacock had wandered into the greenhouse. Dole casually booted it out with a sharp, swift kick. When the peacock shrieked, shedding a few feathers, Dole gingerly picked one up and cautiously sniffed at it.

"Beautiful. But nasty. And such a nuisance. They would nibble away at my bonsai trees" - He protectively caressed one of the small baskets. "Eat them all up, if I let them."

Thurston, still rattled over having his hand snatched away from the vine, stammered a little as he repeated the unfamiliar word. "B-b-bon - sigh?"

Dole lifted one of the weird, twisted trees from out of its basket and held it in front of Thurston's face. "Bonsai. Dwarfed trees. Trees that are properly trained, if you will." A faint smile played on his lips. "From the eternally patient Japanese. Ah, the refinement, the delicate arts of cutting and pruning back required to reach such controlled perfection -!" Tenderly, he replaced the tiny, stunted tree, and then motioned for Thurston to follow him into the house. As they emerged from the dim light of the greenhouse both men shielded their eyes from the bright tropical sun.

"Damn that light," Dole muttered. "Not quite civilized, somehow."

When they were sitting at Dole's elegant lunch table and the servants had served the soup course, the two men bowed their heads in a short, silent grace. Then Dole glared across at his edgy companion. "Run for office, Thurston. It is the only way we will accomplish anything solid."

Listening intently for his host's next words, Thurston had picked up a teaspoon, dipped it into the soup and almost carried it to his mouth when Dole's hand snaked out as fast as lightning. He snatched the spoon away from Thurston's hand and deftly clattered it onto a nearby bread plate. Shaking his head in stern disapproval he handed his guest the soup spoon.

Thurston, abashed, began to shakily slurp up his soup. Dole winced and made a discreet gesture, which caused one of the servers to instantly whisk the soup bowls out of sight while another replaced them with dishes of roast fowl. Nearly beside himself now with anxiety, Thurston looked with great concern at the neat row of three forks by the side of his plate. Selecting one with caution, he looked to Dole for reassurance. Shaking his head once more Dole fingered the proper fork in his own brace of silverware and nodded almost imperceptibly. Grateful, Thurston grabbed up his corresponding fork and was about to dive into his dish when Dole again stayed his hand.

"For what we are about to receive," said Dole, admonishing him, "Heavenly Father, we thank you."

Thurston was so relieved at knowing exactly what came next that he nearly shouted out his "Amen!"

For a moment the two men ate in silence. Then Thurston, still chewing loudly, remarked to his host, "Good! Chicken?"

"Delicious, isn't it?" Dole smiled. "Peacock! Quite the delicacy. Most of the Hawaiians, though, poor as they are, refuse to eat it." He took another small bite and savored the taste. "Another superstition, one can only suppose."

* * * * * * * * * * * * * * * * * *

Across town that evening at Ainahau the Cleghorn family was having a difficult bedtime. Kaiulani was not tired, not one bit, and her mother was very tired, and nothing Archibald Cleghorn or the harried new nursemaid said could make any peace between them. Though the day had been mild and fair, the night the air had suddenly turned heavy and stagnant, signaling the start of a muggy, threatening storm that even the cool breezes of Ainahau could not push away.

Kaiulani and Likelike were both acutely sensitive to changes in the weather and had been badly distressed by the turn. Each was very strong willed with the potential for dark, stubborn tempers and both were now engaged in an almost violent disagreement, the young twenty-six year old parent and the four year old child seeming at the moment to be about the same age.

"I won't, Mama, I won't!" Kaiulani said with an ominous calm. She clung to her father's bony shoulder. "Besides, Papa says I don't have to."

"Kaiulani!" her father pleaded, knowing the argument would only escalate.

"But Papa, you did! You told me a Princess must always be fair, and make up her own mind."

"Yes, but - "he demurred.

"Well, I also am a Princess," Likelike's eyes flashed dangerously. "And I am stronger and wiser than you and I say you must go to bed. Now."

Emma, the nanny, a myopic young woman with watery eyes and a thin, high voice, held up a little stuffed bear and said in a desperately cheerful tone, "Look, Kaiulani! Little Koa wants to go to sleep, too!"

For a second the child seemed to ignore this remark, but then she turned directly to her and patiently addressed the timid nurse. "No, Emma. His name is not 'Koa.' I never said so. And besides, Emma, toys don't sleep."

The worried nursemaid looked embarrassed and kept her eyes on the bear.

Archibald Cleghorn abruptly placed his petulant daughter down on her bed. "No, no," he said rather sternly. "Now, that's not right. You tell Emma you're sorry."

Kaiulani looked up at him with shining, velvety eyes.

"For - for - well, you say you're sorry for -"

Likelike's silvery laugh unexpectedly shivered out. "Oh, Archie, it's no good. She has my temper and your ridiculous logic. She'll never back down. Will you, my darling?" She spoke to Kaiulani with genuine affection.

Picking her up, she held the child close against her own hot face. "Come on, little girl, come on. We won't argue any more. Sit with Mommy out on the *lanai* and let's see if we can't find a little breeze out there, shall we?"

"And listen to the peacocks?" Kaiulani held herself rigid as she bargained with her mother, who only laughed and hugged her tighter.

"Yes, yes, you silly goose, and listen to your peacocks, too." She placed her forehead against Kaiulani's own. "Though I'll never know how you can stand all that crying."

The daughter at last relaxed and snuggled into her mother's arms, tucking her head into the woman's soft shoulder. "Thank you, Mama. And will you tell me a story, too?" Her hand closed loosely on the sleeve of her mother's lavender silk dressing gown; she had already begun to give in to her fatigue. "I love you, Mama," she murmured.

Likelike laughed again. She spun her daughter around in a circle, holding her in her arms. Then, as she carried her out of the room, she said softly "Of course you do, silly."

Archibald Cleghorn sighed at the sight of the pretty woman and the delicate, fierce child as they disappeared in a flurry of fragrance and soft colors.

"Well, Emma," he said crossly to the perplexed nanny, "I shall never pretend to understand females."

Emma looked terrified but said nothing.

The master of the house lowered his voice a touch. "Especially the Hawaiians." He shrugged his shoulders as if to release something from them. "The weaker sex, the gentler sex; oh, I suppose," he said to himself, for the nanny had already backed herself out of the room.

Cleghorn shook his head as he picked up the abandoned bear and carefully placed it at the foot of Kaiulani's bed.

"Well, perhaps my mother was like that, too," he mused to himself, after seeing that he was alone. "Somewhat."

"So sweet."

He made a disapproving sound, clicking his teeth against his tongue as he bent down to reposition the bear at the head of the bed.

"But those moods!"

Chapter Five

The peacocks' wide spread fans shimmered with color, vibrating in the bright morning sunlight. About a dozen of them circled around the base of the banyan tree. Their shrill voices filled the air with chattering noise, reverberating like the cries of young children. On a low branch of the sprawling banyan above them Kaiulani giggled with delight. She was six years old to the day and her radiant face glowed with pleasure as she jumped down to be surrounded by her pets. She ran around in the center of the darting birds with the peacocks following her like puppies as she teased them, making them chase her.

"Oh, no, *pikakaes*! No, no!" Kaiulani laughed at the creatures that jostled her. "You can't yell at me!"

She stopped and held the handfuls of grain behind her back, playfully dodging the birds with her shoulders and neck as they mobbed her, nuzzling for their treats.

"You know why you can't yell at me?!" She darted at them and they fluttered away cawing. "Do you? Because - "She rolled on the ground, laughing as they moved in again, this time allowing them to open her hands and take the food. "Because," she shouted with joy, "I am the Princess! And I say so!"

Likelike appeared at the door of the *lanai* and called for her daughter. Kaiulani sprang up, brushed off her dress and hurried over.

"All right, Mama, all right. I'm coming."

Upstairs in her mother's bedroom Kaiulani fidgeted as the seamstress held up a sky blue velvet dress. Likelike nodded with approval while Kaiulani screwed up her mouth with distaste.

"Oh, Mama, not that one," she cajoled. "I like the green one better."

"This one!" Likelike cried, looking at the light blue velvet against her child's golden face. "For once, on your birthday, you will listen to your mother!"

Kaiulani smiled sweetly, snuggling against Likelike's soft shoulder. "I always listen to you, Mama," she purred.

"Oh, no. You never do. You never listen to me." Her eyes sparkled as she took in her daughter's face. "But I just might have something here - "She flashed a tantalizing glimpse of a small package which she held cupped in her palm, "- that will make you listen!"

Kaiulani tried to reach for the package. "Oh, Mama! Give it to me! Please?"

Likelike made her guess which hand before she would turn over the gift.

"Earrings!" the girl exulted after she had unwrapped the package.

"More than just that, baby." Likelike held the obsidian black teardrops up to the light and their iridescent surfaces reflected a dark, glittering green.

"These are the tears of Pele." She spoke softly as she attached them to her daughter's ears. "When the goddess Pele weeps lava flows."

"When she is angry she makes the mountains burn, and some must die so that others may live." She held up a small mirror so Kaiulani could see herself; then pulled her daughter close and whispered into her ear. "Pele's Tears keep a traveler safe. They will protect anyone who is lonely and far from home."

Likelike pulled Kaiulani in still closer, almost hurting her as she grabbed on and held her in a tight hug. "You must be strong, Kaiulani. For your people. Always. It is your sacred duty. Do you hear me, little Princess?"

Eyes blazing, she held the solemn girl away from her at arm's length so she could look straight into her wide eyes. "Do you hear me?"

Subdued, Kaiulani spoke softly, too. "Yes, Mama."

"Good girl." Likelike kissed her cheek. "Now, close your eyes."

The mother pushed another, much larger package tied with huge pink and white bows into her arms. "Open this, now. Let's see what Mama Nui has sent you."

Kaiulani tore off the elaborate wrapping and lifted out of the box an oversized "picture book" hat, which had a large bow off to one side and long satin ribbons that tied at the chin.

"Oh, it's beautiful!" Kaiulani exclaimed.

"No," her mother said flatly. "Too fancy for a young girl."

"But, Mama!" Kaiulani complained as Likelike took the hat away. "That's not fair!"

"Oh, yes, it is too fair. You see? It fits me even better. We will get you a different one, more suitable for a young girl."

Kaiulani scowled, then raced away to play alone.

* * * * * * * * * * * * * * * * * * * *

Kalakaua sat in the dark study of the old wooden palace, which also served as his library and private meeting room. He was discussing his plans with his small inner circle of advisors.

"That way, you see, I will become the first king ever to tour America! By the time I return, Iolani Palace will be completed and we will have a grand, official coronation. With fine new uniforms and a tremendous celebration. This will be very good for everything; I am sure. For our economy, and for encouraging other royal families to meet us - because, of course, we will visit the royal families of Europe as well."

"My King." Paul Nahahuela, the Minister of Finance, was one of the only half Hawaiian, or *hapa-haole*, men there; a paler faces in the circle of mostly full-blooded Hawaiians. "There will be complaints, reform voices that will be quite critical of the expense."

"I know that," the King said. "I know." His face clouded up. "But I am afraid that our people are in grave danger. Every day more of them give up hope and soon after that they are gone. We all know that many of them are dying of despair, plain and simple. We must do anything we can to restore them."

"And who would rule in your absence, my King?" asked Kakani Haupu. A small, elderly man, Haupu was Kalakaua's long time friend and councilor. Like Kalakaua himself, he was a revered *kahuna*, one of the founding members of the Royal Genealogical Society and the Hawaii for Hawaiians organization.

"Princess Liliuokalani will take care of the kingdom and act as regent while I am gone. My sister is very well respected by our people and this will provide her an excellent opportunity to practice being ruler."

Murmurs of approval were heard around the room.

Kalakaua looked with satisfaction at his advisors.

"The foreigners, - with exceptions, of course, -" He paused to nod first at William Green, the German Minister of Foreign Affairs who also happened to be English; and then at Alfred Hartwell, an American who held the office of Attorney General. "The foreigners continue to prophesy the downfall of our nation. Shall we only sit by and watch the structure erected by our ancestors destroyed? If our house is dilapidated we must make repairs! So that our people can come back to life and prosper again in their own land!"

Kakani Haupu looked around at the others and sighed, shaking his head. "I hope it can be done," he said. "Ever since the Reciprocity Treaty with America, it seems Hawaii's business has been booming. But almost none of the wealth belongs to Hawaiians. Sugar plantations and rice fields and new buildings are everywhere, but we see none of the profits."

"We have empty promises while the others keep the cash and take over the land." Haupu shrugged. "We are 'allowed' to sell them sugar and pineapples and rice with no tariffs, but it is no longer our sugar or pineapples or rice. And, in return? They prosper and we lose everything. Where is the justice in that?" he pleaded.

"Our people pass away," Kakani agreed, "and foreigners take their places before the bodies have gone cold."

Haupu looked sadly at the King. "Pearl Lagoon has long been an important place for our people, a sacred *heiau*. We must never give that harbor over, no matter how much they offer us. Let them find somewhere else to keep their coal and repair their damn ships. It is not good to have the Americans holding so much land."

Kalakaua spread his hands out in supplication as he looked into his old friend's face. "I wish I knew what to do," he said simply.

Haupu placed his hand on the king's, then bowed his head to him. "It is a difficult time for everyone," Kakani said.

"Difficult or no," Kipi Nahinu, a young delegate with quick passions, broke in, "We must develop our defenses!" Kipi shot a look at the Minister of Foreign Affairs, who had recently been appointed by the new legislature, which was often hostile to Kalakaua. This new Minister of Foreign Affairs now controlled all of the Hawaiian armed forces. Nahinu's voice rose. "Soon they will abolish our navy, as well as the Hawaiian Board of Health and Genealogy -"

"Please, stop." Kalakaua held up his hand. "None of that now. Let us remember where we are. This is not the legislature. And we will not argue among ourselves."

His eyes flashed as he looked around at his circle of councilors and friends. "While we still live we can vote, and while we can still vote we will not be defeated, not yet! We shall not go down without a fight."

"These are the plans for our new palace," said the king, motioning to an attendant who spread several architectural drawings out over the table. "Our 'Hawk's Nest' - the nest of the bird of heaven - where the flaming torches of King Kalakaua and all the Hawaiians will continue to burn bright and free! Long after we are gone from this earth, Iolani Palace will stand; a monument, I hope, to the righteousness we struggle for today."

* * * * * * * * * * * * * * * * * * *

Kaiulani's sixth birthday *luau* had been underway for hours. Henri Berger and the Royal Hawaiian Band were playing everything from Kaiulani's March and Kalakaua's own rousing patriotic song, *"Hawaii Ponoi,"* to old Hawaiian melodies. They played German classical and folk music, and even the lively new tunes of Stephen Foster. Sets of "My Old Kentucky Home" and "Old Black Joe" alternated with traditional chants and *meles* and then blended with hybrids or hymns like "Glad Tidings."

At the breaks, Berger and Princess Liliuokalani could be seen engrossed in an ongoing dialogue, sometimes drumming out little phrases and beats of music as they talked, laughing and enjoying each others company. Liliu's husband, John Dominis, seemed aloof and haughty as he attended to his querulous, elderly mother, the two of them huddled off in a corner by themselves.

Kaiulani, who was wearing a midnight blue kimono dress trimmed with creamy Belgian lace, looked lovely. But her face became stormy every time she caught sight of her mother wearing Mama Nui's birthday gift hat. The tears of Pele earrings glittered, looking like little, dark, clouds whenever Kaiulani tossed her curls.

Observing the tension between her niece and her sister, Aunt Liliu had quietly asked Likelike if there was something wrong with the birthday girl.

"Oh, no," Likelike insisted blithely, returning to her daughter's side and briskly embracing the reluctant girl. Rebuffed, the mother tossed her own curls and scowled, looking for a moment very much like an older version of her angry, pretty daughter. Likelike adjusted the angle of the new hat; then bustled off to go stand beside Liliuokalani, Berger and the band. "Just one of her moods," she breezily informed her sister.

As the band completed the final stanza of "Oh, Susannah!," Mama Nui, Emelia and several members of Mama Nui's entourage descended on the party. A ripple of excitement raced through the crowd as Kaiulani dashed over to seek comfort from her godmother.

"Mama Nui," she began, but her substantial godmother held up her hand.

"Not one more word," the old woman cautioned in her most dramatic voice. "Close your eyes, my dear," she commanded the little Princess, who did so at once.

Four young men came up and formed a tight circle in front of Mama Nui, who stood with her hands planted firmly on Kaiulani's small shoulders.

"All right," she said, imperious as she waved the men aside. She clapped her hands over her goddaughter's eyes until everyone was out of the way, and then demanded, "Now, open them!"

The most beautiful, perfect, wonderful horse in the world pranced in front of Kaiulani's eyes. White as a gardenia and with a long, silky, gold-white mane, the child-sized pony was a dream come true. Speechless with joy, Kaiulani hugged Mama Nui as hard as she could.

"Oh!" Kaiulani stroked the darling pony's mane and hung on to Mama Nui's hand at the same time. "Oh!" she cried out again.

"Well, my dear Princess," Mama Nui laughed gaily, "Does your pony have a name, then?"

"Oh, yes, Mama Nui," Kaiulani was breathless. "Fairy! This is my kind and lovely Fairy!"

"Ah! An *akua*, eh? A good spirit that will ride you away to happiness! Very nice. Very thoughtful." She stooped down to kiss Kaiulani's cheek. "Truly, you are my goddaughter."

* * * * * * * * * * * * * * * * * * * *

Later that afternoon the guests sat around the *luau* tables waiting for the birthday girl to appear again so the feasting could begin. At the head of a long arrangement of low tables King Kalakaua, Princess Liliuokalani and Archibald Cleghorn sat together.

A buzz of excitement raced through the crowd as Kaiulani and Likelike, hand in hand, strolled onto the scene. Kaiulani had changed into a satiny, golden yellow party dress and looked much brighter and happier than before. Suddenly, she stopped still, broke from her mother's grasp and ran over to her cousin Koa, now a handsome boy of thirteen. They kissed, after which Koa proudly escorted the Princess to her place of honor.

Kalakaua motioned for silence, then rose to propose a toast. "To the health of the Princess on her sixth birthday."

When Kaiulani came and stood beside him he reached out his hand to her and rested it on her delicate shoulder.

"May this Princess grow up with every possible advantage of our times so that she may ably fill her position in the future to the credit of our country and our people!"

Cheers rang out, and then Theo Davies stood and presented Kaiulani with a bouquet of *pikake*, the fragrant white jasmine flowers she loved so well.

"May Princess Kaiulani come to be the Hope of the Nation!" Davies bowed down low to kiss her small hand. "*Aloha nui*," he said, "We all love you very much, Princess Kaiulani."

Then the *luau* began in earnest, going on late into the afternoon.

It was almost dusk when Kalakaua and Kaiulani found themselves a moment alone, in the Japanese garden away from the birthday crowd. Kalakaua told his goddaughter about his plans to travel and a shadow passed over her warm, flushed face.

"But, Papa Moi! I should miss you terribly if you went away!"

"I know, sweetheart. I will miss you, too." Her godfather took her hand. "But I'll be on a royal tour, all around the whole world, - Japan, France, everywhere! Just think what an honor that will be for Hawaii, eh?"

He lifted her chin and spoke to her softly, coaxing a tiny smile. "Iolani Palace will be finished by the time I return; a brand new home for the *ali'i*. Someday, perhaps, for your own daughters and sons as well?"

She smiled in spite of herself.

Encouraged, he added, "And for generations to come!"

Kaiulani played with his fingers, giving up on trying to hold back her grin.

"When you come back, then will we have the crowno - the corno - "

"Yes, baby." Kalakaua laughed. "We will celebrate with a wonderful coronation and a huge *luau* for everyone that will go on for many days. Now, young lady, enough of spending what's left of your birthday with an old man. Go find your cousin Koa and have fun with someone who can keep up with you."

* * * * * * * * * * * * * * * * * * *

The soft pastel colors of pink and lavender tinted the early evening skies and the water as Kaiulani and Koa waltzed, gracefully, formally, alone in the gazebo at Ainahau. They were excellent dancers, so perfectly in rhythm with each other that they seemed to be floating in the muted twilight. Their affection was obvious and the solemn way they spoke to each other made them seem older than their years. Koa turned Kaiulani carefully, holding her with a firm but delicate touch.

"What if someday," Koa said, "you had to leave Hawaii and go far away?"

Kaiulani looked deep into his eyes to see if he meant this as a joke. "Silly! I won't have to leave here, ever. Ainahau is mine. Mama Nui gave it to me when I was born. When I grow up this will be the center of the kingdom."

Koa insisted, stubborn. "All the same. I know that I will soon have to go away."

Kaiulani was so shocked she stopped dancing. "Koa, no! Why?"

"To school." He sighed heavily. "In America, perhaps. Or even England, where it is horribly cold and rains every single day. To learn about - "He pronounced the words meticulously, as if he had memorized them, which he had. "- International Culture."

"How terrible for you," Kaiulani said. They sat down by the water on a stone bench that was carved to look like a large turtle shell. "You will come back?" The question was tinged with infinite sadness.

"Of course," said Koa, holding her hand. "Of course I will."

The cousins sat for a long moment, gazing into the moonlight reflected in the still water.

"Koa." Kaiulani's voice was very soft when she broke the silence. "Koa, can a Queen do whatever she wants?"

He considered carefully before he answered.

"Yes, I think so. Yes."

Kaiulani looked into his dark brown eyes. "When I am Queen, then, I shall marry you."

Flustered, Koa pulled his hand away. "It is not necessarily - good—to try to see into the future." He stood. "We do not know what may come to pass."

Kaiulani, who had risen with him, moved a little away. Half annoyed and half-playful, she lightly pushed him. "Oh, Koa. Sometimes you sound just like my mother."

* * * * * * * * * * * * * * * * * * *

That evening Kalakaua and Kaiulani danced together, the King resplendent in gold and blue and the girl glowing like an exotic flower in her golden dress, her black hair shining in the moonlight.

"Papa Moi, what good is it being a Princess if you can't have what you want?"

"Ah," said the king. "No one can always get what they want, baby. Not even a princess or a king."

Kaiulani looked up at her godfather, the tall, invincible king. "Not even," her voice was wistful, "on our birthdays?"

The stars shone in their eyes as he swept her up into his arms and sadly shook his head.

* * * * * * * * * * * * * * * * * * *

Much later that night, when almost all of the guests had gone home, the royal family and a few close friends sat down by the water to sing old songs. Henri Berger strummed a guitar and Theo Davies occasionally joined in with his ukulele on the livelier tunes. The night was very still except for their singing and the sound of the waves. Koa and Kaiulani had fallen asleep, side by side.

Liliuokalani touched the bandleader's guitar, and he handed it to her at once with a fond smile. An instant spark of understanding and affection flickered between them as their hands touched. Liliu bent in to the instrument, caressing it like it was a precious child. Playing a few simple notes she began to hum, almost to herself, a song that was sweet and sad.

Likelike, sitting nearby, turned her face to better hear the sound.

"Is that a new one of yours?" She asked her sister.

Liliuokalani nodded. "I call it '*Aloha Oe*.'" She began to sing the words in her clear, strong contralto while she accompanied herself on the guitar. Haunting and melancholy, the sound drifted out among the sleepy company like smoke or a spell. Everyone who listened was caught up in its net, the longing, lonesome notes catching at their hearts.

"Farewell to thee, farewell to thee,
Thou charming one who dwells in shaded bowers.
One fond embrace ere we depart,
Until we meet again."

Cleghorn and Likelike joined hands as she wiped away a tear. Kalakaua and Kapiolani leaned their heads in against each other and sat very still. Koa, who had awakened, sat carefully, without moving, so as not to disturb Kaiulani whose hand, even in her sleep, rested against his. Mama Nui, propped up on a bench and cushioned by her little yellow pillows, wept openly as Emelia made soothing little circles on her back.

"Beautiful!" Mama Nui cried out when the song had ended. "But so sad!"

Cleghorn tenderly lifted his sleeping daughter; she shifted in her sleep but did not wake. A *lei* of white flowers fell from her hand and Likelike picked it up.

"Jasmine," she said, inhaling their sweet scent. "My baby's favorite."

"*Pikake*." Mama Nui lifted the *lei* from Likelike's hand and sniffed its wilted, bedraggled flowers. "Peacocks. Peacock flowers. Goodnight - "She kissed her goddaughter's forehead. "Good night, little Princess of the Peacocks."

Chapter Six

When their ship sailed from Oahu, King Kalakaua and Queen Kapiolani and their retinue, draped with layers of flower *leis*, had waved and waved at all the Hawaiians who had come to see them off on their long journey. The dancers and singers who had come to say good-by performed late into the night in their honor. Hundreds came to see them off, and the music of Henri Berger and the Royal Hawaiian Band followed them as they sailed away toward California.

In a few weeks, word came back to Hawaii that a twenty-one-gun salute had greeted them when they arrived in San Francisco's harbor. The entire city had celebrated for days, thrilled to be hosting their first "real king."

Months after they had been gone, rumors floated back to the islands that the king, while visiting in Japan, had promised Kaiulani's hand in marriage to the young Imperial Prince, Yamashira Sadamaro, a fifteen-year old naval cadet who was still in school. Eventually, the King himself wrote to Liliuokalani, praising the boy Prince. He called him "lively and very bright, a promising lad"; but said nothing about any engagement.

When Kaiulani first heard the betrothal rumors she was quite upset and went off alone to ride Fairy and wrestle with this strange notion. But by the time she returned she was calm again, having shrugged off the idea of marrying a foreign prince she had never even met, sure that Papa Moi would never ask her to do anything she did not want to do.

Most of the news that drifted back regarding the tour was of wonderful successes. There were presentations and state dinners with Queen Victoria; with King Umberto and Queen Margherita of Italy; and even an audience with the Pope. When they visited Queen Victoria at Windsor Castle, she presented Kalakaua with two medals of great distinction, the St. George and the St. Michael. Prince William of Prussia displayed the maneuvers of his seven thousand mounted troops in honor of the Hawaiians. In Japan, the royal couple had stayed in a very fine palace surrounded by a moat. The Japanese Emperor had awarded Kalakaua the Chrysanthemum Award, one of the most prestigious honors of his country.

In Greece, in Alexandria, Kalakaua spoke, with the help of a translator, in front of his own membership society, the Masonic Fraternity. He was greatly acclaimed for his humor and wit. China, Siam, India and Asia celebrated the Hawaiians' visit for days. Altogether, the King was well pleased with their reception, and proud of the impression they made for Hawaii in the cities of the world. He took extensive notes on their nine-month tour, and worked on many new plans for ways to support and encourage his people and to strengthen the power of the monarchy.

There were two difficult visits as well. For some reason, the French were quite cool to them. And, in Vienna, the King had deeply offended the Austrian princess when he drank too much at a restaurant and then insisted on kissing several of the women in their party. But the Khedive, or Viceroy, of Egypt, received them with the utmost hospitality, for he sympathized strongly with Hawaii's problem of increasing foreign dominance, as his country, too, had for some time chafed under European rule.

* * * * * * * * * * * * * * * * * * * *

Back home, Princess Liliuokalani had become very popular in her temporary role as leader. Several of the *kanakas* she met in her travels were eager to let her know how happy they were to have a woman in charge again. Implying no disrespect, of course, they explained, toward their King whom they dearly loved. It was just that a woman *ali'i* seemed somehow more in touch with the forces of nature and the land.

Liliuokalani often took Kaiulani with her; together they rode in the city parks to see and be seen by their people. Kaiulani taught Fairy how to stop to curtsy and make a low bow to the *kanakas,* who always clapped and laughed at this graceful tribute.

Princess Liliuokalani wanted to use the time of her acting regency to learn more about her people and so she made plans to visit all of the Islands. But, before she could start out on her inter-island trip, an outbreak of smallpox struck Honolulu. At Liliu's command, communications between the Islands were cut off until the sickness could be brought under control. After the disease had run its course, she was much praised for her swift, good judgment.

As soon as she was able to resume her plans to visit all of her subjects, Liliuokalani set out, taking with her the Royal Hawaiian Band; Mama Nui and Emelia and the pillows; an entourage of attendants; and her favorite cousin, Bernice Paulahi Bishop.

By the time they arrived on the Big Island of Hawaii the lava flows of Mauna Loa were threatening to engulf the entire town of Hilo. Everyone was becoming very concerned about the increasing danger of losing their homes and lands; and they were all very afraid of Pele's anger. Liliu, a lifelong Christian, visited the churches of Hilo and lead a number of prayer meetings in the smoky, acrid, red-hazed air. When the lava abruptly, mysteriously stopped the official story was that Liliuokalani's prayers had saved the city of Hilo. But the Hawaiians knew otherwise.

* * * * * * * * * * * * * * * * * * *

Mama Nui, who many of her people knew as "Princess Keelikolani" or "Princess Ruth", had not been in good health for some time. Only reluctantly had she consented to travelling with Liliu, and "strictly for the sake of my people." When the royal entourage landed on the Big Island, about halfway through their journey, they found a group of representatives from Hilo waiting to see Mama Nui. They pleaded with her to save their town from Pele's wrath. Princess Ruth, they knew, was herself a powerful *kahuna*, and her connection with the goddess was very strong.

Mama Nui sighed and shifted and shook her head. In the end, however, compassion prevailed over good sense, and she agreed to go to the source of Pele's rage. At great personal danger and expense she traveled in a wooden carriage that had to be specially made to accommodate her great size. The trip took several days; by the time they arrived Mama Nui had to rest for a full day to recover from the effort.

At the edge of the encroaching lava's flow, the malevolent volcano burned up the air, singeing the inside of the mouth and nose like hot pepper; crackling like an angry voice hissing into everyone's ears. Mama Nui rested and ate large quantities of food while the natives worried and worried.

At last Princess Ruth went to the edge of the volcano to speak to the furious Pele who spit liquid fire and ashes from the lava's shore. Ignoring the suffocating heat Mama Nui chanted loudly at first; then became soft and cajoling, coaxing the goddess. After what seemed like many hours Mama Nui unwound a long, red silk scarf from her burning throat. Tenderly, she threw it into the volcano's fire where it flared up like a match. She followed that scarlet bandanna with thirty or so more scarves, all of them red, one at a time, watching each one make a small explosion as it burst into flames. When all the scarves were gone Princess Ruth raised up a very old, brown amber bottle of aged brandy. She smashed this onto the hot lava rocks and watched as it exploded into crackling fire. In a low, soothing tone the elderly princess intoned a long prayer, then bowed her head and stood for a long moment in silence. She touched her heart and hand in respect and to say farewell to the goddess Pele. Then she turned away from the molten inferno.

Mama Nui seemed to collapse a little, her oversized frame sinking into itself, so that Emelia rushed over to steady her shaking mistress. Ruth motioned weakly for her retainers and commanded them in a whisper to make up a bed for her right at the edge of the lava's flow. When this was done she sank down into it and fell immediately into a deep sleep, sleeping straight through until dawn. By morning the lava had stopped, halting within two yards of the sleeping Princess.

Those who were close to Mama Nui said that the struggle with Pele changed her; that ever after that she was quieter, slower, subdued. Others dismissed that as nonsense. Whatever was true, after that ordeal with Pele she cut her trip short to return to Oahu.

Princess Liliuokalani, however, decided to continue and went on alone to Molokai to visit Father Damien and his colony of lepers. Liliuokalani insisted on sending the other members of her party back to Oahu, for she did not wish to expose anyone to possible danger. She went with only four attendants; two of these had family members they wanted to see again one last time, and two had expressed a desire to see for themselves the famous community and its legendary priest.

The morning sun was shining brightly when the royal party reached Molokai's shore. An awkward, large, clumsy man with bottle-thick glasses, wearing a badly worn, wide-brimmed, flat hat and a shabby, sack-like priest's robe, waited to meet them. With tremendous energy Father Damien de Veuster of Belgium came forward and made an odd, ungainly sort of bow to Liliuokalani, who gracefully returned the gesture.

At close range Liliu could see the lichen-like patches of the early stages of the incurable disease that had begun to blossom out on Damien's face and hands. More than eight hundred lepers from the colony had gathered in a long line at the landing dock to greet them. These people gave the Princess Regent and her company a rousing ovation, waving and smiling at the visitors. They had even put together a makeshift band to welcome them. One of the attendants clutched his heart and cried out when he recognized his long lost sister at the same time that she saw him. They fell to the ground, kneeling before one another, unable to embrace, and wept.

Liliu had planned at first to stay for no more than an hour, but Father Damien was proud to show off the community. Liliu, intrigued, had scores of questions. She discussed with him at length the capacity of the great pots and bowls in the busy kitchens; the dormitories' orderly, though not very clean, appearance; and the cave-like charm of the candle lit chapel. She praised the many work areas where even the most debilitated members tried to be productive with what was left of their lives. Portraits of the royal family were prominently displayed in the dining hall. There was a painting of the King and Queen; one of Liliuokalani smiling next to a prized rose tree; and one of Kaiulani as a baby nestled in Likelike's arms. Princess Liliuokalani stayed on for the entire day, and sat down that evening to share supper and grace with Father Damien and his flock.

Bonfires crackled on the beach at Molokai that night. *Kukui* nut torches bound with *ti* leaves lit up the darkness to reveal a crowd of lepers who followed Liliu and her group to the boat landing. The melancholy songs of farewell came to an end when Liliu and Damien reached the ship, which waited at the dock. The priest made several quick bows, holding his hands carefully close in and tight against his sides under his cassock. But Liliuokalani, very deliberately, offered him her hand. When Damien hesitated for a moment, he and the princess looked into each other's eyes. Then he accepted, raising her hand to kiss it. Liliuokalani in turn lifted up a medal on a silk cord, the Royal Order of Kalakaua, and placed it around the neck of the shambling old man whose eyes glistened with tears. With a last wave Liliu boarded the ship and sailed away into the night. The bonfires on the beach blinked like cat's eyes, or like stars fading out in the sky.

When Liliu returned to Honolulu she was dismayed to see the city draped in the black crepe of mourning. President Garfield had been assassinated in America, gunned down by a rejected, would-be ambassador at a railroad station in Washington, D.C. Sadly, he had suffered a lingering death, not passing away until eighty days later at his family's seaside cottage on the New Jersey shore. Services and meetings were held throughout the Islands to express sympathy with the grieving American people.

Not long after Liliu's return, the King and Queen also came home, loaded down with gifts and keepsakes from their trip around the world. Kalakaua was a little surprised at how much Liliuokalani's popularity had grown in his absence, and decided it was time for her to concentrate on social and cultural issues, now that he was back to handle the politics.

Happy to return to the projects dear to her heart, Liliuokalani enlisted Kapiolani and Likelike's help. They planned and plotted together over how to finance a maternity home for poor mothers of sickly babies, as another concerted effort to help increase and stabilize the population. Kapiolani was especially committed to realizing this dream, along with initiating her plans for a hospital for the care of all Hawaiians.

Liliu's was particularly interested in building a school for girls, where they would be taught Hawaiian history, language and music. True, there were already *haole* schools for girls; but there they were only taught how to cook, clean and sew. Liliu campaigned tirelessly for a school for "ladies and scholars," reasoning that they should become "domestics by choice only, not by forfeit."

The last project the women organized was their most ambitious - a bank exclusively for Hawaiian women. Many of these women had already been handling money and business affairs for centuries of their country's history. Now, with the untimely deaths of so many of their men, combined with traditional inheritance procedures that upheld equal property rights for all, much of the wealth of the Hawaiian land-money belonged to women. Some of these wealthy women married *haole* husbands, who advised them not to worry their pretty little heads about such boring subjects as property and land, because those things were really the concerns of men.

Likelike knew next to nothing about affairs of finance and property, secretly thinking them very tedious indeed and being glad to leave such dull problems to Cleghorn. But she was happy to help her sister and sister-in-law in their efforts; and even organized by herself several ice cream socials and bake sales with great success. Kaiulani also helped out at these events. After these fund raisers mother and daughter came home together, tired but elated, and full of ice cream and cookies.

Kalakaua had only a nodding acquaintance with the women's' hard work. Kapiolani talked to him often enough about their efforts, but it was usually either late at night or else early in the morning. At night, he almost always fell fast asleep, and in the daytime he would listen and nod, and at times even said "Good show," a phrase he had picked up in England; but he was really only pretending to take in what she said. The King was quite busy with plans of his own. Iolani Palace had been completed at last and plans for the long awaited coronation were underway. Scheduled for February 12, 1883, it would take place exactly nine years to the day that Kalakaua had acceded to the throne.

Liliuokalani was also, as always, busy with her music. One Sunday Likelike and Kaiulani dressed up to visit the Honolulu Church where "Princess Liliuokalani's Singing Girls" were performing their concert in front of a full house. The royal mother and daughter were seated in the position of honor in the front pew.

When the Lady Conductor signaled, a young girl scampered out to the front to announce the featured selection. Curtseying briefly, she shyly announced, "Liliuokalani's Prayer." But when the child started to dart back to her place the conductor violently motioned her to return to center stage. Freezing for an instant, the young performer suddenly realized what she had forgotten and dashed back. With another low bow she stood right in front of Kaiulani and stammered out in a breathless voice, "Lovingly Dedicated to Her Niece, Princess Victoria Kaiulani!"

Kaiulani smiled and waved at her, and the girl, giggling and thrilled, raced back a second time to stand in the choir.

When the choir mistress raised her hand the girls made a humming sound as they struggled to find their pitches. Then, opening their mouths wide like hungry little birds, they began to sing out in lilting, sweet voices.

> "O Lord Thy loving mercy
> Is high as the heavens,
> It tells me of Thy truth,
> And tis filled with holiness.
> Oh! Look not on their failings,
> Nor on the sins of man,
> Forgive with loving kindness,
> That we might be made pure.
> For Thy grace I beseech Thee,
> Bring us 'neath Thy protection,
> And peace shall be our position,
> Now and forever more."

Chapter Seven

The King looked splendid in his custom-tailored, black broadcloth suit as he stood before an impressive crowd of natives, more Hawaiians than anyone had seen in a long time. From all of the Islands they had come, traveling by boat to Oahu, then on foot or by carriage or on horseback. Some rode the new streetcars, pulled by mules, and wondered at the frantic, exciting pace of the city.

"I have studied the royal courts of Europe and Asia," Kalakaua beamed down on his people, "and I come back to you with many excellent ideas about how we can become more secure and independent."

"I am grateful and happy to see you all, and I welcome you with *aloha* and open arms."

The crowd applauded wildly. Cries of "Long live the King!" and "*Hoolu lahui!*" rang out all around.

Although the sun had been hiding behind clouds and drizzling rain for ten days, the light that there was picked up the shine of the epaulets and medals Kalakaua had brought back from all over the world. The metal pieces that winked brightly from his broad chest looked like dozens of blinking eyes.

"I desire to incite you toward the renewal of our nation, the extinction of which has been prophesied by many of the foreigners, a few who live here, many who do not." His powerful bass resonated through the crowd. "Shall we only watch and wait, to see the country cherished by our mothers and fathers fall to pieces?"

A rumble of negative response met his plea.

"That is right!" The King cried out. "If our house is falling down, we must fix it! We must renovate ourselves so that our nation will grow again with renewed life and vigor!"

The applause that greeted this almost drowned out the king's words as he reassured them that he would protect the people's interests for as long as he lived. He would, he promised, see them all again tomorrow for the Coronation ceremony and the dedication of Iolani Palace the next day.

Mark Twain, a journalist who often wrote articles for the pro-*haole* papers, was present for the king's speech. He had just recently referred to the Hawaiians as "luckless, or at least foolish barbarians." After Kalakaua's speech, Twain railed in the press about "the oddity of the King claiming to protect the natives at all costs on the one hand, and bleeding them dry on the other."

When told of the journalist's remarks, the King only shook his head sadly and said, "He is clever, like a politician. But he does not understand us, not at all."

The next morning, February 12, 1883, the sun was hiding again. At the palace an elderly valet brushed off the King's shoulders, sleeves and back one more time. Kalakaua wore the crisp, tailored uniform of the highest office of the King's Guards. His coat, a dazzling white, was hung with medallions of silver, platinum and gold. The King's Cross, glittering with sapphires and diamonds, hung from a blue and white silk ribbon around his neck. A wide, sky blue sash fit snugly across his chest and a watch in the shape of a star was pinned near his heart.

Theo Davies, who was sitting in the King's dressing room, nodded in solemn admiration as Kalakaua turned slowly around to show off the effect of his ensemble in an arrangement of mirrors that reflected his image to infinity.

"Thank you for helping me polish my speech, Theo."

Davies, his light red mustache and mutton chop whiskers the same coppery color as his frizzy helmet of hair, shrugged.

"It is good," the King said with a sly, sideways glance as he sat down beside his friend, careful not to wrinkle his uniform, "to have a friend who can speak English, *haole* and Hawaiian."

Theo returned his smile. "I am always glad to be useful."

When the valet poured them iced champagne, the two men toasted each other in silence.

The King dusted an imaginary spot off one of his medals and slowly shook his head.

"I saw many sad things on my tour around the world." Again he shook his head. "But do you know, Theo, that with all its faults - and there are many, I know - the Hawaiian kingdom is not such a bad place."

The valet draped an ancient cape made from countless layers of tiny golden yellow feathers, soft and plush as thick velvet, over Kalakaua's shoulders. This robe, carefully preserved over centuries, had been the symbol of Hawaiian royalty for hundreds of years. The King touched the cloak respectfully and motioned for the retainer to return it to safekeeping until the ceremony. The attendant then handed the king a white helmet designed with feathers even smaller than those in the cloak, woven into intricate patterns of red, white and blue. Kalakaua himself adjusted the warrior king's helmet into place.

"With all their misfortunes," he considered, "the Hawaiian people are not so badly off..."

The two men walked down the palace stairs to the waiting coach and stepped inside. The horse drawn carriage moved slowly toward the pavilion, which had been designed especially for the coronation. Kalakaua waved and smiled out upon the throngs of people - natives, *haoles*, and foreigners—that jammed the streets. As he greeted the people from the open window of his coach he continued the conversation with his companion who could not be seen by anyone but him.

"They are better off than most, in fact," the king observed. "They have enough to eat and wear and, despite all their recent troubles, and there are many, that cannot be denied, they are happier than any other people I have seen."

As they turned past a wide corner, the faint, melancholy strains of "*Aloha Oe*", played on a solitary guitar, could be clearly heard just for a moment. Then the cheering of the crowds drowned out the lonely sound and the coach rolled on.

"They are never in debt, because no one trusts them. They love music and the outdoor life; they never go to bed hungry; no one robs them. And they have no indigestion, which is very common in America."

Davies momentarily rested his hand on the king's. Gently he said to his friend, "I am afraid your people may be dying out."

Kalakaua smiled at his companion with genuine warmth. "Well, if they are, I have read lots of times that great races die out and then new ones take their place."

The coach pulled up to the pavilion. Assisted by a waiting attendant the King stepped down out of the dark carriage and into the pale, morning light. He spoke softly back over his shoulder to Davies who remained invisible inside. "I think perhaps the best thing is to let us be."

In very high affairs of state it was the custom for the royal couple to travel separately, in case anything should happen to either one of them. Queen Kapiolani had come in her own carriage, accompanied by Princess Liliuokalani and Liliu's husband and consort, John Dominis.

Dressmakers in London and Paris had been busy for months working to provide the royal Hawaiian women with two coronation gowns each, one for the ceremony and the other for the Grand Ball that would follow.

Queen Kapiolani wore a white satin, cap sleeved gown, trimmed at the neck with a froth of Belgian lace and richly embroidered with gold fern leaves down the bodice, with white velvet edging the hem. A sash, the same deep sky blue as the King's, was draped over one of her sleeves, held in close to her shoulder and then tucked in at her waist. A black and crimson velvet train trimmed with ermine had been carefully arranged at her feet. The edges of her cape were embroidered with the *taro* leaf, the symbol of Hawaii, in gold thread. Kapiolani wore gold and diamond pendant earrings, and a circular gold necklace that had diamond starbursts all around and an emerald pendant at the center. Like all of the royal women that day she wore white, elbow length gloves.

Princess Liliuokalani, heiress apparent, glowed in a golden brocaded gown from Persia. A front panel of white silk, embroidered in a slightly darker shade of gold, was done up in an intricate pattern of *fleur de lis*, and a rich crimson velvet train flowed at her feet. The simple diamond cross she always wore hung at her neck. Her earrings were diamond and ruby teardrops, and her headdress was fashioned out of tiny white feathers tipped with seed pearls and gold leaves. John Dominis, who had recently been appointed Governor of Oahu, looked somber and almost painfully thin in his conservative black suit and tie, eclipsed by the lush elegance of the women.

* * * * * * * * * * * * * * * * * * *

At Waikiki, on the other side of the island, the Cleghorn family was trying to get ready to leave. Miss Barnes, yet another in a long line of governesses hired for Kaiulani, fussed over her charge.

Kaiulani looked like an angel in a pale blue silk dress trimmed with lace as delicate as baby's breath flowers. She was flushed with excitement; but she was also seven years old and determined not to be treated like a baby.

"Miss Barnes, please," she said with solemn dignity, "Do not tug at my hair." Her teacher was trying to tie back with pale blue velvet ribbons the dark curls that cascaded to her shoulders.

Likelike looked beautiful in white satin brocade trimmed with ostrich feathers and pearls. A wreath of pink and white roses sat perched at the top of her chignon hairdo. She had ordered her gown from a San Francisco dressmaker, against the advice of both her sister and the Queen. But she had been enormously pleased with the results as, the day before, she viewed the effect of her ensemble over and over again from every angle. Archibald Cleghorn came up behind his wife and tenderly kissed her warm neck. Giggling, she told him to be careful not to mess up her hair.

"You look wonderful, my darling. You will be the most gorgeous woman there."

Princess Likelike's face clouded up with a pouty scowl. "I don't know why Kaiulani has to walk on first, before we do."

"Sweetheart, we've already talked about this several times. Kaiulani is the closest in line after Liliu. I am the Assistant Governor, and so you must stand beside me both as Princess and as my first lady."

"Oh, well," Likelike flicked at her sparkling, dangly earrings and smiled, the storm having unexpectedly blown over in the excitement of the day. "I suppose." She bent down to kiss Kaiulani on both cheeks. "Come on, baby. Let's go."

"Mama," Kaiulani explained patiently, "I'm not a baby anymore."

"Tish, tish," her mother said with some heat.

"Now, you two," Cleghorn warned, "That's enough. No more."

They all stepped out into the hall where their attendants waited, two of them holding the tall white *kahili* fans on long poles, one for each princess.

The Cleghorns arrived at Iolani Palace at nine in the morning, three hours before the coronation was to take place. The streets were packed with people from everywhere. *Haoles*, natives and foreigners had all gathered to witness the most lavish display in Hawaii's history. But the Cleghorns' carriage had traveled swiftly through the crowds, people immediately making way for them as soon as they recognized the "bird of heaven" insignia on the coach. That same royal symbol, in the form of a brass statue of the spread-winged hawk, was posted like a sentry in a prominent position in the palace's main front hall. The imposing creature fiercely guarded the palace entrance, riveting its gaze on all who dared to enter.

Hawaii had never witnessed such a spectacle of beauty, such a stirring display of taste and wealth. The pillars of Iolani palace were Georgian, and every one was draped with an extravagant variety of ferns, flowers and streamers. Decorations of every shape and style waved from all the doorways and windows. The King's red and green monogram was hung on banners everywhere.

The palace's two stories, which were made of bricks and iron with cement facings and concrete blocks for trim, included a basement and an attic. There were square, compact, towers both in front and in back of the building, and open *lanais*, or porches, surrounded it on both levels and all around, interrupted only by small rooms tucked under each of the four corner towers. Corinthian columns supported the balconies; and Persian motifs of intricate carvings decorated the exterior with stars and mosaic-style shapes in repeating patterns.

The Hawaiian flag, with its small replica of the red ensign of the British Union Jack in the upper left-hand corner, waved from the very highest point of the building's main tower. The flag's eight bold stripes of white, blue and red represented the kingdom's main islands; and the flag could be seen everywhere that day.

Inside, the palace was finished with a rich variety of woods. In addition to the native *koa, kou ohia* and *kamani* woods, there was soft, white Oregon state cedar and dark, whorled walnut imported from America's northeastern states. All of these woods were densely carved, as lavish and detailed as any that could be found in Queen Victoria's Windsor Castle.

The massive front doors of the palace were paneled and decorated with extra wide cornices. All the ceilings had been plastered white and then enhanced with moldings that were gilded around the edges. The floors of the *lanais* were Italian marble tiles in mottled shades of pink, white and gray. The hardwood floors inside the palace had been polished to a gleaming sheen. The flurry of decorations, added on everywhere to the inside carvings, included flowers, grapes, royal crowns, coats of arms, crossed swords alongside cupids, egg and dart moldings, and intricate, elaborate combinations of fluted medallions and rosettes.

Wide flights of iron stairs led to the first floor both in front and back of the building. The huge Throne Room extended along the entire length of the Waikiki side of the palace, interrupted only by a small anteroom tucked behind the throne's raised dais. A sitting room painted in the softest shades of blue gave a cool, inviting touch to the other side of the main floor, and an impressive formal state dining room in gold, white and black stood beside it.

An ornate staircase, similar to those seen in the grand opera houses, wound up from the downstairs central hall to another even wider hall on the second level. On one side was the king's suites; his sitting room, bedroom and anteroom, all hung with pale blue silk, faced out onto a view of the Wavanae Mountains. On the other side were the Queen's three rooms, in multiple shades of ivory; these looked out onto Diamond Head and Waikiki. The furniture in both suites was ebony wood inlaid with ivory. The ample bathtubs, copper lined, were encased in dark mahogany; and the washstands were made of rose colored Italian marble with brass fixtures shaped like cherubs and angels blowing trumpets.

In the basement, accessible only from the outside staircases on either side of the building and by a small inner stairway that lead to the first and second floors, were the kitchens, wine cellars and the chamberlain's offices. The remaining downstairs space was taken up by numerous storerooms which held traditional artifacts - ancient feather cloaks and calabashes, helmets, ceremonial robes, *kahilis*, dishes, silver and glasses.

Never had Hawaii been home to such opulence. Most of the natives who witnessed this wonder felt their hearts swell with happiness and pride. Even in those times of such trouble for so many, the people were glad to see their *ali'i* representing them so grandly; putting on such a dazzling show of prosperity and well being.

But a few of the spectators there that day, many of them with light skin and dark hearts, observed the proceedings with grim resentment and greed, bitterly convinced that the king had misused precious wealth that might otherwise have found its way into their own eager pockets.

Eighteen thousand invitations, bordered in red and gold and embossed with the royal seal, had gone out to Hawaiians and *haoles* alike. They had been sent to the American President, Mr. Chester A. Arthur; and to the royals and heads of government and state and all the other dignitaries Kalakaua had met during his trip around the world. More than two thousand copies of the program of events had been printed in both Hawaiian and English.

Into this melee the Cleghorn family came to wait in the Queen's upstairs bedroom. Archie Cleghorn made little clicking noises with his tongue against his teeth, as he often did when he was nervous or excited. Likelike fussed with her neckline and pinned and re-pinned an errant broach, while Kaiulani, impatient and thrilled, craned dangerously out of the window to get better views of everything.

"Mama, Mama," she began.

"Do not ask me again about Ruth! For the last time, I do not know where Mama Nui is or when she will get here. And I'm sure she can take care of herself without you worrying me to death!"

Kaiulani tucked her head in a little. "I only wondered -"

"Well, don't wonder," snapped her anxious mother, who was secretly also concerned about Princess Keelikolani's absence; and even more about her own brief part in the ceremony.

"Now, now, kitten." Her father patted her shoulder.

Kaiulani looked out the window again to search the crowds, hoping for a sign of Mama Nui. She saw stiff, starched diplomats from many countries, with ladies on their arms who looked like fashion plates out of magazines. There were officers and soldiers from all the foreign warships docked in the harbor; and *haole* families, rich and poor; and businessmen, and, of course, thousands of Hawaiians. But nowhere could she find Mama Nui. She waited and waited for her godmother to show up, but there were so many people that day, and so much to see and do, that, eventually, bit by bit, she forgot about Mama Nui in the excitement of the day. Much later, when she remembered again, she felt disloyal and ashamed of forgetting so completely someone she loved so much.

The sun came out at ten o'clock for just a moment, only to disappear again behind a bank of clouds. The Hawaiians, who always attached great significance to changes in the weather, murmured and worried over what this might mean. At ten thirty, when the Cleghorns arrived at the coronation pavilion, the sky was still overcast.

Because the crowds were already spilling over from the amphitheater onto the palace lawns, it was decided to begin before the scheduled time of noon. At eleven fifteen the conch shells and trumpets were blown to announce the opening ceremony.

* * * * * * * * * * * * * * * * * * * *

One by one, in a somber line, the King's Chamberlain, Marshals and Chief Justice appeared at the start of the walkway and began moving down the long aisle that lead into the gazebo-like pavilion.

On the eight-sided structure of the pavilion, on one side, had been written the names of all the kings of Hawaii, beginning with Kamehameha I. Each name and date was circled in laurel wreaths and underlined by two crossed palms with a crown floating above. Oil paintings and frescoes glowed on the high ceiling and a breathtakingly detailed Hawaiian coat-of-arms had been painted dead center in the middle of a white net work that hung down over everything like a gossamer web.

Two thousand people jostled for position in the amphitheater surrounding the pavilion, while another 4,000 stood on the remaining palace grounds. Still others held their places at the open palace gates. At the palace's entrance foreign representatives were seated on the verandah to the right, while government representatives and ships' comrades filled the seats on the left. Altogether, 8,000 people would witness the coronation.

The national anthem, *"Hawaii Ponoi,"* with lyrics written by the King and march-style music by Henri Berger, began to play and thousands of voices joined in.

> "Hawaii's own true sons
> Be loyal to your chief,
> Your country's liege and lord,
> the *ali'i*."

Kaiulani sang along softly, adding "and daughters" to the first line and "chiefess" to the second. Mama Nui had taught her to do this. Princess Ruth had explained that it was mostly the *haoles'* version of things to exclude the women from references to power and respect. Kaiulani had learned from her godmother that, in the old days, it was the women and girls who had done all the hunting and fishing; and the men were allowed to cook, but never to make *tapa* cloth. That had always been the women's exclusive domain. Women could even be shark warriors back then and bring glory to their tribes with acts of great courage and bravery.

Kaiulani was startled to realize that Koa was poking her, nudging her to proceed down the long pavilion walkway up to the throne area where the King and Queen stood waiting. Gliding along, Kaiulani at first managed to effortlessly ignore the crowd; for she was still half-lost in a dream of the past when she could have jousted for honor while riding on the back of a shark.

Kaiulani was the first *ali'i* to make an appearance at the beginning of the procession to the pavilion. Her blue ribbons tossed around in the breeze and she seemed to float down the runway, barely moving, as graceful and light as an angel. Two attendants bearing white *kahili* standards followed close by, fanning her as she made her way to the King and Queen. As she took in where she was, Kaiulani was inwardly terrified by the vast sea of staring faces all around her. Outwardly, though, she only smiled politely and looked straight ahead, as Mama and Aunt Liliu had taught her to do. Then the other members of the royal family began their promenades, each attended by their own *kahili* bearers.

Throughout this procession of the *ali'i* Henri Berger's Royal Hawaiian Band played "Kalakaua's Coronation March," composed for the occasion by Berger, along with Princess Liliuokalani's help. Prince Kekaulike came after Kaiulani, carrying the royal feather cloak that the king would wear, assisted by Princess Poomaikalani. Princess Likelike and Cleghorn followed after them, and then came Princess Liliuokalani and her husband, Governor John Dominis. The young princes, Koa and Kuio, carried the royal crowns. Several other royals of lesser rank followed them, carrying the scepter, *kapu* sticks and royal rings. All of them wore the royal ensignia, as was their right by birth.

A profound quiet descended as the King and Queen them selves at last stepped into the center of the pavilion. The Queen had eight ladies in waiting with her, and there were attendants on all sides for both of their majesties. Kapiolani's exquisite, lace-trimmed fan trembled in her hands.

The Episcopalian choir sang an English song about the rights and rulings of kings while Princess Poomaikelani presented Kalakaua with the *kapu* sticks, the torch of another king and the *kahili*, all symbolizing his right to be King.

Kaiulani, who now stood between Koa and Kuhio, happily inhaled the clean, fresh smell of sandalwood soap that rose up from the boys' sun browned bodies. Koa was so close to her that she could see the coconut oil pomade in his curly, shining hair. At fourteen, he had started to fill out. His muscles were lean and taut under his crisply tailored shirt, and she could make out the shape of his long, athletic legs and shoulders even in his suit. Koa stared straight ahead with focused intensity as he held the yellow satin pillow on which the Queen's crown rested. Kuhio, who was already seventeen, had grown a straggly mustache. He appeared to be very intent on holding the King's crown, on its satin crimson pillow, at a precisely level angle. Kaiulani could see faint handprints and marks of sweat on the pillow where Kuhio's hands had repeatedly adjusted the position. She observed the fine detail on both of the crowns, which had been designed with repeating patterns of golden *taro* plant leaves alternated with a variety of diamonds, emeralds, rubies, pearls and even some darkly polished *kukui* nuts, which gleamed like little black suns.

Kaiulani thought both of her cousins looked very attractive and smart. She stole a sideways glance at Koa, but his smoldering eyes were fixed on the King.

Kaiulani inhaled the warm, familiar smell of him again. His musky sandalwood scent brought back to her a flood of memories from all the *luaus* they had shared together as young children, their long afternoons riding and the many days they had spent at the beach from dawn to sunset.

At Mama Nui's house they had often explored her cabinets of old curios. They made up games and rituals to go along with the fragrant sandalwood fans and carved boxes, the whalebone rattles inlaid with shark's teeth, the coral and pearl necklaces, and the ticklish feathered headdresses from the old tribes worn by *ali'i* generations before them.

Hanging necklaces and capes on each other the cousins, at times playful and laughing, but other times quite solemn, would pretend for hours that they were the king and queen. Mama Nui applauded and encouraged their performances, and always made sure they had wonderful things to eat afterwards - chilled melon soup with dense, buttery shortbread from Scotland, and—

The loud clank of the King's sword as Chancellor Judd pulled it from its scabbard abruptly brought Kaiulani back to the moment. The choir had ended its song. The Chancellor bowed his head briefly, and then moved to stand beside the King so he could administer again, a full nine years after Kalakaua's election, the king's oath of affirmation to his constitution and his country.

At the end of the oath the Chancellor proclaimed Kalakaua "Ensign of Justice and Mercy," then bowed again before placing the sword of state in the King's arms. Kaiulani could see that the sword, made of fine Damascus steel and inlaid with gold, was inscribed with the motto of the realm, "The life of the land is preserved in righteousness."

The King kissed the sword with great reverence and returned it to the Chancellor who kept it unsheathed for the rest of the ceremony. Princess Likelike stepped forward to lift the cape of golden *o'o* feathers, which had first been worn by Kamehahameha the First, from its place on the King's throne. Suddenly shy, Likelike placed it over her brother's shoulders and said to him very softly, "Receive this ancient mantle of your predecessors."

When Kalakaua smiled warmly down at her she at once relaxed, basking in his attention like a peacock preening in the sun. Kaiulani thought to herself that she had never seen her mother look so radiant.

The Chancellor came forward and slipped the King's ring onto the fourth finger of Kalakaua's right hand and delivered the scepter. Then the choir sang an anthem about bringing gold and gems, the symbols of love, to crown the king of the glorious, unfolding isles, he who had been chosen by the Almighty Father. At last the Honorable President of the Legislative Assembly lifted the king's crown from Kuhio's satin pillow and handed it to Chancellor Judd. Excitement tugged at Kaiulani's heart and even Koa shifted a little on his feet. Finally, it was time for the crowning!

The Chancellor handed the crown to the king, for it was an ancient *kapu* that none could ever cast a shadow over the king nor stand above his head, or even put his or her hands above the head of a chief. There had been long debates over the question of how to crown the king. Although no one had objected to the act of the King crowning himself in principle, several members of the government were nevertheless quite concerned about how it would look to the *haoles* and others who might not understand the ritual. In the end, the King himself had made the decision to take the considerable risk.

The King held the heavy crown in both hands as gently as if it was a baby. Then he bowed his head and seemed to be contemplating its weight. He raised his head back up.

"In our ancient tradition," his powerful voice rang out to the crowd, "the *ali'i* are descended directly from the gods. Therefore, no one is allowed to stand above the *ali'i*." Kalakaua held the crown aloft, presenting it to the assembly. "And so it is that, with your blessing, I will crown myself and your queen."

The people roared out their approval.

Slowly, he lifted the crown and placed it on his own head. At that moment the sun flashed out through the cloud cover like a spotlight, illuminating the scene as if it was being played out on some grand stage. Later, there would be those who swore they had seen a single, piercingly bright star beam down from the heavens just before the sun came out. Whatever had happened, a low collective murmur escaped from the crowd and a few even fell to their knees. Time seemed suspended.

Finally, the Chancellor broke the spell, lifting the Queen's crown from the satin pillow in Koa's hands and giving it to the King. But when Kalakaua tried to place the smaller crown over Kapiolani's elaborate hairstyle, piled high on her head, it would not accommodate its weight or size.

The queen's eight ladies in waiting, all dressed in dark green velvet, rushed over to rearrange her hair. The crowd held its breath while the Queen's veil was lifted and hairpins were shifted this way and that. Then the ladies darted out of the way and the King stepped forward a second time to crown his queen. Try as he might, though, it still would not fit. Gingerly, he himself moved a few locks of her hair to one side and then gave the crown another firm tug. Kaiulani saw the Queen wince, but she did not pull away. Seeing Mama Moi possibly hurting, Kaiulani wanted desperately to do something, anything, to help in some way. But she did not know what she could do. Then, suddenly, the heavy golden crown shifted into place.

Looking at the queen's flushed face Kaiulani had an odd, sudden vision of her pony, Fairy, flying away at a wild gallop, unfettered and free, with her young mistress hanging onto her back.

The band played *"Hawaii Ponoi"* again. By the time Kalakaua strode all the way across the grand pavilion, volleys of gunshots from the men-of-war ships anchored at the waterfront signaled that the coronation was over.

Kaiulani looked over at Koa and could not help but admire his supple shoulders and strong back. As if he felt her eyes upon him, Koa turned to her and bent down to kiss her cheek. A brief, bare smile passed between them, full of secrets and sunshine and long afternoons. All around them people were hugging and kissing. Lifting up the satin pillow Koa teasingly touched it to the top of Kaiulani's head.

"It looks good on you." He grinned as they were swept away into the procession heading back to the palace.

* * * * * * * * * * * * * * * * * *

That night the Grand Coronation Ball lit up Iolani Palace and all of the grounds like a thousand fire crackers. The air was charged with heady smells of plumeria, hibiscus, jasmine and bougainvillea mingled with the sweat and excitement of hundreds of revelers. For two entire weeks the merchants and tradesmen of Hawaii kept their shops open, some of them around the clock, as the festivities spilled over from day to night and then back again. The coronation was good for Honolulu; it filled the coffers of the city.

On the first evening, which was the Grand Ball, five thousand guests were entertained at the palace. Princess Likelike wore a stunning gown in a new color called "moonlight-on-the-lake." It was an ethereal, moonstone pale-blue that made her look like a vivacious sprite, all wrapped up in her own cloud. Her feathery pearl and gauze headdress added to the illusion. Likelike seemed almost too light to be human; her feet barely touching the ground as she danced with partner after partner. Cleghorn, who was usually quite reserved in public, sighed every time he caught a glimpse of his beaming, beautiful young wife.

Kaiulani, wearing a rose-colored velvet dress, stood by her father. A souvenir dance card identical to her mother's dangled from her wrist. Too young to be allowed to dance at the beginning of the ball, she fingered the gold-bordered card, reading Hawaii's motto on its cover over and over. *"Ua mau ke ea o ka aina i ka pono."* "The life of the land is preserved in righteousness."

As her feverishly animated mother swept by again and again, never with the same partner twice, the dance songs changed from waltzes to polkas to sets of quadrilles, and then began all over again. Kaiulani watched Likelike with increasing concern. At last she looked so anxious that even Aunt Liliu noticed and told her not to worry so, explaining that her mother had always been like that, a firebrand, even as a child.

Later in the evening Kalakaua made a toast. "I say to you, today and tomorrow, believe it is so and it will be so!"

Feeling a hot breath on her shoulder, Kaiulani turned to find Koa by her side.

"What does he mean?" She demanded at once. "Something either is so, or it isn't so. Isn't that so?"

Koa laughed and kissed her cheek. "You worry too much, my dear cousin," he said, inwardly congratulating him self on using such a sophisticated phrase.

Kaiulani insisted. "All right, but why does Papa Moi say -"

Koa interrupted, feeling he had to assert his point of view as the older of the two. "I don't know." He shrugged. "I don't have to. And it's a good thing, too. I'd hate to be in his shoes, though, that's for sure." Quite forgetting Kaiulani for a moment, he continued, "Threats on his life; and all those meetings, all of the time, with never a minute to -"

Kaiulani turned pale. "What do you mean, Koa? How could anyone think of -?"

Koa covered his embarrassment over having said far too much by putting his finger to her mouth and "shushing" her. Without another word, he swept her onto the dance floor, leaving her so breathless that she made no attempt to ask her question again. But she brooded about it for a long time afterward, deeply concerned that anyone would even dare to think ill toward Papa Moi.

The coronation was, all in all, a tremendous success. Although the *Hokupu*, the traditional presentation of gifts to the King, where each Hawaiian contributed from their best craft, crop, performance or other skill, did not officially begin until February 21, by the first day of the festivities, presents of *taro*, carvings, woven mats and even livestock had begun to accumulate on the *lanais* of the palace and around the grounds.

It was during the coronation week that the Hawaiians were, for the first time, dazzled by electricity. Kalakaua had his throne room lit up with tiny, sparkling electric lights. Kaiulani, dressed in a gown the color of snow-banked firs, threw the switch, then bowed and smiled throughout the applause, as happy as if she herself had invented the spectacle of day for night.

On February 14 the King pulled the wires, which released two flags of Hawaii, unveiling the fine statue of Kamehahameha the Great in front of Iolani, just across from the palace square on King Street.

Fireworks exploded in the sky on February 17. *Hula* dances and competitions were held every night on the palace grounds; and an endless *luau* was constantly replenished to cater to the teeming hordes of guests. For two wonderful weeks all rumors of strife, of foreigners' discontent and *haole* scheming and missionaries' sons grasping for the wealth and power of the kingdom; all were blissfully set aside and even, for a little while, forgotten by some.

The American poet, Charles Warren Stoddard, was there to witness the Hawaiian kingdom in its great moment of glory. He wrote in his memoirs years later praising Kalakaua, calling him "such a king as one reads of in nursery tales; all things to all men, and possessed of rare refinement."

The state dinner at the palace was followed by another grand illumination of Iolani. Surrounded by two hundred flaming torches, the symbol of Kalakaua's monarchy, the palace and the surrounding area sparkled with red, white and blue lanterns. Fireworks lit up the night sky again. The height of Punchbowl, the extinct volcanic crater said to be the geographic point of origin for Hawaii, was outlined with bright lamps as were all the Fire Department buildings and most of the area's elegant, and not so elegant, private homes.

* * * * * * * * * * * * * * * * * * *

One week after the coronation ceremonies were over Mama Nui's specially built carriage drove up to the main house at Ainahau. With a great deal of assistance Princess Ruth managed to struggle out of the coach, very red in the face and panting.

She looked smaller than before and had, in fact, lost a few pounds of her enormous weight. Her wide cheekbones were more prominent and her nose, pushed out all flat to the sides, made her look like an abandoned child who was about to cry.

Kaiulani rushed over to Mama Nui and did her best to wrap her arms around Ruth's stout form.

"Mama Nui, Mama Nui! Where have you been?! Why weren't you there for -?"

Ruth held a finger against her goddaughter's pouting mouth and gently smoothed out the wrinkles from her forehead.

"Ah, baby. Never mind. What's over is done, and whoever knows why. Help your Mama Nui inside. She is hot and tired and would like only to eat ice cream with her favorite child."

Sitting on the cool *lanai*, the young girl and the old woman ate large bowls of ice cream with chocolate sauce and macadamia nuts. Kaiulani was excited as she described the details of the crowning, and almost ran her words together as she told Mama Nui all about it.

"And then Papa Moi couldn't get the crown on over Mama Kapiolani's hairdo, and it looked like he might be hurting her, but my Mama said she was all right."

She looked up from her dish to see that Mama Nui had stopped eating. The elderly princess was gazing out across the *lanai* as she clutched her hand to her chest.

"Mama Nui?" Kaiulani held her spoon quite still as she spoke. She was reassured when Mama Nui looked back at her and softly smiled.

"Yes, baby," she said.

Kaiulani returned the smile, then dived back into her ice cream. "When I get a crown, will you help me pick out exactly the right size?"

Looking up again she saw her godmother lightly tapping her chest. This time Mama Nui winced a little.

Kaiulani put down her spoon. "Mama Nui, are you all right?"

Ruth reached over to tenderly pat Kaiulani's cheek. "A little indigestion, baby; that's all."

* * * * * * * * * * * * * * * * * * *

One week later the Cleghorn family stood outside the same church where Kaiulani had been christened. An oversized coffin was carefully lifted onto the waiting coach as hundreds of wailing, desolate mourners passed by.

Some placed flowers on the wide casket, others wept. A few of the *kanakas* tore at their hair and pounded their fists hard against their own foreheads in the old way of mourning. Likelike sobbed without restraint while Liliuokalani, stern faced and controlled, tried to comfort her younger sister.

Kaiulani, her expression tight and held in, walked over to the coffin to place a bouquet of jasmine and peacock feathers, which she herself had arranged, close to the top of the casket.

Later, back home at Ainahau, Kaiulani wrote to Koa. He had, in fact, been sent away, just as he had predicted, to be educated and cultured, only days after the coronation.

"Dear Koa,

The burial service for Mama Nui was today. I do not like funerals. The noise the people make scares me very bad. You would have been proud of me. I did not let anyone see me cry.

I do not know why you had to go away when we have perfectly good schools here in Hawaii. I miss you very much.

> Your Loving Cousin,
> Kaiulani."

Later still, when she was alone at last with Fairy, Kaiulani hugged the horse's strong neck and sobbed as she buried her face in his long, silky mane.

Chapter Eight

In the shabby, genteel dining room of a Chelsea apartment in New York City, a middle-aged woman was on her knees, frantically pinning the hem of the traveling cloak worn by her oldest daughter, Gertrude. A small army of rambunctious children, ranging in age from two to fifteen, created a deafening cacophony of noise as they played cowboys and Indians, running back and forth, in and out of the small rooms of the apartment.

Gertrude Gardinier, an intelligent, alert, delicately pretty woman in her early twenties, wore her light brown hair pulled back into a loose bun at the nape of her neck. She wore subdued colors in practical but attractive shades of rose and dark blue. When she turned to accommodate her mother's efforts she saw the older woman furtively wipe away a tear as she jabbed another pin into the hem.

"Oh, Ma, now, please don't start cryin' again!"

Her mother responded in the broad New York accent that had managed to keep a slight suggestion of her native Dublin. "It's just so far away! It's the other side of the world, for pity sakes! What if I never see you again?"

Gertrude Gardinier leaned down to hug and kiss her mother. "Aw, you'll see me again all right, Mama! Come on, now, I promise!"

When Mrs. Gardinier raised her face to her daughter, Martin Matthew Gardinier, ten years old and painted to look like what he hoped might appear to be an Apache Indian warrior chief on the hunt, poked his red and blue striped face between them. "Yeah, unless she marries one of them ooga-booga kings and gets to be a millionaress!"

"Those, not them," Gertrude absentmindedly corrected her sibling.

Another brother, Maurice, who was insisting on being called "Red Wing Eagle" at the moment, took a low dive to tackle his younger brother, Martin, and throw him down onto the floor.

As he wrestled with Martin, Maurice's words came out in fragments and gasps. "Or - maybe - she's gonna get - so burnt - in all that sun—"

At last, he managed to pin his brother to the ground, immobilizing him.

"All that sun in—" He mocked his sister's careful pronunciation by holding his nose pinched together as he spoke - "Hah-vhy"—

Gertrude genially attempted to cuff him as he dodged.

"Hah-vhy," he repeated gleefully, "that she'll come back and look like she don't belong here in this house no more!"

Gertrude automatically corrected him, too. "'Doesn't belong,' no 'here', - 'any more.'"

Martin, red faced and wild upon his release, leaped up to his feet and brandished his wooden broomstick 'spear.' "Yeah, or maybe the real natives'll catch her, and she'll get boiled in a pot and et!"

"Eaten," Gertrude said.

"Yeah!" Maurice chimed in. "Or sacrificed!" He made a juicy slicing sound as he drew his finger across his own throat.

Darcy, five years old, who had been listening intently, burst into tears. Gertrude picked her up to console her, while Mrs. Gardinier struggled to her feet to grab Maurice.

"Don't you dare talk like that about your sister!" she said as she shook him furiously.

Maurice, abashed and blushing, shook his head. "Ah, Ma, I'm sorry, Ma. But - -" He began to sniffle and his lower lip trembled. "I don't want Gertie to get leprosy out there and come back dead!" Maurice ran out of the room, crying. When Mrs. Gardinier moved as if to follow him, Gertrude caught at her sleeve and spoke softly to her, without exasperation.

"C'mon, Ma, we have to finish before the cab gets here."

Her mother went back to pinning in silence, with only an occasional sniffle. When she spoke again, her tone was muted. "Just promise me one thing. All right?"

Resigned, Gertrude sighed. "What, Ma?"

Mrs. Gardinier spoke out of one side of her mouth, clenching pins between her teeth on the other. "You won't go wandering off on your own out there." Without even looking at her, she waved away Gertrude's attempt to protest. "I know how you are," she said.

"Yes, Ma." her daughter said softly.

Taking a closer look at her mother's worried face she saw that there were now several pins sticking out of her mouth on both sides, making her look both frightening and frightened as she spoke through her teeth. "And never go swimming alone! There are sharks all over out there!"

* * * * * * * * * * * * * * * * * * *

Back in the dining room at Ainahau another heated conversation was taking place between Archibald Cleghorn and his young wife.

"I don't see why Kaiulani needs another governess!" Likelike sulked as she played with her food.

Archie tried to keep an even tone as he explained once again to his wife. "Because she keeps sending them away, that's why! Miriam, please be reasonable! Ever since Miss Barnes left us -"

Likelike dropped her fork by her plate and sniffed with disdain. "She said she was lonely for England! How could anyone miss a place as cold and dreary as that?"

"That was almost a year ago, darling! Besides, Kaiulani needs the company. We've both been so busy these last months, what with all the new legislation going through, and with all your -"

He paused, uncertain about his wife's activities. "Well, shopping and parties and whatever." He looked at her beseechingly. "She seems - sad, Likelike, dear. Ever since Mama Nui died—"

"Nonsense!" Likelike laughed in a brittle tone. "She just gets moody, that's all. Like you."

Cleghorn stared in amazement at his notoriously temperamental mate.

"Me?" He said incredulously.

"Yes. Yes, you."

Cleghorn suppressed a frown. A clipped Scottish burr cropped up in his voice, as it always did when he was upset. "Well, and she's strong willed, like you."

Likelike glared at him as if ready to fight, then abruptly gave it up and smiled. "Well, never mind," she said. "If she doesn't like this new one, we'll just send her right back."

Cleghorn muttered half to himself, "Like all the other ones, I suppose…"

Likelike continued to smile. "Where did you say this one is from?"

"America," Archie said. "New York."

Likelike only shook her head, already expecting the worst.

* * * * * * * * * * * * * * * * * * * *

When Miss Gardinier finally arrived in Oahu, Princess Likelike herself came to meet her. The coach that picked them up, with its stiffly carved wooden gargoyles and roses, looked both imposing and primitive to Miss Gardinier's tired eyes. Likelike wore a stylish gown in shades of periwinkle and teal blue enhanced with a scattering of feathers, ribbons and flounces. Miss Gardinier's tasteful but somber navy traveling cloak and pleated skirt, with a plain ivory blouse, seemed, by comparison, very dark indeed.

When they were settled in for the ride to Ainahau Likelike reached over and patted the pale young woman's hand. She had felt an instant affection for the governess, taken with her serious, competent demeanor and formal manners, and charmed by her light auburn hair and clear green eyes. Miss Gardinier smiled back at her new employer, but only briefly, for she was exhausted from the long trip and more than a little anxious about her new adventure.

"Well, Miss Gertrude Gardinier, you will find that my daughter is very strong-willed and sometimes moody, exactly like her father. While I, on the other hand, am well known for my easy-going ways and even temper -"

Miss Gardinier had been fumbling about in her bag as she nodded. There was a loud, startling clatter as something fell onto the wooden floor of the carriage. Likelike almost jumped out of her seat as she gasped, clutching one hand to her heart.

"What!? What was that?!" The famously easy-going Princess almost shrieked.

Miss Gardinier blushed as she picked up the offending noisemaker. "It's called a worry stone," she said very softly.

Likelike imperiously held out her hand, then gingerly grasped the object and proceeded to examine it with caution.

"What is its function?" the Princess demanded suspiciously.

Miss Gardinier's tone was apologetic as she explained, clearly embarrassed.

"It's - from my mother. From Ireland, where she was born. One - touches it - sort of, rubs it, actually, - when one is nervous. For good luck, they say. And to calm one down." Her voice trailed off.

"But, my dear," Delighted with the foreigner's strange custom, Likelike was laughing and friendly again as she handed the stone back. "How barbaric!"

* * * * * * * * * * * * * * * * * * *

In the parlor room at Ainahau Kaiulani, ten years old, anxiously awaited her new governess. Impatient, she looked out at the *lanai*, then over at the front driveway and out onto the road again. She checked for the twentieth time the drape of her mauve velvet dress in the mirror, turning in rapid succession to observe herself from every possible angle. She tugged at her lace collar and readjusted the white satin ribbons that hung over the bodice. Staring at her own intense face, she frowned, then tried on a faint smile in the manner, she hoped, of the Mona Lisa, mysterious and all knowing. Holding the pose for a moment and pleased with the effect, she began to rehearse.

Still smiling and affecting a dignified warmth, the young princess lifted her chin a fraction of an inch to one side, then pulled her head slightly back down again as she held out her hand and said, "Hello."

Changing her expression to what she hoped might pass for haughty yet noble reserve, she next tried folding her hands over to one side of her hip. This time her "Hello" came out with an odd, hollow sound that made her giggle. Rearranging herself to appear shy and retiring, she curtseyed deeply, lifted up her eyes and then flashed a look at herself sideways. Choking back a fit of laughter she said to the mirror, "Hello, your self, you princess."

The sound of a door and footsteps in the hall sent her scurrying back to her chair. Frantically she attempted to smooth out her dress and settle herself in to look aloof and composed. But as the doors to the parlor opened Kaiulani was left hanging mid-pose, looking awkward and oddly devious when her mother and the new governess bustled in, chatting away like old friends.

"We really must get you in some brighter colors, dear!" Likelike said. "It will bring out your features nicely, you'll see."

All of Kaiulani's careful plans evaporated at her first sight of the slim, lovely young woman. Kaiulani stood up at once, wide-eyed with surprise.

"But you're so - young!" Kaiulani blurted out. "And pretty!"

"Well, and so are you!' Miss Gardinier laughed as she held out her hand.

Kaiulani tried to regain some of her composure by moving purposefully and deliberately toward her while avoiding her outstretched hand until the last possible moment. But these efforts at formality were belied by the tiny smile that played around the corners of her mouth.

"I am very pleased to make your acquaintance," said the pupil as she carefully shook her new teacher's hand.

Miss Gardinier's eyes sparkled as she grasped Kaiulani's hands in her own. "And I to make yours, my dear."

Both mother and daughter waited expectantly until Miss Gardinier picked up her cue. "Princess. My dear Princess."

"Teacher." Kaiulani smiled as she shook Miss Gardinier's hand again. "*Kumu. Kumu* means teacher in Hawaiian. My" - To everyone's surprise, Kaiulani managed a broad imitation of Miss Gardinier's New York accent, "-'de-ah' tea-chah."

That first night Miss Gardinier sat out on the breezy *lanai* with her young charge close by, watching her intently as she worked at some intricate embroidery on a blouse.

"My!" Miss Gardinier said with boundless admiration. "Tell me again!"

"Victoria Kawekiu Lunalilo Kalaninuia-hilapalapa Kaiulani Cleghorn! Kaiulani means 'child of heaven,' and all the other names are from the high chiefs and chiefesses, except for Cleghorn, of course, which is Papa's."

"My!" Miss Gardinier carefully folded away her embroidery, then looked at her watch and was quite surprised. "Time for bed, already!"

Kaiulani rose at once, excited over the prospect of showing off her room to her new friend.

"Will you sit with me, please? Please? Come and talk to me. Come see my room now."

Miss Gardinier looked out at the hazy moonshine streaming in from Kaiulani's bedroom window. Never in her life had she seen a moon so beautiful and full. In the soft, magical light Kaiulani looked like the princess in a fairy tale, her dark, curly hair spread out against the pillow like a halo. Miss Gardinier, holding Kaiulani's hand, looked ethereal, like a nymph or a fairy watching over the vivacious child who continued to chatter away even as she began to fall asleep.

"And tomorrow we'll go riding." Her eyes were bright with happiness. "I'll teach you; I can, you know. - And you can meet my horse, Fairy. And go swimming with me, too...and we'll get seashells and sponges...and...and..."

Kaiulani's heavy eyelids dropped as she drifted off to sleep. Miss Gardinier gently removed her hand and kissed her forehead, then whispered, "Good night, little Princess. Good night."

Kaiulani seemed to smile in her sleep.

* * * * * * * * * * * * * * * * * * *

Just a few miles away from where Princess Kaiulani slept, watched over by her new *kumu*, the same bright moon that was over Ainahau lit up the night sky outside the Honolulu Lecture Hall. A poster in front of the building announced the evening's subject: "Why Hawaii Must Change - And How" to be given by the honorable "Lorrin A. Thurston, Representative, Legislative Assembly."

Inside the smoky hall Thurston, a few years older, with a slightly receding hairline and the beginnings of a paunch, stood stolidly at the lectern as people filed in. Considerably better dressed than in his early days as a fledgling lawyer, he ostentatiously adjusted the scarlet flower in his lapel with an air of smug self-satisfaction and righteousness.

Looking out over his audience he saw the usual collection of mostly American and British businessmen, a few with their women; a handful of scruffy, street thug types; and a smattering of sullen "*hapa-haoles*," half Hawaiian and the other half who knew what.

In a shadowy place near the back of the hall, Sanford Dole stood flanked by men on both sides. Occasionally, he exchanged quiet conversation with them, making remarks about the size and make-up of the assembled body. When everyone had settled into their seats, Dole gave the barest nod, his signal to Thurston, who immediately flashed a supercilious smile at the company in general.

"Welcome, good friends. We are gathered here tonight to try to understand the profoundly convoluted situation faced daily by all of us in this increasingly complex place -" He spread his hands wide to include his listeners - "- called Hawaii. What It Is, and Why It Must Change, as we all know, indeed, that it must."

He dropped into a more confidential tone. "My friends, friends of these islands; the question of what we must do here in Hawaii is not, in any way, an issue of race! Nor ever has been! It is, rather, in every way, a question of economics! Why, in this very room tonight there are dark-skinned people who are members of our own Reform Party!"

Thurston's eyes glittered as he leaned further forward on his podium. He had developed the timing and dramatic rhythms, - emphasis and pause - of a fire and brimstone minister. These things he had learned instinctively in childhood at his missionary father's knee; but they had been honed and polished under Dole's expert tutelage.

Thurston would give this same speech, with a few minor alterations, depending on the audience and on Dole's perception and "read" on each community where it was presented, again and again, ad nauseam, for the next several years.

* * * * * * * * * * * * * * * * * *

In Washington, Thurston's tone would be more formal. There, he wore a more tailored and expensive suit as he lectured in a hall filled to capacity with stern-faced men - bankers, politicians and businessmen. Approximately eighty-five percent of the Washington crowds wore exactly the same hats, tipped at precisely the same angles.

For these lectures, entitled "Washington Citizens for Change Presents Hawaii, Our Present Duty," and subtitled "Important Commercial Facts In Favor Of Annexation," Thurston used visual aids to illustrate his talk.

"Here in Washington, gentlemen; here, of all places in the world," he explained in a confiding tone, "We all know that the best—and perhaps the only? - method for judging the future is to look to the past."

"In the past eighty-five years Hawaii, - also called, of course, the Cross Roads to the Pacific - has been taken possession of: - by Russia, once." He flipped through several maps and charts of countries as he continued at a brisker pace. "Once by England. Twice by France. Earlier still, by Germany, Spain and Japan."

Thurston flipped another page to reveal an artistic sketch of a bare-breasted Hawaiian woman dancing the *hula*. Cued by gasps and snickers from the audience Thurston pretended to be surprised, viewing the drawing with a grim smirk as he explained, "A different lecture for another time.   'Indecency and Idolatry in the Pagan Traditions.'"

Turning away to the back wall the lawyer pulled down another large chart. "The Demise of the Hawaiians," was illustrated with lurid drawings, along with detailed percentages of the death rates from leprosy, consumption, smallpox, measles, syphilis and several other venereal diseases.

"For reasons both unnecessary and distasteful to explain to those of strong moral character, certain, well," Thurston added another carefully timed hesitation. "Shall we say - 'indelicate' - diseases - have decreased the Hawaiian race to a fraction of its original size."

* * * * * * * * * * * * * * * * * * *

New York City was Thurston's favorite arena for giving the speech. In New York he could throw all caution and restraint aside and speak with unbridled fervor. There he was free to talk, as he never tired of describing it, "from the heart." For the New York lectures Thurston had even been allowed to grow a mustache, covering up to great advantage his thin, often tremulous upper lip. He had been taught how to fluff out his mutton chop whiskers a little and toss back his hair for greater effect.

One night in New York he smashed his pointer down and fairly shouted as he declared, "The native Hawaiian race cannot compete with other races! It will soon disappear!"

A man in the audience nudged another to point out to him *The New York Times* headline of January 20, 1881, which read "Princess Regent Liliuokalani Visits Leper Colony at Molokai." The beginning paragraph said, "One thousand lepers came to greet her. Sadly, Father Damien himself was found to be infected." The two men shook their heads in sympathy at this tragic, yet timely, news.

Thurston's voice was also filled with compassion and regret. He continued in the fond tones of the shepherd who gathers in the sheep.

"With his superficial and incomplete experience at governing, the aboriginal Hawaiian, like all semi-savages, is not capable of controlling the stronger races. Which now, by the way, outnumber him three to one."

He dropped into a brisk, businesslike cadence as he repeated for emphasis. "In his own country, three to one."

The lawyer returned to his former unctuous tones. "The Hawaiian dies easily, leaving few or no offspring."

Now he segued into the sepulchral sounds he had listened to his father use so often at funeral services; sounds guaranteed to reduce any but the sternest listeners to tears. "The handful of infants that remain are sickly and weak. Most of them, too, are doomed to failure to survive."

In the back of the room Sanford Dole and his companions listened with gratification to the sounds of sniffling and sighing, which were invariably the predominant response at this point in the lecture.

Thurston concluded with sad but firm conviction. "The Hawaiian has already passed from the stage." He straightened up slightly to add with crisp efficiency, "Although, under strong and capable leadership, he does not make a bad citizen."

A few days later Dole and Thurston sat in a meeting in the very expensive offices of the Wall Street Business Association Committee. The ten men sitting in the room with them included several prominent leaders in politics and commerce. Dole stood before them, his exquisitely tailored suit of fine Italian merino wool showing him off to great advantage. Although it was just noon and quite sunny, the blinds were drawn to spare the assembled from the harsh glare of natural sunlight.

Thurston, whose suit was perhaps a shade too flamboyant for this austere setting, was impatient and fidgeting until Dole shot him a warning glance, after which he sat up straight, perfectly still, his hands folded in his lap, like a child on good behavior.

"Gentlemen, if I may." Dole, with a nod, referred the assembly to a neat prospectus, which was covered in gold leaf and bound with a rose-colored grosgrain ribbon. One lay in front of each of the men like an elaborate menu for some very exclusive dining.

Dole opened to the first pages, indicating charts and statistics as he spoke. "American business interests in Hawaii account for three-quarters of all land and property, 98% of all exports and 75% of all imports and trade."

Dole sat down at the head of the table and meticulously folded his narrow aristocratic hands together in front of him.

"Gentlemen, the situation is simple. Hawaii is already ours. All that remains is for us to formalize the relationship. Tie the knot, as it were, with our new," - He allowed an infinitesimal smile to gather at his lips -" - albeit reluctant - bride."

"We would also gain, from this arrangement, the potentially invaluable benefit of exclusive and permanent rights to Pearl Lagoon, also known as Pearl Harbor. This location is uniquely well-situated for an American naval base."

A heavy-set man leaned in toward Dole. Well-upholstered with a tight jaw and an unusual number of small white teeth, he asked, "Is this all constitutional?"

Bored with the question he had heard so many times before, Dole shrugged. "It can be made so."

An anxious man with the rapacious look of a weasel stood up at the other end of the table. "Mr. Dole," His voice was high and breathy. "Does the U.S. dare consider annexing a, - well, to put it bluntly, - a mostly colored population?!"

Dole barely smiled again. "Those people can work and pay taxes, sir, just like you or me."

Appreciative laughter greeted his remark. And then the gentlemen got down to business.

* * * * * * * * * * * * * * * * * *

Several months had passed since Miss Gardinier had come to Ainahau to teach Kaiulani. The two of them had become inseparable - "thick as thieves," Likelike called them, laughing again every time she used the strange phrase.

Kaiulani had taught her governess, who was game though somewhat physically timid, to ride. Miss Gardinier often watched with great admiration as Kaiulani and Fairy showed off for her, performing a series of highly choreographed moves, ending with the deep, elaborate bow which they always performed for the *kanakas* with Kaiulani on Fairy's back.

"My! That's very lovely!" Miss Gardinier laughed with pleasure. "Especially the bit at the end with the bow!"

"That is our salute for the Hawaiians only." Kaiulani was proud.

"Bravo!" Miss Gardinier clapped. And then she had to explain to her curious charge what that word meant, and from there, all about the operas and plays she had seen in New York.

They passed many long hours together, reading, studying or gathering stones and seashells at the beach. At other times they snuggled in, talking for hours or just enjoying each other's company in cozy, peaceful silence. Miss Gardinier had become an important part of the Cleghorn household, adding an element of joy and comfort to their lives with her gentle, supportive nature. She brought harmony to their table, and sang along in her light mezzo-soprano while Likelike accompanied her on the guitar and Archibald or Kaiulani picked at the ukulele.

For her eleventh birthday Kaiulani was allowed to take Miss Gardinier as her guest to the King's box at the Opera House. Papa Moi and Queen Kapiolani were delighted to have their goddaughter and her charming teacher along; and everyone agreed that "Rigoletto" was the best performance they had ever seen. King Kalakaua swore that he must have done something spectacular and gone to heaven for it, to rate the company of the three most beautiful women in the world.

Late that night Kaiulani and Miss Gardinier returned to Ainahau by carriage under a full autumn moon and discussed every detail of the evening all over again on the way home, going to bed at a very late hour.

A few days later at the beach, Kaiulani and Miss Gardinier were adding seashell turrets onto their sandcastle.

"I think this must be the most perfect place in the world," Miss Gardinier stretched luxuriously and closed her eyes in the sun. "Is the weather here always so wonderful?"

"In Hawaiian there is no word for weather, because it is always the same." Kaiulani smiled. "Almost always, anyway."

Miss Gardinier marveled at the bright, delicate mists of colors that arched across the late afternoon sky. "I have never seen so many rainbows in my life!"

"There are more here than anywhere else in Hawaii," Kaiulani said with pride. "I have seen as many as five at once. The *kanakas* say there are more here because of all the high chiefs and chiefesses who are buried in the lost caves along the coast."

She repeated the line she knew by heart from one of her favorite stories. "'The god Lono sent the rainbows to guide the *ali'i* on their pathway to heaven.'"

"What a pretty story." Miss Gardinier sifted sand through her fingers.

Kaiulani suddenly stood, closely observing the angle of the sunlight. "It is almost six o'clock," she said, excited and taking Miss Gardinier's hand. "Come with me!"

Pulling her governess along she raced across the shore rocks to a secluded area.

The sun dropped lower and lower in the sky, and then a fin suddenly appeared in the water, soon followed by a long line of others twisting and turning, churning up the water as a parade of sharks swam by.

"Almost every day some of them come by here at this time! They are on their way to the sea caves to look for food." Kaiulani laughed with delight at the sight of all the silvery, flashing fins. "Mama Nui told Koa and me all about it. In the old days, the king and the court would watch while the sharks were driven into the shallows. Then the bravest gladiators would jump right onto their backs and joust!" She laughed happily and turned back to look at Miss Gardinier. "Today," Kaiulani said, "I am the teacher -"

Pale and trembling, Miss Gardinier sat down a few steps away on some flat rocks.

"Miss Gardinier!" Kaiulani rushed to her. "Are you all right?!"

"Oh, quite all right." Her voice was faint. "Just fine. Only too much sun, perhaps."

Kaiulani took her kumu's hand. "I hope it is not indigestion?"

This unexpected question, combined with her breathless anxiety, caused Miss Gardinier to burst into laughter. In fits and gasps she laughed until she cried. But at last she looked at Kaiulani and saw how upset she was.

"Oh, no, no, Kaiulani." She struggled to compose herself. "I am so sorry. I'm all right, dear. Truly."

It was Kaiulani's turn to fight off tears. She could not look at her teacher but kept her eyes fixed on their intertwined hands.

"What I told you before -" Her voice was muted and low; for a moment she could not speak.

"What I said about Lono and the rainbows?"

"Yes, Kaiulani?" Miss Gardinier nodded, encouraging her. "What about the rainbows?"

"When Mama Nui died there weren't any rainbows!" Her words spilled out in a rush as she fell into Miss Gardinier's arms. "Not one! And she was a princess!" Kaiulani wept bitterly. "Oh, Miss Gardinier! Does that mean Mama Nui didn't go to heaven?"

"Oh, no, sweetheart, no, no." The governess rocked the sobbing child, gently stroking her hair. "I am quite sure Mama Nui went to heaven."

Kaiulani looked up at her with anguished eyes. "How can you - how do you know?" She pleaded.

"Because you loved her so much." Miss Gardinier made soothing sounds as she patted her head some more. "That's how I know."

Chapter Nine

Miss Gardinier was reading out loud to herself a letter she had been writing to her mother.

"Kaiulani is the fragile, spiritual type, but very vivacious and beautiful, with large, dark expressive eyes. She proves herself affectionate and high-spirited, though also quite willful at times. Usually, though, she is reasonable and very impulsive and generous."

"Her mother, Princess Miriam Likelike, is small, graceful and stylish with pretty dimpled arms and hands which she likes to show off. She has an imperious and impulsive nature, and is considered quite haughty by some. But I find her to be generally very genial and thoughtful in her own home, and almost always considerate of those she likes. Unfortunately, however, she is under a great deal of stress at the moment."

"I have met a very nice gentleman here. He is originally from New York but has lived in Hawaii for several years. He is in the tailoring business and owns three stores already, although he is only thirty-two years old. His name is Albert Heydtmann, and he is-"

"Miss Gardinier, Miss Gardinier!" Kaiulani burst into the room.

Miss Gardinier immediately folded the letter away and tucked it into the sleeve of her dressing gown. Although Kaiulani's excitement was infectious, Gertrude Gardinier struggled to keep a sense of decorum.

"Kaiulani, you know you must always knock, to be respectful, when a person's door is closed -"

Kaiulani flung herself on the bed. "I know, I know. I'm sorry, I am. But look at this - look what Mama Moi - Queen Kapiolani - has sent me for my birthday!"

She held up a small golden brooch designed in the shape of a peacock with a fanned out tail. A spray of diamond chips formed the crested top of its crown, with garnets and emeralds inlaid in the feathers of its luxuriously outstretched fan.

"That's lovely, Kaiulani." Miss Gardinier was uncomfortable, for there were a few things she wanted to add to her letter before she forgot them. "Perhaps you could bring it back again a little later -?"

Wounded by this uncharacteristic lack of interest, Kaiulani leaped up from the bed, her face flushed.

"First, Mama is too busy - she never has time for me anymore! And now you! I thought you were my friend!"

Propelled by this fiery outburst, Miss Gardinier rose from her chair. "Kaiulani," She moved toward the flustered girl, "You know I am your friend -"

But Kaiulani had somehow managed to prick her finger on the back of the pin and was now feeling even more forlorn and unhappy. She rushed out the door, calling back to her teacher in a hurt voice. "Papa will play with me!"

Miss Gardinier pursed her mouth for a moment; then resolutely sat back down at her dressing table, tugging the letter out from her sleeve. She skimmed it briefly, then carefully underlined 'very' in her description of Kaiulani as "very vivacious."

Kaiulani ran down a long hallway, almost skidding in her hurry to reach her father's library. Bounding in to the dimly lit room where the well-stocked shelves of books muffled all sound, she dashed over to her father.

"Papa, Papa! Look what Mama Moi gave me!"

She stopped short when she realized that her father was not alone. Sitting beside him was Lorrin Thurston.

Kaiulani's tone shifted at once to a careful, formal reserve. "Good day, Mr. Thurston." She nodded slightly at the intruder and kept her treasure tightly wrapped in one hand.

"Mr. Thurston was just talking to me about how he has been lecturing people all over America, telling them what a fine place Hawaii is." Cleghorn smiled as he reached out for his daughter and kissed the top of her head. "And what good opportunities we have here to do business."

Thurston smirked. In an apparent attempt to be friendly he held his hand out to Kaiulani. "Let's have a look at your little gift then, shall we?"

Kaiulani coolly handed the golden peacock pin to her father who laughed a little and held it up to the light. The tiny diamonds, garnets and emeralds in its fan sparkled next to slivers of semi-precious stones - amethysts, tiger's eyes and citrine. The bird's eyes were flashing flecks of red rubies.

Her father returned the pin to her and she reluctantly handed it over to Thurston. The lawyer held it close to his eye, examining it and assessing its value with a cursory glance.

"Very pretty." Thurston tried to pat Kaiulani's head as he handed it back to her but she deftly slid away. "Quite a fine present for a young girl."

Kaiulani moved closer to her father.

Thurston's expression of warmth seemed forced and artificial, which it was. He looked quickly at his watch as he stood. "Well, Cleghorn, I'd better be going. Too much to do these days; too little time for all." He shook his hand. "We'll be in touch." He reached out another time to Kaiulani who pulled back again, just enough to avoid his grasp.

Thurston's laugh was thin and hollow as he backed out of the room. Assuring his host he could find his way, he called back over his shoulder, "Good-by" as he left.

Cleghorn scooped up his daughter in a hug and sat her down in her usual place across from his desk.

"All right, Miss Kitten. Time for our business lesson for the day."

"Today, "he pulled out a chalkboard, "I am going to teach you about what it means to be a stock holder."

Kaiulani folded her hands under her chin and settled in to listen.

Later that afternoon Kaiulani and her Papa worked together in the garden, taking frequent sips of sweet, tart lemonade. Kaiulani played with a small shovel, imitating her father's moves as Cleghorn dug up weeds from around the base of the biggest banyan tree. An attendant kept Kaiulani's custom-sized tools in order, neatly straightening them out each time she put one down.

"You don't remember," Archie Cleghorn began, pulling a handkerchief out of his pocket to wipe his brow, "when I planted this tree for you, because -"

The familiar phrase was so routine that Kaiulani automatically finished it for him. "I was just a little baby."

"That's right," he nodded in approval.

She continued by rote. "And five hundred banyan trees were planted all over Hawaii for me that very same day."

"Week, sweetheart," Her father corrected her gently.

"'Week.'" she repeated. She tugged at a particularly recalcitrant weed. "Papa? Why does Mr. Thurston look angry when he smiles?"

Cleghorn sat back on his heels. "Hmmm. I really don't know. He does seem to be in a terrible hurry most of the time, though, doesn't he? Curious. But I suppose he is working hard to try to help Hawaii."

Kaiulani yanked at the weed with both hands and finally uprooted it. "Papa Moi doesn't like him."

"Well." A flicker of concern passed over Cleghorn's face. "Your godfather doesn't understand business. Never has, never will." He pulled hard at a stubborn weed, sniffing a little, his voice querulous.

"Thinks you can just give a big party and then everything's all right. And you can't tell him a thing. Not a single thing. Oh no. He just smiles and thanks you for your advice, and then does exactly what he planned to do from the beginning!" Archie crouched back again, exhausted from his exertions, and tossed the weed into a pile.

"That's why I try to teach you about money and politics and business," he said, waving his trowel about for emphasis. "So you'll never be foolish about those things. Right, Tiger?"

"Yes, Papa." Kaiulani smiled. "I won't ever be foolish."

He ruffled her hair. "Well, you're your Scottish father's daughter there, my dearie."

* * * * * * * * * * * * * * * * * * *

That Thanksgiving at the Protestant Church, the Reverend Sereno Bishop, in a very bad mood, lectured sternly to a full house of members, all of them fair-skinned.

"On this Thanksgiving holiday, when many of you are so far away from home, in this the year of our Lord, 1886, let us give special thanks. I give particular thanks, myself, that I am not a heathen!" His voice rose sharply.

"I disassociate myself from, and absolutely condemn the so-called rulers of this country who raise extravagant palaces in their own selfish honor and place golden crowns upon their own vain, idolatrous heads while Hawaii's funds are so shamefully mismanaged."

The angry, set faces of the congregation nodded at the Reverend in grim agreement.

"Our missionary parents did not permit those of us who were born here, or who came over as children, to even learn the native tongue of Hawaii until our later years, when we were mature enough to pass judgment. Why? To prevent our mental contamination, that is why! Then, like today, the vilest topics were and are freely and openly discussed in the Hawaiian language, without discrimination or reserve, even in the presence of children! On a daily basis!"

Reverend Bishop looked wrathful as the devil himself, shaking his finger at the churchgoers as he admonished them. "The gross impurities of these aborigines have gone on far too long! They must—and shall be - stopped!"

* * * * * * * * * * * * * * * * * * *

Two months after Kaiulani's birthday, the southern slope of Mauna Loa erupted. It was one of the worst explosions in years, bringing with it a long, dreary period of endless rainfall and severe bouts of thunder and lightning. The air became thick and smoky, with every breath tainted with the dry volcanic ash that choked in the nose and throat. The people were very frightened that Pele was so angry. In her rage she was burning down and taking bites out of the land everywhere, with sudden, wild eruptions and a constant boil of hissing, molten lava. The dark, flowing streams wiped out all the roads and farms in their path for miles around and breathing the air was like swallowing hot smoke.

Ainahau was in turmoil, too. Very soon after Pele's eruption, Princess Likelike began to act strangely. She would be absent from the estate for mysterious, extended periods, once even staying out all night with no explanation at all. There were rumors that she was visiting the old *kahunas*, trying to find some way to placate the goddess' rage.

Cleghorn did not know what to make of his wife's explosive, mercurial moods. He was very upset by them and desperately wanted to help her. But she began to refuse to even talk to him, and he retaliated by staying away from Ainahau himself, away on business. Or sometimes he would stay shut in, working silently in his library or his room, often till late at night, and always alone.

On one of these gloomy, overcast days Kaiulani and Miss Gardinier were sitting at the beach. Kaiulani was wearing one of the new, lighter, looser dresses that Miss Gardinier had convinced Likelike to have made for her, to replace the stiff, formal satins and heavy brocades she had worn before the governess came.

Kaiulani listlessly sifted sand through her fingers while her governess tried for the fifth time to read a page of her book, *Spirit Tales of Old Hawaii*. Miss Gardinier finally gave up and tossed the book down beside her in the sand. She picked out some ribbon from her mending basket and tried to arrange a braid from some stray pieces of fabric, but soon gave up on that, too.

"Well, Kaiulani," she said gently, "Where's your lovely weather today, dear?"

"Nothing is ever perfect," Kaiulani sulked.

Miss Gardinier looked dubiously up at the clouded sky. "Well, that's true. It almost looks like a storm."

Kaiulani stood, brushing sand from her hands and bare feet. "No one can always have what they want. Do you want to come swimming with me? Will you? Please?"

"Not today," Miss Gardinier replied.

Kaiulani kicked lightly at the ground and then raced away down the shore, shouting back over her shoulder, "You never do!"

"Not too long, Kaiulani!" Miss Gardinier called out. "And stay in close!"

Anxious, Miss Gardinier peered after her charge, then gave up on watching for her to reappear and picked up her book again. Within minutes she had fallen asleep. Waking abruptly with a start, she ran down to the beach and called out the Princess' name several times. But the only response was the sound of the wind and the waves. Very concerned, Miss Gardinier sat down on a rock and wiped away tears of frustration.

Then the wind began to blow up higher still, whipping the water into a frenzy. In the harsh whistling of the high winds Miss Gardinier heard her mother's voice, far away and muffled with fear. "Don't ever go swimming alone! There are sharks everywhere…"

The wind seemed to repeat and multiply the words: "Sharks…There are sharks…sharks, sharks, sharks…"

Relaxed from her long swim, Kaiulani came up quietly behind Miss Gardinier, holding a conch shell she had found for her. But when she softly said her teacher's name, Miss Gardinier jumped off the rock and whirled around to face her, furious and afraid.

"Don't you ever disobey me again!" she said sternly, in a tone she had only heard her own mother use once. Still unable to release her tension, she lightly slapped Kaiulani's wrist. The princess turned pale, dropped the conch shell and ran off.

Later that day, in the parlor at Ainahau, Miss Gardinier and Princess Likelike sat stiffly across from each other like wooden statues. The curtains were drawn and the blinds were all shut.

Her eyes hooded and opaque as a lizard, Likelike coldly repeated her judgment. "A Princess can never be punished."

Miss Gardinier's face flushed a bright rose, but her voice remained firm. "I am sorry, then, Princess Likelike. But if Kaiulani will not learn obedience, especially when it is for her own protection, then I cannot continue on as her teacher."

Likelike nodded once in recognition. "I will need to think this over at greater length," she said.

The governess rose, excused herself and left the room.

That night the air had cleared a little and in the evening sky a few stars faintly shined. Miss Gardinier sat at her bedroom window gazing out with a sharp sense of sadness and longing. In the dim light she looked very young, almost like a child herself, as she whispered, "Star light, star bright. First star I see tonight, -"

A knock at the door interrupted her. She dropped the curtain and turned away from the window. "Come in," she said softly.

Kaiulani entered the room, dignified and composed, but looking very unhappy. She could barely meet her teacher's eyes. "Miss

Gardinier, I am sorry I disobeyed you this afternoon. It was wrong of me to do so."

"Yes, it was, Kaiulani. If you do not learn to respect and obey others, how can you expect them to obey you?"

The princess caught her lower lip in her teeth for an instant before she spoke. "My mother said - she told me you might - "She struggled to stay calm, but this time she looked directly into her governess' eyes with an even, steady gaze.

"You are my *kumu*, Miss Gardinier." Her voice was very quiet. "But you are also my good friend. I hope you will not decide to go away."

Kaiulani made a short, simple bow and left the room.

Miss Gardinier looked out her window again. From far away she heard a peacock crying. Then she sat at her desk, took out paper and pen and began to write.

"Dear Mama," she read out loud as she wrote, "I have decided to stay on at Ainahau for another year. It is very beautiful here. And I believe Kaiulani needs me."

The rains continued for days along with the hazy, oppressive skies. One morning when there was a brief period of sunlight, Kaiulani came outside to the *lanai* to find Miss Gardinier deep in conversation with an attractive American man who was introduced to her as "Mr. Albert Heydtmann." Although she was civil to him, Kaiulani greatly resented the way he whispered in Miss Gardinier's ear to make her laugh.

That afternoon, when the sky had clouded up again, Mama came home from running around all day in a wild burst of unusual energy. She rushed over to Miss Gardinier and held up to her a lacy white gown.

"This would look lovely for your wedding!"

Miss Gardinier looked stunned and Kaiulani looked up from her French conjugation exercise.

"What wedding?" she asked her mother.

Likelike had become increasingly unpredictable. By turns, she would be brusque and sullen; then extravagantly lively and flirtatious.

"She is engaged to be married!" Her voice shrilled out. "To Mr. Heydtmann!"

Kaiulani struggled to conceal her feelings. "I am very happy for you." She said politely to her governess. "Mama, may I go out and see Fairy now?"

"Not in the rain," her mother responded absently. A sharp clap of thunder had distracted her, and a brooding look clouded up her face.

"Then I will go to my room," Kaiulani said and she quickly walked away.

Miss Gardinier looked after her charge, downcast. "I wanted to tell her later, myself - "she began.

"Oh," Likelike said, with desperate, false gaiety. "Better to get it over with!" She attempted to pose and was coy again as she held a bright lavender dress up against her own form. "What do you think? Does this one suit me?"

Upstairs, Kaiulani rose from her bed and walked into Miss Gardinier's room. On the vanity table was a framed picture of a smiling Mr. Heydtmann. She picked it up and looked at it for a long time. Then deliberately, without expression, she scratched a long mark across his face with her fingernail.

Early that evening when Kaiulani walked into the parlor she found Miss Gardinier and Mr. Heydtmann sitting on the couch together, talking. Walking straight over to them Kaiulani looked directly into Mr. Heydtmann's eyes and coldly announced, "Mr. Heydtmann, I hate you."

Mr. Heydtmann's soft, brown eyes became very sad. His tone was crestfallen and low as he asked her, "Princess Kaiulani. What have I done that you should say that?"

"She came to Hawaii for <u>me</u>, not you!" Her eyes were burning as she ran from the room.

The next day Mauna Loa erupted again, in an even worse explosion. Anyone who was able to fled to Oahu to stay with relatives, friends, or even generous strangers who were taking people in. The word raced around the islands that this time Pele could not - or would not - be appeased.

A group of refugees sheltered in an inlet by some craggy rocks saw the wild water turn a deep, blood red. It was the red of the *aweo aweo*, or *akule* fish, churning up in the tidal waves that had followed the volcano's explosion. The tiny, bright fish were suddenly everywhere on the shoreline, darting about frantically in the crashing waves.

An old woman hugged herself tightly and rocked back and forth as she gave voice to everyone's fear. "*Akule* fish very bad. Means some *ali'i* going to die."

Her young granddaughter tugged at the old woman's hand, her voice anxious. "Maybe it will be the King, Tutu? You think so?"

The grandmother shook her head and held the girl close as she rocked her. "You never know. Never know till it's over and too late."

* * * * * * * * * * * * * * * * * * * *

Cleghorn sat alone in his library reading a newspaper. His mouth was pursed up as if he had eaten a lemon. The bold headline across the front page read, "Opium Scandal - King Kalakaua Suspected of Selling Licenses to Sell Opium to Highest Bidders!"

Cleghorn tossed the paper down and shook his head as he muttered. "Well, he's really done it this time."

A few miles away, in a smoky basement room lit by candles and kerosene lamps, a sullen group of men had gathered to discuss the news. Thurston and Dole were off to one side with an angry knot.

A handful of laborers, Hawaiians, *hapa-haoles* and foreigners were also scattered throughout the room. Almost hidden in shadows in the back were some sinister looking thugs who stood guard over several stacks of rifles and other guns. At the head of this group stood Colonel Volney Ashford, a tall, sinister looking man, half Hawaiian and half Portuguese, with a spiky red mustache that curled up the sides of his scarred face. A bright red scarf was tied tightly at his throat. Ashford kept his arms folded close across his broad chest as he exchanged a few rough remarks with his companions.

When at last the door was closed on the crowd, Thurston strode to the front of the room. Although he shouted for quiet several times, it was not until Ashford gave the surly crowd a nod to shut up that he could speak.

"We shall call ourselves the Hawaiian League!" Thurston blared out. "Our purpose is to force the King to reign, not rule! Or suffer the consequences!"

Someone snarled out, "Yeah, that's right; suffer the consequences!" An ugly cheer rose from the crowd.

Volney Ashford raised his fist in mocking salute as he called out, "And my volunteer militia are just the men to do it. Aren't we, boys!"

A large man standing next to Ashford held a rifle high as he shouted, "Let's hear it for the Honolulu Rifles!" Others followed his lead, raising weapons as they called out, "The Rifles!" "Here's to the Rifles!" "Surrender, or else!"

These same men were gathered together early the next day for the official royal drill. They were the Honolulu Rifles in the daytime and the Hawaiian League at night. Now sober and neatly dressed in smart uniforms, they paraded on the exhibition field while King Kalakaua and his dignitaries watched from the stands.

Colonel Volney Ashford, still wearing his red bandanna from the night before, took his men through the full performance of their marching drill with meticulous precision. When he signaled them at last to halt, Ashford strode over to the King and his entourage and stood before them. Kalakaua handed to him the flag of Hawaii.

"In honor of the dedication and patriotism of your most impressive company of Honolulu Rifles," the King said.

The Colonel responded with a deep, mocking bow. "Your highness, it is we who must thank you for this beautiful emblem of the unity of all the many people who have blended together to form this Kingdom of Hawaii."

That same afternoon, in a parlor room near the palace, the secret committee of the Hawaiian League met for several hours. The group of about twenty included American and British businessmen, Volney Ashford and several other hard-looking types, along with a handful of Chinese and *hapa-haoles*. This was the same group from the night before, with a few new members. The table was littered with papers that included a diagram of the interior of Iolani Palace and an illustration of the king's personal quarters. Attended by two sidekicks, Ashford was playing with a large, sharp knife, occasionally gouging deep nicks in the edge of the wooden table.

Thurston read laboriously from a heavily edited paper. "Our new constitution calls for an end to such shameful actions as the king's most recent bill, passed by a corrupt legislature, for licensing the sale of opium.

Irritated by the monotonous drone of Thurston's voice, Ashford viciously stabbed his knife into a corner of the table. Annoyed and restless, he was sick of the hours of endless talk.

Ashford sneered at Thurston as he spoke. "They'll sell it anyway." His voice was sullen and compressed. "Only the Chinks'll make all the money. Two of 'em already bribed him; one lost out and ratted to the papers." He looked around, hoping that someone would challenge him. When no one did he shrugged and added, "That's just the way things are around here."

A Chinese businessman sitting near Dole slapped his hand down on the table, but Dole stopped him before he could speak.

Thurston nodded at Dole's commanding look and began to read again, louder than before. "And we demand that the king at once dismiss Premier Gibson and rectify immediately his unjust policy of a Hawaiians-only cabinet. Furthermore, the Treaty of Reciprocity with the United States shall be renewed posthaste, and the king shall turn over to America indefinite term rights to maintain Pearl Lagoon as a military base."

"Under our new constitution," Thurston continued, "qualified voters shall include only those who have annual incomes of $600 or more or taxable properties worth $3,000."

Unbearably bored and disgusted, Ashford expertly threw his knife into the wooden wall very near the podium where Thurston stood. A shocked silence filled the room as the Colonel casually strolled over to retrieve his knife.

"There is an easier way -" his voice was heavy with sarcasm— "gentlemen."

Pulling the knife out, he turned back to the others and smiled. "Let's just kill him - and it's over. Done with. No - more - King. No more -" With a sneer, he kicked at a pile of discarded papers on the floor. "Extravagant waste - of paper - and time."

Dole immediately rose from the table. His voice was icy.

"Those words were never spoken here. If there is going to be this kind of talk, I have no choice but to resign from the committee."

"Fine, Mr. Dole." Ashford spoke in the same, deeply caustic tone. "But you and the League will still continue to have the service of my excellent—"

Casually, he sheathed his knife and smiled again. "Honolulu Rifles."

Chapter Ten

Six weeks had passed since Mauna Loa's terrible eruption. Princess Likelike, distraught and distracted, had visited several *kahunas* in the first few days following. She would say nothing to anyone about these interviews, but only became more fanciful and unstable afterwards, and then remote. At the end of two weeks, after the second eruption, she took to her bed. Not long after that, she refused to eat.

All the Hawaiians talked about Likelike's condition. Some of the *kanakas* believed that one of the *kahunas* must be "praying her to death." Others were sure that Pele, in her rage, had demanded of the Princess some terrible sacrifice. A few of the people scoffed at these explanations; and, like the *haoles*, would only say that Likelike had always been foolish and flighty, and was a stubborn woman, besides.

Archibald Cleghorn was beside himself. He begged the doctors to give him some reason or hope. He scolded and cajoled Likelike, pleading with her to take nourishment, to try for their sake if she wouldn't for her own. But his wife only shook her head, sadly at times; or pursed her parched lips tightly together. Other times she would just glare at him, silent, fierce and determined. Daily, she grew thinner and weaker. And then came the times when she did not even recognize her husband, or anyone at all.

Alone in his study Cleghorn cried. Soon after that, he began to write letters. When he had finished he asked Kaiulani if she could keep a secret, and then described to her the elaborate plans he was making, plotting a "travel cure" to San Francisco for April. Surely her mother would be well enough to travel then. Even sooner, perhaps, if the doctors gave her permission to go. He spent many hours in consultations with these doctors, demanding explanations, begging for solutions.

"But she's only thirty-six!" he would object, angry or pathetic by turns. "How can this be?!"

King Kalakaua and Princess Liliuokalani took turns at their sister's bedside; one or the other was always there. They talked in low voices, or softly sang the old songs and held her hand, or just sat quietly with her for hours. The King gently chided his sister, saying that such a fine dancer as herself must eat to keep up her strength, so she could dance again. He tried to coax her into eating something, anything, even a little spoonful of broth, promising her a trip to the mainland, or even to New York or Boston, as a reward.

The first time Kaiulani came to visit her mother was with Miss Gardinier. After that she went alone. She would try to pique her mother's interest, telling her about parties that were coming up or that were over. She talked to her about the stained glass windows that Likelike and the other princesses had agreed to donate to the new cathedral at St. Andrew's church. Likelike had chosen for her subject "The Resurrection." But when Kaiulani tried to engage her mother with news of plans for the execution or design, Likelike only patted her daughter's hand, then turned her face away to the wall to brood or sleep. The stale, dead air in that shuttered room where her mother lay for so long disturbed Kaiulani, sometimes making her cough so that she had to leave.

All of them watched and waited, helpless as the mostly silent Likelike wasted away. Archibald clung to Kaiulani as if his daughter's youth and good health could somehow save him from, or alter, his wife's dreadful, willful starvation. But whatever the force that held Likelike so fiercely in its grip, it would not let her eat or drink, and allowed her only brief, fitful moments of sleep.

After one of the worst nights Likelike whispered to Liliuokalani early in the morning that she must see Kaiulani. Liliu, who had been the sentry at her bedside for hours, attempted to dissuade her but, even in her feeble, emaciated state, Likelike would not budge.

Kaiulani had not visited for two days and almost could not recognize the frail, inert figure on the bed. Her once vivacious, volatile mother now looked like one of the ragged, end-of-the-season scarecrows in the sugar cane fields.

When Likelike became aware of Kaiulani, her eyes focused on her daughter like narrow beams of light, unsteady, flickering in and out of the shadows. Trembling in her agitation she motioned the girl to sit beside her on the bed. When Liliuokalani bent over near them, Likelike looked straight into her sister's eyes and laboriously, only once, shook her head no. Reluctantly, Liliuokalani left them alone.

Kaiulani looked at her mother's cadaverous frame with almost unbearable anxiety. It seemed to her as if her real mother had disappeared, leaving behind her this frightening, preternatural stranger, some ancient spirit of flame. Kaiulani's real mother was being burned away, relentlessly smoked out of her fragile, shell-like body from the inside out, disintegrating even as she lay there.

The wraithlike Princess indicated with the slightest movement of her head that she wanted her daughter to move in closer.

"Kai - Kaiu - lani." Her breath came in staccato gasps, struggling to fight its way out from between her dry, cracked lips.

"Must tell you -" She grasped her daughter's wrist in talon-like fingers with a remarkably strong hold and pulled her even closer. Her eyes burned like hot coals and she spoke into the girl's ear with a low, breathless hiss.

"I have seen things -" She stopped to suck in air until she could speak again. "You will never - be -Queen." Her fingers were impossibly powerful as they dug into Kaiulani's hand. "You must not - ever—marry - one you do not - love." Likelike's fierce determination to deliver her message gave way a little as she looked deeply into her daughter's terrified eyes. Her tone became softer and she released her terrible grasp. She shook her head in a tiny, side-to-side movement.

"Sent - away -" Her voice cracked and thinned out, so that Kaiulani could barely make out the next whispered words. "Exiled..." "Poor - - baby." With tremendous effort she tapped a weak finger once on her daughter's hand. Then Likelike's grip loosened entirely and her head lolled to one side as a faint rattling sound rumbled low, deep in her throat.

Kaiulani tried to say her mother's name but could not shape the word in that still, suffocating air. "Mama- "Her own dry lips hurt as she also fought to breathe. "Ma - ma!" She cried out softly as her mother sank into a stupor. Kaiulani ran from the room. As soon as Archibald and Liliuokalani saw Kaiulani's face, they rushed into the sickroom with the doctor.

Kaiulani's hands felt like they were on fire where her mother had touched her. She ran through the house, half-stumbling and almost blind in her fear, until at last she found Miss Gardinier sitting alone on a sofa in the living room. Wordlessly, she slid in close beside her, hiding and clutching her hands, which continued to burn her.

The young woman tenderly supported the grieving girl, wrapping her arms protectively around her. Kaiulani leaned back against Miss Gardinier as if she was a tree, pressing her head and shoulders tightly against Gertrude's front. Without tears, their faces solemn and wounded, they sat in silence and waited for the news they knew must come.

* * * * * * * * * * * * * * * * * * * *

On a cool, gray morning two days later Kaiulani stood in the throne room at Iolani Palace, rigid beside her mother's funeral bier. Princess Likelike was laid out in white satin. Royal bearers, stationed all around the room and at every side of the dead Princess, incessantly waved their tall yellow and black *kahilis*. The large room was filled with the white jasmine and pale gardenia flowers Likelike had loved.

A steady procession filed past the casket as Kalakaua, Liliuokalani and Kaiulani stood close by. Queen Kapiolani sat beside Archibald Cleghorn and patted his narrow shoulder while he wept. By nightfall the wailing of grieving Hawaiians would echo throughout Oahu. For the present, although Kaiulani watched the people as they walked by to pay their respects and could see that many of them were crying, their tears to her were silent. She heard only the sound of their footsteps as they passed and passed on by.

Later that afternoon the bearers carried the coffin to the Royal Mausoleum, a dark stone building at the top of a hill, flanked on each side by a solitary tree. The royal family stood together at the tomb's entrance as Likelike's coffin was slowly lowered down into a shallow crypt. A volley of gunshots rang out, followed by the mournful tolling of bells, which continued to echo as the casket disappeared into darkness. When the attendants closed the heavy stone doors and a final volley of gunshots was fired, Kaiulani felt a hard, tight weight begin to tug at her chest and throat until, at last, she, too, began to cry.

Several weeks after Likelike's funeral, Miss Gardinier requested a meeting with her employer. Wishing to cause no further upheaval in the household, she had waited as long as she could to discuss her plans.

The April breeze promised a balmy day as sunlight streamed in the cantilevered windows of Cleghorn's study. The employer and the governess sat in heavy oak chairs on either side of his massive mahogany desk. Miss Gardinier had just explained that she could extend her stay a little longer but was unable to alter the time of her wedding, when a thunderous volley of gunshots rang out. Cleghorn leaped up and angrily slammed down the window.

"Damn them, with those drills! Why must they keep firing away like that?!"

Miss Gardinier pulled her shawl closer around her as though the sound of the gunshots had made her cold.

"Honolulu Rifles, indeed!" He indignantly sniffed. "'Hawaiian Hooligan's League' is more like it!" Stiffly he resumed his chair and turned to his daughter's governess. "I'm sorry, Miss Gardinier. You were saying -?"

"I will be able to stay here with Kaiulani until my wedding in May." She spoke gently to the agitated man.

"Ah, yes, of course. Kind of you. Very good. Since the King has appointed me Collector General of Customs, I expect I shall be even more occupied than before - "A headline in the newspaper on his desk caught his eye.

"Look at this!" he exploded again, tapping furiously at the offensive article before him as he twisted it around to show Miss Gardinier. "'Thurston Leaves Law to Edit Bulletin'!" Cleghorn threw the paper to the ground and glared at it as if he would like to kick it. "He's the one at the head of that opposition party, I'm sure of it!

"What's he up to now?" He worried to himself. After a long moment Miss Gardinier delicately cleared her throat to remind him that she was there.

Archibald looked up from his dark reverie. "I am so sorry, Miss Gardinier. Of course I will make some appropriate arrangements. Thank you, it is so good of you to let me know."

A few miles away the Honolulu Rifles continued to practice their drills. Kalakaua watched the exhibition with great interest, applauding often. Colonel Volney Ashford took the men smartly through their routines. The Colonel was thinking to himself as they executed their moves that, if all went as planned, by tomorrow or next week at the latest, and possibly even as soon as the next day, the League would have taken control of the palace and banished the king's cabinet.

Kalakaua smiled warmly at Ashford as he presented him with another honorary flag in tribute to the excellence of the militia. The King, in fact, was also aware that the men parading in front of him as the Honolulu Rifles, shouldering their sharp bayonets and hoisting and firing their guns, were the same men who made up the infamous Hawaiian League. And that these men waited and eagerly plotted to divest him of power in any way they could.

Ashford bowed low to the king as he accepted the flag and thanked him yet another time for the "beautiful emblem of the unity of the many peoples who are blended together - ".

For an instant Volney Ashford scowled. Thurston had insisted that he add this next part, and he really hated to say it. Deliberately, he cleared his throat before he resumed.

"On a benignant basis of racial and political equality," - Ashford relaxed again as he returned to his original speech - "combined to form the Kingdom of Hawaii." The Colonel's emphasis on "kingdom" was noticeably exaggerated.

The King, for his part, had made sure the palace was barricaded, that the royal guard was out in double force, and that the miraculous new invention of electricity was turned on promptly at sunset and used to light the entire palace after dark, turning night into day.

None of these precautions would make the slightest bit of difference. By September of that year a new constitution, aptly named the "Bayonet Constitution," would be forced upon the King and his people. This new constitution did not discriminate along any racial lines, either; none at all. Under the new laws, those who were allowed to vote needed to meet only two simple conditions. They had to have earned income of $600 per annum, or to own taxable property valued at $3,000. Any person setting up residence in Hawaii who met these qualifications could, in a remarkably short period of time, make their voices heard by their vote. And a man's oath to his country of origin would never, in any way, compromise his "citizenship" in the new Hawaii.

Out of this new citizenry, only one out of three or four or five or so Hawaiians born in Hawaii were qualified to vote. But for the others, those who did not qualify to vote; well, it was understood that they must look upon these conditions as an opportunity; an inspiration, even, to better themselves, to work harder and thus earn the right to be responsible and to vote.

Positive economic changes came quickly under the new rule. The treaty of commercial reciprocity between Hawaii and America was renewed almost at once, and the exclusive rights to the use of Pearl Lagoon were soon turned over to the USA. The king's cabinet minister, Walter Murray Gibson, was immediately replaced. The king's cabinet, which had been made up of older Hawaiians who had no income to speak of and no ownership whatsoever, was voted out in the name of progressive change. So was every one of the king's myopic "all Hawaiian" programs, such as the board of genealogists and the native Hawaiian board of health. Adjustments like these, of course, it was only logical to expect.

But this was only April of 1887, when the Honolulu Rifles, under the leadership of Colonel Ashford, performed their drills for their King.

And the king's contentment was mostly unsullied as he applauded Colonel Ashford and his riflemen and their drills. He wished Queen Kapiolani and Princess Liliuokalani could be with him to witness this fine spring morning. But they were away in London, serving as the king's personal representatives at Queen Victoria's Jubilee. He had wanted to go with them, both for the pleasure of their excellent company and also to be anywhere as far away as possible from the recent tragedy of his sister's death.

But it was a king's duty to "Hold down the fort." He smiled as he remembered his writer friend, Robert Louis Stevenson, telling him about this quaint saying from the American Civil War.

And, indeed, the king reflected, there were many things that needed to be held down in the fort of Hawaii at present.

Chapter Eleven

May brought the usual changes to Oahu. The air became fragrant with spring flowers, and Kaiulani very much missed her mother's way of weaving jasmine and gardenias into her dark, curly hair.

The "Opium Scandal" dealt a serious blow to Kalakaua's already troubled reign. In June the King was officially accused of selling a license to sell opium to a wealthy Chinese businessman; shortly thereafter he had apparently sold the same license all over again to another Chinese merchant. Although nothing was ever proved on either count, the king found himself regularly on trial in the haole-owned papers.

The Hawaiian Gazette, known throughout the Islands as the Opposition Party's mouthpiece, alleged that the King and his Premier, Walter Gibson, had been "on a course of plunder and defiance with the intention of destroying Hawaii." According to all the anti-royalist newspapers, the king and his followers were not only ready but actually eager "to shoot down the citizens of the community" without the slightest qualm.

The new season also brought for Kaiulani the bittersweet event of Miss Gardinier's wedding. She was, at last, able to be happy for her good friend's joy. Since Mama had died something had shifted and was changing inside the young princess. She was less quick to anger, more self-contained and even subdued in some ways. But she also felt a deeper sadness than she had ever experienced before.

First, with Mama Nui's death, and now, even more with her mother's, her heart had been wounded. Sometimes just the sight of

Papa's grieving face made her want to run from the room in tears. But she tried to keep her feelings to herself. Her loss, she understood, had opened her up, leaving her more vulnerable but also wiser. She could grasp better now, for instance, the intensity of Miss Gardinier's desire to be loved.

Originally, the wedding was going to be held in the loveliest gardens at Ainahau, the ones that bordered on the main house. After Mama's death, though, the location was changed to St. Andrew's Church for eight o'clock on a Saturday evening in the beginning of June. This was done to give Miss Gardinier a longer time to spend with Kaiulani before leaving Ainahau for good.

* * * * * * * * * * * * * * * * * * *

The wedding was just a week away when the Opposition Party, ignited by the daily news of the Opium Scandal, gathered its forces together one dark, moonless night. By ten o'clock hundreds of armed militiamen had formed an angry mob.

Their main rallying place was the gazebo where the royal coronation had been held. The once resplendent area was now dirty and littered, barely recognizable. The frightened people who ventured out into the streets that sullen, humid evening had to duck out of the range of surly, armed men, sometimes even running away from them. Occasionally, one of the thugs would push and bully an anxious, fleeing citizen while his cohorts stood by and jeered. Every once in a while a member of the mob, usually one who had had too much to drink, fired a shot into the air to make his comrades laugh and cheer.

Lorrin Thurston stood at the gazebo's highest elevation and looked around at the rude men who jammed the streets. Most of them carried rifles with bayonets attached; others held knives or clubs. Volney Ashford stood off to one side at the head of a small, organized group that kept apart from the milling crowd.

Thurston was grateful for his long days of practice at violent argument as a lawyer, for it made him able now to pitch his voice at a volume and tone that blared out above the raucous roar of the mob.

"Orderly fashion!" He barked. "No firing without the signal!" he threatened. He positively snarled as he took in Volney Ashford's patronizing grin. "We will win our cause without the need for battle!"

Hoots and sarcastic whistles greeted his remarks. One of the riflemen drawled out in an ugly, whiskey-soaked voice, "That's for sure!" Another man, his voice full of icy rage, added, "Damn well better be right. After all, we got all the weapons."

Thurston held his right hand high, and then sharply dropped it to his left side. This was the signal for Colonel Ashford to marshal his forces.

"Bear arms!" Volney Ashford shouted in a lusty tone. Hundreds of men shouldered their rifles while dozens more fell into a loose crowd behind them.

"To the Palace!" Ashford cried, and the march began.

* * * * * * * * * * * * * * * * * * * *

Outside Iolani Palace a brace of silent men handed out the few, last weapons from the king's storeroom of armaments. Most had been "liberated" earlier by the Honolulu Rifles. Almost all of the palace guards, unarmed and terrified, had run away. A few had stripped off their uniform jackets and fallen in with the mob.

Inside the palace, the King and Queen lay in bed in their dressing gowns, catching up after her long absence away in London with Liliu at Queen Victoria's Jubilee.

Musicians with guitars, ukuleles and traditional "*hana*" drums played in the hall outside the royal chamber. Most of the sounds of turmoil in the streets below were muffled by the soft, soothing music that flowed into their room.

Kalakaua picked up a letter from the bedside table and read the return address. "From my writer friend, Robert Louis Stevenson!"

Kapiolani snuggled in against his solid chest. "That odd-looking poet you told me about, from Scotland?"

"The thin one, who always coughs." He read for a moment in silence and then smiled.

"Listen to this, my dear!" 'So long as we love, we serve; so long as we are loved by others, I would almost say that we are indispensable.'" Kalakaua reached his arm around Kapiolani's shoulder and held her closer in to him still. "'And no man is useless while he has a friend.'"

Stomping footsteps abruptly echoed from the downstairs hall. The King dropped the letter and got up out of bed. The music had disappeared, drowned out by the sound of hammering boots. A heavy hand pounded on the door.

Kapiolani turned pale. "The guards - why don't they -"

Lorrin Thurston himself threw open the unlocked bedroom door. He was flanked by Ashford and several men who carried bayoneted rifles.

The King drew himself up with dignity and assurance, genial as ever.

"Mr. Thurston -"

Kalakaua indicated his frightened wife. "Surely we can - discuss matters—elsewhere?" He pressed Kapiolani's hand to reassure her. "- Perhaps in the hall?"

* * * * * * * * * * * * * * * * * *

Two hours later Thurston was still droning on, reading out every detail of a long, verbose proclamation. Exhausted and tired of listening, besides, the king leaned against a railing, bracing himself by holding on to the top of a stair post which was carved into a likeness of the royal hawk. Even the militiamen and thugs lounged about haphazardly, or stood only wearily at attention. The civilian crowd outside the palace had long since gone home.

Oblivious to the boredom and fatigue of everyone around him, Thurston turned the page again.

"And the King shall no longer interfere in the election of representatives;" Thurston rattled on in his grating voice, "or in any way unduly influence the legislation or the legislators; or use his position in any way for any kinds of private ends.'"

Finally, the lawyer stopped talking. An echoing silence thundered around him. One or two men who had nodded off woke and jolted upright.

Kalakaua peered at the interloper with a curious mixture of disbelief and hope. "Is that all, Mr. Thurston?" he asked politely.

Thurston glared, turned to a last page of codicil and resumed his pompous drone. "Your personal response to this committee's proclamations and your acceptance of our constitution is required within twenty-four hours, by means of your own signature. Failure to answer will be construed as—"

Kalakaua quietly interrupted. "There is no need for all this—formality, - gentlemen." He smiled in a melancholy way and held his hand out for the document which Thurston reluctantly handed over.

"I am sure we can - "For a moment the King's gaze became as piercing as that of the carved wooden hawk under his hand. He peered evenly and steadily at Thurston, recalling their history. "- What was that saying of yours, Mr. Thurston?" Kalakaua took in the sneering face of Volney Ashford, and then smiled again. "I am sure we can - Ah, yes, now I remember it—I am sure we can 'set things straight' - as we go along."

The King signed the proclamation.

A few days later Kaiulani sat in her father's library trying to hide her anxiety as he explained again about the upheaval of her godfather's reign.

"But Papa Moi is still the king, isn't he, Papa?"

"Of course he is. But some of the - procedures - will be different, from now on."

Kaiulani wanted to reassure her father that she understood. "And what does it mean, then, that Mr. Thurston will be—'Minister of the Interior - of the - Formed-?'"

"Of the Reformed Party." Her father corrected himself. "The Reform Party."

Cleghorn picked up the newspaper and angrily shook it. "It means that he will be getting every one of your godfather's programs voted out!" He hit the paper on each point, as if he might in this way be able to erase the bad news. "The Genealogy Board! The Native Hawaiian Board of Health! Even The Children's Education Fund!"

Furious, he read from the paper. "'All Hawaiian children who have been sent to be educated in Europe will be ordered home to defray unnecessary expense.'"

Kaiulani looked up at her father, her eyes shining with happiness, forgetting for a moment to be understanding. She could hardly contain herself, smiling for the first time in months as she said her cousin's name. "Koa!"

That afternoon she galloped around Ainahau in high spirits, giddy with the anticipation of Koa's return. When she returned Fairy to his place in the stable she whispered Koa's name into the horse's ear. The pony seemed to catch her excitement and neighed with a low, pleased whinny.

* * * * * * * * * * * * * * * * * * * *

The next day was Miss Gardinier's wedding. Despite the good news of Koa's return, Kaiulani, dressed and ready, found her self feeling terribly abandoned. She was glad for her governess' happiness, but nevertheless she felt horribly left out. The morning events had already begun, but Kaiulani refused to come out of her room.

Exasperated, Cleghorn rattled his daughter's locked door for the third time.

"Kaiulani, please! Everyone is waiting!"

The unhappy girl threw herself onto her bed and said miserably. "I'm sorry, Papa. I just can't."

After a long moment of quiet there was a single knock, followed by the clear, commanding voice of Princess Liliuokalani.

"Kaiulani," Liliu said, "I must speak with you now."

Her aunt's voice could not be denied.

Inside Kaiulani's room Liliuokalani carefully rearranged her niece's tousled hair. A full-length mirror reflected their images back to them as they spoke. By a trick of the bright morning light, they were magnified and lit up as sharply as if they were standing under spotlights or on a stage.

Liliu spoke in a gentle, almost hypnotic tone while she brushed Kaiulani's hair and rearranged it around her unhappy face.

"I know you are sad right now. I know that you will miss your friend very much. And I know how hard it is for you now that your Mama is gone."

Kaiulani pursed her lips to keep from crying.

Liliuokalani laid her hands on her niece's shoulders, focusing her gaze in the mirror. She spoke kindly, although she made no attempt to soften the resolve in her words.

"But you must also think of your country, Kaiulani, and of your people. These are difficult times for everyone. And there will be more to come."

The girl turned away from the powerful, reflecting light, to lean back against her aunt and be held.

Liliuokalani embraced her for a moment and stroked her head. Then she turned Kaiulani around again to look back at their reflections in the mirror.

"So, my dear niece, we will dry your tears," - Liliuokalani's voice trembled for an instant until she could catch it - "- and you will hold your head up high."

"You are a Princess of Hawaii—beautiful and proud -"

Kaiulani managed a tiny smile to answer her aunt, who returned it with her own.

Liliuokalani's voice was again assured as she grasped her niece's hand. "- And much stronger right now than even you can know."

At the service that night Kaiulani stood beside Liliuokalani, cheerful and gracious as the minister pronounced Miss Gardinier and Mr. Heydtmann man and wife.

When it was over, everyone crowded around the bride and groom. But Miss Gardinier broke away at once to rush over to Kaiulani and give her a hug.

From inside her sleeve Kaiulani took out a small sandalwood box and handed it to Miss Gardinier. Inside was the golden peacock pin Mama Nui had given to her on her birthday.

"Oh, Kaiulani! I couldn't!" Miss Gardinier tried to return it. "It's from Mama Nui!"

Kaiulani folded her hands behind her back. "It would please me for you to have it." She shook her head when Miss Gardinier tried to give it back. "Besides - "A glint of the old mischief twinkled in her eyes. "In Hawaii you are not allowed to say no to a Princess."

At the wedding *lua* King Kalakaua and Queen Kapiolani sat at the table of honor with Liliu, Cleghorn, Kaiulani and the newlyweds. Although the King appeared as dapper and robust as ever, there was an underlying sadness in his face that shadowed his efforts at good cheer and made him seem older than before.

"To the bride and groom!" The King raised his glass of champagne and nodded toward the newlywed couple who sat close by. Kalakaua was every inch a king as he declared, "Another success for Hawaii!"

Chapter Twelve

Koa returned home to Oahu in the late fall of the year just after Kaiulani's eleventh birthday. She was surprised to find herself shy and awkward in his presence. The favorite playmate of her childhood seemed to have vanished from her world. He had been replaced by a handsome, assured young man. Koa had grown a mustache that tickled when he kissed her, very lightly, on the cheek. When she played guitar for him, showing off the musical skills she had learned while he was away, he listened attentively. But he rarely smiled or joked anymore, not even when she reminded him of the fun they had had at Mama Nui's, playing at being King and Queen. On the contrary, he seemed more reserved and thoughtful than ever before. He even patted her hand one time in a very grown up way, saying he would do his best, always, to take care of her and serve her in every way.

Only when they danced together or rode horses did she recognize her boyish friend who had been replaced by this serious stranger. Then, when he twirled her around in his arms, or raced beside her as they rode in the wind, her hair streaming out wild and the intoxicating, boy-man smell of him beside her - only then did Kaiulani feel free with him.

Papa had taken to spending hours, days and weeks in long, arduous conferences with Papa Moi and his many advisors. The King, for his part, never seemed to have time to visit Ainahau anymore. To Kaiulani, he appeared always to have his mind and thoughts somewhere else whenever she saw him. On the rare occasions that he did notice her, he kissed her as warmly as ever and never failed to call her "My Princess of the Peacocks" or "My little *Pikake*." Everyone seemed much busier these days, with less time for visiting or parties or Kaiulani.

Another year passed and Kaiulani could not imagine where the time had gone. She had learned more about "proper behavior" under Koa's strict tutelage. He had become extremely particular since his time abroad about things like which glass went where and how to hold your knife and fork so you ate like a European. Aunt Liliu, too, would remind her, on the visits they made together to the Reformatory School Boys' Sporting Competition and the Photography Club luncheons and so on, about how to hold her hands in her lap in a ladylike fashion; and how to fold up her napkin after teas or ice cream socials for the Orphans of Hawaii or the Japanese Culture Society.

Then Aunt Liliu went away to visit the poor people at Molokai again, for the sad news had come of Father Damien's death from leprosy; so she was not able to attend Kaiulani's twelfth birthday. By special messenger she sent her a highly polished ivory box, inlaid with abalone and mother-of-pearl. Inside was a beautiful necklace of pearls and pink coral with tiny chips of diamonds set into the clasp. Aunt Liliu's card explained that pearls were said to be good luck, especially for growing girls. The necklace was the most grown up jewelry, besides Mama Nui's golden peacock pin and Mama's Pele's Tears earrings, Kaiulani had ever received. She thought it made her look very sophisticated and refined.

The New Year came and with it the news that old Mr. Gibson, Kalakaua's former premier who had been exiled from the kingdom for some time, had died in San Francisco. Many of the older Hawaiians and the royalist supporters grieved the loss of their old friend.

On March 23, 1888, all of Honolulu was lit up for the first time by electricity. A strange sort of unspoken truce had been made between the royals and the "Reformers" of the Opposition Party. Lorrin Thurston, in his new capacity as Minister of the Interior, had actually accompanied the Princesses, Liliuokalani and Kaiulani, to the switch-throwing ceremony at the shiny new "electricity station" in the valley. No words had passed between them and they rode, of course, in separate carriages; nevertheless, they came together. Princess Kaiulani had to stand on a high chair to reach the switch. But, with the aid of the station's superintendent, she threw the lever that connected all the circuits.

Later, in the spring of that year, the King's good friend, Robert Louis Stevenson, sailed into Honolulu on the yacht, *The Casco.* Only days before his arrival, Kalakaua had announced that the heiress apparent, Princess Kaiulani, would be sent abroad to study, to "receive the kind of training traditionally given to the children of European monarchs" in preparation for her ascension to the throne.

The King and Queen hosted a *luau* at Ainahau in honor of Stevenson's return and to celebrate the good news of the upcoming European education for their young *ali'i.*

Kaiulani was shocked by Papa Moi's announcement. She thought at first that it must be a bad joke. To send her away from Hawaii? No Koa, no Fairy, to stay with people she did not know, a stranger in a land she had never even seen? But there was no reassuring private smile for her later from Papa Moi; and no explanation from her own Papa, either, to say it was not so. Mama's prediction of her exile had come true.

So Kaiulani was secretly quite anxious and unhappy about the *luau* that was supposed to be celebrating her good fortune as well as the arrival of Mr. Stevenson. But she smiled sweetly and folded her hands the proper way and accepted congratulations.

Unknown to Kaiulani, someone else at the *luau* was also pretending to be interested in social conversation while he was, in fact, deeply involved in paying attention to her. It was the other guest of honor, "RLS," as many of his friends called him, who intently observed the young Princess.

A tall, extremely thin man, Stevenson wore his usual formal attire - a dark, velveteen jacket, which he kept on most times in most climates because he so easily caught cold. White flannel pants draped sharply over the pronounced bones at his hips and knees, and he wore a loose white shirt with a flowing tie in the style known as "bohemian" or "artistic." His long, silky hair fell down past his shoulders and his dark, almost black eyes, lustrous and shining, looked like coals on fire as they blazed out from his pale, narrow face.

RLS was passionately agreeing with Theo Davies that they must encourage everyone to write letters at once to the American President, Grover Cleveland, and to Queen Victoria, in protest of the unjust treatment of the Hawaiians. But at the same time, he was also busy studying the young Princess. The writer strongly sensed the girl's anxiety, in spite of her glib smile and mild demeanor. He observed the small details of a certain, subtle tightness in Kaiulani's voice and movements, and an intermittent, nervous habit of pursing her lips that indicated to his finely honed sensibilities that all was not as it should be.

Stevenson, sickly and frail since childhood, had traveled to the Pacific Islands in hopes of regaining his strength. He had come to respect and care deeply for the native people who had so warmly welcomed him to their land. And Kaiulani, who claimed ancestry both in his former world of Scotland and in these lush and beautiful South Sea Islands, strangely moved him. He could identify with her graciousness and poise, which reached far beyond her young years. But simultaneously he intuited the frightened child who hid behind a mask of manners; and he sympathized with her loneliness.

The *luau* went on all afternoon. Quantities of champagne were drunk and many toasts were made. The highlight came when RLS presented Kalakaua with a rare, golden pearl and a poem he had written for the occasion which ended with the charming line, "To golden hands the golden pearl I bring. The ocean jewel to the Island King."

Kaiulani felt a spark of pleasure upon hearing the pretty rhyme, at the same time that she felt a flash of disdain for its sentimental phrasing. She wondered what this poet might think if he were taken to see the calabashes of the old kings, many of them lying in Papa Moi's cellars, which were decorated with the teeth of their enemies and inlaid with pearls and shinbones.

Finally, most of the *luau* guests had gone home. Exhausted and distressed, Kaiulani at last was able to steal a moment alone. As soon as she could she went to go sit on one of the benches in the shade of her banyan tree, which had grown into a substantial monument, spreading its roots and branches in many directions. Several of her peacocks gathered around and she rested her warm face near the cool shimmering colors of their fans.

"What good is it, then, to be a Princess?!" She spoke softly to her pets. "What difference does it make, if everyone leaves you anyway and you cannot make them stay? And then -! And then, the very worst of all, - they send you away!" The terrible reality of her impending departure silenced her and she clung to her birds.

Suddenly, the peacocks began to warn and complain in their scolding, cat-like voices. A tall, thin man had materialized beside the banyan, a little way back in the shadows, and was delicately clearing his throat to let her know he was there. His soothing Scottish accent made even the peacocks quiet down when he spoke.

"I beg your pardon, Miss." In the hectic events of the afternoon they had never been formally introduced. "I wonder if you could be so kind as to inform me - is this the original, famous, first banyan tree of the many banyan trees planted in honor of the Princess Kaiulani?"

Not for a moment would Kaiulani even attempt to resume her false smile and artificial, sociable cheeriness. "Yes," she responded flatly.

"Ah, I see, I see." Stevenson put a finger to his lips. His dark mustache made a vivid contrast to his chalk white skin. "By any chance, you don't happen to know," he continued in the same low, polite tone, "If the Princess herself might be along any time soon?"

Kaiulani shrugged, noncommittal.

Stevenson immediately started to bow at the same time as he backed away ever so slightly from Kaiulani and her tree.

"Ah, well, sorry for the intrusion. And thank you very much indeed, all the same. Thank you." Still moving away, he added so softly she could barely hear the words, "My mouse will be so disappointed."

Kaiulani was sure she had misheard him. "Your - mouse?" she inquired skeptically.

Stevenson nodded glumly. "He had so much wanted to meet a real princess."

Dubious, the twelve year old questioned him again. "And where is your mouse?"

Moving a half step back toward the banyan Stevenson patted his jacket pocket.

"Let me see," the suspicious girl demanded.

Instantly, he transferred a tiny, tame mouse from his pocket into his hand.

"Oh! May I hold him?"

Stevenson handed her the mouse, which settled companionably into her palm, nuzzling at her fingers and tickling.

"What is his name?" she asked, beginning to smile in spite of her self.

"He is called Dr. Jekyll. Or Mr. Hyde. Whichever you prefer."

"Mr. Hyde," Kaiulani decided. She looked sharply at the mouse's owner. "My father sounds like you, sometimes. He is from Scotland, from Edinburgh."

"No!" Stevenson exclaimed as he respectfully settled his long limbs off to one side of her banyan. "Why, that's where I'm from, too. How clever of you to notice."

Protecting the warm, furry creature she held in her hands, Kaiulani felt so safe with this odd man that she made no effort to hide her concern. "Is it really so cold there that your hands and feet freeze off in the snow?"

"Ah, no, lassie!" Stevenson reassured her. "It's cold there, yes, but no so cold as all that!"

She wasn't exactly sure what a "lassie" was, but she could sense that he meant her no harm.

"Dunna ya worra!" he said in his coaxing, lilting tone. "There are lovely hills and moors there, and many fine sights in London, too, if you should happen to be down around that way."

England was where she was supposed to go to school. "For the next year or two," Papa had said with an ominous vagueness.

"Like what?" she asked gloomily.

"Well, there's a great, tall Tower in London; and a very beautiful new palace that is all made of crystal; and a long railroad built under the ground which can carry you to ever so many theaters and galleries and shops."

Stevenson suddenly began to violently cough. He had to almost double himself over in order to stop choking. A peacock attracted by the noise strutted over to him and cawed, nudging at his hand for food.

Kaiulani laughed. "He likes you. They're not usually so friendly." She showed the mouse to the peacock, which sent the bird away squawking.

"He doesn't like Mr. Hyde," she observed.

"Well," said RLS in a breathy rasp, "I think, perhaps, he is only - a little - shy - because he does not - know us yet." A deep sigh settled his cough down at last.

"When I first came to your islands," RLS explained, "and not very long ago, either, my health was poor and I was afraid, too; oh, of so many things - the sharks and the sunsets, the volcanoes - even of my own shadow, at times. And once," he smiled as he remembered, "even this little mouse."

Kaiulani laughed at the thought of the tall, lanky man afraid of a mouse.

Stevenson smiled at her as he fed a tiny morsel to his pet.

"But Mr. Hyde began to visit my room every night, and stayed for a bit of supper and to hear me play my flute, and soon we became the best of friends. Now we can talk about anything at all."

He looked at the girl cradling the mouse in her hands. "Even about being afraid."

Kaiulani sighed, moved by his words. "How nice." She held out her hand to him. "I am Princess Kaiulani."

He managed to stand, bowed low and kissed her hand. "Robert Louis Stevenson."

She wrinkled her nose. "That's too long, your name! Like your hair."

Stevenson laughed. "In Tahiti they called me 'Tusitala.'"

"Teller of tales," she translated. "Why?"

"Because I write stories."

"Anything I might have heard of?" Kaiulani asked politely in a very adult and formal tone.

He answered with equal solemnity. "Well, I have one story about a boy who is kidnapped, and another about an island filled with treasures and adventures -"

"Like Hawaii?" Kaiulani asked, hopeful.

Tusitala settled back in to talk. "Very much like Hawaii, as a matter of fact. But first - with your permission, of course -"

Kaiulani nodded graciously.

"- I will tell you a little about the new friends you are bound to make when you visit my island, and how happy they will be to make the acquaintance of a such a lively and intelligent Princess from Hawaii."

* * * * * * * * * * * * * * * * * * *

The next six months of Kaiulani's life passed too quickly. Her father and Tusitala soon became good friends. Privately, RLS told Archie that he felt some concern about Kaiulani's health. Occasionally, she had headaches that forced her to stay in bed, and she had already begun to need glasses for reading and other close work.

Empathetic from his reversed experience, Stevenson worried about Kaiulani's ability to acclimate to the radically different climate she would have to face. He received Cleghorn's blessing to continue to advise the Princess about Europe, talking to her about the new, foreign life she would soon be leading.

Tusitala spent many days and weeks at Ainahau, telling Kaiulani stories about England and the people who lived there and their ways. He played his flute for her and watched her show off the moves she and Fairy had worked out riding, and they visited each other's houses. Sometimes they would spend time together with the King at the horse races in Kapiolani Park, or RLS would visit her on his way to play poker at Kalakaua's boathouse or when he was coming over for one of the King's famous champagne suppers.

Kaiulani was always happy to see him. She watched with great pleasure as his color improved, joking with him that he might yet become Hawaiian if he really tried. They were frequent companions and good friends who went on walks and laughed and told their secrets to each other. The comfort of his companionship strengthened and sustained her as she prepared for her journey and said her many farewells to all she had ever known.

When Papa gave her an autograph book covered in fine red silk to collect remembrances of home, the first person she brought it to was Tusitala, who wrote a poem in it for her. Thrilled, she read it again and again.

" 'Forth from her land to mine she goes,
The Island maid, the Island rose,
Light of heart and bright of face,
The daughter of a double race.
Her Islands here in Southern sun
Shall mourn their Kaiulani gone.
And I, in her dear banyan's shade,
Look vainly for my little maid.
But our Scots Island far away
Shall glitter with unwonted day,
And cast for once their tempest by
To smile in Kaiulani's eye.' "

The inscription underneath was as lovely as the poem.

" 'Written in April to Kaiulani in the April of her age; and at Waikiki, within easy walk of Kaiulani's banyan! When she comes to my land and her father's, and the rain beats upon the window (as I fear it will), let her look at this page; it will be like a weed gathered and pressed at home; and she will remember her own islands, and the shadow of the mighty tree; and she will hear the peacocks screaming in the dusk and the wind blowing in the palms; and she will think of her father sitting there alone.' "

There were farewell parties and picnics and teas to attend. Koa and Kaiulani danced for hours at her final party at Iolani Palace; and they took long walks at Ainahau with the peacocks trailing after them like old friends.

Alone, Kaiulani went for one last ride on her beloved Fairy. The wind was gusty that afternoon as they galloped, careening wildly around the hills and shores of the coast, racing through the warm and balmy breezes.

Miss Gardinier, who was several months pregnant and looked like one of the radiant Madonnas in Aunt Liliu's prayer books, came to help Kaiulani plan her wardrobe and pack her trunks. Kaiulani gave her former *kumu* a wooden horse that she had played with as a child "to remember me and for your baby." To Tusitala, she gave a lock of her hair tied up in a bit of lace and one of the yellow ribbons from her cloak.

"I wear the colors of the little royal maid," he wrote to a friend, "More beautiful than the fairest flower." He told her that he would keep the ribbon with him forever.

Finally, it was time to go. A huge crowd had gathered at the Oceanic Wharf to say good-by. As the Cleghorn carriage drove up flower *leis* were thrown about to her and Papa as everyone wished their Princess good health and happiness and a safe journey.

Henri Berger's Royal Hawaiian Band was out in full dress to play at the dock. Berger chatted with Aunt Liliu who smiled a little despite the bittersweet sadness of the occasion. The lithe sailing ships that studded the harbor that day would disappear in just a few years, vanquished by the age of steam.

The S.S. *Umatilla*, a grand touring boat, was waiting at the harbor. Soon, it would sail for California with Hawaii's Princess Kaiulani, just fourteen years old, on board.

Papa was coming with her as far as San Francisco, she reminded herself as she nervously watched the other passengers loading. She had asked Koa to visit Fairy for her and sometimes remind him that his friend Kaiulani would only be gone for a short time. She had read and reread Papa Moi's letter of authorization, especially the last part, which said "The Princess will travel entirely incognito and be known as Miss Kaiulani." The intrigue excited her, although Papa privately told her that it was really entirely up to her own discretion to tell anyone that she was a Princess, or not. Most important to her of all was the final line of the King's missive: "Her return to the Hawaiian Kingdom," said the King's letter, would be "during the year of Our Lord, One Thousand and Eight Hundred and Ninety." She could bear it, she thought, to be away from Koa and Fairy and Papa and Ainahau and Hawaii for one year.

She clung to the wooden railing in front of her, no longer able to hide her tears as the ship began to pull away from the wharf.

From the crowd Kaiulani heard shouts of blessings, farewells, and her own name, over and over again. Avidly she watched while the land that she loved became smaller and smaller. She kept her eyes on Hawaii long after it had completely disappeared.

Chapter Thirteen

The first thing Kaiulani discovered on her trip across the ocean was that she was susceptible to severe bouts of seasickness. Like most Polynesians, she had lived on the water all her life and took to it like a second skin. But she had never traveled on the ocean for any long distance, only the short time that it took to go from one island to another. During the week's trip from Honolulu to San Francisco she spent several hours each day below deck, so wretched that more than once she wished herself under the ocean instead of on top of it.

When at last the *Umatilla* docked at San Francisco Bay, she was grateful to be released from the noxious cradle of perpetually rocking waves. Once she managed to get down a little light toast and some tea, she found herself caught up in a maelstrom of activity and excitement that hardly left her time to think.

Although she had known, of course, that there were places in the world bigger and busier than Hawaii; and taller buildings, even, perhaps, more impressive than Iolani Palace; she had never really imagined what they might look like. This carnival of sights and sounds and creatures she had landed in was truly astonishing.

First of all, there was the city itself, spreading out in every possible direction, including, apparently, straight up and down, for miles and miles and miles. Kaiulani and her father stayed with family friends in a stately, five-story brownstone that sat up in the highest shade at the topmost point of elegant Nob Hill. From there the sounds of the city were muted and far away, distant and faint as waves. But as their horse drawn carriage clattered down a hill so steep it seemed more like a cliff, the roller coaster that was San Francisco seemed to explode upon Kaiulani's nerves.

She had never seen so many people in all her life, and everyone so incredibly busy! Whalers and businessmen and "old salts;" and craggy old men down by the wharf who looked like they had been preserved in the ocean's brine. Still others, young and old alike, who had been worn down and sometimes washed out, looking as smooth as stones or softly gnarled like driftwood.

They passed rapidly through the infamous Barbary Coast district around lower Pacific Avenue and Broadway. Kaiulani saw dance halls and parlor houses with men and women pouring in and out of shabby buildings in a restless, endless stream. Some of the women were very beautiful, with their red painted mouths, pushed up breasts and low-cut, side-slit dresses. These seductive women, with their bold, direct stares, were raw, exposed and provocative in a way that no *hula* dancer had ever been. Other inhabitants of the area were bruised and battered, some of them desperate and barely able to walk. Many of the people had eyes as unnaturally round and big as saucers, while others peered out of tiny, little slots, narrow, suspicious and swollen, and looked haggard and ill. There was a pervasive smell of whiskey, perfume, sweat and tobacco that lingered in Kaiulani's nose and hair long after they had passed through those grim and hectic streets.

Some of the people lining the alleys and streets in Chinatown looked like the *kanakas* back home. Others, both *haoles* and foreigners, had faces as sharp and edgy as sharks; they looked ravenous, as if eager to devour everything and everyone around them. From a few of the doorways on Sacramento and DuPont Street the heady, sticky-sweet smell of dried herbs and burning flowers wafted out into the streets. It reminded her of the field poppies back home, which were sometimes burned in the rice fields and drifted out into the air in wispy clouds of thin, gray smoke.

The biggest sailing vessels Kaiulani had ever seen were piled high with harvests of grain and goods, and unloaded at every dock. San Francisco was the whaling capital of the world and hosted seamen from everywhere. On many of the piers the long, naked-looking bones of the humpbacks and other big whales dried in the sun.

There were parties and expeditions and sightseeing adventures that made the time in San Francisco pass like lightning. Friends and admirers fought over who would escort the starry-eyed Princess and her fidgety father to dinners at private homes; cable car outings at Fisherman's Wharf; day trips to the famous Cliff House at Land's End; and lavish picnics in sprawling Golden Gate Park.

When they were not riding around in carriages, they traveled all eight lines of the cable cars—up Telegraph Avenue to Russian Hills, far out to the Presidio, then back again to the woodlands and curved roads of Golden Gate Park. From the outdoor markets of Kearney Street and Market they raced over to the social hub of dense, historic Portsmouth Square.

During this time, even with all the excitement, Kaiulani clung to her father whenever they had a rare moment alone. Papa reminded her over and over that Mr. Davies would be there as her advisor and a friend to rely on when he was gone. For it was Theo Davies, the longtime supporter of the royal family, who had accepted with pleasure the honor of traveling with Kaiulani as the King's designated guardian.

Mr. Davies, a financier, was principal owner of the Iron Works in Honolulu. He already spent much of his time every year in his native England, where he had the majority of his business investments and holdings. An energetic man with a fine baritone voice, Davies had always maintained that the Hawaiians should rule themselves and was adamant about their right to remain independent.

Mr. Davies had several annual meetings and other important matters to attend to in San Francisco, and so was able to see little of Kaiulani and her father at that time. Forced to send his regrets for invitation after invitation; he was, in fact, able only to attend the engagement planned for the last night of their stay in the city, - an evening at the opera.

* * * * * * * * * * * * * * * * * * *

When they arrived at the Grand Opera House, Kaiulani thought the atmosphere and setting was, indeed and truly, very grand. She was dazzled by the extravagant costumes worn not only by the performers, but also by the opulent members of the audience.

Formerly Wade's Opera House, which seated a mere 2,500, the building had been redesigned to accommodate 4,000 opera goers, and the theater that night was full.

The opera was Verdi's *Aida*. The dark tale of ancient kings was performed by the Emma Juch Company, a new troupe that was touring the United States, Canada and Mexico. Miss Juch, the famous American soprano who performed the lead role, sang like a sweet, doomed angel.

Kaiulani watched spellbound as the King of Egypt bravely struggled to keep his power and throne while his daughter, the angry and jealous Princess Amneris, plotted to snare the love of Radames, the king's handsome captain of the guards. Aida was the princess' unhappy slave who had herself been a princess in her own land. She was desperately torn between her forbidden love for Radames, the conqueror of her people, and loyalty and devotion to her beloved father, Amonasro, the warring Ethiopian king.

After the jealous and spiteful Princess Amneris caught Radames in a tangle of lies, he was condemned to be buried alive. At the end of the performance courageous Aida, the heartbroken slave girl who was really a princess, stole into her lover's living tomb to share his horrible fate.

Kaiulani felt her own heart would tear apart with passion and pain, so strongly did she identify with the plight of these royals from so long ago. At the same time, she was aware of a still, calm center deep inside her soul, which understood perfectly well that these characters were only mortals, not gods; and, as such, they were caught up in a web of destiny that they could neither alter nor escape.

When the opera ended Kaiulani became very quite. She went through the motions of shaking hands, smiling and receiving compliments, best wishes and fond farewells from the many people who surrounded her to say good-by to a real Princess. But secretly she was off in another world, a realm of the spirit. For the first time she understood that her own life was, and must always be, a poem and a prayer that would honor her land and the people she came from.

That last night in San Francisco, Kaiulani had so much she wanted to say to her father that she did not know where or how to begin. She wanted terribly to make sure he knew how much she loved him, and that she would never forget all the things he had taught her; but she could find no words to tell him.

"Papa -" She began when at last they were alone.

"Yes, dear." He patted her hand awkwardly, uncomfortably aware that it was almost time for them to part. He looked to her, hoping she would in some way release him from this tumult of unwonted feeling.

But she could only shake her head and bite her lower lip, because she was so overwhelmed by the weight of the moment, and by her desire to let him know of her love.

Her father again stiffly patted her hand and struggled to hide his discomfort.

"Now, you must remember that you can always count on Mr. Davies." He could not look at her beseeching eyes as he rambled on. "He will watch out for you, and advise you; help you with any business matters or other problems that might come up -"

He suddenly became speechless, appalled by the realization that his daughter would be so far away from him, and he would be all alone at Ainahau.

"I know, Papa, I know," she said. Shyly, she wiped a tear from her father's cheek. "I know," she repeated, refusing to allow a rueful sob of laughter and tears to escape from her aching chest. "Still," she said, "it is not the same."

Cleghorn thought of the portrait of his child, a profile taken just one week ago, which he had already packed in his valise to take home. Gone forever was his young "kitten," his little tiger who had weeded gardens with him, and listened so patiently as he talked and talked, trying to teach her everything he knew. The young beauty in the photograph, who gazed so solemnly into an unknown distance, was someone he hardly knew, an elegant young woman who broke his heart, so much did she echo the tender, fragile loveliness of her mother.

"No," he agreed as he patted her hand again. "It will not be the same."

* * * * * * * * * * * * * * * * * * *

Kaiulani's journey through America drifted by in a haze. The Southern Pacific Railroad trundled them out of California and through the Rocky Mountains where she saw her first glimpse of snow, far away on the distant mountaintops. She slept for many hours, sometimes even in the day, as the lulling, monotonous rhythm of the train carried her past wide open fields, meadows, groves and farmlands, vast and hypnotic. And she never awoke without missing Hawaii. The smells of the wheat fields and pine trees and all the strange, exotic plants and flowers reminded her unceasingly that every day, every hour, took her farther away from home. In her restless sleep she would sometimes hear dogs barking and dream she was back at Ainahau, sitting under the banyan tree with her peacocks. Or she would reach out to wrap her arms around Fairy's warm neck and wake to find herself clutching a pillow.

Mr. Davies was helpful and kind, constantly checking to make sure she had enough to eat and drink, and pointing out to her all the sights, like the grain silos or early summer crops coming up from the rich, loamy soil of America.

In Chicago they took a boat ride on the great Chicago River, which had thirty-five moveable bridges across it and two giant tunnels winding underneath its circuitous expanse. They went to see the new, twelve-story Rookery Building downtown, and drove by Fort Sheridan's massive exterior. The military base had recently been built to insure the safety of the city's citizens and prevent the destruction of their property by violent strikers and other rabble-rousers; such as the bomb-throwing Anarchists and Communists who had recently wreaked havoc at Haymarket Square. Seven policemen had been killed and seventy people were wounded.

In Chicago everyone seemed to talk out of one side of their mouth, and almost no one ever looked you directly in the eyes. Their flat, hard voices seemed to be permanently stuck somewhere in their noses; and the twanging, braying sound make Kaiulani involuntarily wince. For the first time in her life, she became used to a certain kind of privacy. Most people did not pay her any particular attention at all, except, of course, when she spoke. Her years of dealing with a wide variety of people and situations had left her with an instinctive poise; and her innate graciousness and soft-spoken manner made her sound like the Princess she was.

She noticed only a few changes in temperature and terrain on the shorter leg of the trip from Chicago to the East coast. There were more hills, for one thing, and the trees seemed denser and darker green in color. But New York City jolted her attention like a bolt of electricity. It seemed impossible that so many people and so much action could be crammed into one small place like that; and on an island no bigger, really, than Lanai!

Where San Francisco had been rambling and loose, New York was as tightly packed as a ship carpenter's shelves. Not one particle of anything was unaccounted for. Space was at a premium in every neighborhood, from the haughty, high priced luxury shops on Fifth Avenue to the rickety slum houses on the Lower East Side. Dialects and accents in the city seemed to change from block to block and even each borough seemed to have its own distinct accent. One day, when they had visited quite a lot of places, with appointments for breakfast, lunch, dinner and in-between, she counted eight different languages that she had heard spoken besides English.

With amazement and admiration, Kaiulani remembered that Miss Gardinier had actually grown up in this complicated city. She loved to imagine her former governess navigating the labyrinthian streets with ease and grace, walking about with confident strides as she shepherded her younger siblings.

Most of their time in New York was very purposeful, spent making arrangements of all sorts for their travel and for Kaiulani's school in England in the fall. She heard about many friends and supporters who would welcome her and wanted her to visit them overseas. There was such a long list of people to call on, Kaiulani felt tired just thinking about it. But she conscientiously wrote down every name and address, along with their association or connection to other, also sometimes unknown, foreign or New York friends. She was moved by their generous feelings and reassured to know that Hawaii's struggle was not going unnoticed.

Mr. Davies, though still quite busy with business affairs in New York, somehow found time to take her to art galleries, fine restaurants and several of the city's excellent museums. As they traveled about the congested, beehive-like city, she observed that even its streets were, for the most part, laid out in tight, structured grids.

Unlike the Chicagoans, who almost never made eye contact, New Yorkers seemed to take two sides. Either they looked right at her, taking her in with their assessing, almost critical stares; or they glanced at her and then away at once, as if they already knew who she was but had dismissed or discounted her. She could only wonder at the incredible pace of Manhattan, and lay awake most of one long night trying to determine if her heartbeat had indeed accelerated since she had come to the city.

While they were in New York, Mr. Davies asked Kaiulani to please call him "Theo" if she liked. She tried but could not get used to the informality of the address. One afternoon Mr. Davies and Kaiulani met with a charming young matron, Mrs. T. R. Walker. The wife of the British vice-consul, Mrs. Walker was returning to London and her husband. A talkative woman with a lively sense of humor, she at once engaged Kaiulani in conversation, telling her all about England and the English people. It was soon decided that they would all travel there together, Mrs. Walker bringing along her young daughter and infant son.

At last it was time to set sail for Europe. The steamer ship from New York Harbor to Liverpool ran into rough weather the first few days, and Kaiulani again spent many hours in her berth. But a few days into their journey, the skies cleared and the water became as still and clear as glass. A balmy, pleasant wind sailed along with them and Kaiulani was delighted to find her seasickness gone. With Mr. Davies, Mrs. Walker and her children, she strolled on the deck in the mild sun and played cards and drank tea. Mr. Davies, a British subject through and through, often remarked on the healthful qualities of the "bracing sea air" and confided to Kaiulani that he looked forward immensely to seeing his homeland again. She felt a constant, aching loneliness for Hawaii, for Papa and Mama Moi, Koa and Fairy - but decided she must set those thoughts aside, for now, and concentrate her energy on the times ahead.

After they landed in Liverpool the party took a long train ride of several hours into the dusty, smoky city of Manchester, which Kaiulani thought not very nice. On June 18, they finally arrived in London.

Chapter Fourteen

London was the first city on Kaiulani's journey that she came to know well. She felt a new sense of independence there, an exciting and heady sensation of beginning to come into her own. Mrs. Walker proved an excellent companion and friend, introducing her to an exciting world of European art and culture.

The best social circles of the city opened to welcome the charming, exotic child-woman who bloomed in their midst. Kaiulani gave herself over to a non-stop whirl of theater going, sightseeing, musical entertainments and scores of parties. With her new friends, she learned to travel on the city's underground railway, and felt extremely worldly. She wrote long letters to everyone back home to tell them of her adventures.

There were art galleries to go to almost every day. She never grew tired of seeing the paintings, watercolors and sculptures, and developed a passion for rich, saturated colors and noble subjects. Sometimes she wept over the tragic scenes of saints, martyrs and suffering; other times she felt real joy at all the wonderful, intricate impressions of life's simple pleasures and triumphs. She especially loved the landscapes. Whether dramatic, tender, tempestuous, or even of settings totally unfamiliar to her, like snowstorms or the Alps, they always somehow reminded her of home. She longed to be able to paint and draw herself and, soon, at Mrs. Walker's urging, began to keep a notebook of sketches and studies of her own.

With Mr. Davies as her frequent chaperone, she reveled in learning all she could about the London stage. She adored the theater and was thrilled by everything about it. Often, she thought of Papa Moi, who also loved theater and dance. She wrote long, chatty reviews for him with notes on the performances, acting, costumes and plots, and frequently sent along programs from plays she had seen.

Mrs. Walker, a true devotee of visiting, shopping and gadding about town, was delighted to have the articulate, eager young Princess in tow. That summer they became fast friends. Mrs. Walker turned out to have a peculiar fondness for the macabre—or "the dark side," as she preferred to call it. She took Kaiulani on several visits to the gravesites of famous people. They spent hours at the notorious Tower of London listening to the guides tell horrible stories. There were grisly tales - about the beheading of poor Queen Anne by King Henry; the cruel murders of the two Little Boy Princes; the tragic execution of Sir Thomas More, who was later declared to be a saint; and the dreadful imprisonment of Sir Walter Raleigh, Queen Elizabeth I's favorite adventurer and poet. Wrongly accused of treason, Raleigh had been jailed and executed for the crime. Before he died, during the long years when he was "Shut away, yes shut away!" - the guides loved to draw out these words, with great emphasis, for dramatic effect - Sir Walter wrote the *History of the World* in his tiny, cramped cell, which felt to Kaiulani like a dark, dank cave. The stone ravens on the Tower seemed to glare evilly at Mrs. Walker and Kaiulani, and to watch them come and go on their many trips to the sinister stone tower.

Mrs. Walker also took her to the weird Museum of Madame Marie Tussaud, commonly known as the London Wax Museum. A Swiss wax modeler by trade, Madame Tussaud had been forced to make death masks of quite a few of the guillotined aristocrats during France's hideously bloody Revolution. When at last Tussaud was allowed to leave Paris, she moved at once to London and used the terrible events she had witnessed and her unique, unusual art to create mysterious, often frightful tableaus. Kaiulani thought of the shark warriors and the human sacrifices of her own people; she was grateful to see that none of them were represented at Madame Tussaud's.

Another high point of that summer was a visit to the Crystal Palace. Designed by Sir Joseph Paxton for the Great London Exhibition of 1851, this breathtakingly beautiful exhibition hall was made mostly of glass. It was the first time that a cast-iron frame had been used for building; and the Palace was also the first structure to have prefabricated units made elsewhere, then assembled together on site.

The Crystal Palace positively sparkled with light, and Kaiulani felt like a Princess in a fairy tale when she was there. She received many admiring glances at the Crystal Palace and elsewhere, too, for she had grown into a lovely young woman, and had also begun to look quite stylish as well. Mrs. Walker had asked permission to "take you under my wing," and proceeded to tutor her in everything she needed to know and do, teaching her the fine points of fashionable dress and behavior, and often admonishing her to "Smile, my dear, and show off your curls!"

They went to concert halls and fancy parlors for tea and rode about the streets of London in Mrs. Walker's carriage. One day the Shah of Persia passed by, glittering with innumerable, priceless jewels. He made a swift, odd bow to them, his black eyes riveted on Kaiulani from beneath his snow-white turban. Gems flashed around his neck, on his wrists, and in his fingers and hair. When they described the encounter to Mr. Davies later at dinner, he joked and said he "would have liked to have seen his toes, too!"

Another day Queen Victoria drove by them, propped up and bouncing about in her carriage, looking like a little toy or a doll. She seemed extremely frail and old. Kaiulani thought of how Aunt Liliu and Queen Kapiolani had visited London for the Queen's Jubilee, and that the Prince of Wales himself had been Mama Moi's escort to the grand ball. For a moment she felt sad to realize how long ago all of that seemed, when, really, it was only a few years! Mrs. Walker observed that she had "gone away into your dreams again, dear." Gently she coaxed her back around to the present, as one might wake a sleepwalker from a trance. Then Kaiulani smiled at her and told her everything she could remember about the royal Hawaiian women visiting the Queen's Jubilee and attending the gala at Buckingham Palace.

There were trips to seaside resorts, where Kaiulani drank in deep draughts of the fresh, crisp sea air. There was a damp coolness here that she had never experienced in Hawaii; it made her pull her shawl or jacket closer around her shoulders and neck. She even took to wearing the lacy, frilly gloves that Mrs. Walker had given her;

encouraging her to wear them for "protection in all seasons." Mrs. Walker often reminded her, "One can never be too careful, my dear!" They visited Blackheath and Tenby; then returned to London to see St. Paul's Cathedral, the Houses of Parliament, the Law Courts and Westminster Abbey, built in 1245, where so many English kings and queens had been crowned and buried.

As all good things must come to an end, so did Kaiulani's summer in London. The leaves were beginning to fade and there had been a sharp nip in the air for several nights in a row; and then it was time for her to go to school. For the first time in her life Kaiulani would attend classes with other young ladies, at the Great Harrowden Hall in North Hamptonshire.

Chapter Fifteen

Harrowden Hall was a sixty-mile drive from London, about eight miles from Mr. Davies' country home just outside of Wellingborough. Built in the fifteenth century as the main estate of Baron Vaux, the hall was an imposing, three-story stone building covered with dark green ivy and twisting vines.

The Vaux family was descended from a long, distinguished line of Catholics who had been courageous in their efforts to shelter and hide a succession of priests during several intense periods of persecution of their faith. With its secret chambers and maze-like, sequestered rooms, Harrowden Hall felt like a place that had been a setting for romance, danger and intrigue. For the last century it had served as a school for sons of nobility and the well to do. About six years before Kaiulani's arrival the Hall had been leased out to a new headmistress, Mrs. Sharp. So, when Harrowden Hall's days as an elite school for daughters of very good families began, Kaiulani was still small enough to ride about on the backs of the giant turtles at Ainahau.

Harrowden was tucked away in a rustic park at the end of a long, winding driveway lined with oak trees, many of them older than the building. These trees stood guard over the fortress-like Hall like towering sentries. They spread out their branches to shade and shelter the stately building, so solid and integrated into its surroundings that it seemed to have grown out of the ground.

The main gate of the Hall was made of wrought iron, intricately designed and embellished with curlicues interwoven with a pattern of *fleur-de-lis*. These complex, stylized designs looked to Kaiulani like the codes and symbols of some very old religion or clan. She had seen signs similar to these carved into the bows of ancient canoes that had been passed down through the centuries, either by the *kahunas* or royalty; and, eventually, to King Kalakaua. She thought she remembered Mama Nui explaining to her once that these were the signs of secret membership, and they included a severe warning to all who did not belong to stay away.

Winged angels carrying spears stood at attention on top of the two tall pillars that framed the gate on either side. A few meticulously clipped bushes had been planted at precise distances from the walkway on either side of the glass-paneled door. The lawn was perfectly manicured.

Mrs. Walker and Mr. Davies settled Kaiulani in at Harrowden Hall, making sure she had everything she might need. They arranged to visit her the first Saturday of every month, and more often if she wished, if she became lonely or required any special attention or care.

* * * * * * * * * * * * * * * * * * * *

Mrs. Sharp, the school's headmistress, was a compact, athletic-looking woman with a keen sense of fair play. She was an ardent champion of equal rights and education for women and girls. Despite her matter-of-fact nature, at Harrowden Hall she was the focus of persistent and colorful rumors.

Some of the girls swore that she was the illegitimate daughter of a high-ranking Jesuit priest, or else a nobleman's rebellious daughter. Others scoffed at the idea, convinced that Mrs. Sharp, a widow, had been raised a scullery maid's child who had somehow managed to capture the heart of her mother's wealthy, elderly employer. She married him at a very tender age; mourned him when he died under unusual and possibly suspicious circumstances, and consequently inherited his vast fortune, which included Harrowden Hall. There were those who insisted she was the only child of foreign-born merchants who had run some lucrative but shady business, something to do with children and/or women of loose morals. According to this contingent, she had been orphaned after a dreadful accident that killed off both her parents, leaving her an independent woman of considerable means.

With her brisk, no-nonsense attitude and the crisp, white collars she wore fastened high around her neck, Mrs. Sharp seemed an unlikely candidate for any of these romantic and glamorous theories. The reality was that no one knew anything about her background or her past.

"Let me go directly to the point, here," Mrs. Sharp said, after they had exchanged minimal social pleasantries. She had called Kaiulani in for an interview to discuss the circumstances of her stay at Harrowden Hall.

"You are, despite and apart from anything to do with your true position and personal - well, status, I suppose, we might say, - You are here to get an education, are you not?"

Mrs. Sharp peered sharply at Kaiulani from behind her thick pince-nez glasses. She did not wait for a response.

"That is absolutely all that matters to me. We are all here at the Hall in that capacity and for that cause, whether as educators or educatees. Anything else, to my mind, and as far as I can see—"

Her pointed look seemed intended to challenge or badger Kaiulani's lack of response.

"From my point of view, there is nothing which outranks the importance of that single, solid fact." She leaned in to make her point even more clear, pronouncing each syllable of every word with distinct vigor as she tapped lightly on the top of her desk. "We are, all of us, above all else, here to learn."

Kaiulani wondered what could possibly have happened in Mrs. Sharp's life that made her become so adamant. What circumstance of error or compromise could have left the school's founder so definitive, outspoken and so extremely careful in her selection of every word?

At just that moment Mrs. Sharp suddenly relaxed as she sailed in to port with her final, favorite inspirational catchphrase.

"To the one the many, To the one, the all." She said this with great satisfaction. Mrs. Sharp was not entirely certain of what it meant, but she had always liked the sound of it. And it rarely failed to impress the students.

"What does that mean?" Kaiulani's curiosity was greatly piqued.

"Well, *naturellement*, of course," Mrs. Sharp was the tiniest bit flustered, "it means that we must all look out for each other, mutually, at all times."

"Yes, of course," Kaiulani agreed politely, deciding she approved of the idea even though it did seem rather obvious.

The first few months of school were one of the most exciting and fulfilling times Kaiulani had known. To her surprise she found that she was quite content and even relieved to be part of a group. She enjoyed being a student: attending classes and studying, not at all set apart, no different from the others. With her honest, open nature she easily made friends, and discovered that she had an avid thirst for learning. She loved to spend hours poring over books about history, art and literature. She also had an affinity for languages and soon became one of the best students in her French class. Everyone at school apparently knew that Kaiulani was a princess from Hawaii but, as there were many others of noble or privileged birth there, no one paid any special attention. They accepted her as one of them, and she was grateful.

She soon became good friends with a young woman who had been born in London and raised both there and in Paris. Miss Miranda de Courcy's father was an English duke, her mother a lady of high rank in French society. Kaiulani and Miranda sat next to each other in their classes, as the listing for the seating order was alphabetical and "de Courcy" had been made, questionably, in point of fact, to follow "Cleghorn."

Miranda had golden red hair, an easy smile and a quick wit. She thought Kaiulani "terribly beautiful" and very amusing as well, and the two soon became inseparable, walking along the country roads and telling each other fascinating stories from their lives.

One glorious weekend they rode horses for two days with Mr. Davies and friends at his country estate. Soon after, Mrs. Walker came to visit at Harrowden Hal and decreed that Miranda was "quite smart" and "immensely clever." The three had a fine time together and promised to meet again soon.

Kaiulani and Miranda had secret nicknames for each other - "Randa" and "Kai." Both felt that few people ever really understood each other; or had anywhere near as much in common as they did, since both came from "double" backgrounds and cultures. They each had noble blood on one side only, as well; and both felt that they had, in effect, been "exiled" to Harrowden Hall. They vowed they would always be best friends.

Early at the start of the fall session, a few of the less refined girls whispered stories about Kaiulani behind her back. Some criticized her "unruly" hair; or mocked her pronunciation of "Hawaii," imitating the way she said the "w" like a "v", and then laughing among them selves as if they had made a joke. But when Kaiulani did not react, since she was far too busy with her studies and old and new friends and writing letters home, they soon gave up on their childish games.

Kaiulani was thrilled to hear that Koa and Kuhio had been sent to school in London. Despite the Reform Party's demand to return all Hawaiian children being educated abroad, Aunt Liliu and Papa Moi had been firm in insisting that both Kuhio and Koa be sent overseas again to continue their education. The brothers' first time studying away from Hawaii had been at the San Mateo Military Academy in California, for two years.

Kaiulani wrote to Koa at her cousins' new London address to tell him about how hard she was working in her classes, especially French. She had also begun to paint and draw a little, but could never hope to be as accomplished an artist as her good friend, Miranda de Courcy, who was not only gifted and talented, but probably brilliant besides. Several weeks later she received a brief note from Koa saying that he was well and also working hard, and would see her over the holidays in London when they would be "taken around" under the auspices of Mr. Davies. Kaiulani had to look up "auspices" in the dictionary, and wondered if Koa might some day wish to consider a career as a lawyer or a judge, or perhaps be interested in politics. When she showed Miranda the picture Koa had sent her, Miranda remarked that he looked exactly like her older brother, Toby, only just a little shorter and darker and heavier and possibly more serious around the eyes.

The Christmas holiday with Koa in London was a dream. Her handsome cousin had grown several inches taller and all of his former boyishness had disappeared. She felt her heart beat faster when she was with him. She liked him much better, and he seemed much more relaxed with her, too.

He was not as formal, nor as stiff as before, and they laughed and danced together like the old days. When he held her hand in his and they walked through the London streets, she felt happy and excited. She imagined that she could feel the warm sunlight of Hawaii radiating from his cocoa-brown skin. When they looked into each other's eyes after long talks, or sat silently alone, content just to be in the presence and company of one another, she felt a profound sense of comfort and peace. He was the only person in the world who knew her so well that he was like a brother.

Mrs. Walker, with whom Kaiulani stayed while in London, declared Koa "quite good-looking, my dear!" Kaiulani was surprised to find her self blushing at these remarks, even though she and Mrs. Walker were quite alone. Even Mr. Davies was able to arrange a little extra time in his busy schedule to escort them all to an elegant restaurant near the Crystal Palace for lunch. Later, in private, Mr. Davies told Kaiulani that "Mr. Kawananakoa" was "coming along nicely. Quite well. Very good." And then, for some reason, he seemed flustered and changed the subject.

The troubling news that Koa brought from home was that the King was not feeling well. Burdened by all the stress, Kalakaua's stamina was not what it had been. He had sent Kaiulani a shawl of beautiful *o'o* feathers for her fourteenth birthday with a note saying how happy he was to be her godfather and asking her to take care.

"When do you think Papa Moi will make the arrangements for me to go home?" Kaiulani had to ask Koa the question she most wanted an answer to. Her year abroad would be over in June.

"I do not know." Koa looked off to one side. "I wish I could tell you. I myself have been missing Hawaii every minute and hour that I am gone."

The thought that either one of them might not be able to go home soon was more than she could bear.

"Oh, Koa! You don't think -!"

He touched his finger lightly to her lips, the way he used to when they were children and he wanted her to listen.

"It is not for me to think about, my dear Princess. I must only work hard to develop my character and abilities so I will be ready when the day comes to use them to serve Hawaii."

A slightly dizzy sensation made her shake her head. Koa at once protectively cupped her arm in his own.

"Do you need to sit down? Some water, perhaps?"

Kaiulani smiled wanly. "Koa -" Her voice was wobbly and uncertain, like a child's.

Her cousin touched her mouth again as he returned the smile. "There is not a minute of my life that I am away that I do not long for Hawaii. We must stay strong, and learn to be patient. I will always be here for you," his liquid eyes warmed her like a fire, "My beautiful Kaiulani."

He kissed the tip of her nose, breaking the solemn mood. "And that, dear cousin, is a message to say hello from your horse, Fairy, who misses you, too."

Kaiulani's heart stood still. Then she stretched up to reach her cousin's cheek and kissed him.

"And that, dear cousin, is my hello to cousin Kuhio."

The holiday was over much too soon. Back at Harrowden Kaiulani applied herself to her studies. Under Miranda's tutoring she became fluent in French. She survived her first English winter and wrote to Papa Moi and Queen Kapiolani to tell them how she loved to curl up "like a cat" by the fireplace with a book and hot tea. The cold weather outside was, as her friend Miranda often said, "Nothing to laugh at."

It was strange to think of her friends at home out in the sunshine and riding the surf while she navigated drifts of snow. But by spring she was able to write to Aunt Liliu and say that she had done exceptionally well in her studies. Mrs. Sharp herself even wrote to Papa to tell him that Kaiulani's efforts were "first rate, indeed."

When school ended in June, Kaiulani spent the first month of the summer in London where she saw Koa only a few times since he was very busy working as an apprentice law clerk for an old London firm.

For the rest of the summer she stayed with Miranda in Paris, giggling over the strange characters and fashions they observed, taking rambling strolls along the Champs Elysees and visiting the cafes and shops.

The two friends haunted the theaters, and were fortunate enough to see the great Sarah Bernhardt perform. The famous actress was tiny and stunning with an odd, cat-like face and masses of curly, coppery red hair. *"La Divina"* was said to sleep in a custom-made satin and rosewood coffin. "Kai" decided this was "ghoulish" but "Randa" thoroughly approved.

As they watched the passionate woman capture, seduce and hypnotize the audience, the idea came to Kaiulani that, had she not been born a princess, she might have pursued a career on the stage. The freedom to rage, cajole and weep, and the authority she saw in Bernhardt's expressions appealed to her enormously.

"Oh, well," the often-fatalistic Miranda said when Kaiulani confided this, "That's blood under the bridge, isn't it?" When Kaiulani questioned her about the colorful phrase, Miranda said she thought it had originated in the gruesome French Revolution.

Kaiulani was thrilled with the vibrant life of the Paris city streets and especially taken with the posters they saw for the myriad of theatrical events. She never failed to be moved by the bold, vivid colors in the advertisements for music hall entertainments by Monsieur Henri de Toulouse Lautrec.

Miranda, who knew everything there was to know about any French person of interest, explained that Monsieur Lautrec was a tragic, fascinating man. Born into a noble family, a dwarf, he had managed against great odds to develop himself into a talented artist. Kaiulani told Miranda that his powerful, uncompromising colors seemed to her "real, true colors" like the flowers and sunsets and the feathers in the peacocks' fans back home.

From Miranda Kaiulani learned a thousand different ways to be sophisticated and "chic." Miranda taught her how to tie a bow at precisely the right, most flattering place under her chin, and showed her the perfect angle at which to tilt her hat "for optimum effect." She showed her how to add lace to extend a collar and sleeves, and educated her in a plethora of "beauty techniques," such as pinching her cheeks to cause a flush that would make her complexion glow, or lightly biting her lips to make her mouth rosy and inviting. "Showing off your colors," Miranda liked to call it.

Still, there was no word from Papa Moi. Kaiulani's father wrote to her about all the changes taking place in Hawaii now. Honolulu was growing rapidly, with new businesses and buildings coming in every day. John L. Stevens, a stern and glowering military man from the state of Maine, had recently been appointed as Minister to Hawaii when Mr. Merrell left his post. Papa promised he would come to visit and take her to Scotland for a nice trip "very soon," but was unable to commit to a date at this time.

So Kaiulani waited. But all the time they were dashing about London and Paris she was secretly, eagerly anticipating daily the news of arrangements for her return home. Miranda, who had put on a little weight from all the fine pastries and rich sauces they had enjoyed in the Paris cafes and at the lovely afternoon teas in London, was more playful and flirtatious than ever.

Miranda remarked to Mrs. Walker, their frequent companion and chaperone, that Kaiulani seemed *"un peur pensif."* Together, they asked her if something was wrong. Reluctant to reveal her anxieties lest they might think her ungrateful for their company and friendship, Kaiulani smiled sweetly at her friends and attributed her moodiness to the humid, unfamiliar weather.

When they finally returned to England in mid August, Mrs. Walker took Miranda to visit her mother in London and allowed Kaiulani to travel on alone the few hours more to Mr. Davies' estate. School would begin again in two weeks, and the Princess still did not know of any plans for her return home.

* * * * * * * * * * * * * * * * * * *

As soon as she had arrived at the estate, Kaiulani sought out her guardian and requested a private conference.

Mr. Davies observed to himself that the Princess had changed dramatically during the summer. He had the awkward sensation of being alone with a commanding, powerful woman, instead of the girl-child who had left such a short time ago. Kaiulani had filled out in places and thinned down in others. Miranda and Mrs. Walker had taught her to dress well and showcase her hourglass figure with the cinched in waists and tight, full-bosomed fashions of the day.

Kaiulani was wearing her traveling costume, a comfortable, cream-colored muslin dress with a V-shaped, navy, sailor-style ribbon that emphasized the shape of her bodice; and delicate Belgian lace at the collar to frame and accentuate her features. Her long hair flowed down over her shoulders and she wore a boater-style straw hat at a jaunty angle that seemed to filter all the light in the room onto her radiant face. The wide velvet band around the hat's crown was tied again inside with a smaller, pale blue satin ribbon embroidered with the word, "*Immortalité*," a souvenir of their recent outing on a French luxury yacht.

Despite her appearance of worldly elegance and refinement, the Princess was solemn and direct in her manner and speech.

"Mr. Davies, I am grateful for your guardianship and care. But I need now to know what plans are being made for my return to Hawaii."

Theo Davies was disconcerted and more than a little in awe of the beautiful woman who stood before him. But he, too, had the tact to maintain his composure.

"Please, Kaiulani, I beg of you," he said with the utmost gravity, "Please, do sit down."

When she complied, Mr. Davies sat across from her.

"Your cousin, Koa, came here to visit last month -"

Kaiulani paled. Koa? And no one had told her?! She nearly stammered, so unnerved was she at the thought of her cousin in Mr. Davies' house, without her, in a place where she had never seen him before. The idea of Koa being here with Mr. Davies when she was not disoriented her sense of balance.

"What did he have to say?"

"Not very much, I am afraid. There are, as you know, many difficulties to sort out in your homeland."

Respectfully, he took her hand in his own. Although she acquiesced, she felt herself recoil a little inside, for she could sense that his move was meant to soften a blow.

"I believe," he said quietly, "for now, the best thing would be for you to continue your studies at Harrowden Hall."

The despair that crushed Kaiulani did not reveal itself on her face. Already she had become adept at not expressing emotion; she had learned to be cautious, to put on a mask and hide her heart and feelings away from view. With a formal, practiced smile, she thanked her guardian and rose, all graciousness and poise.

"Well," she said, "Do you suppose there is time before supper for me to ride?"

Only when she was completely alone in the lush English countryside, riding her favorite horse from Mr. Davies' stables, only then did she allow her sorrow to spill out into sound and tears. Furious, frustrated, she felt she had been abandoned and disregarded by those who she thought she could trust.

Then she remembered a prayer to Pele that her mother had sometimes repeated when she was very angry and had no other recourse for her pain. As she spoke it out loud, she could hear the echo of her mother's voice in her own, and she felt her spirit move through her.

The chant felt like a veiled threat to her; and, as such, it was a balm to her disrupted mood. Surprised that she remembered all the words, she pounded them out like a wild drumbeat while she galloped around the estate.

"Pele, goddess from Kahiki,
Spread forth your lava rocks.
A resounding, a reverberating in Kahiki!
An island red with heat
Where dwell the gods and goddesses,
the chiefly gods.
Sky, spill your content upon the earth.
Kane, hold up your firebrand to light the sky.
It is Pele's fire that burns at Kilawea.
Sharp-pointed are your teeth, oh stone-devouring goddess.
Who dares enter Pele's house?
Kahiki glares up with flashes of Pele's fires.
The *lava* pours forth, pours forth.
Awe possesses me."

The prayer was wonderfully satisfying and she chanted it full out three times. When at last she had worn out her anger, she came back to herself and was calm.

Then she was able to return and meet Mr. Davies for supper as if nothing had happened at all, and she had not a care in the world.

Chapter Sixteen

So Kaiulani, her heart filled with longing for home, began her second year at Harrowden Hall. She immersed herself in her classes with a vengeance; they included German and English composition, singing, grammar, art and French. Her eyesight, which had been fair, grew mediocre and then became worse. By the end of her second year at school the Princess needed glasses not only for reading but also to see anything at all up close to her face.

Miranda would often remind her anxious friend, Kaiulani, that she, too, was a member of the human race and of the world they both presently lived in, in addition to being the heiress apparent to Hawaii and a princess in exile.

When Kaiulani's moods became very dark, as they did when she was listless from weeks of staying indoors with no sun or exercise, surrounded by stacks of paper and huge piles of books, Miranda was always there to help.

She would shake her loose from her melancholy with a boisterous pillow fight, insisting loudly on "a surcease of withdrawal!" Kaiulani laughed at her dramatic exaggeration but then pummeled her with a pillow in return while she demanded "a surcease of sweets!" For Miranda had grown increasingly fond of desserts, while Kaiulani usually only picked at her food. When Miranda was able to coax her into putting aside her work, they would go to spend to spend a weekend at Mr. Davies' house, getting dressed up and spending time with some lively and interesting people. Occasionally, there would be a few young men with whom they drank tea and talked, or strolled in the garden, weather permitting. Miranda enjoyed flirting with these young men in her friendly, casual way, but Kaiulani preferred to engage in serious conversation. Although she did enjoy Miranda's playfulness, she easily became restless or bored with frivolous or strictly social talk.

At Harrowden Hall the two friends would take long, brisk walks out in the bracing, fresh air, even when it was so cold that they could see their breath. Kaiulani had grown a few inches taller while Miranda had developed out an inch or so wider, her contours as round and soft as a dove's. "Kai" playfully complained that her "South Seas bones" were not equipped with the enviable and attractive protection that "Randa" had managed to put on. Indeed, the Princess' teeth would begin to chatter and her shoulders trembled while Miranda only grew livelier and pinker trudging through the cold wind and snow.

Both young women came inside with rosy cheeks and high spirits. They sipped honeyed tea or hot chocolate, and were cheerful and animated as they snuggled in close to the fireplaces in their rooms. Miranda loved to listen as Kaiulani told stories about Fairy and Ainahau, Miss Gardinier, Mama Nui and the gardens and sharks and volcanoes. In turn Miranda told Kaiulani her family's legends, many of them revolving around the aristocrats in France who had miraculously survived the Revolution, others about great romances, blood feuds and duels in the high society circles of London and Paris. Kaiulani was fascinated by these stories, so different from her own, though she often shook her head at their conclusions. She was grateful, she told Miranda, that the Hawaiians were not so complicated, for she could not imagine how she would have survived in that heady, treacherous world of endless gossip and intrigue.

* * * * * * * * * * * * * * * * * *

For Kaiulani's fifteenth birthday the King and Queen sent her a beautiful, very old jade bracelet with matching jade and pearl earrings. The letter that came with them was written in Queen Kapiolani's fine script. She congratulated the Princess on her success at school, and explained that the bracelet had belonged to Kapiolani's own mother, and the earrings were a present from King Kamehameha

I to Queen Kaahumanu for her twenty-first birthday. They hoped Kaiulani would wear them in good health and happiness always. Kapiolani had signed her own name and then the king's.

A few weeks later Kaiulani received a cryptic and disturbing letter from the King. In an unsteady hand he advised her to be on her guard against "certain enemies I do not feel free to name in writing." She could not imagine what Papa Moi meant, and went to Mr. Davies for counsel. He gently suggested that the King had not been well and was under tremendous stress, with so many problems to sort out in Hawaii. Perhaps the King was not entirely himself, or possibly he was not thinking as clearly as usual when he wrote to her.

She wrote back to Kalakaua, "I am at a loss to know to whom you refer as not to be relied upon. I wish you could speak more plainly, as I cannot be on my guard unless I know to whom you allude."

She waited and waited for Papa Moi's reply, but nothing came back from Hawaii. When she returned from her Christmas holiday in London with Miranda she received from Koa the sad news that Papa Moi was very ill.

* * * * * * * * * * * * * * * * * * *

Back in Honolulu, Kalakaua's aides were concerned as they watched the once robust regent grow gaunt and pale. The king was listless, often silent and easily discouraged. Lorrin Thurston, with his rude voice and bullying ways, continued to be a thorn in the king's side. There were times Kalakaua felt he would actually be willing to leave the government in the hands of the reformists, if only it meant he would be spared from ever having to hear Thurston's voice, so like fingernails scratching on a blackboard, again.

The friction between the cabinet members, now equally divided between Missionary Party Reformers and native Hawaiians appointed by the King, had become nearly unbearable. Not a day went by without someone screaming and yelling, or at someone else's throat. Thurston, as usual, was the loudest and worst. But it was Sanford Dole, elected to the cabinet right after the storming of the palace "overthrow," who was unrelenting in his efforts to transfer all power from the king to the cabinet.

Dole's cold, meticulous insistence cut through matters like a surgeon's blade as he reinforced again and again the idea that the actions of the King and the state must be divided and made separate at every turn. His large, angular hands would slash at the air as he spoke, like giant knives slicing away at some invisible foe. Sometimes he would hold his grasping, clutching hands clasped tightly down at his sides, or carefully hide them from view behind a book or in his pockets.

Princess Liliuokalani's steadfast support had always been a great comfort to Kalakaua. Even that counsel, though, had been severely cut back, for Liliu's husband, Governor John Dominis, was plagued by such debilitating attacks of rheumatic pain that she had to sit by his bedside for days at a time.

Robert Wilcox, an avid supporter of the royals and arch-enemy of the Missionary Party, had unhappily only made a delicate situation worse when he insisted again and again that any peaceful communication with "those scoundrels" no longer served any purpose. The child of a Hawaiian mother and an American father, Wilcox had been educated in Italy. He was notoriously in love with the idea of overthrow, revenge and theatrics, and in favor of grand, political gestures - a highly unfortunate and volatile mix.

Colonel Volney Ashford and his many men immediately squelched Wilcox's abortive rebellion. Seven native Hawaiian activists were killed. A few sticks of unlit dynamite were tossed back and forth between the Opera House, where the heavily armed militia of the Honolulu Rifles' Royal Guard was stationed, and the ramshackle storage bungalow on palace grounds, where Wilcox and his pathetic crew of Liberal Patriots began and ended their revolt. The King happened to be out of town overnight when this useless "action" occurred; and as the rebellion was over in less than twelve hours, it was finished by the time Kalakaua returned to his Palace the next morning.

The King was worn out and discouraged, drinking more than ever but no longer finding any pleasure or solace in it. Robert Louis Stevenson, his loyal RLS, had long since departed for other South Sea shores. There were no more horse races or poker games, no *luaus* or festive champagne suppers to give Kalakaua any kind of relief or break. With Likelike dead and Kaiulani gone away, Ainahau provided no haven or shelter for him, and his brother-in-law, Archie, was constantly harping at him, always arguing about one thing or another.

By the time the Legislative session closed on November 14, 1890, the King had never been so exhausted in his life. Liliuokalani came to visit him and was shocked by his appearance. His hands and shoulders shook when they embraced, and the simple act of walking up stairs left him winded and wheezing.

Liliu stayed for two days, refusing to leave until he had promised that he would accept a friend's invitation to get away and travel for a short time in an effort to regain his fragile health and spirits. At first he had refused, unwilling to leave Hawaii for any time at all. But when the news came that the McKinley Act had been passed by the U.S. Congress, thereby posing a serious threat to the future of Hawaiian sugar and its economy, Kalakaua changed his mind. He became convinced that he must repeat his long ago visit to Washington, D.C. He was sure that, if only he could meet with the President and reach out to the American people, he could again speak out against the injustice being forced upon Hawaii.

Leaving Princess Liliuokalani in charge, the King set sail for California on the U.S. cruiser and man-of-war, the *Charleston*. With him was his good friend, Rear Admiral George Brown. Kalakaua explained to his people that he would only be gone a short while, trying to rest and regain his strength for the long journey to Washington. Some Hawaiians wept as they watched the *Charleston* sail away from Honolulu Harbor; for they had again seen the shoals of *aweo aweo* fish turning the water blood red at the shore, and they feared that their king might not return.

* * * * * * * * * * * * * * * * * * *

At first, the sea air and change of place began to rejuvenate the King. He ate with a better appetite, and even smiled and laughed a few times. But by the time the *Charleston* landed in San Francisco, Kalakaua was so weak that several assistants were needed to lift and carry him up to his suite at the Palace Hotel.

One of his oldest retainers, a wizened old man named "Nene" after the Hawaiian goose because of his shyness and easy laughter, insisted on staying by the king's side throughout all hours of the day and night.

"You make me tired," the King feebly joked. But although he wished the doddering old man would rest, he could not bring himself to order Nene to leave him. The New Year came and went and the king grew more fragile each day.

One of Kalakaua's aides brought to his bedroom a new mechanical contraption called an Edison cylinder, or phonograph. The hand-cranked machine for recording sound had just come out. Knowing Kalakaua's fondness for gadgets, the man hoped to arouse the King's interest and distract him from his pain.

Kalakaua coughed incessantly as he examined the strange-looking cylinder. He nodded his approval and motioned them to set it up for him to use.

His breathing was ragged. "I sound like - a - *haole*" he gasped to Nene, who did not even try to smile at the joke. The aide held the speaking device up very close to the King's mouth as the regent struggled to talk, for he wanted to send his regards one more time to his people back home.

"*Aloha kaua!*" He paused, supported on both sides by assistants as he valiantly struggled to sit up in bed.

"We greet each other - *ke hoi nei no paha*" - the King's soft, almost inaudible Hawaiian sounded like the refrain to a sad song. Nevertheless, he waved away Admiral Brown when he pleaded with him to stop.

"Now," Kalakaua whispered, smiling a little at the rotating machine, "go to Hawaii, to Honolulu … tell my people," his voice grew more faint, "Tell them - I tried -"

Possibly he wanted to say more, or perhaps he had come to the end of his thoughts. The cylinder was barely moving until, with a difficult, grinding noise, it stopped. Old Nene passed a soft cloth over the King's damp brow, tending to him as delicately as a mother caring for her child. With his last, fading strength Kalakaua managed to grasp old Nene's hand in his own. When he spoke his voice was heavy with regret. "I tried to be - a hawk for my people—to look out for them - to fly - to the heavens - and save them."

A tear spilled onto Nene's ancient, wrinkled cheek and another glittered in the king's cloudy eyes. Kalakaua smiled at his faithful,

old friend. "Unfortunately, good Nene, my wings have been clipped."
Then the king sank down and slipped into a final inertia.

A few days later the *Charleston* turned back for Honolulu bearing
its heavy freight. Because of the new Transatlantic cable the news of
the King's death reached London long before anyone in Hawaii knew.
Mr. Davies came to Harrowden Hall for Kaiulani as soon as he heard
and took her to his new home near the city in Southport at Hesketch
Park.

At "Sunset," as the mansion was called, the Princess would have
some privacy and time to herself in her grief. She telegraphed for a
wreath of orchids to be sent and placed on Papa Moi's coffin; it bore
the traditional message, "My love is with the one who is done with
dying."

On January 29 the *Charleston* was spotted turning around the
outermost curve of Diamond Head in Waikiki. Honolulu had been
preparing for the King's return for days. Brightly colored bunting
draped the streets and shops to welcome him home. A huge wreath of
fragrant evergreen branches arched over and across the Inter-Island
Wharf. In the center of the pine branches was an oversized drawing
of two hands clasped together, representing the friendship between
America and Hawaii. A crisp white banner, on which "*Aloha Oe*"
had been painted in royal blue and white, streamed across the arch on
one side. On the other half of the arch a similar banner proclaimed in
red letters, "Hawaii Greets Her King and His Guests." Another
banner had been raised high at the intersection of Fort and Merchant
Streets; it also read, "*Aloha Oe*." A grand ball had been planned for
eight-thirty on the day of Kalakaua's return.

As the *Charleston* rounded the curve at Diamond Head, a murmur
of concern and then of despair spread through the streets. For the
people could see that the flags of the ship were flying at half-mast; all
except for the royal standard, which was never lowered, to honor the
belief that the King never dies. By nightfall the city's bright banners
had been replaced with black mourning. Princess Liliuokalani, now
almost the last of her line, was soon proclaimed Queen.

The King's casket, made of black koa wood and inscribed with a
silver shield, was placed on a cloth of royal feathers - *o'o* and *iiwi* and
mamo, - and carried to Iolani Palace. Twenty guards watched over it
there, in twenty-four hour shifts, holding aloft the entire time the large

feather standard *kahilis*. The weather that afternoon was so overcast that it looked like a night sky. But as the bearers carried the King's body through the palace gates, a triple rainbow rose up out of the gloom and wrapped itself like a soft blanket around the palace grounds. The people wept with joy at this indisputable sign that King Kalakaua had been received into heaven by the gods, who were pleased with him.

When the Royal Hawaiian Band played "Nearer My God to Thee" their mournful music mingled with the wailing of the Hawaiians. Liliuokalani's sorrow over losing her brother was like a deep wound. She stayed close to his casket throughout the services, while beside her Queen Kapiolani wept and prayed.

At last the bearers came to carry the king's bier with slow marching steps through Nuuanu Valley to the Royal Mausoleum. Kalakaua's Masonic brothers placed sprigs of pine on his casket to honor him. Then the royal family was left alone behind the closed doors of the tomb to grieve. When they emerged about fifteen minutes later, the military escort accompanying the mourners fired three volleys high into the air above the casket in a final salute of farewell. The Royal Hawaiian Band played the mournful chords of Henri Berger's new composition, "The Kalakaua Funeral March." And even as the funeral procession began its somber return to the palace, the Reformers plotted to overthrow Hawaii's new Queen.

The native people brought many gifts to Admiral Brown as tokens of their respect and to thank him for the care he had given their king in his final days. When the *Charleston* sailed from Hawaii its decks were laden with these spoils of the people's *aloha* - *tapa* cloth, jewelry, shells, carvings and food.

Three days after the beginning of Queen Liliuokalani's reign the San Francisco Chronicle, a notoriously pro-Reformer paper, carried an article "from an anonymous source" about "Mrs. Dr. Bully-King." The article confirmed the new queen's "rabid" ill will toward "most of the citizens of Hawaii," describing at great length how she had hated her brother so intensely that she had "worked with her *kahunas* to have him prayed to death."

By the beginning of March Admiral Brown, who had long since eaten, given away or sold the food and gifts from the decks of the *Charleston*, wrote to Mr. John L. Stevens, America's new minister to

Hawaii. In his letter the Admiral archly suggested that, "Her Majesty should be taught a lesson which will do her good." Mr. Stevens, a man who had not once but twice before been recalled by his own government from foreign posts under highly questionable and controversial circumstances, gravely thanked the Admiral for his advice and replied that he would be only too glad to comply.

Chapter Seventeen

Kaiulani received a letter from her father, full of his worries about the future of Hawaii. He was, for one thing, he explained to her, quite concerned about Aunt Liliu being Queen and entirely in charge right now. And that probably was the main thing he was worried about, at that. Of course, it was all right and proper, and she had immediately and publicly proclaimed Kaiulani as heir apparent, so all was as it should be on that account.

But he was afraid that the Queen - how strange to call her that, after all these years - that her aunt simply did not, well, fully grasp, or comprehend, he supposed, the seriousness of the forces she was up against, that opposed her. It was all well and to the good, her Hawaii for the Hawaiians campaign, and her desire to restore the land and the vote, etc., to the native people was admirable. And, at fifty-two years of age, she certainly must know her own mind by now; no doubt about that, was there. But why must she always be so complicated! So absolute and unyielding in her attitudes! For the fact was that there had been, and continued to be, a tremendous financial investment in Hawaii by outside sources, and not just a few of them, either. Foreign businessmen had sunk piles and piles into the economy, and she was a fool, really and truly a fool, he was sorry to say so, but there it was, if she thought everyone concerned was going to just go away or back out and give up on their extremely vested interests at this late stage of the game!

He didn't want to worry Kaiulani; that was never his intention, so she should please forgive him if all this constituted only more distressing news for her. But she had better keep an eye on her aunt's dealings, he admonished, lest there be precious little left for her to rule over when at last it became her own turn.

He was sorry that they could not afford a new coat for Kaiulani for the winter; perhaps she could have alterations made to her old one, as money continued to be very tight and her school fees, which were already high, had been raised yet again another time. He hoped she would be able to make do and be brave and strong during this difficult time for all.

Kaiulani felt rather drained after reading his letter. It was difficult enough for her to be living so far away, unable to cheer him up or even just encourage him to take time out to work in his lovely gardens. She had come to worry, really, more about her father's well-being and health than about Aunt Liliu's ability to rule. Her Aunt, she knew, was a strong and determined woman, fired with steel and tempered with a fierce resolution in her every move. Papa, on the other hand, was often ruled by his emotions, becoming anxious and overwhelmed by his unfortunate habit of always considering the entire range of possibilities, without ever admitting that there was only so much he, or anyone else, for that matter, could do to control the world around them. She felt badly for him and wrote right away to Aunt Liliu, apologizing for her own boldness in the matter but asking her please to keep an eye out for Papa, as he always seemed to be worrying so much.

Kaiulani also had a short letter from Koa in which he explained with some excitement that the Queen had insisted on and won the resignation of several "Reform Party" members of the Cabinet. And then she had chosen members of her own, all true to the crown, of course. Samuel Parker had been made Minister of Affairs which was quite excellent as he was three-quarters Hawaiian himself, with one-quarter Portuguese, and had always, of course, been loyal. Her cousin had signed his letter "David Kawananakoa" and then, as an afterthought, added a postscript to say just "Koa" in parenthesis.

What was she supposed to do then, she would like to know, with all this troublesome information?! Kaiulani felt a heat rising from inside her and spreading throughout her entire body. She felt a little angry, if the truth be known, there was so much expected of her on the one hand - stay well, get a good continental education, become polished and smart. At the same time, on the other hand, she was a sounding board for everyone concerned, hearing everything about this problem and that change, but still treated like a child who must keep her hands folded neatly in her lap!

Oh well. She could wear the old coat from last season again; only Miranda would have to help her be clever about adding some sort of hem or extension, perhaps some rabbit or beaver fur, for more length. She had grown taller again and more beautiful, too, as she blossomed into a woman. Though she shook her head when she thought how Koa - or was it to be "David," now?! - How Koa and her friends back home would think her much too thin.

She had a natural, wholesome beauty, unaffected and unselfconscious, to which she paid no more attention than to the color of her eyes. Except that Miranda or Mrs. Walker might at times tell her how pretty she was, and point out admiring eyes or longing glances that came her way when they traveled about together. She had a perfect hourglass figure, with broad but fine-boned, delicate shoulders; a narrow waist; lush, full hips and long legs. There were few of the most stylish fashions that did not suit her, although several of her costumes were borrowed from Miranda and had to be altered with a few neat tucks or pins or sashes here and there.

The Princess often had a faraway, preoccupied look in her eyes, which at times could appear hooded like a falcon's, or shaded and pensive. Some of this was worry and homesickness for Hawaii, and some could be attributed to her increasing problems with near sightedness. Miranda affectionately teased her, preventing her from brooding too much by insisting that they take off on day trips and to concerts or other amusements at Mr. Davies' and visit friends in London, like Mrs. Walker, when they could.

Kaiulani found herself turning more often to Mr. Davies for advice to help her sort out her perspective on the troubles back home. Like her father, Davies, too, anticipated a heavy conflict between Queen Liliu and the Reformed Party Opposition forces, given all the business affairs and financial risks that were at stake. He reassured Kaiulani, however, when he told her that the one person who remained unequivocally respected and trusted in Hawaii by everyone was she, herself, the Princess and heiress apparent.

* * * * * * * * * * * * * * * * * * * *

The main event of Kaiulani's sixteenth year was the summer visit of her father. Together they toured his Scottish homeland which, Kaiulani wrote to Miranda, was "quite romantic and beautiful, but so wet and cold!" Papa talked to her at length about his concerns that Liliuokalani, "in her zeal to reclaim Hawaii for the Hawaiians, might just overplay her hand." The idea of stern, staid Aunt Liliu playing any game at all, much less cards, seemed absurd to Kaiulani, though of course she did not say so.

She had been quite shocked by Papa's appearance, not having seen him for more than two years. From the first moment of their meeting she felt herself hiding her real feelings, as she did not wish to upset him or add to his troubles. He seemed much older to her now, in every way, and considerably more nervous than she had remembered.

She had always thought of her father as strong, tall and sure of himself. But now, - why, they were practically the same height; really only a few inches difference, when she wore Miranda's bronze kid evening slippers with the high heels. She was startled to realize that, at her current height, she would have towered over her mother who must have been, now that she thought of it, only Miranda's height or even shorter.

Papa seemed so fretful and anxious that most of the time she felt she was looking out for him, rather than the other way around. At the beginning of his visit Papa came to see Kaiulani at Harrowden Hall. He made a very good impression on Mrs. Sharp, who later told Mr. Davies that the Scotsman was "worthy of his daughter" and they shared "a similar sense of great purpose."

At Cleghorn's request the headmistress had recommended a chaperone for their visit, a Mrs. Rook. She was a soulful and intellectually highly developed widow who had long been a devoted advocate of Harrowden Hall and women's rights. Archibald, Kaiulani and Mrs. Rook made the Langdon, a fine London residence hotel on Regent Street, their temporary home. A lively crowd of visitors, including old friends from Honolulu and elsewhere, as well as many new admirers from all over who supported the Hawaiian cause, made their time there a flurry of activity.

Papa had been given many business concerns and commissions from the Queen to execute in London, so there were visits to the Foreign Office and Windsor Castle, the House of Parliament and the Royal Gardens, and daily rounds of lunches, dinners, theater and concerts. Kaiulani had come to especially love the musical events. The deep, unquestioning passion she felt for music and the enduring comfort and order she found in it had never left her, as natural as breathing, bred in her bones.

One afternoon when Papa was away on business, Mrs. Rook and Kaiulani received the Parker sisters, Eva and Elizabeth, from back home. Kaiulani and the Parker girls had been playmates since early childhood, spending many pleasant hours together at Ainahau and the Parker Ranch in Waimea. The sisters' father, Samuel Parker, was now Queen Liliu's Minister of Affairs, and their spacious ranch in the mountains of lovely Waimea had been like another home to Kaiulani. Nevertheless, she found herself strangely reserved, almost shy with them now. Although both women were in their early twenties and one was already betrothed, they seemed awkward with her, and in awe of the Princess. And she felt suddenly like a child again in their presence.

Papa and Kaiulani undertook the ten-day visit to Scotland alone, while Mrs. Rook stayed in London. Father and daughter traveled throughout Scotland as a kind of team; both of them stirred by cherished memories of their days together at Ainahau. They stayed at Dreghorn Castle with the Honorable R.A. McFee, who flew the Hawaiian flag from his castle tower the entire time in their honor. They visited the two lovely pine trees King Kalakaua had planted during his visit there only a few years ago. Mr. McFee requested that the Princess also plant a tree near the King's and, with considerable assistance from the expert gardener, her Papa, she was happy to do so.

They visited Glasgow, the Highlands and Edinburgh. The tenacious roots of history in these places thrilled them both. Archibald delighted in showing off to his daughter such treasures as the original Act of Union of Scotland and England, and a book that had been written in by Good Queen Bess herself. He also took her to the tomb commemorating the unfortunate King Charles I who had been executed by his own rebellious subjects. Kaiulani touched the fine linen shirt the King had worn and held the watch he had looked at every day of his life. When she was allowed to hold a lock of the king's thick, wavy hair, she thought how sad it was that everyone eventually died. Papa seemed to catch a spirit of melancholy, too, and, shortly after this visit he was laid up with a bad cold, which came and went, never really leaving him throughout the rest of his trip. Papa's mood seemed to rather flag after that, and he began to talk to Kaiulani again about their financial straits. He confessed that he had recently petitioned Queen Liliu to consider him for a higher post than his present situation as a customs official, one that would hopefully involve not only a title but also a more substantial salary.

When they returned to London they resumed their busy social schedule. Among the new people they met was an Irish playwright, John Millington Synge. Kaiulani thought he was charming but Papa dismissed him as "rather common, in the long run," put off by his rolling bass voice and thick Irish brogue.

The sad news came that John Dominis, Aunt Liliu's husband and Oahu's governor, had died. Iolani Palace was again the setting of an elaborate lying-in-state. Papa became quite agitated about this development, concerned not only about Aunt Liliu's lack of protection, for now she stood truly alone, but also worried over anticipating to whom the well-paid, plum position of Governor might go. There were rumors that David Kawananakoa was under consideration as the Queen's first choice.

The idea that a possible boon to Koa could leave Papa at a disadvantage pulled at Kaiulani like an undertow. She would be glad to see her cousin making his way in the world, if that was the way things turned out, but didn't Papa deserve some good luck and fortune, too? She wrote Aunt Liliu a letter expressing her sympathy and sorrows. But the matter constantly preyed on her mind, until, about a week later, she wrote to her again. She begged to be excused for asking favors at such a time as this, but nevertheless hoped that Aunt Liliu would think of Papa for the post of governor, as well as letting him keep his customs job, for she knew he would be quite competent, and at the present time he needed both positions as their finances had dwindled very low.

Cleghorn went out one evening in London with a police detective acquaintance, curious to observe the workings of law enforcers in the slums of the greatest city in the world. By the time he returned in the early hours of the morning his cold had come back full force. The doctor who was called in diagnosed the sordid vapors and filthy streets as the cause of Cleghorn's relapse, and insisted that his patient take an entire week to rest in bed or "no one could be responsible for the consequences." So it was that, by September's end, Archibald Cleghorn, sniffling continually into a camphor-soaked handkerchief, bade his daughter a reluctant good-by and boarded the *Umbria* steamer headed for New York City and then on to the long journey home.

* * * * * * * * * * * * * * * * * * *

That fall, for the first time, Kaiulani approached Mr. Davies not with a petition but with a plan. After careful consideration, she had decided to leave Harrowden Hall at the mid-term January break. She would study privately, residing, if he concurred, at the home of Mrs. Rook who had kindly asserted her eagerness to oversee the continuation of Kaiulani's education. This would be a tremendous help in defraying expenses and, besides, Kaiulani felt it was time for her to establish some personal independence and autonomy in the eyes of the world. After all, she was a Princess of her country and not a simple schoolgirl. There was nothing wrong with being a schoolgirl, she assured him; but she needed more time and privacy of her own. She was quite certain her father and the Queen would acquiesce to, if not wholeheartedly approve of her plan.

Mr. Davies was so impressed that he actually bowed to Kaiulani at the end of her speech, although he did not realize he had done so. He was her servant, he said; ready to assist her in every way with whatever course she chose. As her advisor and guardian, he did wish to respectfully suggest just one small alteration to her excellent plan. Did she think Miss Miranda de Courcy might agree to accompany her on her journey, to stay with her as both good friend and companion? For he felt, given the nature of their close connection to each other, Miss de Courcy might be happy to do so; with the requisite permission, of course. And he himself would be very pleased to think of Kaiulani having the comfort and company of one so dear to her heart.

So the plan was made, with Miranda relieved to be free of the constraints of "regular school" at Harrowden Hall, and excited to be able to accompany the "sister of my soul."

Miranda's brother Toby came to visit her that fall at Harrowden Hall, to help settle his sister's affairs and to anticipate the girls' midwinter move to Mrs. Rook's house in Brighton. Although she was six years younger, Miranda and Toby were very close. She had often told Kaiulani about their childhood when Toby had entertained and looked after her. Always, no matter where they were or with whom, he could make her laugh like no one else in the world. Kaiulani loved the idea of her friend's kind older brother providing such protection and warmth, and sometimes wondered to herself how much his good influence might have contributed to the sweet, sunny nature of her friend.

The first time Toby came to visit at Harrowden Hall Miranda was away at class. Kaiulani, as was usual for her those days, sat alone reading and musing in her room. While she had no regrets about her decision to leave school, she could not help but worry about what the future might bring. Mrs. Rook was sweet and sensible, and thank heaven Miranda would be there as her study mate and companion. But still she worried about Aunt Liliu and Papa and Hawaii and, most of all, about when she would finally be able to go home.

When Toby found that his sister was not in her room he started off down the hall but was caught up short when he heard a low, musical voice somewhere close by. He stood perfectly still until he located the source, then moved quietly to the doorway it was coming from.

Kaiulani was reading a poem from her Ancient Literature of the World course. The passion and rhythm of the words left her breathless. It was from one of the five books of the Chinese Confucian Classics. The *Book of Songs'* temple hymns and ballads, from the Chou society of 600 BC, were written in plain language, and meant to teach about the pains, desires and pleasures of everyday human life and spirit. The poem that Kaiulani read out loud was the lament of a noblewoman who had been forced by her family into a loveless marriage when she already loved another. Enchanted by the power of the poem, the Princess read softly, with deep feeling.

"My heart is not a mirror,

To reflect what others will.
O sun, ah, moon,
Why are you so changed and dim?
Sorrow clings to me like an unwashed dress.
In the still of the night I brood upon it,
Long to take wing and fly away."

At the next stanza of the ballad, intense emotion flooded her soul so that she could hardly speak for the sensation of heat and fire that pulsed through her body and blood.

"My heart is not a stone,
it cannot be rolled away.
My heart is not a mat,
it cannot be folded away."

A ragged sob escaped her. She lifted one hand to the base of her throat and held it there as if she was trying to protect her own heart.

Toby, who was a gentleman through and through, could bear it no longer. He cleared his throat to signal his presence and then stepped into view in the doorway.

Kaiulani looked up at the startled young man, so impossibly tall and slim. With his light, thin eyebrows, high peaked forehead, wide, pale eyes and white-blonde mustache and hair, he looked like a newly hatched chick that had just pecked its way out of the shell. A few brown and gold feathers from the chic Parisian hat he held in his hands, brought as a gift for his sister, had entangled themselves in his hair, making him look even more like some wild, strange creature from another world.

In spite of her own predicament Kaiulani could not help laughing at the comical, unexpected sight of the anxiety stricken young man who stood before her. She laughed so long and hard that tears spilled down her cheeks. Struggling to gain control, she clutched her hands against her aching sides. But the longer Toby stood there, dumbfounded and blushing, looking like a giant child caught at some terrible misdeed, the more Kaiulani laughed.

"Oh, please, do stop, please," she cried, gasping and laughing at the same time. "Please, sit down; do, at least, sit down." She patted the chair beside her. But when Toby awkwardly folded his long, gangly frame into the small chair, he looked so much like a flamingo from back home, trying to accordion itself into a space that was much too small, that Kaiulani dissolved into gales of laughter all over again.

"Oh, I do so - beg your pardon," she spluttered, "You must think me - just awful." But every time she looked again at his wounded baby face again she laughed.

Toby swallowed hard and shook his head in a baffled sort of way that only struck her as funnier still.

"I do so awfully beg your pardon," he said softly, tucking his head in as if he wanted to bury it in his narrow, lanky chest. Then he looked at her again and was so dumbstruck by her beauty that he actually whistled.

"I thought a man had to die and go to heaven to see an angel," he murmured.

"Where I come from," she said merrily, "a hundred years ago a remark like that could have gotten you killed."

Emboldened and immensely cheered by her good humor, Toby put one hand up as if to shade his eyes and struck a meditative pose, like a swami.

"Ah," he announced sonorously, "I see it now. Yes, it must be - it is—she is - the Princess from Hawaii! All comes clear." He raised his other hand as if to ward off any protest, then brought both hands together on his high forehead in a prayerful attitude and bowed his head as if worshipping at a holy shrine. "Nevinson William de Courcy sees all and knows all," he intoned. Then he peeked out at her from behind the fingers of one hand. "Lord," he sighed, "You are phenomenally beautiful."

This set her off laughing again for several minutes, this time with the added embarrassment of having loud hiccups at irregular intervals. Toby just smiled at her in such a sweet and silly way that she only laughed some more.

At last she managed to collect herself.

Toby sheepishly held out his long, thin hand. "I am-"

"Yes, I knew exactly who you were as soon as I saw you. You look just like Miranda, only really not at all."

"I've always thought so, too!" He smiled at her irrefutable logic and agreed with unfeigned pleasure, ready to resemble the Eiffel

Tower if only she would smile at him some more. "Well," he sighed heartily, "I believe I have finally found my mission in life!"

"And what would that be, pray tell?" Kaiulani's eyes sparkled even as she tried to look stern.

"To make you laugh," he answered without hesitation.

That was how Kaiulani and Toby met. They talked for hours that day, about everything and nothing, nonstop from that moment until Miranda came home. It was as if they had known each other forever, as though the tall civil engineer and architect in his stiffly starched high collar and pince-nez glasses and the dusky, beautiful princess with her halo of wild black hair had always been friends.

From the first day on she called him her "Father Confessor" and poured out her feelings to him without reserve. After Kaiulani met Toby, the brother, sister and the princess were ever after the best of friends. When they could not be with each other they wrote long letters back and forth. Kaiulani told Miranda that Toby was her sweet "clown prince," a warm, steady light that never failed to chase away the shadows, and made her always feel safe and cared for.

Toby was a constant visitor to their home in Brighton. Even Mrs. Rook, who tended to be critical, especially of men, thought highly of Toby, and referred to him as "Kaiulani's favorite beau."

Chapter Eighteen

Just before Kaiulani left Harrowden Hall, Mrs. Sharp called her in for one of her famous "*Tête-À-Tête*" conferences to tell her how much they had all enjoyed having her as a student, and to commend her for being "a model of superior intellectual application and exemplary behavior." She also said that they would miss her.

Mrs. Sharp expressed her "tremendously committed involvement" with the Princess' ongoing academic career, and her eagerness to participate in any way possible to support Kaiulani in all her future endeavors. Mrs. Sharp adamantly pledged and then avowed again and then reiterated her unyielding desire to be of any help whatsoever, at any time, under any circumstances at all. Then Mrs. Sharp gave Kaiulani a firm hug and both women laughed for no reason at all except as a token of their mutual understanding and affection.

The journey to Mrs. Rook's townhouse in the seaside resort town of Brighton at South Sussex, No. 7 Cambridge Road, went smoothly. Kaiulani, Toby and Miranda were excellent traveling companions. They pointed out noteworthy scenery to each other, discussed at length the state of the world and the universe, and sang. Kaiulani was not used to this kind of close, familial camaraderie, and she loved it. She was so grateful for her new and old best friends that she was sure she would be happy doing anything at all with them.

One night when she was restless and unable to sleep, Kaiulani thought for a long time about what the de Courcys had come to mean to her. With her playfulness and practical bent, Miranda was like a sister. Toby was an anchor for her, a stable, solid presence in the kaleidoscopic shifts her life continued to take. In her heart she knew that their friendship would always be there. She was aware, too, that she and Toby were probably a little in love with each other, or could be. Her sense of these connections was something she felt deeply. Her friends constituted for her another home in her life.

* * * * * * * * * * * * * * * * * * *

When Toby was sure that Kaiulani and Miranda were comfortable in their new quarters, he reluctantly returned to London to attend to business affairs. Mrs. Rook, as thorough and efficient as ever, had already taken charge of organizing a full schedule of tutoring for the two young ladies that included music, history, art, literature, singing, French and German.

Kaiulani was relieved to have a place of her own again, even though it was only a spacious bedroom nestled away in the cozy domestic comfort of Mrs. Rook's home, with Miranda just a few steps away. Mrs. Rook's little dog, Sammy, a Yorkshire terrier, made the household lively with his antic behavior and usually slept all night curled up just outside their bedroom doors. His silky-soft, straight coat and his sweet, gentle nature sometimes reminded Kaiulani of Fairy back home, and then a twinge of longing and loss mingled with her pleasure.

At first, she did not mind the frequent rainy weather and dense, low fogs that were so prevalent in Brighton. After a while, however, she realized that she always scanned the dismal, gray skies during and after the rains, searching in vain for traces of the breathtaking rainbows she was used to at home. Here, there were occasionally a few faint stripes of color that ended in a vague haze, but the English rainbows were only pale shadows compared to the rainbows of Hawaii.

Kaiulani continued to enjoy her studies, but she loved the hours of her singing lessons best. She was in her element when she sang, neither worrying about the future nor remembering or regretting the past.

Her voice teacher was an old man from Switzerland, Mr. Sergei Tyrol. In his mid-eighties, Sergei wore dark, shiny, exquisitely tailored suits that had been the height of fashion thirty or forty years ago. He moved like a spider or a monkey, animated and very alert, and maintained a fluid grace in his every gesture and glance. Although Kaiulani was several inches taller than Mr. Tyrol, she looked up to him in every way and felt very fortunate to be his pupil. He praised her full mouth and lips and always encouraged her to smile "because it is not only good for your constitution, it also helps mine, too." Her wide, voluptuous mouth had often made Kaiulani feel self-conscious, especially here in Europe where it was such a strong contrast to the many thin-lipped people.

"No, no, schveetie," Mr. Tyrol said when she confided this to him. "Zat is vonderful, schveetie," he told her. "You know vhy I zay so? Because zat is all singing voice, your beautiful mouth."

'Mouth' sounded like "mouse" when Sergei said it, but Kaiulani felt no impulse to laugh as she hung on his every word, strangely pronounced or not. "You vill zee." he assured her. "You vill zee, mark my vords."

Kaiulani had never been called "schveetie" before. She basked in the warmth and affection that never failed this lovely, diminutive gentleman. He had the beginnings of a brilliant career in opera but an untimely illness had halted his progress for several years and his career never recovered after that. Sergei would ask her again and again his two simple questions: "Is it easy?" and "Is it natural?" She felt honored to study with him and made fine improvements in their work.

Mrs. Rook decided to teach Miranda and Kaiulani how to embroider.

"A useful skill for anyone," she declared, "even a princess or a queen."

Kaiulani smiled to herself as she tried to imagine Liliu working with minute patterns of needle and thread and was sure that her aunt would have infinite patience. Miranda, however, was definitely not patient with the degree of concentration and detail required to learn the stitching, and gave up on her project when she was only on the first letter of "H" for "home."

But Kaiulani enjoyed the soothing monotony of the manual task. Working with her hands seemed to free her mind, which allowed her to indulge in hours of daydreaming as she sewed; visiting in her thoughts the people and places she so sorely missed. She made a lovely pillow cover for Mr. Tyrol, embroidered in green and gold thread with an ancient proverb from India, "God respects me when I work but he loves me when I sing." Sergei was very pleased and kissed her hand several times in gratitude.

That March Kaiulani wrote to Aunt Liliu to tell her about her life in Brighton. "It is wonderful to have Miranda here with me. I have also become good friends with her brother, Toby, who is very clever and never fails to make me laugh, regardless of the weather or my mood or anything else at all."

"My singing teacher, Mr. Tyrol, has helped me immensely with my voice. He is quite extraordinary and very accomplished. I do wish you could somehow meet him. He says I have a sweet soprano voice, which I tell him I must have inherited from you and Mama as that is the side of the family that is musical."

"I am so looking forward to my return next year, as I am beginning to feel terribly homesick. I shall be very glad to see you, although I wonder if you will even recognize me as I have changed so much. Your Loving Niece, Kaiulani."

To Papa she wrote about the weather. "When it was cold over here, from about December until the end of March, the wind blew such color into my face that Miranda and Toby would tease me by pretending that I must be a Princess from 'the wilds of America' since my face and hands turned red from the cold."

"I do prefer the intense cold to the intense heat. When I am too hot, I feel sluggish and stupid and every movement I make is so slow that I feel like a sponge soaked in water. But when it gets too cold I can always warm myself by the fireplace, or with a cup of hot tea or a walk."

"How is Fairy? I miss her awfully. Papa, would you please make sure that someone nice is grooming her and gives her some sugar now and then? None of the horses here can 'hold a candle' to her, as the saying goes. I would give almost anything to ride Fairy again."

"The indomitable Mrs. Rook has found us even more tutors, this time for classes in dancing and 'deportment,' so-called. I must say I find the whole idea highly amusing. I always thought I carried my self, if not exactly <u>well</u>, then at least serviceably. You can imagine my shock when my friends here told me that my posture is much better when I am walking in the street than when I am in a drawing room. So, at the present moment, I am doing my very best to walk into a room without too much noise and move quietly and gracefully."

"Papa, do you remember how I used to run around the halls at home? I miss you so much and love you and can hardly wait for the day when I shall at last be back home. Your Loving Daughter, Kaiulani."

* * * * * * * * * * * * * * * * * * *

As winter turned slowly into spring in Brighton the townspeople began to scrub and air out and set up the hotels and cottages, which had lain dormant since the end of last year's tourist season. In spite of Miranda and Mrs. Rook's company, Kaiulani felt strangely alone here in a way that she had never felt before. Although her friend was her constant companion, and they regularly practiced German and French together, talked about their classes and shared secrets, she nevertheless felt a strong sense of isolation, sometimes exciting, at other times disturbing.

Mrs. Rook made sure to invite a few appropriate and congenial companions over for the occasional small supper or tea; and Toby was both a frequent visitor and the official, pre-approved escort to accompany Miranda and Kaiulani to any social events.

Even with all this, Kaiulani found herself in the new and novel situation of venturing out into the world alone, really for the first time in her life. Out on her own she encountered an ugly kind of prejudice from which she had previously been carefully insulated.

She went to pick up a packet of sewing needles and thread for Mrs. Rook at the general store and noticed that the clerk whispered something to another customer and then made a point of waiting rather ostentatiously before coming over to assist her. She had no idea what had been said, but she felt an unpleasant note of emphasis when she explained her order and the clerk responded with, "So, you must be <u>Miss</u> Rook, I presume?" The other customer, who had been listening avidly to their exchange, snickered a little as she turned away and went out the door.

A few times and only briefly, Kaiulani had been surprised, both in Hawaii and America, by peculiar, disdainful looks, or by faces which either stared at her quite indiscreetly, or turned sharply away from her on the streets. She had not cared or wondered about it for very long as she was much too busy with her own affairs to be overly concerned about other people's rudeness.

But in Brighton, off-season, there were those among the townspeople who relished every shard of gossip. The smallest sliver of rumor or intrigue became their main livelihood during the long, dull winter months. Mrs. Rook firmly insisted that Kaiulani ignore any low-minded people who tried to put their noses into other people's business where they most emphatically did not belong. Mrs. Rook explained to her that these were the exact same people who would fawn over and be horribly obsequious to the summer trade tourists, but then would make up lies about them and promote nasty rumors behind their backs. Kaiulani took her advice and ignored those few who attempted to snub her. Still, she could not help but wonder how it was possible for anyone to want to hurt or be cruel to people they did not know, had never even met or talked to.

Kaiulani was glad to hear from her father that he was beginning to develop his plans to build "a proper house" at Ainahau. She wrote back to him how happy she was and that it had always been her desire to have a house at Ainahau that would be worthy of his exceptional gardens.

One day when Miranda was away at a class Toby came by and took Kaiulani out for tea in one of the quaint little shops in the town's business district. She confessed to him that the idea of Papa building a new house at Ainahau had begun to trouble her somehow, making her feel alternately both happy and sad.

Toby was in a silly, florid mood. "I see," he considered. "You are a damsel in the midst of a paradox, albeit a very fine damsel who is admirably strong and certainly brave enough to tolerate and handle contradictions."

Kaiulani smiled at him, but only just, and the anxious look remained on her face. Toby poured them more tea from the delicate china pot, which rested on the table between them. The teapot was designed to look like a wide-eyed calico cat with one uplifted paw serving as its spout and a cap-like lid on its head.

"There, there, ducks. Do tell Uncle Toby what's the matter."

He lifted the linen napkin from the table and deftly shaped it into a high, pointed, pontiff-like hat, which he held above his head. "Father Confessor is all ears."

Kaiulani leaned in toward him to speak; then abruptly pulled herself back to sit up straight in her chair. "Deportment," she explained with a wry smile. "I mustn't forget."

"Oh, dear, please, <u>do</u> forget deportment! At least while I'm around, please?" He played at being exasperated. "Besides," he could never resist the opportunity to tell her, even obliquely, how he felt, "you look so fetching when you slouch."

At last Kaiulani laughed. Then she took a deep breath and began, her words tumbling out in a rush.

"My dear, dear Toby, you are so generous to let me tell you all about my petty thoughts and daydreams and never judge me ill or lacking because of them. I am afraid that I am really very selfish." She blushed a little and paused before she continued again.

"You see, of course I am glad that Papa is building a new house at Ainahau. But I keep worrying about the old place, which I know so well; that it will not be the same when I return! Or, worse still, that everything I know might be torn down or gone away or rearranged! It's almost as if the old house will be sacrificed, in a way, for the new, before I can get back home!"

"Oh, now," Toby patted her hand as she sighed. "Now, now. Hardly sacrificed, my dear. No one really sacrifices any more, here or there; didn't you know?! It's so passé! So cliché, if you will, ever since those French revolutionaries made such a horrible, botched job of it with all that 'off-with-their-heads' guillotine business."

She smiled just a little but still did not meet his eyes.

"At any rate," Toby said, desperate to cheer her up, "I defy any mere house, or even the entire estate, for that matter, old or new, to resist being utterly loyal to such a delightful, wonderful personage as you! Even a stone or a block of wood would have to pay homage to your sweetness and grace!"

He snatched up the cat teapot from the table and declaimed to it theatrically. "You blocks, you stones, you worse than useless things!"

Kaiulani started to feel better as she always did when she had someone she could talk to. "Julius Caesar. 'The fault, dear Brutus, lies not in our stars...'" she began.

"- but in ourselves." Toby smiled back at her as he finished the quote.

"D'you know," he said in his normal voice, "I am generally a rather sensible chap, really, under most circumstances. But I am giddy most of the time with you. You bring out my silly side."

"And a very nice, lovely side it is, too." Kaiulani patted his hand. "You and Miranda are alike that way, with your sunny dispositions. Sometimes I feel like there is a dark cloud over my head that only lifts away when you and Miranda are near to make me play."

"On the subject of play," Toby said, "I wonder if you would like to accompany me to the young Duke's wedding in London? P'rhaps I might introduce you to Princess Mary and the Duke, if that would be all right? It's not until mid-month, January, so you have tons of time to decide, if -"

Kaiulani touched his hand again lightly as she spoke, "Since it is only now late December and I have no immediate plans either for this or the next year, thus far, I think I may safely say yes."

"Stunning!" He exclaimed. "Everyone will be there. The groom is the Duke of Clarence and Avondale. Now that I think of it, he's a bit in the same boat as you, as a matter of fact! He stands to inherit Victoria's crown next in line after his father, the Prince of Wales. Very pleasant chap. I know you'll like him. He's engaged to Princess Mary, who is ever so jolly. Miranda and I grew up with her; they were just down the road when we were children. I should be so happy to arrive with my own, most charming princess in tow," he said with great satisfaction.

"I'd prefer to be on your arm than to be towed, if it's all the same to you," Kaiulani laughed.

She looked forward to the royal wedding with pleasure. Mrs. Rook designed a midnight blue silk gown for her, which wonderfully accentuated her dark eyes and skin, and a peach chiffon dress for Miranda, who would attend with an old friend of Toby's named Lionel who they had also known since childhood.

But, alas, there would be no wedding for the young Duke. There was a funeral service instead. A sudden pulmonary congestion turned into pneumonia and, within just a few days, he was gone.

Feeling very sorry for the ill-fated young couple, Kaiulani redoubled the intensity with which she immersed herself in her classes. To Aunt Liliu she wrote of her ambition to study as hard as she possibly could. "When I come home I shall try to help you as much as I can, though it may not be much as I am afraid I do not understand state affairs very well."

The days passed slowly and Kaiulani constantly anticipated the time when she would be allowed to return home. A spring holiday in Jersey, across the Channel, proved very pleasant for Mrs. Rook and the two students, except that rough weather on the way over confirmed the Princess' tendency to be seasick. By the time they arrived, however, the weather had turned mild. Jersey Island delighted Kaiulani, reminding her of home with its rocky shoreline and numerous reefs, inlets and small bays. She returned from their two-week trip refreshed and renewed.

The news from home continued to be of struggle. Aunt Liliu wrote to her, happy and proud that the Royalists had won in both houses of the legislature. But she was equally furious over the crude threats and antagonistic behavior of Minister Stevens, the new U.S. Foreign Minister who had the gall to publicly declare his readiness "to aid the annexationists at any time."

Summer passed by quickly with mostly sunny days and mild, balmy weather. Miranda and Kaiulani were, as Toby liked to say to make them laugh, "ravishingly gorgeous" in their light, thin blouses and summer dresses the color of blue skies, berries and sunshine.

Kaiulani and Miranda spent several weeks at Mr. Davies' house, eager to get acquainted with the new wife who he had recently brought back from San Francisco. Madeline, or "Maddie," as she was called, was many years younger than Mr. Davies. She had a generous, easy-going nature and it was heart-warming to the two young romantics to see Mr. Davies in love after he had been a widower and on his own for so long.

They all worked together that summer to raise funds for charity. Kaiulani alone brought in more than 400 pounds, which, Mr. Davies explained, was more than $1,000.00 in American money. The vacation time passed too quickly. Maddie, Miranda and Kaiulani pledged their friendship at summer's end and promised to regroup again soon.

* *

Back in Brighton, Kaiulani found packages and letters from home. Aunt Liliu had sent *"A Brief History of the Hawaiian People,"* a new book by Charles Bishop. Kaiulani looked forward to finding out more about her people and their history. From Papa there was a recent issue of the journal, *Paradise of the Pacific*, which featured a long, glowing article about the heiress apparent. The article was full of affection and respect, calling Kaiulani "Hawaii's Hope." It stated how much the people of Hawaii looked forward to her coming home "to celebrate her eighteenth birthday in the land of her race."

Although Kaiulani was moved by the article, she repeated the last line several times over and felt a disorienting sense of irony. All right, she thought, but which race was that? Who was she, really, and where did she belong? She knew there were those at home who considered her too mixed to be a true Hawaiian, and questioned her right to rule because she was half-Scottish. Since she had been in exile, living out in the world, she also knew that there were people who dismissed and disregarded her because she was not light-skinned enough, or fair-haired or blue-eyed or thin-lipped like they were.

Even Tusitala, who most certainly was a friend, had written in his poem to her that she was "the daughter of a double race." Did that really make such a difference? Did it make her feel or think or act differently? Did it make her any less or more than anyone else in the world?

She decided it was an unfortunate subject. Prejudice was basically stupid, a wanton waste of energy and time. It was a subject that seemed to occupy people who either had little else in their lives to engage in or worry about; or others with bad manners, who had in some way been disappointed or were angry at life in general. It was not an issue she cared to be involved in. If there were others who were, who sought out that kind of negativity, well, that was their concern and not hers.

The time in Brighton at Mrs. Rook's house was a period of intense transition for Kaiulani, although she did not realize it until later. When she left Harrowden Hall she had been left without moorings. The fact of being perceived, both by herself and others, as still a child had shifted and changed when she decided to leave school. In doing this she had, in a way, left her childhood behind, and it was both disturbing and exhilarating to be cut loose.

She had her connections, of course, with Mrs. Rook and Toby and Miranda, and still a full schedule of classes. But she came and went as she pleased in a way that she had never done before, with a freedom that she was experiencing for the first time. These things, combined with her age, conspired to give her a new sense of herself. At times she felt that she was floundering, uncertain of how to behave anymore. For the first time in her life, she was outside the circumscribed parameters, released from the boundaries of her roles in her family - as princess, daughter and student. She was separated from the persona she had lived with all her life; free, if only temporarily, from both the burden and status of her position.

For her seventeenth birthday Mrs. Rook and Miranda gave her a lovely print of a painting she had long admired. Called "The Soul's Awakening," it was a picture that Kaiulani had seen on her first trip to London with Miranda. They had both been fascinated by it's haunting, ethereal beauty and the eerie, otherworldly nature of the scene.

"The Soul's Awakening" was an example of that popular genre which represented women as angels or saints, sometimes adorned with lacy wings, other times as veiled Madonnas or martyrs. Usually, these women were dying tragically for some noble cause.

The young woman in "The Soul's Awakening" was beautiful, tender and fragile. She appeared to be weightless as she floated in the air; suspended high above a marsh-like pond and shrouded in a mist that made her look like a ghost or a deathly pale consumptive. A wild, tangled garden rose up beside the dark, threatening marshland and a lush forest could be seen outlined vaguely in the distance behind her. The marsh, the garden, the looming, sinister, shadowy forest - all seemed about to engulf or overwhelm the lovely young woman. Her soft features were fixed in an expression of pensive, melancholy brooding. Above her halo-like curls a wreath of buds and tiny roses hovered like a sacred crown. She looked as if she would be blown away by the next strong wind. Even so, the barest suggestion of a smile played at the corners of her mouth. She gazed off into the distance as if she saw something far away that was pleasant to look on and brought her comfort in her vulnerable condition. Although wrapped up everywhere in danger and confusion, she appeared as if she kept to herself some small but powerful secret.

Miranda and Kaiulani had talked about the painting for hours. When they were in London they never failed to visit the shop where it was displayed. Kaiulani saw the picture as a tribute to the idealized quest, whatever it might be, of the self-sacrificing maiden who, for her, represented pure spirit or soul. She did not tell Miranda that, since the first time they saw it, images from the painting kept recurring in her dreams, oppressive at times, at other times freeing.

Miranda, who was pragmatic and down to earth, thought the maiden was intended to be the soul of art, or possibly a muse for creative endeavors. On one visit when the weather was bad and Miranda was out of sorts and cranky, she perversely insisted that the soul was tired and hungry, that was all, and was probably trying to figure out a way to get out of the damp mist. Or maybe she was hoping for it to clear up so she could search for food, berries or bark or something like that, in the forest behind her.

Kaiulani wrote to Aunt Liliu about the birthday gift and said she had placed the picture on the wall beside her bed so that the woman's lovely face was the first thing she saw every morning.

* *

Winter weather came early that year. By the beginning of November, a few weeks after Kaiulani's birthday, a light blanket of snow frosted the trees and roofs of the houses. Kaiulani's resistance was low and soon she was laid up in bed for a few days, and afterwards stayed for several weeks mainly in Mrs. Rook's front parlor by the fireplace, staving off a cold and feeding little bits of toast and jam to Sammy. The little dog often slept curled up on or near her feet, and she was always grateful for the warmth of his small, soft body.

The rumors from home were rampant. Kaiulani had asked Mr. Davies to send her some American newspapers to supplement the news she received from Hawaii. In the Washington Star, a pro-annexation paper, Kaiulani read that Mr. Thurston had declared that the Queen was "pig-headed, stubborn, stupid, tricky and totally without knowledge that there was trouble in the country."

Another anti-royalist paper, the San Francisco Observer, carried a grotesque, insulting cartoon which depicted Aunt Liliu as an obese creature labeled 'half-woman, half sacred cow' that was swallowing down copious amounts of money and sugar cane. The crudely drawn picture jarred Kaiulani, both by itself and also because it somehow made her think of Mama Nui's girth and unhappiness, and she felt guilty and disloyal for even thinking of her loving godmother in such a perverse context. The article below the hideous drawing read, "It is said that she is well known to be much more stubborn than her brother." The writer concluded with smug assurance. "She will finally have to yield and place herself in the hands of the conservative and respectable men of the country as this is the only way for her to retain her throne."

Furious, Kaiulani ripped out the page, crumpled it into a ball and tossed it in the fire. The sudden flare-up made Sammy wake up and whimper.

"I'm sorry, sweetheart." Kaiulani petted the dog's soft ears. "I didn't mean to scare you." The Yorkie snuggled into her arms and was soon back asleep. The touch of his silky hair and the faint, earthy smell of him calmed her.

She stared into the fire as if she might find a message in its flames.

"It is said, it is said," she angrily murmured. "Who says it then, and does not have the courage to put their name on the slander?! And what makes them think they know?!" The little dog twitched in his sleep and she patted his coat to soothe him.

Picking out another newspaper, one from Hawaii that she knew would be staunchly royalist, Kaiulani skimmed a story about the Queen's second good will trip to Molokai. An excerpt from a speech Samuel Parker had made was all about "our beloved queen" and included a public statement she had made to the lepers. "I deeply grieve your afflictions," she had said to them. "Your sorrows are mine, and your joys are mine, for a Queen is powerless without a people to rule over." Mr. Parker had asked "all true Hawaiians" to "rally round this excellent and honorable lady," and declared that all gathered there must "unite in upholding her throne for there are yet hopes for your tears."

Stunned by the dire tone of even these positive remarks about the "situation" in Hawaii, Kaiulani wondered if this could really be happening, or was it only a bad dream? She knew that the so-called "overwhelming majority" who were trying to wrest Hawaii from its queen was a handful of greedy, grasping cowards who schemed to rob her family, her people and her country of their rights and power.

The Princess felt the first, dreaded signs of a severe headache coming on - a light-headed feeling combined with slightly blurred vision and the constricting sensation of huge hands that gripped her head and pressed down hard on her temples.

She slowed her breathing, closed her eyes and tried to imagine that the pressure she felt was a strong, stormy wind that was already beginning to ease off and dissipate even as she focused on it. Once again, she was grateful to Mr. Tyrol, for it was he who had given her this image "to use vhenever you are vorrying too much." With a mischievous glance he had added, "By 'too much,' of course, I mean at all. Any vorrying is too much vorrying for you." As she began to breathe easily again, deep into her diaphragm, Kaiulani opened her eyes. She picked up another Hawaiian paper and read yet another interview with Lorrin Thurston. In this one he complained that the Queen was "partial to sugar barons and her own little pets." Kaiulani was incensed by his unjust, ludicrous treatment of her aunt, and remembered the unpleasant sound of Thurston's loud, abrasive voice.

Let them say what they wanted; Kaiulani would soon be home to give her support to the Hawaiians' cause. Aunt Liliu and Mr. Davies had written to say that plans for her return were already underway. She was to stay in Brighton through the holidays, then travel in Europe for a month or two, to be presented in society, with a formal presentation, of course, to Queen Victoria. Soon after all that had been accomplished, she would be summoned back home.

She also knew that Aunt Liliu, in a recent address to the legislature, had called for many economies; including a voluntary cut of ten thousand dollars from the Queen's own personal funds. She knew that one of the Legislature's final acts before the session was over would be a vote to arrange a four thousand-dollar payment that would provide for Kaiulani's expenses and her return to the islands. She knew that Aunt Liliu was seriously considering granting a new constitution to her people, one that would do away with the grossly unfair stipulation that those who did not own property, or made less than a certain income, could not vote. Aunt Liliu had explained to Kaiulani that, ever since the '92 cabinet elections a year earlier, petitions had been pouring in from all of the Islands to request a new constitution, one that would truly serve the people. Even out of the 9,500 registered voters, the great majority of voters, about 6,500, - a full two-thirds - had signed petitions to ask that the constitution be changed.

Papa had also written to Kaiulani and referred to Aunt Liliu's actions as "very foolish, or, at best, not well thought out."

But there was only so much figuring out that Kaiulani was able to do. There was too much to think about and consider all the time; so many differences of opinion, even between Papa and Aunt Liliu, though neither would openly admit it. And Aunt Liliu had made Papa Governor of Oahu, after all, so Kaiulani wished he would be more grateful and positive about that.

Well, she thought as she settled a shawl closer around the sleeping dog. Sammy had twitched a little in his sleep, for the fire had burned down low. She could only wait and be patient. The holidays were almost upon them. Soon she would see Toby again, and he and she and Miranda would be jolly and gay and go to see the Davies for a lovely while. And then it would be the New Year, and they would all see what they would see.

Chapter Nineteen

The holidays were a welcome distraction to Kaiulani, as the news from home continued to be equivocal at every turn. She would receive letters from Papa that were full of complaints about Aunt Liliu's "secretiveness." He questioned the Queen's "apparent indifference to communicating anything about either her plans or her intentions" to the cabinet. Or, he could only presume, to anyone else; and most certainly not to him who was, after all, only "the lowly Governor of Oahu!" After broadly hinting that Kaiulani might "soon, very much sooner than we thought, be back in Hawaii," he added the cryptic postscript, "Though I cannot say how or why just now." Papa often concluded his letters with further criticism of the Queen; and once had even written, "I do not and cannot understand her." Another time, when he was especially frustrated with Liliu, he wrote, "I am sorry to say so, but sometimes I think she is to blame for all our troubles."

Then Aunt Liliu would write to Kaiulani telling her how well things were going, enclosing money "to help you enjoy the holidays" and encouraging her to have courage and good faith. The Queen wrote long, cheerful explanations of how busy she was at work on all the new changes in the legislation, which would, she hoped, help the Hawaiians at last.

"I believe we shall finally be able to restore the powers lost to our people and to ourselves when that despicable 'bayonet constitution' was forced upon us." Aunt Liliu signed her letters, as she always did now, *"Omni pa'a."* This was the official motto she had chosen for her regency. It meant "Stand Firm" in Hawaiian.

Even Mr. Davies, usually so calm and self-contained, was perturbed by the contradictory reports of the fray back home. As her guardian, he felt it his duty to let Kaiulani know he had heard "some British sympathizers" had suggested that she should replace the Queen as acting regent, "as a possible way to solve the problems of the regency as it stands." While the idea of displacing Aunt Liliu was both absurd and terrifying to her, it was only slightly less fearsome than the malignant rumors of annexation, or the threats that Hawaii would be made a republic of America.

Kaiulani knew that her Aunt's determination was unshakable. With a keen awareness of the irony of the situation she confided this to Toby, telling him, "'The problems of the regency as it stands,' indeed! My Aunt's will is constant and unswerving. *'Omni pa'a'* is her reply to them. 'We stand firm,' "She explained to Toby with great pride.

Toby loved to see Kaiulani's usually mild manner and subdued energy ignite as they always did when she spoke of Hawaii. Her eyes lit up with passion and her muted voice grew in timber and strength until it was clear and resonant as a bell. Miranda, pretending to be afraid of her friend's intensity, would shield her eyes and tuck her head down as if to avoid a bright light. "Watch out for the volcano!" she would say, trying to make Kaiulani laugh, sometimes succeeding, at others not. But Toby always loved to see her so excited. On fire and fearless, reckless like that, she was more beautiful than ever to him.

* * * * * * * * * * * * * * * * * * *

At the Davies' New Year's Eve party Kaiulani found herself underneath the mistletoe with Toby by her side as the stroke of midnight closed out the old year. Toby's chaste, soft kiss barely skimmed her lips and she smiled at him, happy to welcome in the New Year with such a good friend. Then he kissed her a second time, holding her close against him for a moment. She was surprised to feel a tingling sensation, as if a small electric current or shock had traveled from his mouth to hers. She felt her throat tighten up and drew away from him with a questioning look.

In the same breezy tone he always used with her Toby said lightly, "You really are quite extraordinary, you know. I adore you so much."

Kaiulani felt heat rising from her chest up into her face, and suddenly realized she was about to cry. Toby held only her hand now and lifted it to his lips to kiss.

"Might I hope -" Toby's voice was very soft. Kaiulani's eyes were bright and roses flamed in her cheeks as she touched his mouth with her fingers to stop his words.

"Ah, my dear, good Toby. For now, with so many things uncertain, won't you love me like a brother? Just for now?"

"For always, if you like, my dear." He struggled to remain composed and his voice came out in a near whisper. "Forever, if that is your wish."

Just then Miranda came over and demanded that her brother partner her for the first dance of the year. As they spun away into a waltz Kaiulani thought again how fortunate she was in her friends. She knew that Toby meant exactly what he said; that he was as true and constant in his affection as his sister. She also felt flattered and excited to know how much he wanted her. Those feelings, though, she must put away for now. She had to conserve all her energy for the struggle before her. Later, perhaps, she might indulge in thoughts of her own desires and longings for love and comfort. For now, though, she needed to be strong. She did not know how soon that strength would be put to the test.

* * * * * * * * * * * * * * * * * * *

January passed uneventfully, except that Miranda and then Kaiulani caught mild colds again and were nursed by Mrs. Rook and entertained by Sammy. But on January 30th, in a single day, Kaiulani's life was changed forever when Mr. Davies received three consecutive telegrams.

As soon as he received the first message, he contacted Kaiulani at once, sending his private coach to pick her up in Brighton and bring her to his home in Southport. She was certain that Papa or Aunt Liliu or Koa had died. Outwardly calm, she was trembling inside when she arrived. Mr. Davies' demeanor was so somber it only accelerated her fears. Unable to hold back her anxiety any longer she asked in a quavering voice, "Papa -?"

"No", Mr. Davies said, almost inaudible, and handed her the three telegrams. Two more had arrived within the time of her travel. He tried to help her sit down on the sofa, but she was too agitated and indicated she would stand.

The first telegram read, "Queen Deposed." Kaiulani's hands shook as she looked at the next. "Monarchy Abrogated."

She stared at Mr. Davies in disbelief.

"Abrogated?" She questioned. "But doesn't that mean - abolished? Repealed?!?" Her words sounded wooden and her voice seemed to echo in her ears.

Mr. Davies looked miserable as he nodded yes.

Stunned, she began to read the third telegram. It began, "Break the news to the Princess." Much to her own dismay, Kaiulani began to laugh. The unnerving sound of her silvery, trilling laughter rang out hollowly in the silent room.

Concerned, Mr. Davies guided her to a chair into which she fell rather than sat, immediately ceasing her outburst as she caught her ragged breath.

"For some reason -, "She tried to explain but the breath caught again in her throat and made her sound like she had just been pulled back in from drowning. "That word - 'break' -" Helpless to continue she could only shake her head. Mr. Davies sat down beside her as she looked again at the last telegram. "Islands transferred," she read. "Princess provided for."

"'Provided for?!'" she read again. "But how dare they -! Oh, Mr. Davies," she bolted up again, crying out in a plaintive wail, "Who would do such a thing—and why?!"

She gasped and then released a wrenching sob, which brought on a torrent of tears. Mr. Davies could only stand by. Then Maddie, who had just heard the dreadful news, rushed into the parlor. The two young women fell into each other's arms and wept.

It took several days to piece together the patchwork of conflicting reports and information.

* * * * * * * * * * * * * * * * * * *

In the opening session of government on January 14th, Aunt Liliu had made good on her promise of the new constitution, which had been requested by the natives and many other factions. The first item of business on her agenda had been the provision that, in Hawaii, as everywhere else in the world, only Hawaiian citizens would be allowed to vote in Hawaiian elections.

The *haoles'* rage knew no bounds. They struck swiftly and cruelly at the weakened monarchy. Within hours of the Queen's announcement a "Committee of Safety" had been formed, made up of a hundred or so foreigners, mostly businessmen, the majority of them Americans, and a handful of Germans and Brits, all with vested interests and loaded weapons. The Committee had provided for, of course, the requisite militia, and called for a mass meeting of their few supporters the night of that same day the Queen had proclaimed the new constitution.

Loudly declaring that "American lives and property were in grave danger," U.S. Minister John L. Stevens took it upon himself to sail his ship, the *U.S.S. Boston*, from the Big Island, where it had been docked for some time, and anchored it in Honolulu Harbor. Stevens justified this action by claiming that the Queen's proposed new constitution was an illegal, revolutionary act, and so put her and her supporters outside the protection of him and his troops. The huge cannon on board the ship was right away trained in the direction of the palace. Within forty-eight hours, the city's streets were choked with armed marines. More than half of the troops were positioned with their arms aimed at and around every angle of Iolani Palace, surrounding it from all sides with loaded weapons pointed at every window and door.

The Queen was loath to call for gunfire in the Honolulu streets, unwilling to risk having blood shed in Hawaii. As she refused to put her handful of household guards or her people in danger, Aunt Liliu hesitated rather than attacked. Her terrified Cabinet offered no advice other than caution. Liliuokalani's official statement, printed in the pro-monarchy and PG papers alike, was that she had been forced "to yield to save the lives of my people, and my supporters."

The "Annexation Club" held a meeting that night at the armory, drawing 1,500 people who listened as Thurston and the others railed against, in the lawyer's own words, "this disgusting Monarchy!"

Thurston admitted in his inflammatory tirades that the Queen had already agreed to uphold the previous constitution "for now." But in the same breath he furiously denounced her word as "worth less than nothing."

"Last week," Thurston pounded on his high podium, livid with excitement and rage, "Last week the sun rose on a peaceful and smiling Hawaii! Today it is otherwise, and it is all the Queen's fault!"

A savage roar came back to him from his supporters in the crowd; many of them were drunk, some were armed marines.

"It is not because of her that the streets do not now run red with blood!" He fairly shrieked, sounding like a banshee or an evil spirit. "She wants us to sleep on a slumbering volcano which will one morning soon spew out blood and destroy us all!"

Dropping back into a hoarse shout the missionary's son exhorted his listeners. He was in the pulpit now, milking his performance for all it was worth. "Has the tropical sun cooled and thinned out our blood?! Or do we still have flowing in our veins the warm, rich blood that loves liberty so much it will die for it?!"

The crowd howled approval of Thurston's confused and tortured metaphors.

Within twenty-four hours of the formation of the Committee of Safety, Judge Sanford Ballard Dole had accepted the nomination to be President of the new regime. He resigned from his position as a member of the Queen's court to do so. The new government was henceforth to be known as the Provisional Government.

Minister Stevens and his troops had soon taken possession of the government buildings and the palace. Of his own volition Stevens had personally, gleefully pulled down the flag of Hawaii and hoisted the American flag in its place, over the main government building. While some of the Reformers did not approve, no one took it down.

Honolulu was under armed guard. The new Provisional Government announced that it would maintain control of Hawaii "until terms of union with the United States of America have been negotiated." Before another day passed, the "PGs" had sent several representatives en route to Washington, D.C. to attempt to negotiate the terms of annexation. On the less inhabited outer islands of Hawaii the people still had no idea that a "revolution" was underway.

* * * * * * * * * * * * * * * * * * *

This horrid story of betrayal and brute force left Kaiulani feeling exhausted and ill. Now that she knew that Papa and Aunt Liliu and Koa were all right, and the Hawaiian people were in no immediate danger, other concerns began to gnaw at her. First of all, what could she possibly do?! What could she do?! Feeling almost numb with rage at the injustice of it all, at the same time she felt powerless and distraught over her inability to grasp what she herself might do to help. What could she do?

After much debate and consideration Mr. Davies made a suggestion. He asked if she would be willing to go to America with him to speak to the people and the President about what was happening in Hawaii. He and Mrs. Davies would, of course, accompany her, and do everything in their power to help her deliver the message about Hawaii's plight.

Her first reaction to Mr. Davies' proposal was negative. She would love to go to America and tell the people there of the bad decisions and actions that were threatening to violently rip apart her homeland. But she had been feeling so run down lately, body and soul, really. She didn't know how much energy she could muster, and doubted that she had any in reserve.

Kaiulani had been very tired the last several weeks, certainly more than was usual for her. Toby and Miranda had both noticed that she was less vivacious, even occasionally inclined toward lethargy of late. She had lost her appetite for food, or anything else as well, really. The simple pleasures of painting, studying and even singing had paled, she presumed in the stress of her constant anxiety about Hawaii. She was rarely able to sleep through the night, and often woke at three or four in the morning to lie in bed for hours imagining new, worse reports from back home.

When she felt like this it was as if she lived in a separate world from others, shut off by invisible but dense layers of air. It was as if an almost palpable, physical space came between her and the rest of the world. And, on those dreadful occasions when she could actually feel herself starting to slide into a mood of despair, she felt as if she was missing a layer of skin. At those times she felt horribly vulnerable and became acutely, uncomfortably aware of sensations, especially smells and sounds. If this acuity went on for long she could be sure that another wretched headache would follow in its wake.

Kaiulani told Mr. Davies she would need to think it over, about going to America. She was still reeling from the terrible turn of events.

That night she had a strange, clarifying dream. She was being pulled in some sort of cart or tumbrel, moving slowly down a very old road. The Hawaiians who lined the road on both sides for miles were all looking up at Kaiulani in the cart as it rolled past them. She could feel that her hands were either tied or held behind her back in a way that made her feel, by turns, exposed and then very open and proud. She stood tall in the cart and began to sing. The song was a light, sweet tune, rich with melodies and grace. A strong, soft light began to pass back and forth from Kaiulani's face to the uplifted faces of the sad natives all around her. She felt a ray of pure energy and hope shifting from her to the people, and then radiating and reflecting back to her again.

She slept all through the night and woke the next morning feeling tremendously eased and comforted by her dream. At once she dressed and went to find Mr. Davies.

"I know now that I can and must do this, Mr. Davies. I am very sure that my will is strong enough to overcome any obstacles or fears, and that I can count on the energy I will need to have to do this."

Mr. Davies grasped her hand in his own and thanked her for her courage.

"It is not mine alone," she demurred. "Perhaps someday the Hawaiians will say that Kaiulani could have saved us but she didn't even try! I will go with you to America."

There were many arrangements to be made for their trip and only a few days to make them. While the conditions in Hawaii continued to change every moment, Kaiulani and the Davies rushed to make their preparations.

Kaiulani was on her way to America, again.

Chapter Twenty

Rumors about the upheaval flowed like lava from an eruption. In the course of just a few weeks there were wildly conflicting reports about the conditions in Hawaii, which shifted on a daily basis. There was no way for Kaiulani to know what was true.

According to one account Sanford Dole, in his new office as President of the PG, had immediately advocated the swift return of Kaiulani to serve as acting regent, now that the Queen was deposed. Another story held that Kaiulani's father, distressed by Liliuokalani's declaration of a new constitution, had taken it upon himself to call on Lorrin Thurston. Cleghorn was supposed to have pleaded with Thurston, explaining that Princess Kaiulani was held in universally high esteem and could be made acting ruler, to replace Aunt Liliu. This action would require, of course, the appointment of an appropriate board of regents to advise her. They would be carefully selected from the heads of the Provisional Government. And they could make any ultimate decisions regarding all actions that might occur during the brief period until the Princess reached her majority.

Thurston was alleged to have responded to this by assuring Archibald Cleghorn that, although he personally had only the highest regard for the young Princess, matters had already proceeded much too far for such a plan to be considered. The abrogation of the monarchy was "in essence, already completed." Cleghorn was supposed to have been seen leaving Thurston's office - in the new Government Building, which was really Iolani Palace - with bowed head and tears in his eyes.

Upon hearing this last version, the ever-pragmatic Miranda asked how it would be possible to see that someone was crying if they had their head bowed. When Miranda tried to attempt a demonstration of this improbable position, Kaiulani, even in her anxiety, had to laugh at her friend's stubborn practicality. But Toby admonished his sister to "Just forget it, please" and so she did.

Minister Stevens, the Marine troop leader who had taken over the Palace, was said to have sent a repugnant letter to the American State Department. In it he referred to Hawaii as "a fully ripe pear" and gloated that, "Now is the golden hour for the United States to pluck it."

Yet another report claimed that Benjamin Harrison, the soon-to-be-former U.S. President, was very warm to the idea of annexation and had given it his whole-hearted support. The president-elect, Grover Cleveland, however, who would be sworn in within a month, was said to be strongly opposed. Harrison and his Republican administration had even gone so far as to make a public statement that the consideration of statehood for Hawaii had never really been a question at all, since the Hawaiian population was, as the conservative papers so delicately put it, "nine-tenths non-white." In early February, President Harrison sent the first draft of an annexation treaty to the Senate. Cleveland promptly withdrew it when he took office in March.

Although she had every reason to feel discouraged and perplexed by these disparate reports, Kaiulani was surprised to find herself becoming bolder and more determined with each new development. Now that the worst had already happened, in a way, she could face it and begin to struggle with the problems. Kaiulani knew that Aunt Liliu would never give up fighting the gross injustices done to Hawaii; and neither would she.

Papa Cleghorn had only reluctantly approved his daughter's trip to America. His tepid letter advised her to "try to do what you can. I myself am at wit's end and stymied by the apparently endless layers of the whole situation." Not wishing to sound disinterested, perhaps, he advised Kaiulani to "keep your eyes open, talk as little as possible, and never disparage your Aunt."

Kaiulani puzzled over Papa's peculiar warning. Why would she ever speak unkindly of Aunt Liliu, who had always been only loving and kind to her? Why did so many things conspire to confuse her, just when she was trying her hardest to think clearly and sort everything out?!

"Even though I am only seventeen and perhaps considered naive in the eyes of the world," Kaiulani explained to Toby. "Still I can tell what is right and what is wrong. I am not a president or a king, but I can speak out to tell the American people the plain truth."

Before leaving Europe she issued a gentle statement of protest to the London papers. With Toby and Miranda as her eager audience, Kaiulani carefully crafted her first efforts at formally addressing the Americans. Miranda, who had always been fond of poetry and acting, turned out to have an excellent ear for the "*bon mots*" of a speech, and helped Kaiulani in her fervent attempts to say exactly what she meant in a simple, natural way.

Toby assisted a little in terms of logic and clarity, - "the sense of the thing," - he called it. Mostly, though, he loved to listen to Kaiulani's sweet voice and watch her move about as she rehearsed. Mr. Davies served as her proofreader and editor, suggesting that she be more specific on some points, such as referring to Mr. Thurston by name.

Her brief statement to the press was first printed in the London newspapers, and then circulated throughout the American journals as well.

"Four years ago, at the request of Mr. Lorrin Thurston, then a Hawaiian cabinet minister, I was sent away to England to be educated privately and fitted to the position which, by the Constitution of Hawaii, I was to inherit. For all these years I have been patiently in exile, striving to fit myself for my return this year to my country."

"Now I am told that Mr. Thurston is in Washington asking you to take away my flag and my throne. No one even tells me this officially. Have I done anything wrong, that this wrong should be done to me, and to my people? I am coming to Washington to plead for my nation. Will not the great American people hear me?"

The very bad news that Aunt Liliu had been forced to yield and surrender her authority came just a few days before Kaiulani and the Davies' scheduled departure to the United States. Only under adamant protest had the Queen acquiesced, appealing to the government and the power of the American people to restore the monarchy that had been so unjustly torn apart.

The Queen had unequivocally declared her surrender to be "conditional until such time as the Government of the United States shall, upon the facts being presented to it, undo the action of its representatives and reinstate the monarchy." She had sent as her own personal ambassadors to Washington the young *hanai* prince, David Kawananakoa, and Paul Neumann, a trusted attorney and longtime advisor of the Queen.

A shiver ran through Kaiulani at the prospect of seeing Koa again so soon. When she thought about the circumstances in which they would meet, she was sorry that they would see each other at such a sad and stressful time. But it could not be helped; there was nothing to do but be brave and strong and try to weather this storm.

* * * * * * * * * * * * * * * * * * * *

The *Teutonic*, the ship that took the Davies and Kaiulani from London, arrived at New York Harbor in the afternoon on March first. The pier was jammed with newspaper reporters, well wishers and thousands of curious people who had showed up hoping to see Hawaii's Crown Princess.

One of the reporters in the mob that afternoon was the author and journalist, Stephen Crane. Only twenty-two, Crane possessed a fervid desire to know and write about life in all its tawdry, naked passion. His insatiable lust for "experience" made him determined to be "a testing ground for all the sensations of life."

Crane's usual beat was the low-life Bowery district and its many flophouses, as well as several other slum areas of the city. He had come to know these places in the process of researching prostitution and poverty for his first novel, the self-published *"Maggie: A Girl of the Streets."* Having just completed the first draft of his second book, a grisly, realistic story about the American Civil War, he needed to distract himself until he could face tackling the revision. He had been thinking of calling it *"The Great Red Death"* or *"A Badge of Courage"* but wanted to give himself a few more weeks before he committed to a title.

Crane had heard about the half-Scottish, half-Hawaiian Princess who was being educated in England and wanted to see for himself this exotic blend. His own background included preachers and rabble-rousers. His father had been an incendiary Methodist minister and his mother, a minister's daughter. She had also been an avid organizer in the temperance movement; and had died just the previous year. Crane's father succumbed to diphtheria when Stephen was just ten. So Crane had been on his own from an early age. He had ghost written articles for the *New York Tribune* when he was only sixteen. He felt a deep empathy with the half-breed princess who had come from so far away and now was apparently being displaced in her own country when she wasn't even there to fight back. He was also curious to hear what a seventeen-year old, and a royal one, at that, might have to say about such a volatile political situation.

There had been lively debate for some time now on the subjects of "Manifest Destiny" and "Our Expanding Territorial Acquisitions." In England they called it "The White Man's Burden." Everyone in the country seemed to have an opinion on this loaded topic, from streetwalkers to the president. Crane had heard the issue bandied about by the clergy, politicians, newspapers and businessman of every stripe.

America had already conquered its own prairies, forests and wilderness, and damned bad luck for all the former residents. Almost every tribe in the original Indian nation had been ruthlessly destroyed in the process. Now the raging question was whether to "annex" territories overseas.

The conquerors used pompous terms like "solemn duty," "the burden of responsibility" and, - his own personal favorite, - "the inevitable manifestation of destiny." And they all made off with big winnings. But no one called it what it really was: plain, low down robbery. Stealing. Whether it was the British in Africa or the "Reformers" in Hawaii, it all came down to the same thing. Theft, that was all, when you got right down to it. Crane could hear his clergyman father's voice echo in his head, quoting verse.

"'If riches come to you by theft, they will not stay the night with you. They made themselves wings like geese, and flew away to the sky.'" Well, one was never very far from one's personal history, was one, he mused sardonically, no matter how hard one tried.

That almost lustful greed to conquer was certainly what seemed to be the order of the day in Hawaii. He had recently seen a disturbing cartoon in a San Francisco "anti-manifestation" magazine. In this drawing, Hawaii was pictured as a swarthy-skinned, miserable-looking young woman lying flat on her back, suspended in thin air with only a wispy, fragile grapevine weed for support. A nasty, dour faced octopus, with the word "GREED" blazing across its low, furrowed forehead, reached its tentacles of varying sizes and lengths at, into and around the disconsolate figure of the woman. Growing out of the octopus' upper tentacles, which jutted in the opposite direction, were the heads of three "Reformer" leaders. In the middle was Sanford B. Dole, the PG's new president, looking angry, arrogant and smug all at the same time.

A vapid expression graced the mustachioed head of Lorrin Thurston; Crane gathered he was supposed to be the "muscle" of the operation. To Thurston's right was the head of a bearded, sulky looking character called "The Colonel," who wore a red bandanna around his neck. The middle tentacles of the octopus were tightly clenched around rolled-up deeds labeled with the names, "Banker," "Planter," "President," "Marshall" and "Secretary of State." The cartoon left no doubt at all about the way in which the highly organized economic powers - about 98% foreign, he knew, - were "taking" the prone and defenseless Hawaii. To him, it looked like a singularly repulsive depiction of a woman being violated by a beast.

The peculiarly sexualized nature of the "overthrow" was reinforced by another cartoon, which he had seen only the day before in *"Puck,"* England's journal of political satire. No punches had been pulled here, either. A sour-looking, half-blind minister was forcibly "marrying" an old, arthritic, disgusted-looking Uncle Sam, who knelt painfully at the altar and held on tight to the arm of a stooped-over, half-naked, young, black woman with bare breasts. The woman had caricatured, distorted large lips and a fearful, trapped expression. "Another Shotgun Wedding," the caption read, "with neither party willing." An obese businessman stood close behind the couple, lording his weight over the whole sordid affair, grasping a shotgun and sneering as he made sure that the service was carried through.

* * * * * * * * * * * * * * * * * * *

"Well," Crane thought, as he tried to angle himself for a better look at the steamer, he hoped he would see this Princess, after such a long wait. Ah, there she was. She looked like she was trying to say something but he couldn't hear any words at all. He cupped both ears toward the spot where she stood alone on deck. People to all sides of him pulled their collars up against the wind and cold and shielded their eyes from the bright, winter's end sunshine.

Kaiulani tried to speak but felt faint when she looked out at the hordes of people who had come to hear her. Dizzy and disoriented, she was sure she would fall. Then a sharp wave of recognition shot through her as she took in the afternoon sun that sparkled back at her from the water. She suddenly remembered the way the sun had glinted off Papa Moi's crown, when he lifted it up to show it to the people at the coronation in Honolulu so many years ago.

"Unbidden," Kaiulani began in an uncertain, quavering voice, "I stand upon your shores today, where I had hoped so soon to receive a royal welcome."

Almost choking, she gulped down a ragged, uneven breath. Hundreds or thousands of faces, an ocean of faces, waited for her to continue. One jangled thought after another raced through her mind. She was terrified, she was going to pass out...

As if it came from inside her, she heard the calm voice of her singing teacher, Mr. Tyrol, Sergei, telling her to "always connect it with something you love." Thinking of Mama Nui and Ainahau and Koa and Miss Gardinier and Miranda and Toby and Fairy, she felt her fear drop away; a sense of grace and assurance replaced it. Though her heart fluttered with the gravity of the moment, when she spoke to the crowd again her voice was loud and clear as a bell.

"I come unattended except for the loving hearts that have come with me over the winter seas."

A deep, attentive silence settled over the crowd as people stood still and strained to hear.

"Commissioners from my land, I have heard, have for many days been in your country, asking you to take away my little vineyard. They speak no word to me, and leave me to find out as best I can from the rumors of the air that they would leave me without a home or a nation or a name."

A sob caught deep inside made her tremulous words seem to shimmer in the air like haunting, sweet, sad music. Even the reporters in the crowd stopped writing for a moment to listen to the young princess.

"Seventy years ago Christian America sent over Christian men and women to give religion and civilization to Hawaii."

The flashing spirit of a warrior woman moved through the Princess like lightning, striking and informing her speech, which grew stronger and fiercer with every breath.

"Three of the sons of those missionaries are at your capitol today asking you to undo their fathers' work. Who sent them?" She barely recognized her own voice, which echoed back at her as if she was standing in a valley or a canyon.

"Who gave them the authority to break the Constitution which they swore to uphold?"

"Today, I, a poor, weak girl with not one of my people near me, and all these Hawaiian statesmen against me, have the strength to stand up for the rights of my people."

The depth of her feeling transformed her words into a brave and steady cry. "I can hear their wail in my heart." She shivered as something moved through her again.

"It gives me strength and courage; and I am strong. Strong in the faith of God, strong in the knowledge that I am right, strong in the strength of seventy million people who, in this free land, will hear my cry and will refuse to let their flag cover dishonor to mine!"

The applause was deafening, coming at her wave upon wave. Mr. Davies, as pre-arranged, fielded questions from the reporters. He told them they would be staying at the Brevoort House on the East Side where he would be glad to arrange interviews. Then he shepherded his party through the crowds and into the waiting carriages.

Another crush of reporters and curious citizens had to be navigated when they arrived at the hotel. Kaiulani felt exhausted but happy, as if she had run a long race and won. She was excited, exhilarated, - and, at the same time, triumphant over some deep, underlying sadness which she overcame again and again, each time she spoke out.

* * * * * * * * * * * * * * * * * * * *

Her time in America had a magical quality about it. The eighteen days of the visit, as they traveled from New York to Boston to Washington and then back to New York again, passed like a dream. A spirit of *aloha* touched her and through that spirit she was able to reach out to the people of the land. All who heard her speak about Hawaii with such passion and so much love were moved; even those who believed her mission was doomed to fail; even those who thought her brave but foolish.

Kaiulani knew, for the first time since she had left Hawaii, exactly what she was doing and why. She felt blessed, in a way, comforted and strengthened by her sense of mission. She was Victoria Lunalilo Kaiulani, Hawaii's Crown Princess, searching out the kindred spirits of those who might hear and help her people; revealing her heart and the hopes of her tribe to be made whole and happy again.

There was something ethereal about her. But there was also an earthy sensuality in the mix of cultures and realities she had known in her short life that transformed her into a powerful magnet.

Wherever Kaiulani went people turned out to see her, to catch a glimpse of the vibrant young princess. Men and women alike were drawn to her rich, velvety voice and the riveting, compelling gaze of her deep, dark eyes, which had seen so much sorrow but still remained wide with wonder.

The press went wild. In New York they wrote, "The Princess impresses one as tall and slight with decidedly good eyes, which are a soft brown. Her hair is almost black and somewhat wavy. Her complexion is dark but not more so than many girls one meets every day on Broadway."

Another report said, "The Princess is a tall, beautiful young woman of sweet face and slender figure. She has the soft, dark eyes and dark complexion that mark the Hawaiian beauty."

Even Stephen Crane, the reporter who was best known for his acid tongue and caustic wit, could not help but admire the brown-skinned princess. He was uncharacteristically full of praise, even loquacious as he described her demeanor and style.

"She wore yesterday, when she left the steamship," Crane enthused, "a simple, gray traveling gown with a dark jacket and some sort of fluffy hat which was not unbecoming. She talks in a very simple, dignified way and seems possessed of decidedly more common sense than most young women of seventeen or eighteen."

Before they left London Mr. Davies had sent word ahead to Dr. John Mott-Smith, Queen Liliuokalani's minister in Washington, to let him know when they would arrive. His response had been a curt telegram that said only, "Cannot use assistance yet." Despite this brusque reply, Dr. Mott-Smith was waiting to greet them at the Brevoort House.

Another crush of reporters had descended like locusts, filling up the hotel's parlors and public rooms. Mr. Davies and Dr. Mott-Smith dealt with them, while the ladies went to their suites to rest and bathe. Later in the day Mr. Davies was unpleasantly surprised by a terse exchange with the doctor. They had worked well as a team together all afternoon, deftly fielding the reporters' questions while remaining genial and forthcoming. But as soon as the newsmen were gone, Dr. Mott-Smith glared at Mr. Davies and coolly asked him for a moment alone.

"With all due respect, Mr. Davies," the doctor said in a tight, clipped tone, "It was not perhaps the best idea, or even in particularly good taste, for you to have brought the Princess here at this juncture."

Mr. Davies was amazed by his outburst. Quite unused to being addressed in such a way, he, too, became cold.

"I hope you will remember, sir, that it is her country, too, which is endangered."

"Nevertheless," Dr. Mott-Smith continued through clenched teeth, "there are certain unspoken matters of protocol."

Blushing to the roots of his fine, thin red hair, Mr. Davies was very angry. "Well, speak of them now, then, Dr. Smith, or be good enough to have done with them."

Dr. Mott-Smith's response was to grab his hat and pearl-buttoned gloves, nod sharply at Mr. Davies, then turn on his heel and leave.

Around eight o'clock that evening Prince David Kawananakoa arrived to pay his respects to the Princess. Mr. Davies had barely had time to change his clothes and was leaden with fatigue from dealing with the crowds of callers all day long. He was also still wounded by Dr. Mott-Smith's angry words. He soon made the Prince apprised of his feelings.

"Well," Koa said, taken aback and feeling extremely awkward, "You must know there are rumors and such about the Reformers asking the Queen to step down and replacing her with my cousin, with Kaiulani, and then instituting—" He could not keep a sneer out of his tone - "a supposedly temporary board of *haole* advisors to 'help' her rule."

This time it was Mr. Davies who turned on his heel and walked out of the room. Koa was forced to wait restlessly with the remainder of the still considerable crowd in the public rooms of the Brevoort. It was nearly ten o'clock when Mrs. Davies finally came down and spoke to the disconsolate Prince.

"Kaiulani is in the parlor upstairs," she explained politely enough, but added with a definite edge. "She will have only a few minutes to see you."

Koa twisted the sterling silver duck's head of his stylish walking cane as he sheepishly followed Maddie Davies up the long, winding staircase.

Refreshed after a long bath, a short nap and a light supper, Kaiulani eagerly awaited Koa's arrival. She wore a pale-lavender gown, embroidered with pink roses, tiny green leaves and vine tendrils, which was very becoming. Koa had on light, finely tailored pinstriped trousers with a smartly fitted cummerbund at his waist and a dark, contrasting cutaway jacket. His fedora hat was tilted a little to one side and he looked dapper, in spite of his long wait. In fact, with his mustache waxed and carefully curled up on both sides, an Italian silk scarf at his neck and a white linen handkerchief in his breast pocket, he looked very fine.

Kaiulani smiled happily as she stood up to greet him and was shocked to find that they were now almost the same height.

Koa laughed a little and gave her a light, pecking kiss on the cheek. "Well," he said, "I hope we shall still dance well together!"

He was much too polite and formal with her; and Kaiulani understood right away that, for some reason, he disapproved of her visit. But the rich, sandalwood smell he brought into the room with him was like an independent message from home.

How she wanted to touch him! She needed him to hold her in his strong, familiar arms. She felt that she had to rest, protected and content in the safety of his muscular arms, peaceful again in the intimate, tender world they had shared.

Instead, they chatted like total strangers, hardly even seeing each other, allowing their few precious minutes to slip away.

"Oh, Koa!" She longed to say to him, "Look, please! It's me, Kaiulani! Don't you go away from me now, too!"

But they only went on about the length of their visits, their busy itineraries, the weather and the lobbying they would both do for Hawaii. They agreed that they would meet again for a longer visit if they saw each other in Washington, or perhaps when she returned to New York.

Then Mrs. Davies was at the door again, clearing her throat and saying that it was time for him to leave. Kaiulani pleaded with Maddie, begging her with her eyes to leave them alone again, just for a moment. Although Maddie gave her a disapproving look, the new wife took pity and acquiesced.

The second she had gone the Princess moved in closer to the Prince. Abandoning her reserve entirely she held on to him lightly, a delicate hug. Suddenly, surprisingly, he relaxed and dropped his stiff, artificial posture of *bonhomie* to return her gentle embrace.

The voice in her ear was so low that she was not sure, at first, if he had spoken at all. The Hawaiian words were so muted they felt like a soft wind that whispered by her face and hair. She released Koa's shoulders and put her hands on his warm, close face and looked into his wide, dark eyes.

A slow, easy smile floated onto his face, just like in the old days; like the early morning sun beginning to rise. He said to her again, *"He pili wehena 'ole."*

"'A blood relationship'," she translated, gladly returning his smile.

"'A relationship that cannot be undone'," He corrected, kissing her cheek one more time before he left her alone in the room.

Chapter Twenty-One

Asteady, soft snow began to drift down as their train left Grand Central Depot in New York. By the time they reached the outskirts of Boston more than two feet of powdery-white had piled up, sparkling like wet diamonds in the late afternoon sun.

On the train ride from New York to Boston Kaiulani had been lost in thought. Their last day in New York, Kaiulani, Theo and Maddie made a brisk sight seeing tour of the city, which included a stop at the new, monstrously large Seventh Regiment Armory where hundreds of American troops were stationed. The soldiers on duty had seemed to her like a giant colony of ants, swarming into, out of and around the imposing mortar and brick building. The vision of so many young, male bodies, all alike in their stiff, heavy uniforms, every one so determined and implacable in their ceaseless, energetic movements, made Kaiulani try to imagine what Liliu must have gone through a few weeks earlier in Hawaii. How had her Aunt felt when the American troops surrounded her home, her own Iolani Palace?

Had Aunt Liliu been afraid of the American soldiers? Had they pointed their guns at the palace, or at Liliu or the few guards who remained, unarmed and defenseless, staying with their Queen until the last possible minute? Perhaps Aunt Liliu had been haughty and disdainful, looking through the young soldiers with steely disregard, as if they were not even there. As if the soldiers were only wind ghosts, noisy but invisible and harmless, fit only to frighten small children and babies.

The thought of all that aggressive, volatile energy around Iolani Palace; and the idea of the soldiers perhaps daring to train their sights on her stern and dignified Aunt, trying to threaten her, disoriented Kaiulani. It seemed so uncalled for, so inappropriate - like using a huge, heavy lasso, the kind for rounding up wild horses, to catch a small, still peacock which was not even trying to go anywhere.

The Princess tried to clear these distressing images from her mind. She noticed a newspaper from Washington on the seat beside her and picked it up to read. Inside was an interview with Koa who had told a reporter that Mr. Davies had "acted unwisely, to say the least," by bringing his cousin, Princess Kaiulani, into the "unpleasant confusion of the moment."

Poor Koa! Didn't he understand that they were all caught up in this storm together? Only the memory of his warm breath in her hair and his familiar voice murmuring of their "blood relationship" comforted her, a little.

When the train stopped at Providence a statuesque woman, her hair a mass of dark, auburn curls, came on board. She wore a vivid, garish purple traveling suit and had a commanding presence. From the familiar way she began to chat with Maddie and Mr. Davies, Kaiulani assumed she must be someone they knew. But she was soon introduced to her as Miss Marcy Smithson, a reporter from *The Boston Globe*. Although Miss Smithson tried several times to engage Kaiulani in their conversation, the Princess held herself aloof, put off by the woman's familiarity and her overly-modulated voice.

Sensitive to Kaiulani's discomfort, Maddie kindly trundled her friend off to the other side of the car under the pretense of showing her the view. From their secluded spot Kaiulani caught bits of Smithson's interview. When she heard Mr. Davies say, "She sings very well, unless she thinks someone is listening," she realized with a start that he was talking about her, and sounding like a doting father. A few minutes later she saw the woman lean forward and nod, her red hair spilling over her notebook as she scribbled away while Mr. Davies confided, "Yes, very high-spirited. Much like her mother, who was the sister of the late King and the present Queen."

To hear her guardian talk about her and her family made Kaiulani feel weirdly invisible. Mr. Davies' remarks seemed to be about someone she did not know, a stranger, some other young woman who had nothing to do with her.

* * * * * * * * * * * * * * * * * * * *

Washington was a flurry of activity anticipating Cleveland's second inauguration and some of that liveliness had affected Boston as well. Despite the messy weather the citizens of that city had turned out in droves to greet the Hawaiian Princess. Mr. Davies' handsome son, Clive, from his first marriage years ago, was waiting at the station to meet them with a group of his friends. Students at the Institute of Technology, they were falling all over themselves, one more excited than the next at the thought of escorting or serving or just being near Kaiulani and her entourage.

Twilight had begun to fall as their train pulled in to Boston Station. Clive and his companions held up a purple and yellow banner; in large, uneven letters it proclaimed, "Welcome, Princess Kaiulani! From Friends and Supporters of Hawaii!" The sight of the tall, exotic woman, her complexion the color of *cafe au lait*, in her closely fitted, midnight-blue serge suit and her hat plumed with ostrich feathers made the young men cheer and applaud as she descended from the train. Kaiulani smiled at them all, graciously repeating the names of each one as a suddenly tongue-tied Clive shyly introduced them.

The party was whisked away to the Brunswick Hotel where the concierge at once showed Kaiulani to her private quarters. The rooms of the Venetian Suite were richly paneled with cherubs and roses, and grape leaves were carved everywhere into the dark mahogany and cherry woods of the window frames, doorways and arches. She looked out through the lacey Irish curtains that covered the tiny, elegant windows, some no bigger than in a ship captain's galley that ran the expanse of one side of the sitting room.

Kaiulani saw an exciting panorama of city life below her on Boylston Street. Hundreds of Bostonians, undaunted by the weather, trudged through deep snow bundled in woolens and furs, wearing sturdy boots or snowshoes. Boys and girls fenced with makeshift ski poles or played and made angels in the snow, while well-dressed, refined couples of all ages came and went in carriages. Some rushed off to the opera or grand charity balls. Others hurried to quiet evenings with twenty or thirty of the town's other most distinguished citizens in one or another of the city's lovely old mansions, where they indulged in lavish eight course dinners accompanied by hours of chamber music.

Even while the rush in front of her made Kaiulani's heart race, she felt alone. She longed for Toby and Miranda; she wanted to be with her old, dear friends. She felt suddenly drained and dizzy from the journey and the non-stop pace they had maintained since leaving England.

Grateful to have a light supper in the hotel's dining room with Maddie, Mr. Davies and the starry-eyed Clive, she excused herself early to snuggle up by the fire with a book in her soft, warm bed.

The next day, Saturday, was Cleveland's Inauguration. Boston was colder than when they had arrived but a bright, strong sun made the snowdrifts almost blinding in their dazzling whiteness. Kaiulani rested, taking care to ward off a cold by drinking cups of hot tea laced with honey and lemon. A note came mid-morning from Clive. He invited them to join him and his friends for a "proper, old-fashioned Boston sleigh ride."

Cheered by the prospect of being outdoors, even in the cold weather, Kaiulani forgot about her sniffles and eagerly conferred with Maddie about what to wear. She persuaded Kaiulani to borrow one of her fur coats, a heavy, very dark-brown sable. It was wonderfully becoming, highlighting and accentuating Kaiulani's colors. Maddie was delighted with the effect and Mr. Davies declared with enthusiasm that Kaiulani looked exactly like an Eskimo queen. Maddie laughed, kissed her husband's cheek and demanded that he tell them at once when he had ever seen any Eskimos at all, never mind their queen.

An old, ornate Russian carriage, generously decorated with carvings and painted folk art designs, picked them up at the hotel. Kaiulani, Maddie and Mr. Davies sat in the seats of honor in front while Clive and his gang clustered behind them, jockeying for position to be closest to the ladies, showing off and flirting with them. The crisp air blew roses into everyone's cheeks as the rickety wooden sleigh jangled and bounced along, sluicing through the snowy streets of Boston. Everyone - Clive, the other students, even Theo - was eager to point out the many historical sites to Kaiulani and Maddie, who had neither of them been east before except to visit New York.

They dashed down Boylston Street and saw the delicate spires, pillars and intricately cut stones of Trinity Church. Then they flew past the plain, Puritan grace of Old South Church. Turning off at Charles Street they cut across the famous Boston Common "where cattle and sheep grazed in the 17th century," Clive informed them in a tone so unduly solemn and grave that everyone, including him, had to laugh.

They raced past Beacon Street and Beacon Hill, then on to the State House with its gleaming golden dome. They dashed down Park Street to the white steeple of old Park Church at the corner of Tremont and Park; then on to Brimstone Corner where the American Colonial army had kept their gunpowder supplies stored in the old Meeting House during the War of 1812. On Charlestown Heights they saw the obelisk-shaped tower, which stood tall in memory of the battle of 1775 and the brave soldiers who had fought down to their last bullet.

Near the end of the ride Michael Arthur, III, a handsome young man who had not said a word when Clive's group met the train the day before, presented the Princess with a bouquet of colorful hothouse flowers. This unexpected reminder of the approaching spring filled Kaiulani with joy. Graciously she accepted the flowers from the arms of the smitten young man, held them close to her heart and told him, "I will keep them warm, here."

Overwhelmed, Michael was so in awe of the Princess that it seemed he would not be able to speak. Clive pushed gently at his shoulder and tried to prompt him.

"What, did you forget your speech, already?"

Michael swallowed hard and collected himself. Bowing low to Kaiulani laboriously stammered out, "They are - n - n-n- n - ot - as s-s-s-sweet - as - - -" He sighed and tried again. "N-n-n-n-o - m-m-match for your b-b-beauty."

"Nor for your thoughtfulness," the Princess returned.

Made bold by her praise, Michael spoke again with only a hint of his former struggle.

"I w-was b-born in - Hawaii!"

"I see." Kaiulani lifted one of the flowers from the bouquet and tucked it into his lapel.

"You must be one of my subjects, then." Her low, flirtatious voice surprised no one more than her. "Isn't that right? You belong to me."

Clive and Mr. Davies looked shocked but Maddie beamed with admiration and Michael nodded happily, charmed by the Princess' easy wit. Despite the rocking motion of the sleigh, he managed to lower himself onto one knee in front of her and respectfully kissed her gloved hand, much to his comrades' rowdy amazement.

"Y-you m-m-must - allow - me to p-p-prove my l-l-l-loyal, loyal-l-l - my all-liegence, then."

"Ah!" declared Clive in a mock-serious tone, "The swain needs a task! A trial, a tribulation! A grail for the Princess Kaiulani!"

Clive's father cuffed his son playfully, as if intending to chide him, but instead entered into the boisterous spirit of the moment as he pretended to whisper into Michael's ear.

"She is very fond, you know," Theo said to Michael, "of musical events and the opera."

Michael rose, flushed with daring. His sense of mission almost defeated his trembling tongue so that his stutter was barely noticeable.

"If you w-w-will p-p-permit—allow me, I believe I can s-s-secure tickets for the opera - t-t-t-tomorrow n-n-night." His cherubic face flushed with pride.

So, on their last night in Boston, Kaiulani, Maddie, Mr. Davies and the Princess' adoring subject, one Michael Arthur, III, were seated in a private box at the Boston Opera. The program, "Manon Lescaut" by Jules Massenet, was being performed for the second time, having premiered a year or two earlier at *L'Opera Comique* in Paris. "Manon" was the story of a tender young woman who loved pleasure too well and so came to a tragic end.

Looking out over the opulent crowd, Kaiulani was grateful that Maddie had insisted that they shop for one "special occasion" ensemble for their trip. She had even treated Kaiulani to a day of shopping in Paris.

* * * * * * * * * * * * * * * * * * *

"My dear," Maddie had overridden Kaiulani's protests about time and money, "Once we actually get to Paris, we will only need to make a few stops in a matter of hours, I promise you! And never mind, please, about money. We have plenty to go around. I won't hear another word about it, not one."

"Besides," Maddie said firmly, "It's extremely important for you to be properly dressed for this tour. This is no minor affair, you know, your going about to meet the American people and talk to them about Hawaii."

When they arrived in Paris Mrs. Davies, who was well acquainted with all the best shops, took Kaiulani right away to the gleaming, huge "*Le Bon Marche*," the largest, first and only store of its kind in the world.

Many believed that the real future of merchandising was embodied in this unprecedented phenomenon. "*Le Grande Magasin*" was a veritable temple of commerce, a palace of worldly goods. Sectioned into mazes of separate, individual "departments," the *Bon Marche* boasted row after row of clothing, accessories and house wares. Each row was designed with artistically arranged displays that showcased everything from fashions to shoes, coats and dishes in an overwhelming variety of sizes, shapes and colors. *Le Bon Marche* was the epitome of *au courant* style. The women spent several hours there, and returned with a staggering load of packages, tired but triumphant, as if they had been on a long hunt.

Maddie had demanded that Kaiulani join her in picking out at least "one really good dress" for the theater or whatever other fancy event might come up.

"My dear," she decreed, "you absolutely must." They had been wildly successful, and Maddie was thrilled now that the opera in Boston provided the perfect place to show off their "*haute couture*."

* * * * * * * * * * * * * * * * * * * *

Maddie wore a "casino-style" gown of pale yellow with faint overtones of grass green. There was ruffled, beige-gold lace gathered at the cuffs and collar and edging all three tiers of her floor length skirt. The bodice was a fitted, ivory satin shirtwaist with eight rows of gold lace in front and another eight rows on the back. The squared off, fashionably oversized shoulders went out well beyond any natural span of Mrs. Davies' limbs, making her look like she had grown lacy angel's wings. A forest-green, silk sash nipped in her waist. She wore short, white, kid gloves, and her green velvet hat had a pale fuchsia flower off to one side and four deep brown, crushed velvet roses on the other.

Kaiulani's dress was grass green silk trimmed with muslin-colored lace at the low "sweetheart" neckline, which wonderfully showed off her shoulders and throat. A silk flower of a pink shade called "dusty rose," or "roses of ashes," was pinned above her right breast. Her poufed sleeves were gathered and tucked in under her lace-shawled collar, then pulled tight again above her elbow length, white satin gloves. A fall of delicate lacework draped at the edge of the sleeves from the elbows to above the wrists, finished off at the cuffs with an irregular hem that fluttered with every movement.

When they were ready to leave Maddie hugged Kaiulani close.

"My dear, you look so sweet!"

Kaiulani laughed and admitted that she had been trying to decide whether she looked more like a little girl dressed for a birthday party or an extravagant pastry.

They arrived at the opera radiant with excitement. Kaiulani blushed when Maddie pointed out the looks coming their way; but she could not deny that she felt the heat of admiring eyes. It was like a spotlight was shining on their box and illuminating them, though, of course, the strong light was actually reflecting back to them from the brilliantly lit stage. Kaiulani felt as if she, too, was a performer that night. And, with no lines to memorize or actions to worry about, she found that she enjoyed both the attention and her heightened sense of visibility and power. Young Michael Arthur, III could hardly take his eyes off her long enough to glance at the stage.

The opera was the story of Manon Lescaut, a pretty country girl with an eager, open heart, who loved to laugh but was just as easily moved to tears by suffering. Her tender response to all creatures flowed easily and naturally. Manon's poor but respectable family was troubled by what they perceived as their daughter's excessive sensuality. Her headstrong behavior - rescuing stray animals, talking to strangers, being uninhibited in her vast curiosity about life, - all this made them fear that Manon's simple nature would make her vulnerable to the whims and temptations of others not as pure as she. They decided to send her away to a convent, both for her own protection and for their peace of mind.

On her way to the convent Manon has an arranged meeting with her cousin, Lescaut, who is one of the Royal Guards. Lescaut leaves his attractive cousin alone when he goes to search for her luggage; soon, a wealthy, bawdy old man propositions her but she merely laughs at him, taking his overtures as a joke. Not long after the old man leaves in a huff a handsome young aristocrat, Des Grieux, discovers the high-spirited woman and they fall in love on the spot. By the end of Act One, Des Grieux and Manon have run away to Paris.

At the first intermission a spirited discussion began about whether or not it was, in fact, possible to "fall in love at first sight." Mr. Davies and Kaiulani were skeptical that such a thing could happen; while Maddie and Michael, both staunch believers in romance, argued in favor.

When Michael and Mr. Davies returned with hot cocoas and a paper twist of chocolate creams for the ladies, Michael shyly told Kaiulani that her earrings were the most beautiful he had ever seen. Kaiulani touched one hand to her ear and flushed with pleasure as she remembered they were a gift from Toby.

* * * * * * * * * * * * * * * * * * *

As soon as he heard she was going to America, Toby had secretly commissioned an exclusive London jeweler to design them.

"Oh, Toby, they're so beautiful!" Kaiulani's eyes sparkled as she held them up to catch the light. From a rose-gold wire a square-cut garnet hung, rich and red as blood, suspended in a gold, rectangular setting. Below the garnet a seed pearl was attached with a tiny loop of gold.

"I had them made for you. I wanted to give you something as unique as you are. And garnets are good luck for travelers! I have it on the best authority that they will ensure a successful trip abroad and your safe return home."

Kaiulani turned from side to side to show him how they looked.

"Even better than I had hoped." He delicately touched her cheek. "Though nothing could ever be as lovely as you. The pearls are for your precious Hawaii, that beautiful jewel which informs and is the foundation of all you do."

They kissed, as they had so many times before, in friendship and love, once again putting aside the tremors that stirred their blood when they embraced.

* * * * * * * * * * * * * * * * * * *

The intermission lights blinked signaling the second act and brought Kaiulani back to the present.

"Are y-y-you f-feeling w-w-well?" Michael was looking at her with some concern.

Kaiulani nodded.

"You seemed very f-f-ar away just then," he said. Are your ear-r-rrings r-r-royal heirlooms? P-p-perhaps you are w-worried about l-l-losing them?"

Kaiulani smiled and shook her head, taking his arm as they made their way back to their seats. "Thank you," she touched the earrings again, "they are a gift from a very dear friend. He says they will make me lucky."

Michael was relieved that Kaiulani had returned from her reverie. "W-w-ell, I s-s-suppose even a P-p-p-princess can use s-s-ome l-l-luck."

In the second act Manon and Des Grieux are happy together in a small apartment and plan to marry. But an older, wealthier aristocrat, who has been secretly watching Manon, lures her away. The pleasure loving Manon is not strong enough to withstand temptation and betrays her lover, abandoning him for the promise of a more glamorous life. By the third act Des Grieux, devastated and in despair, enters a monastery. A repentant Manon seeks him out and begs to rekindle their love. At first he refuses but then Des Grieux gives in and admits that he has never stopped loving her.

By Act Three they have lost all their money. Des Grieux gambles; through a series of events, the lovers are imprisoned. Des Grieux is released but Manon is kept in jail to be transported to a penal colony overseas. Exhausted and ill, she escapes to find her lover one last time. They remember the happiness they have shared, but it is too late for Manon. Dying, she tells her lover, "It had to be this way."

"What a sad story!" Maddie exclaimed, dabbing away at tears as they settled in for the carriage ride back to the hotel.

"V-v-v-ery s-s-sad," Michael agreed.

"If only she had been less impetuous!" Maddie exclaimed. "And stayed with Des Grieux and been faithful!"

"But then, my dear," Mr. Davies patted his wife's gloved hand, "We should have had only the first act and nothing more to follow."

Maddie and Michael laughed at Mr. Davies' business-like logic. But Kaiulani, who had been silent since the opera's end, spoke out with real passion.

"Perhaps not, though, Maddie. We have no real reason to think that love would have carried them through to happiness in the end. The element of fate, or destiny, or whatever one wishes to call it, seems to have doomed her from the start."

"Perhaps no effort of will or determination on her part would have made any difference at all." Kaiulani seemed to be somewhere far away as she continued in her pensive tone. "If it was meant to be, perhaps nothing could have changed it."

An uncomfortable silence followed her melancholy assessment. Then Mrs. Davies surprised everyone, including herself, when she recited from memory.

> "Riddle of destiny, who can show
> What thy short visit meant or know
> What thy errand here below?"

"C-Charles L-lamb!" Michael's excitement at recognizing the quote was so intense that his stammer all but disappeared. "We've just finished s-s-studying him at school. *'On an Infant D-Dying as Soon as Born.'* "H-he s-s-stammered, too," he said shyly.

"Yes, he did." Maddie smiled at Michael. "He was my grandfather's close friend. My father used to read his poetry to us often, especially at bedtime."

She closed her eyes to remember more. "'I have had playmates, I have had companions -" Maddie opened her eyes again. "Then something else, another line, and then -"

Maddie and Michael spoke the phrase together.

"All, all are gone, the old familiar faces.'"

"Now, now!" Mr. Davies' tone was a bit brusque. "That's quite enough tragedy for one evening. Who wants to go for a spot of tea?"

A mischievous light gleamed in Kaiulani's eyes, her pessimistic mood cast aside. "As far as I'm concerned, I believe that going out for tea is destined to be our fate for tonight."

At the hotel cafe young Michael Arthur, III rambled on and on about all the many pleasures of Boston in better weather, and about all the places he would like to show Kaiulani if she ever came back "when the weather improves." He told her about the Swan Boat rides in Public Park, which ran on bicycle-like paddles that you operated with your feet. There was the brand new Museum of Fine Arts at Copley Square, and Boston's excellent Public Library, both designed in Italian Renaissance style. And the Boston Symphony, of course, and the Boston Pops Orchestra, and so many lovely parks and boating activities that made for splendid good times, in fairer weather, of course.

Kaiulani seemed to listen with interest but she had in fact retreated to a place inside herself. She wondered where Aunt Liliu, Papa and Fairy were right now, what they were doing, and what was happening in Hawaii. If only there was something she could do!

* * * * * * * * * * * * * * * * * * *

On their last day in Boston they visited first Clive's school, and then the Wellesley College for women, where Kaiulani found herself feeling a twinge of regret. Just before she left Hawaii, there had been some discussion that she might eventually be sent to school at Wellesley to finish her education, as well as to become more familiar with "the unique American spirit," as Mr. Thurston had rather obtusely described it.

At Wellesley, an official committee took them through the classrooms and science laboratories, the art museum, libraries and music studios. The cozy, scholarly atmosphere of the campus appealed to her immensely. It was so quiet, she thought, so self-sufficient and complete. Everything seemed orderly and so organized - an independent community unto itself.

When the midday bell rang they were suddenly surrounded by scores of excited young women who gave Kaiulani their best school cheer, shouting out to welcome her again and again. Then the college music club sang a rousing rendition of the school's Alma Mater and a crowd of well-wishers accompanied them to their carriage. The good will of these people enveloped her, making her feel for a moment as if she was back home.

Everything had gone very well in Boston. And though they knew that a handful of disgruntled Provisional Government agents had been trying to stir up sympathies against them, they had encountered no trouble in public or private. Now they were facing what would probably be the most difficult part of their journey.

* * * * * * * * * * * * * * * * * * *

Their train was scheduled to arrive in Washington at about noon. For a moment Kaiulani allowed herself to fantasize that Koa might be there to meet them, although she had no reason to think so. She was not even sure if he was still in New York, or if he had come back to Washington at all.

They arrived at the red brick Baltimore and Potomac Railroad Station at precisely noon on March 8th. Located on the corner of 6th Street and Constitution Avenue, the brand new terminal boasted an abundance of spacious waiting rooms. A long, covered platform extended out for more than 130 feet at one end of the building to accommodate the trains that came and went around the clock.

A gaggle of reporters waited for them, as they had in every city throughout their trip. When they arrived at the Arlington Hotel and Kaiulani stepped down from the carriage, the reporters descended on her like a flock of vultures. Some even perched on her luggage after it was unloaded from the carriage that had followed behind them.

The Washington reporters were very aggressive, greedy for any news.

"How long will you be here?" one shouted to Kaiulani.

Before she could begin to answer another belted out. "Do you expect to see the Prince, your cousin," - the reporter read each syllable of the name out from his notes - "Prince Ka-wa-na-na-koa, - while you're here?"

A lanky reporter with a booming voice and a shiny, bald head pushed his way to the front of the crowd. "Say, Princess," he brayed, "When're you going to the White House and visit 'Frankie'?"

Kaiulani knew that was the Americans' pet name for their beloved first lady. She nodded to acknowledge his question.

"In Hawaii," she courteously explained, "We prefer to wait for an invitation."

"Ah, she probably wouldn't care," the same reporter drawled. "She likes everyone."

"Yes, but I would," the Princess remained gracious. "And for the same reason, I believe, as well as out of my respect for her."

They were soon settled into their rooms at the Arlington Hotel. The hotel was a luxury establishment, which boasted electric lighting, 500 guest rooms and an impressive four, fully equipped "bathrooms" for all the guests to share.

Not until they were unpacked did Kaiulani learn from the concierges' captain that Koa had, in fact, already been there. He had waited for her a long time, carrying a hand made *lei* of pink roses. Unable to push through the relentless mob, he had left the flowers with a message for her at the front desk.

"I am only sorry they could not be *pikakae* flowers. Love, Your Cousin Koa."

More to her chagrin than to her surprise, he had left no information to say where or how to reach him.

* * * * * * * * * * * * * * * * * * *

"What if no one comes or they won't listen? What if the PGs, or others who want to discredit us, become sarcastic or unkind?" Kaiulani had confessed to Maddie and Theo that her concerns about the success of their visit were strongest here in Washington, where their reception and the response could make such a difference.

"I don't know if I could bear being mocked or laughed at, if it came to that."

That night Kaiulani dreamed that she was falling down a deep, dark hole, gripped by a harsh sense of vertigo and unable to catch her breath. The next morning she woke feeling winded and even more anxious than before. She had never been so worried before in her life. It had been very hard to lose Mama, of course, and, later, to leave Hawaii. The sense of isolation and the feeling of being abandoned were overpowering both times. But this knot of fear in her belly was so tight that it felt like a clenched up fist that was hitting and punching her.

There was no question that their time in Washington held the highest stakes of all. Would the President and his new government recognize them and sympathize with Hawaii's plight? The hard truth was that only he could give them any real, effective help. No matter how receptive or encouraging the American people might be to Kaiulani, only the leader of their country wielded the power to take action.

Feeling like her heart was in her mouth most of the time Kaiulani gave her speech over and over to the factions in Washington. The reactions were different here than in Boston or New York. The Washington audiences, who often heard several lectures a week, seemed more jaded and judgmental; not ready to make up their minds or lend their approval to anything on the spot. And there were always a few sullen looking men who lurked at the back of the hall in pairs or small clusters; sometimes they even scowled at her. These, she knew, were the PGs, working day and night, avid to push through a fast conclusion to the matter that could only lead, sooner or later, to the end of Hawaii as she knew it.

The debates were heated. Some condemned Stevens and his marines as scoundrels; some demanded a thorough investigation at once; while others insisted that the whole thing was just a clever move to bring the sugar industry and Hawaii's economy under control. There was speculation that the whole sordid affair was a "sham takeover," an elaborate act, perhaps even engineered by the devious, domineering Queen herself in a base, deceitful attempt to draw attention to the monarchy's dubious cause.

One California paper demanded that Minister Stevens be recalled from Honolulu and brought up on immediate charges of wrongdoing, or even treason. There were barely veiled threats, too, that the

Princess had been careless and foolhardy to dare to appear in public at all, as there were those who would not hesitate to harm her.

Though she was hurt by the ugly rumors Kaiulani stood firm, determined to do whatever she could to influence America in Hawaii's favor. She wondered why, if Koa was still in Washington, she had not heard from him again by now. But she continued to tell Hawaii's story, speaking out for her people. She was frightened, yes. But she was not going to let fear rule or stop her.

On their fourth day in Washington the letter they had hoped and prayed for came. President Cleveland and the First Lady requested the pleasure of receiving Princess Kaiulani in the White House Parlor the very next day.

The White House! Kaiulani was terrified and thrilled. What would they talk about?! How did one address the American President and his wife?! What should she wear to meet them?! In less than twenty-four hours she would be face to face with the leader of the entire United States and the woman they called "The White House Bride," although it had been seven years already since they had married.

Maddie chattered like a magpie as she helped Kaiulani try on outfits for the event. Maddie, who seemed to know everything about everyone, or at least was able to find out rather quickly, eagerly filled her in on the President and the First Lady.

"They still call her 'The White House Bride,' you see, for two reasons. The first is that they were actually married in the White House, June '86 it was, just a few months after he was in for his first term. The second reason is that she's the youngest first lady, ever. Only nineteen when they married! She's supposed to be very sweet - answers all her own mail, everybody loves her to pieces, that kind of thing."

She stood Kaiulani away from the mirror as she ducked under the Princess' elbow and then bobbed over her shoulder to observe the effect of the ensemble.

"Hmm," she mused critically. "I think that's too stuffy, don't you? The dark plum is pretty but that collar is so high and tight. It makes you look like a matron; too reserved, don't you think?"

Maddie circled around the bed where several dresses were laid out, selected a soft peach and brown floral print tea gown, and brought it over for her to try on. Resigned by now to being pushed around by her petite, dynamic companion, Kaiulani accepted the dress without a word and modestly retired behind a wicker screen to change.

"Here's the lively part, though," Maddie tucked herself into a corner of the love seat sofa.

"He'd known her since she was a <u>baby</u>!" She almost sang out in her enthusiasm. "She's the daughter of his former law partner, and Cleveland was thirty years old when she was born! The partner died when Frankie - everyone calls her that, her real name is Frances - Anyway, she was only eleven when her father passed on, so Grover became her guardian, unofficially, and the administrator of the estate. He was great friends with Mrs. Folsom, too, even after the marriage. Can you imagine? Everyone expected him to marry the mother! It was quite a scandal at first. But she's such a charmer, so sweet, that everyone got over it in no time."

She stopped for a moment and then continued in a more subdued tone.

"Actually, there was another scandal, too, earlier. I'd forgotten about that till just now. When he ran for office the first time, there were rumors - well, they said he'd had a child out of wedlock with a woman he never married. A widow who drank too much, that's what I heard. The Republicans had a nasty rhyme about it that the kids would sing in the streets. "'Ma, Ma, where's your Pa? He's in the White House, ha, ha, ha!'"

"I heard that when his people asked him what they should tell everyone about it, he said 'Tell them the truth.'

She must be a real saint, to forgive him something like that, don't you think?

Well, at any rate, they have a daughter, Rachael, I believe, or is it Ruth? And now another newborn."

Kaiulani emerged in the peach floral tea gown.

"Hmm." Maddie motioned for her to turn around and looked from several angles before she spoke again.

"Not bad. A little pale, maybe. A little washed out."

She swooped over to the bed again and lifted up a silky green and blue feathery looking print that shimmered a little in the light.

"Now, this one has some life to it!" She held it up to Kaiulani and nodded her head at once.

"Try it on," she demanded.

Kaiulani groaned in exasperation but headed back behind the screen.

"Now, now," Maddie said. "Remember, dear, it's for the good of both your country and mine."

"I never thought of finding the right dress as an expression of patriotism before," Kaiulani remarked dryly, which made Maddie giggle.

"It's a state occasion, really; only in this case you actually are the state!" Maddie laughed.

"In a state is more like it," the Princess grumbled. But it was only a moment before she emerged again in the light-catching, blue green dress.

"Oh, very nice!" Maddie cried out as she began to tuck and tug at the bodice and sleeves. "Very lovely!"

"It doesn't make me look like a peacock?" Kaiulani worried.

"No, no, no, no, no." Maddie imperiously directed her to turn around and look at herself in the mirror. "This is the one, trust me."

"Now," she said, pleased, "All we have to figure out is the jewelry."

The next afternoon Maddie and Theo rode in the carriage, going along with her as far as the White House gate.

Despite Maddie's protests, Kaiulani had at the last minute chosen to wear the "stuffy" dress, saying that it made her look the most proper.

The dark plum silk dress circled high up at the neck, just under her chin; but a delicate ruffle of the same material softened the severity and framed her face. A mass of tiny pleated ruffles repeated in fine strips down the front of the close fitting bodice, long sleeves and ankle length skirt. For this special occasion she wore for only the second time the Pele's tears earrings Mama had given her so long ago. A new hat in the Gainsborough style, named after the English portrait painter, trimmed with vibrant ostrich plumes, rested on top of her neatly coifed hair.

She wished that the Davies could go with her. Maddie was so much more adept at social conversation, and Theo always knew how to express the political side of things so well...

"Frankie plays the piano," Maddie rambled on. "And she's fluent in French and German - why, you two could speak three languages with each other!" Maddie touched Kaiulani's hand to reassure her but swiftly pulled back.

"Goodness! Your hands are like ice!"

She stripped off her own black kid gloves. "Here, take these, in case you need them," she insisted.

Nervous as a cat, Kaiulani looked imploringly at her friend. "Maddie, what if—"

But they had already arrived at the front door of the White House. So Maddie kissed her quickly and whispered, "Good luck!" Theo helped her out of the carriage and escorted her to the door. Kaiulani felt dizzy, as if she had been running for a long time and then had abruptly stopped short.

A tall, dark brown man, elderly and wearing a liveried uniform, ushered her in the door.

"Good afternoon, Princess" - he pronounced her name very well - "Ka-i-u-la-ni." He made a low bow. His voice was a rich deep bass with an accent that Kaiulani recognized as Jamaican. When the man took her coat, Theo pressed his ward's arm one last time and quietly promised to see her again in two hours.

The Jamaican bowed once more and then respectfully motioned for her to walk in front of him down a long, wide hall with many tall windows.

"Mis-tah President Cleve-land is very sorry he could not meet you himself," he explained cordially as they slowly made their way down the corridor. "Little Es-tah - she their baby - has a touch of colic so they needed to keep her in close by the fire."

The old man's gentle, slow movement and melodic voice soothed her like a soporific. By the time he slowly opened the door onto a remarkable Blue Room, lit up by a blazing, crackling fire, Kaiulani was peaceful and calm.

The President was right there to greet her. The baby cooed in a bassinet near the fire while her sister and mother watched over her.

President Cleveland was fifty-six years old, short and stocky with a pronounced double chin, heavy neck and jowls. He had a straightforward gaze under his long, bushy eyebrows, a well-receded hairline and a thick mustache under his distinctive patrician nose. A double breasted jacket did little to disguise his bulk - he was a man who obviously never missed a meal if he could help it - and his florid complexion reminded her strangely of the way Papa Nui used to look after he had drunk rather a lot of champagne. The President gripped her hand and shook it with great vigor.

"We welcome you, Princess Ka-i-u-la-ni." Like the Jamaican, he pronounced each syllable. "You honor us with your visit."

Kaiulani felt awkward and too tall as she looked directly into the president's eyes and returned his strong handshake.

"Thank you, President Cleveland, for your graciousness in receiving me."

Then Frankie was at her side, patting her hand, and the atmosphere of stiff formality dissolved.

"Oh, my dear," she said, somehow managing to include both her husband and Kaiulani in the endearment. "We must let the Princess sit down by the fire! Our weather here in Washington is so changeable this time of year," she confided to the Princess.

Whisking Kaiulani over to a burgundy brocade couch Frankie sat her down; then expertly plumped up the pillows beside and behind her as she sat herself close by. President Cleveland, joined by young Ruth, sat in a well- upholstered, plush chair while his oldest daughter lounged comfortably at his feet on an ottoman.

"Well!" Frankie beamed with intense satisfaction, "I had heard you were beautiful but I had no idea you were gorgeous, too!"

Frankie was so warm and welcoming that her presence was like another fire in the room. Her gleaming chestnut hair was piled loosely on top of her head and her clear hazel eyes were frank and honest. The modest neckline of her rose satin dress was covered with a smoky, lace-like net embroidered with ivory *fleurs-de-lis*.

"We are so happy you could come to see us before you return to New York," she said. "You are here for such a short while!" she said with genuine regret.

Kaiulani understood at once why the Americans were so enamored with this vibrant, cheerful woman who answered all her fan mail personally, and so obviously adored her husband and family.

Their time together passed quickly, with no mention of politics or problems. They were soon conversing like old friends. President Cleveland was coaxed into performing some amusing imitations of a few of his colleagues. Kaiulani was persuaded to render a few verses of an old Hawaiian *mele*, and then sang Aunt Liliu's "*Aloha Oe*" to an enchanted Ruth while Frankie played the music quite well on the piano after listening to just one verse.

By the end of the visit Ruth was clamoring to her father to be picked up so she could kiss "Princess Sky" good by. The President solemnly obeyed his daughter's command while Frankie laughed in delight.

"My, my!" she said softly. "She certainly has taken a shine to you! She's usually quite shy with people she's just met."

Then murmuring, "May I?" in her soft voice, Frankie, too, kissed Kaiulani on the cheek.

"It is so wonderful, my dear, what you are doing," Frankie's murmured with warmth and admiration. "The efforts you make on behalf of your people and your country could only come from a loving and selfless nature."

She smiled at the charmed Princess and spoke to her with real passion and conviction. "Education, as you certainly know, is the key to our equality and freedom." Then she wrapped her new friend in a delicate embrace.

Kaiulani suddenly felt as if she might cry, she was so moved by Frankie's candid and generous ways.

"You seem so happy!" she said impulsively, carried away by her feelings. "With your husband and your children -!"

Frankie smiled back at her with shining eyes. "Ah, my dear, I can only wish such good fortune on everyone. My circumstances give me boundless joy. But, as the world has shown me time and again, there are thousands of ways for us to love and help each other. And not all of them come in the form of families."

Kaiulani did not remember very much about returning from the White House to the hotel.

Maddie was puzzled at first when her friend seemed unable to answer her questions about how they looked and spoke and what they wore; and what was she like, really, and did he look at all like his pictures.

She smiled when she realized what had happened. "Oh, I see," Maddie laughed. "You have become a little star-struck yourself!"

Kaiulani could only return her smile, knowing there was no way to translate her overflowing emotions.

By the time the press interviewed her she was able to say that Mr. Cleveland was very clever, and Mrs. Cleveland was beautiful and also remarkably sweet, which was a rare and wonderful combination.

The papers the next day were full of the news that President Cleveland had appointed his own personal representative to investigate and report back to him on the situation in Hawaii. There would be no more talk of annexation or of any so-called "Hawaiian treaty," or an overthrow of the Queen or anything else, he promised, until this investigation was done. Mr. James H. Blount, the Democratic Congressman from Georgia, was already on his way to the islands. Renowned for his impartiality and integrity, Blount had been given President Cleveland's unconditional and absolute authority paramount over all other American officials in Hawaii, including the obstreperous Mr. Stevens and his marines. Within hours the press had dubbed the President's new emissary "Paramount Blount."

When she heard the news Kaiulani wept with relief. Theo applauded and Maddie grabbed Clive and danced an impromptu jig around the room.

All that was left for them to do now was a rush of last minute social events - dinners, receptions and parties in their honor. At the grand evening ball given by former Senator Henderson and his wife, Kaiulani was attended all night by the handsome French ambassador. The Women's Suffrage Association event required police assistance to control the swelling crowd when too many citizens without invitations showed up to get a glimpse of the royal guest of honor.

When the prestigious National Geographic Society gave a reception for the Princess in the main ballroom of the Arlington Hotel, most of the powers of Capital Hill turned out to see and be seen at the important event.

The frustrated PGs were forced to give up, for the time, their tactic of referring to the Hawaiians as "undisciplined savages." Instead, they were reduced to coyly suggesting that "perhaps Princess Kaiulani's true mission was to be a light of high society in America" rather than a royal personage in her own "relatively insignificant" country.

One unpleasant occurrence marred Kaiulani's remaining time in the capital city. She and Maddie and Theo ventured out one morning to see the famous Center Market, two entire city blocks of a street market offering flowers, vegetables, dairy products, fish and meat for sale. At the hectic intersection of 7th Street and Indiana Avenue, Center Market boasted a huge new "Queen Victoria-style" building with more than 1,000 stalls for vendors and merchants who came from all over the country to sell their wares. Hotels, taverns, restaurants and apothecaries had sprung up around this almost incessant hub of commerce. The eager shoppers ranged from coachmen to cooks to fine ladies with their husbands and friends.

The Market was in full swing when they arrived. At first, Kaiulani was thrilled by the tremendous spectrum of energy and activity that surrounded them like a fabulous, makeshift parade. But then she began to notice the hats.

As soon as she noticed the first one, she seemed to see them everywhere. Worn by rich women and poor women and middle class maids; they were even on the occasional gentlemen's stovepipe or top hat. In New York and Boston she had often seen plumes on hats, for feathers had been for some time quite the fashion rage. Indeed, she had even worn them herself.

But here in Washington the women's "*chapeaux*," as Maddie always liked to call them, were decorated with entire dead birds; and sometimes more than one. Sea gulls, sparrows, egrets, songbirds, even hummingbirds, hung suspended in cruel parodies of flight, precariously "perched" on top of, behind and on every possible side of women's heads. Some of the birds seemed to be trying to lift themselves off the hats, giving the appearance of movement and life for brief but unnerving seconds as they dipped, fluttered and swayed in the light spring breezes and winds. Devastated by this grotesque vision, Kaiulani heard herself say she must go home in a small, plaintive voice that sounded like a child.

"Whatever is wrong?!" Maddie rushed over to her after she looked into her face.

But the dead birds had upset Kaiulani so much that she was unable to explain. She would not speak of it to anyone, but was so repulsed that she left her brand new ostrich feathered hat and some feather trimmed gloves shoved far back into a dark corner of the hotel closet when they left town.

* * * * * * * * * * * * * * * * * * *

Back in New York for just one day before they set sail back to England, Kaiulani had another brief meeting with Koa. She was exhausted and feeling a little distressed, for that morning she had read accounts in the papers of several versions of her supposed romantic "affairs."

"It is said that Princess Kaiulani and the Hawaiian Prince David Kawananakoa are unofficially betrothed," one report from Washington read. "If the course of royal affairs runs smoothly and their longtime affection holds, they are very likely to marry."

She threw the paper aside in disgust. But the next one, a reprehensible rag from Los Angeles, California, was no improvement.

"It is said, however," she read out loud, her voice full of sarcasm, "that the Princess harbors a deep affection for a young English count and will never marry her cousin if she can help it." In a third paper she found out that she was engaged - and had been for quite some time, too, - to a mysterious, unnamed Japanese prince.

Kaiulani crumpled the page into a tight ball and threw it on the floor. "It is said, it is said!"

She stormed over to the window to look out at the street. The weather, for the last week or so, had been balmy on the East Coast, and the trees and bushes, even in New York, had at last begun to bud and bloom.

"I will know who said it, then," she murmured, furious at being the focus of such ludicrous, blatant lies.

A knock at the door interrupted her brooding. It was Koa carrying two-dozen red roses. She wanted to be happy to see him but she felt so annoyed by the new rumors that she found it hard to be civil.

As it turned out, he was even more sullen than she. Although he congratulated her on her "success with the president" and explained in an offhand way that he, too, would be leaving America soon to return to Hawaii to "try and help the Queen," it was almost as if he was implying that Kaiulani had somehow not helped Liliu. He had, of course, not been to the White House himself, he explained, but that did not necessarily strike him as the very best choice at this juncture.

She was too tired and out of sorts to attempt to discuss it. Suddenly, she was intensely jealous that Koa was going to return to Hawaii, while she had to go back overseas in the opposite, wrong direction entirely. It dawned on her that perhaps he was jealous because he had not been invited to meet the President and Frankie, and probably felt left out and hurt, besides, that they had had so little time to themselves. That she had been unable to spend more time with him. Well, there was nothing she could do. It couldn't be helped, not right now. And she really couldn't explain it, either, satisfactorily, to herself or to him.

They kissed each other perfunctorily, politely, promising to be in touch quite soon, and then he was gone. Only the sandalwood smell of him lingered in the air.

A last batch of reporters and well wishers had crowded onto the New York dock to see off the ship, *The Majestic,* and to record the Princess' final words as she sailed away from the American shore.

"As I leave your generous country," She had to swallow a lump in her throat before she could continue. "I wish to thank the many hearts that have made my time here so happy."

"The hundreds of hands I have clasped, the kind smiles of so many American people, the generous words of sympathy and support sent to me and my people from so many. It was to the American people that I spoke and they heard me as I knew they would."

"Whatever happens to me," Her face glowed with a radiant light from within and she beamed out at the crowd again like a beacon. "I shall never be a stranger to you again. I am grateful for all you have given me."

She raised her hand and many in the crowd returned her wave good-by. "God bless you for everything. *Aloha. Mahalo nui loa.*"

Then the ship sailed and she was gone.

Chapter Twenty-Two

The trip back to England, for the most part, was over calm and steady seas, unusual for that time of year. Kaiulani had the luxury of staying on deck most of the time. She strolled in the sun and enjoyed the lulling, soothing sounds and salt spray of the ocean.

This was the second time in five years she had traveled to America and then sailed from there to England. Both times she had been impressed by the vital, insistent energy of the United States, sprawling out all over like a puppy that could not sit still for one moment.

What, she wondered, would life hold for her in the next few years? If or when she returned, would America welcome her again with open arms? And what might happen to her if things were not made right in Hawaii? She could not even imagine what she would do if such a dreadful thing occurred.

In this pensive mood her thoughts returned to the warmth of the Blue Room with Frankie, the fireplace, President Cleveland and their sweet daughters, Ruth and baby Esther. For the first time in her life, she felt a powerful longing for children of her own. The tender affection of the first family gripped her with a desire to have a baby that was like a strong, physical ache of hunger or anger or lust. The idea of having a family of her own became a palpable need for her. To have a stable, happy home, to be a mother and wife and hold her own babies and husband folded close and safe in her arms...

But how could she possibly do that? And with whom? For some time now her life had been tangled up in loose ends, some unraveling further even as she thought of them! For several years now all she could be certain of was that her circumstances were likely to change from moment to moment and that her life would continue in a constant state of flux. She could hope and dream, naturally, like anyone else in the world. But she never knew what might come next, or where she would be tomorrow.

Well, she reflected, I am grateful to the higher powers for my family and friends. Without them, I might die from sheer loneliness.

Not long before they arrived in London a small steamship delivered a load of mail on board the *Majestic*. Kaiulani received two very large bags; more, she was sure, than she could read in an entire year, even if she devoted herself only to correspondence. Aunt Liliu's letter was very gracious; she thanked her for her hard work and all her efforts and told her how much she was missed in Hawaii. Liliu had enclosed one of the songs the grateful Hawaiians had written in honor of their Princess's journey.

As she read the lyrics out loud Kaiulani felt the tempos and rhythms of her islands drift back, echoes of a precious, half-forgotten dream.

> *"A Song to Kaiulani"*
> Let us sing in praise of Kaiulani
> Lovely child of Princess Likelike -"

The old, familiar sound of saying her mother's name brought tears to her eyes.

> "To our Kaiulani, rose of Ainahau,
> fair *ali'i*, Royal daughter of Hawaii.
> She is as lovely as the morning dawn,
> This Princess, our Princess,
> flower of our beloved land.
> Wonderful news comes of your achievement.
> Word of it spreads to every island.
> We laud your success, dear Kaiulani,
> In helping to restore our Queen to her throne.
> Prayerfully and in unison we say,
> 'Long may the flag of Hawaii fly!'

We cry it, so the world may hear us.
We cry it, our hearts overflowing with love.
For we are deeply grateful, Kaiulani.
You have won all, with your charm and beauty.
Kaiulani, Princess, you have captured every heart!"

The song had been written on March 11, just a few days before her visit to the White House.

* * * * * * * * * * * * * * * * * * * *

Toby and Miranda were there to meet her when the ship docked. Miranda bounded up to kiss her friend and exulted that they were very glad to have her "home at last!"

"Is this my home now?" Kaiulani mused.

"Well, then," Toby encouraged her, "Your <u>second</u> home, at least!"

Something was going on with Toby; Kaiulani sensed it right away. He had some secret that he was keeping to himself. Soon after they had settled in to Mrs. Rook's house in Brighton, he said he was frightfully sorry to have to run off so soon, but he had some important business to attend to in London. He promised to return by Friday or Saturday, at the latest.

Miranda rolled her eyes in mock despair at her brother's "busy-ness," and told him that it was becoming rather tiresome and boring to have him away so often these days.

Toby just laughed and kissed his sister's hand. He made a low bow, then pecked Kaiulani on the cheek and assured them again, "Friday or Saturday, at most." Looking mischievous, he added, "And perhaps with some news!"

Miranda and Kaiulani caught each other up with news and gossip from both sides of the continents, and soon Miranda was asking her friend to tell her all over again about America, especially the parts about "Frankie" and the parties and the balls.

That night Kaiulani realized she was thinking about Toby in a different way. What if he had fallen in love with someone in London and she could not see him anymore? They were more than friends; she knew that was true. But neither of them had ever declared anything more than friendship and loyalty to each other. She couldn't face the idea of losing Toby, too, of not being able to confide in him and talk as they had always done since the first time they met.

On Saturday the mystery was solved. Miranda and Mrs. Rook had gone into town to take care of some errands when Toby came dashing up to the front door of their house, his color and spirits high.

"I am so pleased to find you home alone!" he exclaimed to Kaiulani. "There is something I've been dying to tell you!"

They sat across from each other in the parlor sipping tea while little Sammy sat watching their conversation as avidly as if it was a tennis match, until he drifted off to sleep.

"Kaiulani," Toby held her hands in his and began in a low, confidential tone.

What would she say, the question raced through her mind, if he declared his love to her today? Or even asked her to marry him? Her heart stopped for a second as she imagined it. Oh, it would be so terribly complicated. She was not free to speak her mind about anything yet, not until she knew more about what the future would hold. And yet—

Toby broke through the hectic confusion of her thoughts when he let go of her hands to take out of his jacket pocket a small, burgundy leather box.

She found a bracelet inside, rose gold with a narrow band of exquisite white gold, studded with garnets alternating with seed pearls. It was the perfect complement to her earrings.

"Oh, Toby! It's beautiful!"

Toby blushed, a deep color staining his cheeks, face and neck.

"Well, it's kind of a thank you, really; and a sort of going away present, too. Only this time it's me, - well, I am going away."

She felt like the breath had been knocked out of her. The blood drained down from her head toward her torso and then to her toes.

"None of this would be happening," Toby eagerly clasped her hand, "if not for you."

"What do you mean?" Kaiulani wondered if he had noticed her trembling hand.

"The economy, you see, has been in rotten shape here these days, and for quite some time now, too." Toby's words spilled out. "I hear it's not much better in America lately, either. And it seems to be heading for another downturn fast?"

Kaiulani had an abrupt, fleeting image of the dead birds on all those hats in Washington. She could only shrug at his question, loath to comment on a subject about which she knew so little.

Toby, chivalrous as always, continued on as if he has not asked the question.

"At any rate, I've hated to see it in London, myself, - Marylebone and Whitechapel are dreadful slums, with mothers on the streets feeding gin sops to their babies just to make the poor things a bit more comfortable as they cough their lungs out, or starve, even, some of them...And the men are so desperate; no regular work, no money or place to live, and the families going to pieces. But just blocks away, there are all those bourgeois, well-mannered homes in Kensington and Bayswater..."

"The bad winters these last few years have only, of course, made it worse. And the immigrants; the Jews fleeing persecution in Eastern Europe, as an example, add to the poverty that the Irish have never gotten out from under -"

He stopped himself, and took her hand again.

"The university settlement people - I'm an alumnae, you know - and the social reformers have finally pulled together. About four years ago, in '89, we joined forces to set up the London County Council as a kind of beginning effort, a way of at least attempting to try to do some good, to start to dig out from underneath."

He saw that she did not understand.

"It's a building program, you see, Kaiulani! My part of it, anyway. They're desperate for architects to design and build schools, fire stations, technical colleges and housing, especially, for the working classes. I think I've found a way to be really useful, to give back a little, at last."

"But, Toby, how can this be connected to me?!"

He seemed suddenly shy, as if revealing a secret.

"It came clear to me when I watched you get ready for your trip. I must admit, at first my heart ached for you and I wondered incessantly if all that effort could really do you or Hawaii any good."

"More than anything else, though," he said softly, turned away from her eyes, "I worried about you."

He faced her again, smiling now.

"Then, gradually, I begin to really listen, carefully, to what you were saying in your speeches; and to think about it and question why it began to strike me as so exceedingly important. Something began to happen to me then, Kaiulani, because of you, and I am glad to say it has changed me."

"Ever since I've known you, dear, and heard about your beloved Hawaii and the injustices being forced upon your people, I have started to think differently about my own place in the world. About my responsibility, in fact, to help out. I felt what a strong direction you have in your life and I found myself quite lacking by comparison."

He tried to sound off-hand but his voice was unsteady. "Except for my connection with you and Miranda, you see, I had begun, rather, well, floundering, somehow. Oh, I had loads to keep me busy, of course; I always do. I've never not worked, making some kind of a living and not such a bad one, at that. But there was a sense of -" he struggled to find the word - "of participation, I suppose, really, with others, and with the rest of the world, if you will, that was lacking."

"It was your influence, really, your example, which made me come to think differently about my part in looking out for others. That I also have, well," he seemed almost embarrassed by his words but was determined to speak his mind, "a responsibility, too; perhaps even an obligation, to do my bit to help out."

"A lot of things have come to me very easily in my life, Kaiulani." He gazed into her eyes with a forcefulness and purpose she had not seen before. "In all fairness, I want to try to give something back."

Kaiulani felt numb, dreading what she knew was coming next.

"Does this mean you will be gone a great deal more often?" she asked almost in a whisper.

"Oh, yes. I shall have to leave Brighton altogether, quite soon, as it turns out. I'll need to live in London, on location, as it were, and probably in some rather "iffy" digs. Or near them, at any rate, to study the situation in-depth, up close, absorb myself in the reality of it. So I can come up with some practical and really useful solutions."

She felt an undercurrent of sadness pull at her with the idea of Toby gone. A childish part of her wanted to scold him severely and ask him how, if he cared about her, too, as much as he said he did, how could he leave her, too?

But she told him how happy she was for his decision and that she was moved by his choice.

"You have done me a great service, dear," said Toby. "I will forever be grateful."

Kaiulani turned away to hide her emotions.

"I hope," she said lightly, "we shall be able to correspond on a regular basis?"

"Oh, my dear, of course! Every day, if you like! Or nearly!"

"Well," she sighed, her face lighting up with a playfulness she did not feel, "I should hate to lose my Father Confessor like that, even to such a good cause."

Toby folded her in an embrace that made her heart flutter. A sob caught and then stifled in her throat.

"You will never lose me, Princess. I am yours for as long as we shall live."

Kaiulani stepped aside a little as she placed her hands on his high shoulders and smiled. "Perhaps, then, someday someone will say that even I was an inspiration to someone." Her voice quivered a little in spite of all her best intentions. "That I, too, did something useful and good with my time."

Toby looked so destroyed by this remark that she sat him down beside her and held his hand. "Oh, there, now, don't you worry about me. I am only feeling a little sorry for myself, that's all."

She looked at him with a spark of mischief in her eyes. "Remember, please, I am Hawaiian."

He looked at her, uncomprehending.

"Don't you know," she was desperate to deflect his grim mood, "that all Hawaiians, even if we get knocked off our feet, can always get back up again to surf, or else we swim?"

"You must give me your promise, though," his voice was solemn with concern.

"Of what?" She tried to sound casual.

"That you will be careful not to sink, or swim in waters too deep or dangerous."

Just then Miranda walked into the room.

"News!" she was elated and flushed. "We just saw Mrs. Sharp in town! She is going to live over at The Yews in Kettering now! She lost the school, had to give up Harrowden Hall. I must say, though, she seemed quite cheerful about everything, nevertheless. Mrs. Rook invited her to lunch with us next week, Monday noon."

She bounced onto the couch beside Kaiulani and Toby.

"She is so looking forward to seeing you!" she said to the Princess.

For the first time, Miranda paused and looked carefully first at her brother and then at her friend.

"Oh, my. You two look like a jolly good time. Where's the funeral?"

* * * * * * * * * * * * * * * * * * *

Within days, everything in Kaiulani's life had completely changed, again. An urgent letter from Papa informed her that they were now in dire straits financially as he no longer had any income, none at all, and please to do anything she could think of to help economize.

So the lunch with Mrs. Sharp turned into more than just a reunion. Their former principal was as enthusiastic as ever. When she heard about the Princess' plight, she insisted that Kaiulani come and live as her guest at her newly rented cottage in the "garden community" of Yews at Kettering, less than ten miles from the old school.

"It would be such a help to me, dear. I'm finding it quite peculiar to go from managing an entire educational institution to living '*tout seule*,' completely alone with only my own thoughts and no company at all."

Mrs. Rook apparently began to feel in competition with her old friend, Mrs. Sharp. In fact, Mrs. Rook had very much enjoyed the time spent with her two young boarders and the always-helpful Toby. Recently, she had become particularly fond of the reflected glory of serving as landlady and housekeeper to the now renowned princess. Mrs. Rook started to question Mrs. Sharp intensely on a number of points regarding the arrangements and safety of the new abode at "The Yews in Kettering," a name she pronounced with the slightest *moué* of distaste.

Was it properly fenced in, for instance, she wanted to know, especially all those garden areas? Were the windows sound, and sturdy enough to provide adequate protection when the cold weather returned? Some of those older houses, as Mrs. Sharp must certainly be aware, were inclined to be drafty and damp if the mortar holding the bricks was of a certain vintage or otherwise not quite up to snuff.

Mrs. Rook reminded her friend Mrs. Sharp that Princess Kaiulani was inclined to contract colds. Consequently, she must remember that Kaiulani needed not only sufficient time by the fireplace on a routine basis, but also plenty of hot tea and honey to bolster her health. In fact, said Mrs. Rook, sniffling a little herself, she was very much of a sensitive flower, Kaiulani was, and she hoped Mrs. Sharp would take that into serious consideration.

Kaiulani and Miranda exchanged a few furtive looks, amazed that the usually reticent Mrs. Rook had suddenly become so proprietary and even motherly, in her own way.

"What a regular mother hen Mrs. Rook turned into!" Miranda exclaimed later that night when she and Kaiulani were at last alone.

"Indeed!" the Princess laughed. "Well," she reflected, "I suppose we have all been rather nesting here together these past few months," thinking how lonely and quiet the house had been without Toby.

"I miss my brother," Miranda sighed.

"I do, too," Kaiulani said.

At lunch Mrs. Sharp, who was quite used to her friend's spontaneous and sometimes volatile lectures, had patiently and politely assured Mrs. Rook that all was as it should be at The Yews. Kaiulani felt grateful for Mrs. Sharp's aggressive, take charge attitude and was soon listening avidly as her former principal began setting up with her the arrangements for the move.

At first, Miranda seemed sulky and out of sorts regarding the whole venture. But later she admitted to Kaiulani that she had, in fact, already been considering an extended visit to her mother's home in Paris, long before Kaiulani even thought about moving.

When it was time to say good-by they wept and hugged each other, promising to write all the time. Little Sammy yelped and scampered about while Miranda and Kaiulani packed. Later, the diminutive dog stationed himself like a sentry in front of Kaiulani's largest trunk and refused to leave his spot until he was forcibly dislodged.

* * * * * * * * * * * * * * * * * * *

As soon as Kaiulani had settled in at The Yews, another shipment of letters, most of them from Aunt Liliu and Papa, arrived from Hawaii. They were filled with contradictions and retractions. Papa said he had no idea what Aunt Liliu was hiding up her sleeve, and had given up on trying to advise or understand her. Liliu hinted that it might be well for Kaiulani to begin to think about marriage prospects. Koa, of course, might be a possibility. But an alliance with a powerful future leader from another country; for example, a prince or a lord from Europe or Japan, could also be advantageous, especially if such an alliance helped them further Hawaii's cause.

Kaiulani wrote back to the Queen at once, explaining that she had no interest in considering any possibilities of marriage at the present moment.

A few weeks later Aunt Liliu sent another letter telling her that she had recently heard rumors that Kaiulani might be asked to ascend to the throne. If this were to happen, Aunt Liliu would appreciate it if Kaiulani would be very circumspect and careful to respond in a guarded manner. "Think before you say or act," she advised, "and keep cool at all times."

Petitions had been circulating throughout the islands, Liliu explained, to have her restored to her position as Queen, post haste. The Provisional Government already seemed to be losing some ground. Commissioner Blount had ordered them to take down the United States flag and raise the Hawaiian flag in its place; that had been promptly done. And, although Blount would not express any opinions regarding the issues, he had been very busy examining all sorts of witnesses to the events; from both sides, it was true, but his report was alleged to be shaping up quite positively in favor of complete restitution.

Kaiulani was hurt by her aunt's letter and replied the same day.

"June 15, 1893

Dear Aunt Liliu,

I have never received any proposals from anybody to take the throne. I have not received a word of any sort from anyone except my father and the letters and poems sent by you.

I have been perfectly miserable these last four months. I had been looking forward to '93 as the end of my four years of exile. Now it seems as if nothing is settled, and I am so longing to see you all and be home again, at last. I will try to be cheerful, but I am so homesick!

I am staying with Mrs. Sharp at her new home in Kettering, working as hard as I can, plugging away at my reading, practicing languages, painting, drawing, gardening and sewing.

Please be sure that I shall always remain,

Your Loving Niece,
Kaiulani."

Two days later she received the news from Mr. Davies that the PGs had taken over Iolani Palace. On June 2, nearly two weeks before she wrote to the Queen, they had moved into Iolani to claim it as their headquarters and rename it 'The Executive Building,' also known as 'The Government Building.'

"Apparently," Mr. Davies explained to her with regret, "quite a lot of pilfering and looting took place. Many of the art treasures and silver and gold pieces have disappeared from the palace and are said to be turning up on display at the PG's offices and houses."

King Kalakaua's crown had been mutilated by one of the first looters, who stripped off the gemstones and left the golden crown a twisted, broken shell. Queen Kapiolani's crown had disappeared. All of the national insignia had been pried loose from the iron gates of the palace and kept or sold as souvenirs. The gilt mirrors from the throne room were all gone, and whatever of the royal stationary that had not been ripped up or shredded was showing up as "scrap paper" for the schoolwork of the PG's children.

* * * * * * * * * * * * * * * * * * * *

That summer at The Yews was exceptionally balmy. Until the middle of the season the sun stayed out very late, sometimes not setting until 10 or even 11 at night. Kaiulani and Mrs. Sharp spent hours together in the garden, coaxing, clipping, weeding and tending to an abundant crop of lush roses and excellent vegetables, along with a great variety of other flowers and herbs.

Theo and Maddie Davies had rented a house for the summer in Killiney, Ireland at the seaside a few miles from Dublin. When Kaiulani joined them there for two weeks in midsummer it was pleasant to see young Clive again; but, although there were picnics, tennis, cricket games and horses to ride, as well as a fair number of would-be suitors, Kaiulani could not relax and enjoy herself. She constantly brooded about Hawaii.

Papa sent a letter to say that Aunt Liliu had become a recluse at her own home in Washington Place. Soldiers were camped out both at the Kawaiahao Church and at the Central Union Church, which was right across from the Queen's house and had been converted into a PG lookout. Aunt Liliu's enemies spied on her day and night, twenty-four hours, watching her from the church spires through their binoculars.

Kaiulani wrote to the Queen at once to commiserate.

"My Dear Aunt,

How you must hate the sight of the Central Union Church. What a shame that a place meant to be a house of worship should be turned into a spy tower. I suppose it is wise for you to remain at Washington Place, but how you must long to get away to some other place! If I was in your place, I am afraid I should pine away and die.

I could not stand it. I am so tired of waiting."

When "Paramount" Blount's report was delivered to President Cleveland that July, the Commissioner minced no words in entirely condemning Stevens and the marines and the PGs. The vast majority of Hawaii's citizens were, he explained crisply, by a huge margin, totally and absolutely opposed to annexation. In his opinion, there existed no discernible moral or legal grounds upon which an annexation of the Hawaiian Islands to the United States could be justified.

"A great wrong has been done to the Hawaiians," he said in his report. His unequivocal recommendation was that the Hawaiian government and the monarchy should be restored at all speed.

At stake, President Cleveland later informed Congress, was "nothing less than America's honor, integrity and morality."

Mr. Grisham, Cleveland's Secretary of State, issued to the press the statement that "The Queen's submission was thus coerced. The affair was discreditable to all that engaged in it. It would lower our national standard to endorse the selfish, dishonorable scheme of a lot of adventurers."

That October, on her eighteenth birthday, Kaiulani realized with some surprise that she was looking forward, for the first time, to the winter season. With everything that had been going on in her life and with Hawaii, cold weather and gray skies seemed more in keeping with the increasing harsh times.

Chapter Twenty-Three

It was a chilly fall night and the two women had been working by the parlor fire for some time. Kaiulani took a break from her drawing to glance at yet another new article by the Reverend Mr. Bishop, but she soon threw down the paper in disgust. She tried to return to her work but was too angry to go on.

"How dare he?!" she exploded. She tossed the charcoal she had been using, to sketch Mrs. Sharp at her needlework, onto the ledge of the easel.

"It is he who is the savage! And a terrible liar to boot! Just look at this!"

Mrs. Sharp adjusted her glasses and read out loud.

"*An Editorial by the Reverend Bishop.* It is constantly urged that, by the annexation of Hawaii without the full consent of the natives, the United States would be committing a robbery of their rights of sovereignty and independence, taking away their cherished Flag, etc., etc.'"

Mrs. Sharp paused to fan herself with one hand, for she was feeling a bit vapor-ish that evening. "He certainly is verbose!"

"And a very bad writer," Kaiulani burst out, "as well as a man who will lie about everyone and anything, at any time!"

Kaiulani crossed her arms over her chest and began to pace around the room. "Go on!" she commanded.

Mrs. Sharp squinted a little until she found her place. "'Such a weak and wasted people prove by their failure to save themselves from extinction' - Oh, my!" she interjected softly. Disapproving, she read ahead silently for a few lines and then picked up further down the page.

"'Is it not an absurdity for the aborigines, who, under the most favorable conditions, have dwindled to less than one-third; actually, probably as low as one-fourth now, of the whole number of males in the Islands, and who are mentally and physically incapable' -"

Dismayed, Mrs. Sharp skipped ahead again, hoping to find some less incendiary part; for she, too, like Mrs. Rook before her, had been watching Kaiulani with an eagle eye and had come to have concerns about her health and well-being.

"Well," Mrs. Sharp said, reluctant to continue, "he finishes with a part about -"

"Read it to me, please. It is important to remember what we are up against," Kaiulani said.

"'It would seem that the forty millions of property interests held by foreigners here in Hawaii must be delivered from native misrule.'"

"First they stole our land, then our lives, and now they mean to justify it as 'righteous!'" Kaiulani shook with anger.

"And from a man of the cloth, too!" Mrs. Sharp said sorrowfully.

"He once called my Aunt 'the debauched Queen of a heathenish monarchy.' Reverend Bishop claimed that she was ruled by sorcerers, manufactured and distributed opium, and was sired, along with my godfather, the king, by an African coachman!"

She flung herself down on the couch beside Mrs. Sharp. "I've heard that Aunt Liliu told Mr. Willis, the new American Minister that the usurpers should all be beheaded and their properties confiscated at once." Kaiulani laughed deep in her throat. "One can only hope it is true!" she exulted, but stopped short when she saw Mrs. Sharp's expression.

"I only mean I hope she said it," she reassured her. "Aunt Liliu would never dream of doing such a thing. Unlike the Reverend Bishop, the Queen actually does have charitable values which, for better or for worse, do temper her loyalty to justice."

Mrs. Sharp retrieved her needlepoint and Kaiulani went back to her charcoal sketch.

"At least," the Princess shook her head, "Mr. Thurston is an honest foe. For all his failings and they are myriad, I must say, he has never claimed otherwise than that racial enmity and economics are, and always have been, at the base of our conflict. 'Failure to save themselves,' indeed! I'd like to see Mr. Bishop try to save himself in an ocean full of greedy sharks!"

* * * * * * * * * * * * * * * * * * *

For the rest of that long winter Kaiulani willed herself to be content resting with Mrs. Sharp at The Yews, immersed in reading, studying, sketching, painting and biding her time.

The news from Hawaii continued to be erratic, hopeful one day and filled with contradictions the next. Finally, after several good reports in a row, it seemed that at last the restoration of the Queen had been agreed upon and settled, with only a few formalities remaining to be gotten out of the way.

A February letter from Aunt Liliu explained that there would be only one more short delay.

"We are only waiting for the 'good news' and then you may come home." The Queen urged Kaiulani again to think about the possibility of marriage. She hinted that she might consider seeking out the Japanese Emperor's nephew, referring to the long-standing story that King Kalakaua had, years ago, spoken with the Emperor about perhaps betrothing this boy and Kaiulani. Aunt Liliu had recently heard that this nephew was said to currently be in England pursuing 'a continental education,' just like Kaiulani. "I do not know his name," she wrote, "but should you manage to meet him, and think you could like him, I give you full leave in advance to accept him, should he propose to you and offer his hand and fortune." She encouraged her niece to always remain candid with her and "never hesitate to open your heart to me."

After a while, try as she might, Kaiulani found herself beginning to get numb and lose interest in staying current, as best as she could, with the constantly shifting news.

Appropriately suspicious of any crowd activities, the Provisional Government banned all large gatherings throughout the islands. In 1894, there were no birthday or holiday luaus, parades or parties anywhere, unless they had been initiated and sanctioned by the PGs themselves.

Kaiulani's birthday and the holidays came and went with a welcome visit from Toby and Miranda and a lovely holiday party at the Davies' new home. Toby's hairline had receded a bit and he was almost painfully thin, but he was in high spirits and regaled them for hours with fascinating stories about his work in London, which made every day an adventure for him, he declared, whether happy, sad, or both.

Miranda had grown a bit taller and slimmed down, though her capacity for anything sweet was undiminished. She moved with a new languidness, sighing often, and soon admitted she had fallen desperately in love with a young Bohemian painter but was keeping it a secret because her mother, determined to have Miranda come out in society, would never approve. Miranda confessed, with a little prodding, that she had, in fact, been in love "perhaps two or three times, at most," in the last few months.

"There are too many good-looking men in Paris!" Miranda complained when Toby and Kaiulani laughed at her and charged her with an irrepressible tendency to flirt.

At midnight they toasted each other with glasses of Theo's fine Madeira sherry, which made them bold. Toby held Kaiulani in a close embrace under the mistletoe for a long kiss.

"I will always wait and care for you, dear, and I will always be your friend," Toby's mustache tickled her ear.

Also feeling the effects of the sweet, rich wine, Kaiulani giggled and playfully held her finger against his lips.

But when they became tangled up in each other's gaze, she became suddenly very serious.

"We only can wait, Toby. Be patient and see what will come." A lighter note eased back into her tone. "And, my dear Father Confessor, my good, sweet Toby, you must promise to forgive me in advance if it all comes out strangely, or even to naught."

Toby looked crestfallen but obediently nodded in agreement. Then he took from his pocket a slim, leather bound volume of verse tied up with a velvet bow.

"It's Tennyson, dear, for you," he intoned glumly. "He died just last year, you know."

* * * * * * * * * * * * * * * * * * *

Later, when she examined the book she saw he had inscribed on the frontispiece, "To My Dear Kaiulani, From Her Very Own Shepherd (I Hope!). Love, Toby, New Year's 1894." He had marked a passage for her to read in a poem called *The Princess*.

"Come down, O maid, from yonder mountain height:
What pleasure lives in height (the shepherd sang).
In height and cold, the splendor of the hills.
But cease to move so near the Heavens, and cease
To glide a sunbeam by the blasted Pine,
To sit a star upon the sparkling spire;
And come, for Love is of the valley, come,
For Love is of the valley, come thou down
And find him; by the happy threshold, he."

What was Toby trying to tell her? That she was cold, that she lived at some high, unreal level that made her seem unapproachable to him? Was there something, really, that might come to grow between them, if they were willing and able to wait? Could Toby be her loving Prince and might the two of them together create a "happy threshold"? If only time would reveal its secrets and she could feel sure of something, for a change!

Toby wrote again, right away, from the train returning to London, to say how good it was to see her and to half apologize for his inscription and the book.

"I hope I have not been too forward, dear. I find so many of Tennyson's poems to be otherworldly and even sad. But somehow I was sure they would move you, as they have touched me. With all my love, Your Toby."

All through that long winter at The Yews Kaiulani read the Tennyson often. Seeking out other of his poems as well, she was especially taken with the thrilling ballad, "The Charge of the Light Brigade." The story of those heroic warriors never failed to stir and excite her, there in the midwinter doldrums of the sleepy English countryside.

Late at night when she was still wide eyed and far from sleep she would recite out loud softly, almost chanting, as a way of comforting herself. Sometimes even in the daytime she would find herself recalling those haunting lines which repeated themselves in her mind like an ancient *mele*.

> "Boldly they rode and well,
> Into the jaws of Death,
> Into the Mouth of Hell,
> Rode the six hundred.
> When can their glory fade?
> O the wild charge they made!
> All the world wonder'd.
> Honor the charge they made!"
> Honor the Light Brigade,
> Noble six hundred!"

When spring came at last and buds blossomed out and fresh, new creatures were all around, everything vibrant and alive, Kaiulani began to ache for adventure.

She wanted to be in the sun, not the shade, to slough off winter's stale dreariness and warm her body in the heat of summer. Restless and filled with yearning, she felt as if she was ravenously hungry, almost starving, in fact, but had no idea of what she might eat. She only picked at her food and either slept for hours, even during the day, or almost not at all.

She felt guilty and selfish for wanting to escape Hawaii's troubles for a while and find some fun and pleasure of her own. But she could not suppress the energy and excitement that coursed through her blood and bones like sap in a flourishing tree.

In May more bad news came from home. Despite the long months of patience regarding the Queen's reinstatement, the Provisional Government had continued to scheme to ill effect. They held a convention that spring to present a complicated declaration, written by Thurston and Dole, which asserted the legitimacy of their Council's rule. If the declaration was accepted and approved, it would mean even greater losses for the Hawaiians. Kaiulani had no recourse, once again, except to wait and hope.

Maddie and Theo returned to England in early June after a stay of several months in San Francisco visiting Maddie's family and friends.

After their first hellos Maddie soon got Kaiulani alone and insisted that they go off for tea, cookies and "a good, long talk."

"Darling," Maddie grasped Kaiulani's hands firmly in her own. "It is all well and good, your studying so hard and being so noble and self-sacrificing and all that.

"But you are really much too pale and you look a little under the weather, I must tell you. I'm sure Mrs. Sharp can manage to let go of you for the summer. That's how long we will be touring Europe - all the major cities - and Theo and I absolutely insist you must come."

Kaiulani was thrilled by the prospect, but immediately began to worry what Papa and Aunt Liliu would think of such apparent frivolity given the dire circumstances at home. Before she could even express her concerns, however, Maddie, as was her wont, charged ahead with the plans.

"You'll be happy to know that Theo has already cleared it with your father, and the Queen thought it was a lovely idea, too." She began to unfold a much pored over map. "Now, just look at this itinerary I've planned!"

* * * * * * * * * * * * * * * * * * *

Their first stay was at a gentleman's estate in the lush farmlands in the south of France. For days they did nothing but lounge about in the mellow sun and mild breezes, indulging themselves in rich, delicious meals, usually out of doors, with plenty of fresh baked bread with new butter and cream and sugar in their coffee several times a day.

"We shall all get quite fat!" Maddie declared more than once, happy to see Kaiulani's color and softness begin to return.

Even the Princess had to laugh when Maddie pointed out how her hips and bosoms were starting to fill out, "Plump as a little dumpling!" Kaiulani felt expansive and daring as she luxuriated in the sunshine, lapping up the excellent food, fresh air and easy-going company. After a few weeks of these idle delights the party gathered themselves together and took off for Paris.

"The City of Lights - and Love," Maddie announced with a coy, sideways look at Kaiulani who appeared not to notice.

In Paris they visited galleries, museums, restaurants and scores of shops where Maddie relentlessly educated everyone about the latest styles, outfitting them all in the most *"au courant"* fashions.

At one of the shops, Kaiulani was being fitted for a golden yellow, silk tea gown designed to Maddie's specifications, when the tailor accidentally brushed a pinpoint too close against the Princess' wrist. For an instant Kaiulani's eyes flashed and her nostrils flared. She looked like a fiery, thoroughbred horse, a beautiful but high-strung filly about to burst forth from the starting lines at the races. With considerable effort she managed to collect herself and accept, albeit a little coolly, the unhappy tailor's profuse apologies. Maddie was concerned when she saw the hairline scratch on Kaiulani's wrist and commended her on her self-control.

"I know he did not do it on purpose." Kaiulani said, but a slight flicker of anger still lingered in her eyes. "But as a representative of my nation and people, it is my duty to remain calm at all times."

"Well," said Maddie, for she did not know what else to say in light of such a serious declaration. "Well," she said again.

At the end of their first week in Paris Theo was called away to London on business, so Maddie and Kaiulani decided they would visit Miranda at her mother's estate on the Seine.

The ride from the city to Madame de Courcy's was only an hour but Kaiulani, lulled by the motion of the coach, drifted off into a nap. When the carriage lurched to a halt in front of the DeCourcy's home, she woke to see Miranda waiting there with her mother to greet them.

Kaiulani was amazed at the changes that had taken place in her friend, and in such a short time, too. Miranda looked absolutely wonderful, radiant and with an air of calm serenity that Kaiulani had never seen before. She behaved differently, too, hugging Kaiulani in an almost diffident way, and introducing her and Maddie to *"Ma Mere"* in a formal yet altogether charming, soft tone. She even gave a low curtsey as she made these presentations, much to Kaiulani's surprise. The lively rowdiness she was used to from her old school chum and former housemate now seemed to be entirely missing.

As soon as she could manage it Miranda made an excuse to leave Mrs. Davies and her mother to admire the gardens while she bundled Kaiulani off to see her private quarters. Her bedroom was lavishly decorated in pink satin and white velvet with frills of white lace everywhere.

Miranda grabbed Kaiulani by the waist and spun her around in a wide circle, then kissed her cheeks and laughed wildly.

Here, Kaiulani thought to herself, Here she is, my old friend, 'Randa.

"Oh, Kai! Only guess what has happened to me?!"

"You've fallen in love?" Kaiulani asked in a comically bemused tone.

Miranda was shocked by her keen intuition.

"How did you know?! She demanded. "Even Toby doesn't know!"

Kaiulani sat on the edge of the frilly pink and white bed. "Well, let's see," she said, pretending to examine some elaborate embroidery on the coverlet, "Perhaps it is because the last time we saw each other you had been in love - oh, - three times in one season? I believe." She looked up innocently at Miranda. "Or was it four?"

Miranda laughed and bumped into the Princess as she threw herself down onto the bed. "Oh, all right! Enough! This time, though, -"

She drew a delicate gold chain necklace from where she had hidden it under her camisole. "This time it's real!" she said. "The genuine article," she sighed, showing Kaiulani the fragile, antique chain from which hung suspended a lavaliere pendant with one black and one white pearl.

"It belonged to his great grandmother! He says the pearls represent Venus and love. The white one is the goddess and the black one is the reflection of her beauty in a mirror held up by Cupid, the God of love! Could you die?! He says one pearl is him and one is me. And he loves to think of them both resting so close to my heart and he longs for the day when he will nestle beside them!"

Kaiulani was not prepared for this burst of romantic fervor from her formerly down to earth companion.

"Does he have a name, this knight?" she queried dryly.

"Oh, yes!" said Miranda, oblivious to everything but her own joy. "Viscount Maurice Cartier-Rouget." "Maurice," she said again, fingering her necklace as if it was the most precious object on earth. "We plan to marry a year from next summer, or in the fall at the latest. You must be there, Kaiulani, of course! Oh, please, would you be my bridesmaid; please, promise you will! I wouldn't feel right without you by my side, like we always used to."

Kaiulani was not sure what to say. "Have you cleared it all round?" She asked rather tentatively, imagining herself, for some reason, standing on a very high hilltop in a white dress. "Is it all right with - "She could not bring herself to call Miranda's beloved either 'Maurice' nor 'The Viscount' - "with him?"

"He only wants whatever makes me happy," Miranda sounded dreamy with bliss.

"Why will you wait another year?"

"Well, *Maman*, as you know, has always wanted me to 'come out' in society here at one of the Debutante Balls. I promised her I would and Maurice—"

She began to giggle like a young girl - "Maurice says it will be amusing, my coming out and then becoming engaged and marrying him right away after! It will be so lovely, Kai!" she sighed.

"The Debutante Ball?" Kaiulani asked, feeling rather confused and dazzled by this new burst of ecstasy.

"No, the wedding, of course, silly!" Miranda put aside her own happiness long enough to focus on her friend. "You know, Kai, the Deb Ball -" she said slowly, "You really should be there, too. To come out, with me. Mama's chosen the one in May, year after next, in Paris, of course. It would be so much fun to do it together! We'll get all dressed up and there's this funny promenade kind of thing everyone does where all the girls walk up and down a sort of plank-type arrangement, just like prize hens, I swear it's true! But everyone does it so it's not like you're being ridiculous all alone. There are tons of eligible men, too, of course," she mused thoughtfully.

Miranda grabbed her hand and held it fast and close.

"Do say you will! Promise! I know Mama would be thrilled to arrange it!"

"All right, all right!" Kaiulani had to smile again at Randa's avid, insistent nature. "If I'm still here, and not back home, I'll come. If I'm not home by then, heaven knows I'll need some distraction to keep me from going crazy."

The terrace where lunch was served looked out over the edge of the river. A steep rock embankment rose up sharply on one side of the estate and a pristine, meticulously cultivated garden was on the other. Sunlight streamed over the terrace and dappled in the winds that shifted through the tree branches, highlighting one section at a time, sometimes playing over the water as it alternated beams of light and shadows throughout the gardens and far and wide over the rocky hill.

Kaiulani felt oddly detached from the company. Although she listened, responded and even initiated a remark here and there, she had the old sensation that she was playing out a scene. All the conversation and events seemed like they had been scripted in advance; they felt rehearsed and completely predictable. Once or twice she thought she saw Maddie look over at her with a keen curiosity, when she thought Kaiulani would not notice her questioning glance.

Several immaculate and silent servants, all of them dressed in shimmery pearl gray and starched white linen, served the light, delicious meal. An excellent grilled salmon "*au poivre*", in a delicate sauce of lemon butter and shallots, was their first course, followed by a cold salad of new potatoes and string beans *a la vinaigrette*. Dessert was a strawberry cream tart, still warm from the oven, served with coffee and liqueurs. When they had finished Miranda shyly asked her mother what she would think of the possibility of Princess Kaiulani coming along as a welcome addition to the Debutante Ball. If the princess was able to do so, of course.

Madame de Courcy, with a sharp look, made a rapid and calculating assessment of the foreign princess. Mentally, she tallied up the enormous *caché* she would gain, and what a feather it would be in her cap to formally introduce such a rare, exotic treasure to Parisian society. A glint of pleasure and triumph gleamed in her eyes. However, because she was a well-bred woman of the aristocracy, she merely responded, "Yes, of course. I shall see to it."

* * * * * * * * * * * * * * * * * * *

On the ride back to Paris Maddie rattled on about the de Courcy estate and its decor, speculating on the family's holdings and position, until she realized that Kaiulani had only nodded and" hmmmed" for the last several miles without saying a word. Only the abrupt cessation of Maddie's chatter shook her from her reverie.

"I'm sorry," Kaiulani said, "They owned what property previously in Italy? Or did you say they do now -? "She hoped Maddie would fill in the information and resume, leaving her again to her own thoughts.

"All right, my little cabbage." Maddie smiled as slyly as a cat taking a bead on a bird. She examined Kaiulani as intently as a jeweler poring over a fine diamond with his loupe. "You can fool many of the people most of the time, but not me today. You're a million miles away."

Kaiulani protested but Maddie held up a hand to stop her.

"That attentive, civilized routine may work on some but it is absolutely lost on your old friend Maddie. What on earth is so preoccupying you this afternoon?"

Kaiulani hesitated, desperate to keep up her charade, but suddenly found she could not. The mask-like expression on her face fell away and tears welled up in her eyes as she poured her heart out in a wild rush.

It was all very well that Miranda was so much in love, she breathlessly explained, and with such a wonderful man, too; a count who was going to marry her! She was happy for her happiness, she was; but what about her, what about Kaiulani, then!? What was going to become of her, who had no one who wanted to lay his head pillowed against her breast where his great grandmother's pearls had once nestled! And what if, what if, back home; that is, if she ever even managed to get there -!"

"Now, now, now!" Maddie said mildly as she put her small hands on the Princess' strong shoulders. "Such a thunderstorm for one who remains at all times calm!"

To her immense surprise Kaiulani began to cry with abandon; great, wracking sobs rose up from deep inside her. The petite woman rocked the statuesque one as if she was holding a child and talked to her in the tones used to comfort a baby.

"Oh, now, sweetheart. It's all right. There, there. What's wrong, dear? You can tell your old friend Maddie."

The story came out in fits and starts with gales of weeping in between. Kaiulani's heart was breaking; she was so lonely! She knew she shouldn't be; with so many people who were so kind and thoughtful to her, like Maddie and Theo and Mrs. Sharp, of course…But she would never marry; she was starting to feel sure of it! She would never be Queen, either, not with the way things seemed to be going now, falling apart every time she turned around! She would never go home again but would always have to stay exiled from her people and Hawaii -!

After a while Maddie had soothed Kaiulani to the point where she could speak without dissolving into tears. Sighing often, she confessed her worries and worst fears about the future to her sympathetic friend.

After Maddie helped her pat away the tears, powdered Kaiulani's nose and adjusted her hat, she spoke to the Princess in a low, firm voice.

"My dear Kaiulani, I can only imagine how difficult things have been for you, and all that you have been going through. I am terribly sorry about all of it. You are so sweet and thoughtful and you've been working terribly hard at all of this for such a long time with no resolution or change -"

Then Maddie had to stop talking for a moment to regain her own composure, so moved was she by her friend's troubles.

"There is nothing," she said softly, "I can say or do to help you about Hawaii. I am sorry to have to say that, but it is true."

"However," she carefully adjusted her gloves in a precise, determined manner and then took Kaiulani's face, tilting it gently toward the carriage window to catch the afternoon light. "This marrying business," Maddie positively glowed with ambition and pleasure, "Well, that's a different matter entirely!"

"If you are considering prospects for marriage," she said carefully, "or even if you would only like to line up some potential, possible suitors for future reference; well, don't you see, it would be impossible for you to wed some minor lord or unimportant count, like your friend Miranda plans to do. You'd have to look much higher than that. A prince would do, of course - where could we find you some, I wonder? Or, at the very least, someone famous or wealthy - which sometimes is the same thing, by the way, though not invariably, and wealthy is always better, if you have to make a choice. At any rate, a great man of some sort of culture. A composer, perhaps, or a poet, - well, no, not that, not a poet, nor a composer either I suppose, not really. There was a time when a poet might have done, but not any more, I'm afraid, and for some time, too, actually."

Kaiulani, tears forgotten, only listened, intrigued by Maddie's sophisticated plan.

"So." Maddie began to sound a little dreamy, as if she was perusing some huge catalog of fashions. "An artist, possibly, but only if he's quite well off or enormously talented, which hopefully would amount to the same thing in the long run. Or a fabulously wealthy and powerful sort of "lord" of business, you know; that might be all right, too."

Kaiulani laughed, despite herself, at her friend's matter-of-fact offerings of imaginary men who would change her life for the better.

"And where might all these fine matches be found?"

"Darling," Maddie said cheerfully, "We are on the continent, you know, and on vacation for the entire season, after all!"

Kaiulani felt a delicious thrill of excitement and anticipation at the start of her quest for appropriate potential suitors. Under Maddie's more or less watchful guidance, she was wined and dined by a number of important and well-placed men - counts and lords and businessmen, mostly from Europe and America. Some were avuncular and tried to give her advice, which she loathed. A German count, almost as old as her father, proposed marriage to her on the first, last and only evening they went out. Many of her prospective suitors brought her expensive gifts, often jewelry, which she would never accept.

At times she felt like a terrible flirt. She wrote to Toby about the "silly situations" that Maddie had set up so she would have "suitors on the hook," rather like fish, really, she supposed, in the event that circumstances or "a rainy day" sometime decreed that she must marry. Which, *naturallement*, she explained, she had no intention of doing at this point in her life. But she had been advised a few times now by her aunt, the Queen, to take a look at what prospects might be out there, just in case.

"Dear Toby," Kaiulani wrote, "You would not even know me, I think, if you saw me 'out-on-the-town,' as I have been all this summer. I smile and chatter away but this kind of living - the socializing and clever banter - is not and never will be natural to me, not at all. If I ever succeed in getting home to Hawaii, whatever the circumstances, you must come and see me there. For I know it is only back home that I will be myself again."

After several weeks of this hectic, demanding schedule Kaiulani came to dread the assignations and events, even ones she had previously enjoyed. She soon grew tired of the sporting or hunting aspect, and became bored to the point of numbness with the mostly predictable conversations, compliments and remarks. She discovered no one who truly moved her or to whom she could really talk.

"If you want to make an omelet, though, darling," Maddie admonished, "you must break some eggs."

"But I have been out four times already this week alone! And, yes, I am becoming wonderfully well versed in the performance of classical music and operas of all sorts. But if I have to eat one more late supper of roast quail on toast points, or sip another glass of champagne or May wine with a strawberry stuck to the side of the glass, I think I shall scream!"

Maddie acquiesced to a break in their plan, but reminded Kaiulani that staying home and studying would make her no new friends at all, or even casual acquaintances, that much was for certain. She agreed, however, that they would take some time off from their quest. And even, if they must, give it up, if Kaiulani so desired.

Cheerful again, Kaiulani immediately wanted to set up activities for just the two of them, as Theo was, as usual, out of town on business.

"I know the very thing!" Maddie was excited. "There's supposed to be a lovely art exhibition in Paris next week. The Impressionists, I think they call them. Theo saw some pictures in London recently and liked them quite a lot. They paint with light in the background, or tons of white, anyway, to represent the air or something, and they use scores of pretty colors for a change. Anyway, everyone worth talking to in Paris should be there."

Kaiulani thought for a long time about what to wear to the Exhibition. In her travels and experiences with other cultures she had discovered that Parisians were, on the whole, notoriously fashion-conscious. Also, she had spent so much time with Maddie recently in interminable consultations about costumes and cloaks, and how to present oneself in various "looks" and which accessories to wear on what occasions for her many appointments and meetings in search of suitors, that she was really very tired of putting on facades and shows for the world.

"I want to look and feel completely like myself again," she told Maddie, "with no attempt, for once, to seem or be seen as anything but who I am!"

Recalling that Kaiulani, for all her worldliness, was still not yet twenty, Maddie smiled and agreed, leaving the Princess on her own, but "for this time only."

As she tried to chose a new dress for the Paris Exhibition Kaiulani discovered, much to her surprise, that she was not quite sure exactly who she was anymore, independent of her many roles and duties and responsibilities as Princess, daughter and student, or even prospective lover or possible future wife.

She selected a simple tea gown of soft, cream-colored muslin accented with subtle ivory stripes. It had puffed, gathered sleeves, a cinched in waist and a skirt that flowed in a long drape to the ground. The only decoration was a slim sash at the waist and a high collar. The trim was delicate lace in a pale blue robin's egg color. Her ivory hat had a small band of pink silk roses off to one side, and she carried a silk "garden party" umbrella with a polished golden bone handle that looked like it might have fallen from a nest high up in a tree.

She felt very romantic in this outfit, and more comfortable and at ease than she had been in weeks. It pleased her to feel that many eyes turned toward her when she made her way through the halls of the exhibit.

The Impressionists' work, as Maddie had promised, was lovely, filled with soft shadows and warm light. Released from the constant exertion of presenting herself - what was it Miranda had said about the Deb Ball? - "Like a prize hen at market" - she could just see herself, all decked out in feathers and bows, offering herself up like some prime livestock hoping to fetch a good price! Released from the burden of displaying herself to others, Kaiulani enjoyed taking in the energy and beauty that surrounded her. She was reminded of long walks in Hawaii with Koa, Papa, Tusitala and Miss Gardinier around the grounds at Ainahau and at other places on the islands.

Maddie wanted to visit another part of the hall to see some friends who Kaiulani did not know, so the women agreed to meet in an hour for tea, near the main entrance.

As the Princess strolled, taking in the paintings, she had a sense both of observing and being herself observed. It was as if the world she saw and moved in at that moment was a multi-layered scene on a living canvas, a painting that had come to life.

Her eye was caught by one of the most tender portraits she had ever seen. Arrested by the vision before her she stopped dead, standing still as a stone to drink in the details with every part of her body and soul.

The painting was simple, almost plain. A mother sat beside her young daughter and cradled the girl in her lap as she washed her feet. The child, who was around three or four years old, stood in a small basin. An old pitcher took up the foreground. A worn rug on the floor showed muted tones of rose and brown, and a carved, much-used wooden dresser painted with faded pink roses stood behind all. But it was the warmth of the scene, the powerful feeling of serene and peaceful connection that riveted Kaiulani's attention.

The girl's right hand rested above her knee, while her left was angled behind her, bent at the wrist, fingers spread out, firmly supported on her mother's strong knee, with everything in perfect balance and harmony. Dark head leaned in against smaller dark head, and the mother's downy cheek was tucked in against the daughter's plump, bare shoulder, their faces so close they seemed to be touching.

Kaiulani's mother had held her and bathed her like this, sometime, once, at least; she was sure of it! Where had they been? On the beach, or in the parlor at Ainahau? Was it in summer or fall or spring?

A terrible ache of loneliness and desire washed over her like a wave of surf. More than anything in the world she wanted her mother's arms around her, holding her in easy and close; her mother's fingers touching her toes, comforting and protecting her in a timeless moment.

Not even breathing, she was transported as if by some generous - or perhaps cruel - magic into the vibrant portrait. At the bottom of the picture was clearly painted in an even, steady hand, "Mary Cassatt."

All at once, Kaiulani sensed that she herself was being scrutinized, and at very close range. Furious at the intrusion, she wrenched herself away from the picture and spun around to rage against this invasion, only to find herself an arm's length away from one of the most compelling and handsome creatures she had ever seen.

A big man, he was as robust as a peasant. He had the widest, most open face she had ever seen and his luminous eyes were round as saucers. The wild, bushy eyebrows that angled close above them were like unruly caterpillars trying to wriggle away off his face. He looked somehow merry and desperate at the same time, as if he might break into tears or laughter any second.

Even more startled, if that was possible, than she was, he lifted up his shoulders in defense, ungainly as a lumbering bear. Yet when he moved, wary and instinctive, a step or two away from her heat, he did so with the grace of a jungle cat. Not until then did Kaiulani notice the tiny, vividly dressed child dangling from the end of one of his paw-like hands and the woman, all darting, fluttering movement, like a bird, who was attached to his arm.

The hummingbird woman, her rosy, delicate, aristocratic face and massive, gingery halo of curls set off by an impossibly high, wing-like collar, wore a slinky, sheath-style dress. Her long, low cut gown was patterned with fabulous, glittering designs of multiple geometrics: irregular shapes overlaid with swirls of richly saturated color - sea green, copper, aquamarine, turquoise and gold. Next to this exotic vision in her hypnotic flurry of sparkling colors, Kaiulani felt suddenly like a child, like a young girl all primly and properly attired, dressed up for an afternoon party in her ivory and white muslin frock.

When the woman opened her small, rosebud mouth, a high soprano voice as brilliant and colorful as her clothes shivered out.

"There, now, you see, she is just as I have told you!" Her breathless, vivacious energy and voice seemed to vibrate in the space around her. She spoke German in a heavily accented Austrian dialect.

"Beautiful, exotic and strange, all at the same time! Come on now, Gustav, you must admit it!"

The bear-like man responded in a low, pleasant growl that made Kaiulani think again of a lion or a wild cat. His fluent German was smooth, slightly accented with the same Austrian dialect as the woman. Despite his unusual demeanor, he was obviously very cultured; and a man of some status in the world, enormously comfortable in his own body and skin.

"Yes, of course, you are right, Emilie." He nodded his head demurely to the Princess, who suddenly realized they thought she did not understand what they were saying.

"But the eyes," he murmured softly, "So sad."

Kaiulani bristled at his somber tone, feeling like a cat herself. She answered in perfect German.

"And you, sir, I suppose, consider yourself a bastion of perpetual happy feeling?"

"Oh, my heavens," he said in a tremulous English to his companion, "She speaks German! We have insulted her, I fear!"

"And English, as well, Mr. Gustav. So wouldn't it be a minor improvement," she said, graciously offering her hand, "If we were at least all properly introduced?"

He had an air of almost desperate concern as he fumbled around in his eagerness to pull a calling card from his pocket.

"Gustav Klimt, mademoiselle. I am terribly sorry. I do decorative work, mostly buildings," he said apologetically. "I also can paint and draw."

"And he designs any number of other useful and charming things, too, including my dresses, on occasion!" Emilie swooped in again by his side to show off. "And he is ever," she looked like a playful kitten holding on tightly to his arm, "so clever and nice." There was something calculated yet charming about the way she flirted with him. She did so with all the focus and concentration of a professional musician, tuning him up as if he was some finely calibrated violin, a highly refined instrument that was tremendously fussy and fragile.

And he did, indeed, seem to be regaining his equilibrium as he smiled broadly at the slender woman beside him, basking in her praise.

"Well, yes, thank you, dear Emilie."

He looked over at Kaiulani, preening a little now and entirely back at ease. She felt a strong force of animal magnetism coming from him and had the sensation of being physically drawn into his sphere.

"You looked to us so like a Princess, visiting royalty of some sort. Or - "He was embarrassed but determined to say what he meant, - "Well, I said," his voice became softer, even dreamy, and he seemed all at once to be touching her everywhere with his eyes, half-looking through her as his glances moved over her here and there, maddeningly teasing and tender. "I said a goddess, even, perhaps. We are so sorry to have disturbed you -"

"Gustav! Is that really you? And Emilie and, oh! This must be little Emilie, no? I am so happy to find you all here!"

Kaiulani smiled, relieved that his eyes had turned elsewhere and not a bit surprised that Maddie Davies, who knew everyone, was friends with this unusual couple, half glamorous, half gothic, and their tiny, ethereal looking child.

Maddie did not need to insist that they all go out for tea together as everyone was more than willing.

Kaiulani had the disorienting sensation, repeatedly, of trying to prevent herself from leaning against Gustav Klimt, or falling into his arms, so strong was her attraction. He was like an undertow that constantly threatened her balance. She could not at first believe that no one seemed to be aware of this electricity between them. She could neither look into his eyes nor turn his direction without feeling dizzy and light headed.

Conversations ebbed and flowed. Kaiulani hoped she was responding intelligently, but would not have been surprised to find out later that she had been making incoherent sounds the whole time. Little of what was said, those two or three hours they were in each other's company, existed on a level of logic or familiarity for her. Nevertheless, she was able to piece together that the hummingbird woman - Emilie Floge was her name, - was not Gustav Klimt's wife or mistress, but the widow of his late brother. The child, therefore, she reasoned with considerable effort, was apparently his niece and her daughter, and not their offspring; yes, she thought that must be how it went.

Never in her life had Kaiulani been so entranced by another human being. She felt giddy with excitement at the same time that she felt an aching pain, so overwhelming was her desire for this calm man who sat beside her, eating cookies and sipping at tea as though nothing out of the ordinary was going on. As if sitting beside someone while invisible, crackling currents of energy shot back and forth between them was a normal, everyday occurrence. When he took a breath she felt her own lungs expand and then contract. Every time he moved she experienced a mild vertigo, felt the vortex of his power surround her and threaten to engulf her. She could have sworn that she heard his heart beat.

And no one else - including - or perhaps even especially him - seemed to notice or mind! Maddie and Emilie Floge chatted on about dressmakers and boots; Klimt patted his little niece's head and fed her pieces of sweets with his paw-like fingers and beamed out beneficently on everyone. A man of few words by nature, he had an all-consuming lust for soaking in everyone and everything around him. He loved to eat and drink and revel in the colors and rhythms and chemistries of all the life that came within his range with unending joy and delight.

Kaiulani was almost unbearably aroused. When they finally parted, with promises to visit Klimt's new studio in Vienna at an appointed time in the relatively near future, all of this negotiated between Emilie and Maddie, Kaiulani was trembling in every fiber, feeling both miserably overwrought and more acutely alive than ever before. All she could manage to say to Maddie when at last they were alone was to ask her, who on earth was that man?

Maddie chuckled low in her throat.

"Oh, now, don't tell me he's gotten to you, too. Ah, I can see he has! Very charming, that one. And quite a good business building up; very steady, in his own way. He paints unusual pictures... Wonderful, really, but quite, well, daring, to put it mildly. Lots of symbols and mythology, I suppose." She smiled, thinking of his pictures. "He is something else, isn't he? Everyone adores him, of course, especially women, and, naturally, children, too. There's just something about the man—attractive, exciting, even dangerously so, in a way, if you consider how -"

She broke off, pausing for the first time in a while to look closely at her friend's face.

"Oh, dear," she said in a much more subdued tone. "He really did get to you, didn't he?"

Kaiulani could only nod.

"Well," Maddie considered thoughtfully, "Anything is possible, isn't it, I suppose. He's well off enough already, and sure to become more so. He is a painter, which isn't ideal, but he has a very solid hold, too, as an interior designer, of sorts. He did the new Ringstrasse buildings, as a matter of fact, and won some awards for them, too! Which is much better, really, than- - - -"

She stopped again when she saw that Kaiulani, electrified and beaming, had not taken in a word.

"Oh, my! Hmmm!" Maddie was impressed by the intensity of Kaiulani's response. She had never known her to be speechless before. "My, my, my, my dear! Well, then!"

She patted Kaiulani's hand. "Well," she said brightly. "We shall just have to go to Vienna, then, so you can see him again, and then - and then - well, we shall see what we shall see!"

The two weeks between the Paris exhibit and the trip to Vienna slipped away like quicksand. Kaiulani lived for the night time and her dreams—which were of lush, exotic settings in which she and Gustav laughed, danced and held hands, pouring themselves into each other like twin fountains or two rivers that flowed into the ocean. Other times, Klimt came to her in the shape of an owl that flew all around her, resting in her hair, perched on her back or shoulders, or rubbing against her feet like a puppy or kitten. Or she would search for him, traveling through dark caverns or caves, blindly seeking his light and warmth, on fire with desire and the frustration of needing to be near him. Another time he appeared as a robed, hooded *kahuna,* or priest, who undressed her with great care, attending to her as if they were involved in some ancient, intricate ritual of sacrifice and birth.

Once she was cloaked in a robe of shivering, living fishes that felt like lava dripping over her body, burning and cooling her all at once. In another dream they wore garments woven of grass and leaves and moss, damp and moistly alive; and then their pelt-like furs, their outer skins, began to merge and turned them into a single, entwined, mythical creature.

She hardly knew where she was most of the time and cared not at all. She would eat nothing, or else be ravenous, unable to stop feeding herself, filling herself up until hiccups and laughter forced her to stop. She felt awful and wonderful, excited almost to the point of sheer exhaustion.

Maddie, at first, laughed at her new lack of reserve, for she had never seen her so wild and beside herself before. But she was also secretly thrilled to see Kaiulani come so vibrantly alive. Maddie came to view Kaiulani's intense infatuation with a deep respect, and did not try at all to advise or direct her.

"You must find out about this one alone, dear, and see where it takes you. With my blessings and best wishes as always, of course."

* * * * * * * * * * * * * * * * * * * *

At last they arrived in Vienna. There was a heady, intoxicating quality in the air that Kaiulani had not felt anywhere else in the world, not even in Hawaii.

The citizens of Vienna seemed more acute and alert in some mysterious way. A long tradition of respect for history, culture and art was evident everywhere. Kaiulani had never seen so many palaces, monuments and churches; so much inspiring architecture; and such an awareness of balance - - - from the carefully executed and tended gardens to the lovely classical music that was played, hummed and whistled all over, indoors and out.

Maddie and Kaiulani visited the breathtaking Baroque splendor of the Belvedere Castle, with its extraordinary, lavish gardens. They saw Prince Eugene's winter palace and its painted, gilded ceilings, dramatic staircases and grand, great halls. They went to the magnificent Church of St. Charles Borromeo and the Cathedral of St. Stephen and the steeple of the Minorite Church, still in the same spot where it had fallen during the Turkish artillery siege of 1529. There was the Trinity Column which Emperor Leopold I had built in gratitude for Vienna being spared the terrible Plague; and the Capuchin Crypt where twelve emperors and fifteen empresses rested in eternal silence. They saw the sumptuous new Burg Theatre on the amazing, incredible Ringstrasse, with buildings designed and decorated by Gustav himself, with goddesses and angels and wings!.

And everywhere they heard the pervasive, enduring passion of the Viennese people for music.

When Theo finally returned again from business to rejoin them and met Gustav for the first time, he was put off by the artist's curiously slow movements and soft-spoken words. Toward the end of their visit, when Klimt quietly inquired if the Princess might honor him by posing for a few sketches in the afternoon hours of their stay, her guardian barely concealed his displeasure. Kaiulani, though, could hardly contain her delight.

Maddie managed to convince Theo to put aside his chaperoning duties for the few days they were in Vienna. She distracted him, keeping him occupied with tour after tour of the city's ornate architecture. When he questioned whether it was wise for Kaiulani to spend time alone every afternoon at Klimt's studio, Maddie soothed him. She explained that, although he was certainly a genius when it came to business affairs, neither one of them understood the first thing about art. Whereas Kaiulani had been a devoted student of it for years now. Gustav Klimt was, after all, Theo must remember, the leader of an entire new movement of art! The "*Jugenstil,*" the "youth style," of course! Which she positively dared Theo to say he knew anything about! And how, did he suppose, could Gustav possibly develop an adequate impression of the Princess for a painting unless he had time to sketch out a few poses?!

"Besides," Maddie said. "Kaiulani is not a child anymore. Yes, you are her guardian, and that is well and good. But you are not her keeper, my dear, so you must let her be a little independent. If Kaiulani is to become Queen and rule anywhere, or even make a life for herself, she must be allowed some freedom now."

So this gift, to be released from being watched over and directed for once in her life, was given to Kaiulani in a city that already placed the highest value on such individualism and freedom. After the obligatory morning sightseeing and museums and monument visiting with the Davies, the Princess was able to spend her afternoons alone with the object of her recent dreams, the artist, Herr Gustav Klimt.

* * * * * * * * * * * * * * * * * * *

Klimt's studio in the Josefstaderstrasse was mostly hidden in front by a small, dense, lush garden. A breathtaking array of flowers in every color, shape and size grew luxurious and wild. These flowers were some of the painter's favorite models. Never any fewer than eight cats roamed about the grounds and inside the bare, modest studio. All the furniture was black, simple but sophisticated. Klimt's friends had provided him with a few plain tables and chairs and two or three comfortable couches tucked away in discreet corners, - all designed by his artist friend, Kolo Moser. The only other decoration was the pictures on the easels.

A man of strong and regular habits, Klimt began each morning before six in all weathers with a brisk walk out to Tivoli near Schonbrunn. Max Nahr, a photographer and his best friend from childhood, was almost always with him. The two men consumed a substantial breakfast at the nearby dairy; after which Klimt took a short carriage ride to his studio. There he worked all day long until dusk, taking breaks only to eat a few apples or exercise with his Indian clubs while his models took brief rests, or wait a few minutes for some color to set or for the light to change. He loved the theater and concerts and attended every art exhibition that he could, firm in his belief that, "One has to see everything, even the bad, from which one can learn how not to do things."

Klimt's enthusiasm was contagious to Kaiulani. His high spirits lifted her heart, and his charming smile was enough to trigger her joy.

Klimt wore, as he always did when he worked, a sack-like, floor length, dark blue, monk-style robe, which he called "My artist's smock." As he worked, he frequently held or petted his adoring cats. Kaiulani told him about her peacocks at home; how they followed her around like puppies, and scolded and begged for food, and at once he insisted that he would include their beautiful feathers in her portrait.

Klimt had given all his other models the afternoons off for the duration of Kaiulani's visit. By the time she arrived around one o'clock he was the only person there. But she could see the sensuous, exotic women in their provocative, seductive poses in the paintings that surrounded her. Their gorgeous, intense faces resembled the beautiful flowers, fruits and designs all around them. Their skin and flesh glowed, lit up from within by sparkling shades of rose, gold and green. She could still smell the lingering perfumes of their earthy, powerful female bodies, blended together with the musky, pungent odors of Klimt, his paints and his cats.

The only interruption during their three afternoons of work was the occasional ring of the doorbell. Klimt, who cursed like a fisherman when he went to answer, would open to find yet another down on his luck beggar. Every time, he would reach into the bowl of change that stood always by the door and hand "the poor devil" a silver coin, cordially inviting them to come back for more anytime.

At the beginning, Kaiulani was shy about modeling. The problem was not the loose, draping robe he gave her to pose in; that only reminded her of clothes the *kanakas* wore back home. The trouble was that she was not sure how to look or at what or what to do.

"I never sat for a painting before. Only photographs."

"It is very easy." He smiled at her. "You must only think about nothing and then everything will be fine. I will be sketching from many angles, so you must be at your ease to move about, except when I ask you to hold for a bit, within that small area."

His gesture indicated the couch, chair and a few backdrops; all of which had been carefully arranged to catch the best light.

She was content to be there with him, and to have him look at her with such intensity. Inside, a volcano of emotions made her weak with excitement. Just as he had done in Paris, he seemed to be able to look right through her, or perhaps into her, somehow. Occasionally, he would make a slight adjustment of her arm or hand, or tilt her chin a little.

"Just so, just there. Yes! Thank you. Perfect." Each time he came close or touched her, she caught her breath in response to the bluff charge of his powerful animal nature.

When they had finished working on the second day, he took her for a walk along the misty shore of the Danube River. He talked about his brother, Ernst, who had passed on a year ago exactly and how much he missed him still, all the time, every day. His brother, who had also been his partner and model, died just a few days before Gustav's thirtieth birthday; he did not know if he would ever get over the loss. Thank God for work, that was all he could say. He lived at home with his mother and sister and was glad he could take care of them properly, now that his father and brother were both gone.

Whenever he looked at her she felt like he was caressing her, making love to her with his searching, tender eyes.

The summer evening was cool. As dusk fell, hundreds of lights in the heart of Vienna began to light up, - in the railway stations and government offices, the museums and theatres and shops, - sparkling like a thousand strands of loosely strung pearls randomly tossed about. He was courtly with her and careful, which made her long even more for a kiss or a touch or some sign from him that would ignite the fire she knew must be smoldering beneath his skin as it did under hers, threatening to burn them both.

The last afternoon she was there, a heavy, loaded feeling hung in the air between them. It was as if the atmosphere they moved in had become palpable, dense, opaque and thick.

One part of her was desperate for him to declare himself. She wanted him to hold her and kiss her and love her. To ask her to stay with him, and forget about everything but the passion she was sure flowed between them. But what might she say to provoke such a declaration from him? Their first afternoon together, he told her he was a man who mistrusted words. "Not," he explained, "much of a one for conversation." Words, he said, made him feel, for the most part, seasick, whether spoken or written. A mere letter could fill him with fear and trembling.

"Whoever wishes to know something about me must look carefully at my pictures and try to see in them what I am and what I want to do."

How, then, could she ask him for reassurance or promises after such a statement? And what could he say, really, or even do, to hold her? She knew she must eventually return to Hawaii, to stand by what was left of her people and land. Her heart felt heavy as stone.

Seeming to sense her mood, he offered, for the first time, a glass of sherry, which she was glad to accept. The sweet, dark wine slid down her throat warm and slick, and dulled her anxiety. She could feel herself relax.

"Yes, there, like that is very good," he murmured. She was surprised to find him standing beside her, angling her arms out a bit.

"Today you will relax for me a little, yes?" Klimt's voice was very soft. "This time, you will let go. So graceful, so lovely. A true Princess."

She thought she might have drifted off to sleep except that her eyes were still open. There was something hypnotic about him, as if the air around him had a different density, weight and gravity. She was so comfortable and loose and tired that when he rearranged her on the couch she could hardly feel his touch. Strange that so husky and bear-like a man should have such a delicate, releasing way of touching one...

Kaiulani slowly shook her heavy head to clear it, willing her eyes open.

"Such eyes." He talked to her like she was an infant or a skittish animal. "So beautiful, so sad."

He lifted her chin a fraction. His fingers seemed to be covered with velvet or satin, so silky and smooth on her face they made no more impression than soft, downy feathers.

"Athena." His voice was lazy and offhand but his eyes flickered over her face and body, warm and liquid as a cat's.

"You have seen too much, already, too much sorrow. Not enough comfort. Not enough *Gemutlichkeit* for this Princess. Yet you do not give up your vigilant watch."

His voice was so faint and far away she could not tell if the soft whisper was in her mind or real. She did not care.

"You have fire inside. Too much for one so vulnerable. Wise but wounded."

He continued to murmur as he slipped away from her to work.

"Unyielding. Eyes green and gold, like a cat."

There was silence for a while. Later, she thought she must have fallen asleep. In her dreams she was languorous, floating, enveloped by the Rivers of Lethe, of forgetfulness, as she lived and breathed only to be held by his eyes.

From a distance she heard his voice again, light as wind in trees.

"I will give you a golden mask. And a helmet of copper and gold, which will turn your eyes into flashes of bronze and green, malachite and gold. Chain mail will protect you. A shower of golden coins flows over your lovely shoulders and chest. Your necessary armor. Your shield."

Only his voice made her breathe as she drifted in the stillness of the peaceful, waking dream.

"In one hand you hold a spear, for your warrior self. The challenge of the virgin. But also the fierce determination of the goddess, who is always alert, ever watchful, resolute unto death and beyond. In your other hand a tiny, naked figure of your self, unprotected and wild. The naked truth, held close in your own hand. Pallas Athene, goddess of wisdom…"

It was impossible to know whether she really heard these words, which were so like a song, or merely imagined them. Soon she did drift off to sleep.

When she woke she saw the sun slanting low in the sky. Klimt had tidied up his paints and brushes and charcoals, and was now packing away his smock, looking like the *burgermeister* he was: a solid, substantial citizen closing up shop for the day.

After she had changed he asked if she would like to see the portrait.

"Only a sketch, of course," he demurred as he turned the canvas for her to look. "With a little color added."

The woman in the picture was from another place and time. A profusion of peacock feathers stretched out in the background behind her upraised arm. Her face was mask-like, half- helmeted, and her soft green eyes gazed out into the past or perhaps the future. The shadow of a smile lurked at the corners of her fine, determined mouth. The little nude creature she held so firmly in the fingers of her right hand had wide, outstretched arms and a defiant, tilted head. This homunculus was balanced by a tall, imposing staff that the woman gripped tight in her left hand. Her skin tones were inextricably blended with her chain-mail type armor. Everything in the portrait was burnished copper and bronze, overlaid in accents of gold.

It was beautiful but so hauntingly sad that Kaiulani wanted to cry. Instead she only nodded, then looked directly at him; kindly and gently, he returned her gaze. It was the last time they would ever look into each other's eyes.

Maddie was disturbed by Kaiulani's listlessness and her reluctance to provide any but the barest details about the portrait and their sessions.

Klimt and the Princess were perfectly cordial, and even held hands for a moment when they said good-by, as she was leaving Vienna for good. But it was as if they were strangers each waiting for a train, going off to opposite ends of the world. They were civil and polite, but formal in the manner of acquaintances who will never meet again.

Maddie wanted to hear all about it, and was hurt and puzzled when Kaiulani said there was nothing to tell. It had been fascinating to model for him, of course, she explained, and to see his studio and paintings. But they had only worked together so he could talk to her a little and develop a theme for his picture. When Theo asked how everything had turned out, Kaiulani smiled discreetly. Klimt had chosen a Greek motif, she said. Beyond that, she said, they would all just have to wait and see.

On the train back to England she dreamt about him one more time, then put him out of her mind.

* * * * * * * * * * * * * * * * * * *

Back in England Kaiulani felt depleted and worn out, but her terrible spell of restlessness had passed. She never spoke of Klimt again and only smiled when his name came up in conversation, or when Maddie or Theo mentioned him in conjunction with an exhibition or gallery.

With quiet determination Kaiulani again applied herself to her studies. At last she was able to write to Aunt Liliu regarding her position on marriage. She had no plans, she said, none at all, at least for the time being.

"Dearest Aunt,

I am sorry to say it has been a very long time since I received your letter. I have often tried to answer it, but failed. I have given a great deal of thought to what you said about my marrying some Prince from Japan.

Unless it is absolutely necessary, I would much rather not do so.

I could have married a rich German Count, but I did not care for him. I feel it would be wrong to marry a man I did not love. I believe I should be perfectly unhappy, and we would not agree. Then, instead of being an example to the married women of today I should become like them, merely a woman of fashion and more than likely a flirt. I hope I do not express myself too strongly, but I feel there must be perfect confidence between us, my dear Aunt.

I look every day in the papers for news from home, but nothing seems to change. I wish things could be properly settled. It is so hard to wait here not knowing what is happening."

I sympathize with your troubles with your sight, as I know well what it is to suffer from the eyes. Sometimes now, if I look very long at anything I get such a headache I don't know what to do.

Your Loving Niece,
Kaiulani"

There was nothing she could do but wait and hope.

Then, at the end of the long summer of 1894, the bitter news came that, on August 27th, the U.S. Congress had formally recognized that fledgling cuckoo bird, the usurpers' Republic of Hawaii. President Cleveland's impassioned appeal for a different solution had been superseded by the political pressure of business interests; and the "adventurers" had been given hasty endorsement as the legal government of Hawaii.

It only made Kaiulani feel worse to read that President Cleveland, in his speech to the joint session of the U.S. Congress, had said, "Hawaii is ours. As I look back upon the first steps in this miserable business, and as I contemplate the means used to complete the outrage, I am ashamed of the whole affair."

* * * * * * * * * * * * * * * * * * * *

Just before the New Year she received a letter from Fanny Stevenson, curt and to the point.

"Dear Princess Kaiulani,
You may not even remember me, it was so long ago that we saw you.

My husband, Robert Louis Stevenson, was felled on December 4, 1894, by a stroke precipitated by his disease of consumption, less than one month after his forty-third birthday.

He always spoke fondly of your friendship, and at the end of his life requested that I send you the poem he wrote to be engraved upon the stone at his final resting place.

Also, per his earlier request, he was buried with a yellow ribbon in his vest pocket, which he always kept with him, and said it had been given him by you.

Sincerely,
Mrs. Fanny (Osbourne) Stevenson."

Kaiulani felt a light had gone out in the world. She had always expected to see Tusitala again when she returned home.

As she read RLS's "Requiem" she wept away some of her grief.

"Under the wide and starry sky,
Dig the grave and let me lie.
Glad did I live and gladly die,
And I laid me down with a will.
This be the verse you grave for me:
Here he lies where he longed to be;
Home is the sailor, home from the sea,
And the hunter home from the hill."

Chapter Twenty-Four

The beginning of the New Year, 1895, brought no reprieve, as the troubles in Hawaii grew worse. On January 6th, a brief attempt at a royalist insurrection was made in Honolulu.

On Diamond Head and Punchbowl Hill, rifle shots and volleys rang out for three days as the Hawaiian volunteer army and the New Republic leaders fought. The cannons and howitzer of the PG militia soon decimated the pathetic, disorganized straggle of the pro-monarchy forces. Before two days had passed the uprising had deteriorated into a virtual manhunt in the valleys behind Honolulu, where the annexationists' militia easily picked off the few remaining royalists.

A total of two hundred prisoners were arrested, which included the Queen's personal attendants and staff. One hundred and ninety of those arrested were accused of treason and tried by the PG's military court. The Queen and her nephews, Princes Koa and Kuhio, were the biggest catch of all. After a ten-day sweep of Waikiki and the Honolulu mountains, the last of the conspirators had been thrown in jail. A handful of these were sentenced to death; the rest drew long jail sentences and exorbitant fines.

Among those condemned to die was Volney Ashford, who demanded at his short trial that he be addressed as "Colonel" and snarled out several times that he had not been fighting for the Queen, but rather "against the damned, thieving republic!"

At eight in the morning on January 16th, Queen Liliuokalani had been arrested at her Washington Place home. A single guard had escorted her to Iolani Palace, now called "The Executive Building," where she and her attendant were locked up in a few rooms of her former quarters.

On January 24th the Queen was forced to sign a statement of abdication by which she hoped, as she later explained, to save the royalist conspirators who had been condemned to die and to create a climate of clemency for the others.

The PGs claimed to have found at Liliuokalani's residence an arsenal, a regular ammunition dump of bombs, rifles and cartridge belts with at least 1,000 rounds of bullets along with some pistols and swords. According to the testimony of the Queen's servants and personal retainers at Washington Place, however, the PGs had thoroughly ransacked the place and found nothing but Liliu's diaries, personal papers and possessions, which they had promptly destroyed or stolen.

The Queen knew nothing about bombs or any other weapons that were allegedly planted in her garden, and admitted only to making plans to replace the present cabinet.

Her trial was held in the former Throne Room of the palace. Repeated attempts by the military commission to mock the Queen fell flat when Liliu maintained her level tone and civil demeanor throughout the proceedings.

When one of the interrogators scoffed at her denial, and laughed at her as he asked how anyone could not have known about such a stockpile of weapons in their own garden, the Queen fixed him with a cool, steady stare.

"It has been for some time now, sir," she calmly responded, "that we Hawaiians have been banned from our own lands. Why should our gardens be any exception?"

Another commissioner sarcastically inquired why she continued to insist on giving false testimony about the ammunition stash. A spark of anger flashed across her face but she only replied, *"O na hoku no na kiu o ka lani."*

A satisfied murmur from the natives who were present made the irate questioner demand a translation. The interpreter could barely keep from smiling as he translated, "'The stars are the spies of heaven.'" When the nearly apoplectic interrogator, purple faced with rage, shouted at the man for an explanation, Liliuokalani herself politely interpreted.

"'The stars look down on everyone and everything,' sir. I have no reason to lie."

The fifty-seven year old Queen was convicted of conspiring to commit treason and sentenced to five years of hard labor and a five thousand dollar fine.

Determined to make the best of her situation, the Queen spent the many months in 'jail' as productively as she could, writing songs and taking long walks pacing back and forth on the short veranda. After a long time, she was given permission to write to her niece.

"My Dear Kaiulani,

I am sure that by now you have heard more than enough of bad news. So I have set myself the task of searching for positive events to tell you about.

My room here is rather large, though uncarpeted, as most of the furnishings and most of our creature comforts have been removed from the Palace. Mrs. Wilson and I are doing as well as can be expected under the circumstances. We share a bathroom, which is time consuming at best, and she has a small bed sitting room next to mine. Thank heaven for our veranda - it is the only way I can see the sun and skies, which I miss more than anything else.

I am writing songs and prose pieces and trying to put down as many of my recollections of our history and culture as I can remember while I am here. As I am writing music without the benefit of instruments, I must transcribe all the notes by voice alone. I find great consolation in composing. I am adding a little to the song called *"Aloha Oe,"* which I began several years ago as a kind of tribute to your Mama. I am grateful she is not here now to suffer all this; though I do wish, the more I think about her short life, she had been granted an easier time of it. I miss her very much as I know you do, too.

The only thing I cannot seem to get used to are the constant footsteps of the guards for, even here, we are under surveillance twenty-four hours a day. Fortunately, I do not hear them any more, or at least do not notice them, when I work on my music.

Whatever you might hear, my dear niece, about the details of my signing an abdication of power is likely to be untrue. I will say now, as I have said again and again, and will continue to say forever, that I owe no allegiance to any power or anyone save the will of my people and the welfare of my country.

If you do hear, however, that I have sometimes referred to the guards as "snakes," I must confess that is the truth. It is one of the few areas where my Christian patience fails me time and again. Only God is perfect.

Please take good care of yourself. Continue to strive for understanding and keep your spirits hopeful.

I trust God we may see each other soon.

          With abiding love,
          Your Aunt Liliu

P.S. I have enclosed a prayer to be sung by a chorus, which is, my dear Kaiulani, for you."

Kaiulani's hand shook as she picked up the sheet of lyrics that had come loose from the other pages of her Aunt's letter.

She could hear Aunt Liliu's honeyed, dark tones as she read the words of the song.

"*Nu Oli* - The Queen's Prayer
Lovingly dedicated to her niece, Victoria Kaiulani
O Lord Thy loving mercy
Is high as the heavens,
It tells me of Thy truth
And tis filled with holiness.
Oh! Look not on their failings,
Nor on the sins of man,
Forgive with loving kindness
That we might be made pure.
For Thy grace I beseech Thee,
Bring us 'neath Thy protection,
And peace will be our position,
Now and forever more.

Amen."

* * * * * * * * * * * * * * * * * * *

Kaiulani spent most of that winter and spring at the Yews, visiting the Davies at intervals and on the holidays, and reading a great deal of poetry while she tried as best as she could to rest and regain her energy and strength. Though Mrs. Sharp's good nature and companionship kept her from withdrawing entirely, she was often alone with her thoughts as she tried to understand, especially during her many wakeful hours at night, what was happening to her world.

Sometimes she felt as if she, too, was in prison along with Aunt Liliu and Koa and Kuhio, from whom she had not heard at all. She wrote to Papa and Aunt Liliu regularly and included in one of her letters to each of them a haiku, a Japanese poem of seventeen syllables. "It expresses well," she told them, "the philosophy I am struggling to develop."

The haiku was by Issa, a seventeenth century poet, who had written it after the death of his infant son.

> "Dew evaporates
> And all our world is dew,
> So dear, so fresh, so fleeting…"

Kaiulani would often recite the poem to herself when she felt the onset of one of her harsh, unrelenting headaches. They could last for anywhere from a few hours to several days, so she tried hard to calm herself at the beginning to avoid them as much as she could. Sometimes the haiku helped her relax; other times it did not.

Papa wrote in late March to let her know he had filed an account of their personal possessions and estate at the insistence of Mr. Thurston and Mr. Dole. The Honolulu Bulletin of May 17th included an article with an extensive listing of, among other things, what was left of Mama's jewelry. The reporter, impressed with the collection, had rather churlishly written, "Now that Miss Kaiulani is in lawful possession of the above…she ought to be satisfied," adding snidely, "At least, most young ladies would be." He suggested that she could quite successfully open a jewelry store if she cared to, with all her inherited wealth.

Kaiulani thought it not very nice that those who had stolen so much from them and Hawaii begrudged her and Papa the little portion they had left.

Papa sent a telegram to say that he would be coming to see her after the estate business was settled and expected to arrive by midsummer. She was elated with the good news among so much that was bad, and became quite lively again for a time, bicycling everywhere with Mrs. Sharp that summer. They both wore the daring and fashionable new "culottes" or "sporting pantaloons."

Mrs. Sharp was especially enthralled with the new "metal horses" and often went out on her own when Kaiulani chose to stay home and read or write. Mrs. Sharp returned from her adventures "on wheels", or "*a la bicyclette,*" exhilarated and full of praise for the practical, egalitarian transportation.

"It healthfully affects absolutely everything, my dear! Including one's breathing and digestion; and it's an excellent cure for insomnia!"

The headline in the daily newspaper on the table caught her eye, and Mrs. Sharp shook her head ruefully after she had taken it in.

"You know, even if that Lizzie Borden in Massachusetts didn't kill her father and stepmother, well, I can certainly see how she might have wanted to! Can't you?"

Mrs. Sharp shook her head again in sympathy.

"I mean, just think of it! - A hundred and four degrees in August, and all of them locked up in that stuffy old house, and that bad fish they ate! And you know that poor girl was wearing layer upon layer of those thick, nasty woolens, and probably a steel trap of a corset as well! Frankly, I think she did it. Who else was there, after all?! But I can't say I blame the poor child. I'll never wear a corset again! If Lizzie Borden had had a bicycle, I'll bet that never would have happened!"

Papa arrived on August 10th with the news that most of the conspirators' sentences had been greatly reduced and even, in a few cases, dismissed. The Queen's health, he was sorry to say, was somewhat compromised by the stress of imprisonment. She had refused, of course, as stubborn as ever, the PGs' generous offer of a weekly ride out into the countryside. But there were stories that Dole was considering a full pardon for Liliuokalani, too, and might release her soon.

Archibald Cleghorn looked decades older to his daughter. She had not even, at first, recognized him. When he came off the boat, she saw only an old man, stooped and rather pinched looking, and was shocked when she realized she was looking at her father. Almost five years had passed since they had last seen each other, in London - she could not believe how long it had been! From his bowed demeanor she felt bitterly that time had not been kind to him. She longed to make amends, to take care of him somehow. But there was nothing, really, that could protect any of them from what had already come to pass. So the dutiful daughter put on a pleasant smile, and arranged her face into a mask of contentment as she escorted her now entirely white haired father to the Davies' home where they stayed as honored guests for several weeks.

As autumn closed in upon them Papa's spirits seemed to droop in the chill, cooling air. The novelty and relief of being away from the conflicts in Hawaii had begun to wear thin. He longed, he told his daughter, for a "bit of home" himself, so they decided to visit Scotland. The sale of a few pieces of Mama's jewelry had given them some temporary financial freedom so that they were able to come and go more freely. They had no idea what was coming next and both often felt, as Kaiulani admitted in a letter to Miranda, "a little set adrift."

Just before they left for Scotland they received the cheering news that Aunt Liliu would soon be released. Dole had "conditionally pardoned" the Queen, Koa, Kuhio and the rest. Aunt Liliu would be "on parole," which meant she would be permitted to stay at her own Washington Place home, but not allowed to leave the grounds.

This good news made Kaiulani feel easier about her plans to travel with her father and she gave herself over to getting to know him again. Slowly but steadily they began to remember each other's humors, needs and peccadilloes, and relaxed into a new relationship; more equal than they had been before. Papa began to seem more of a companion and friend to her than father now.

"It feels so strange," Kaiulani wrote Miranda, "to be traveling with Papa this way. Almost as if we were an elderly couple! We have settled into quite a regular domestic routine. Meals out, with the exception of breakfast which we generally take at the hotel, and then off for our daily "morning constitutional" as Papa calls it, in every weather, rain or shine, for which we are always "properly and appropriately dressed." (Papa's phrase again, as I'm sure you can tell).

We visit relatives or friends in the afternoons and sometimes in the evenings. They are always kind and polite, though I must work hard to understand their heavy brogues, especially if I am tired. Other times we go out to musical concerts, mostly classical, or to the theatre or a lecture, and then we are usually in bed and asleep by eleven or eleven thirty.

With this mild and soothing schedule combined with Papa's constant company my health, I am happy to say, is beginning to improve at last. I hope to be in tiptop shape again for our "promenades" or whatever it was you called them, and for showing off with you when it is finally time for the Debutante Ball in Paris.

I miss you very much. Please write me with news of your "marvelous Maurice" and your life with him in Paris.

Yours Ever,
Kaiulani ("Kai!")"

She wrote Toby to tell him about an odd exchange that had taken place between her and Papa at the end of their travels. On impulse, they had decided to take a brief detour to Calais, where neither of them had been, before they returned to London.

When they arrived in the northern-most seaport city in France, closer to England than anywhere else, they were delighted. Calais' clean ocean breezes were bracing and the familiar, comforting sounds of the waves on the shore put them both more at ease than they had been in a while. Relieved that the reserve between them from their long separation had worn off, Kaiulani had taken to shyly observing her father. She often admired his strong yet delicate hands, remembering how many times she had seen them at work in their gardens or holding a book, held close against her own cheek or stroking her mother's back as they danced.

They sat on the hotel terrace that overlooked the ocean in the mild, fresh, fall afternoon. Papa was telling her about an amusing incident that had taken place in San Francisco at the start of his trip.

"So there I was, walking through the gardens in Golden Gate Park, anxious and impatient to see you, when suddenly I heard these startling sounds behind me, like children yelling, all at once, or cats fighting with each other. I turned on my heel to see what was happening, and what do you suppose I found behind me, right there in Golden Gate Park?!"

"You must tell me, Papa. I cannot guess."

"Peacocks! Fans all spread out, cackling away, following me like a small army, scolding me to be on my way! As if they knew I was heading out to see you!"

They both shook their heads and laughed together at the bossy, predictable nature of peacocks. Kaiulani felt an emotion swell up inside her, which escaped in a heartfelt sigh.

"Are you all right, dear?" Papa awkwardly patted the fingers of her hand. "You have looked a little pale, of late…"

"It's nothing, Papa," she smiled. "I am overwhelmed at being with you again, that's all," she murmured in a low voice as she looked away from him, out toward the ocean's distant horizon.

The words came out of their own accord, surprising her as she spoke them.

"Papa. I do not know where I belong anymore."

"Belong?" he said a little sharply. "What do you mean, 'belong?'"

"Where I fit in, now that -" She laughed nervously, feeling insecure. "I mean, how I will fit in again, back home in Hawaii."

"Oh, nonsense," he said briskly. He took a pouch of fragrant tobacco from his vest pocket and began to meticulously tamp it into his pipe.

"You are sometimes a little fanciful, I am afraid; like your mother, with all her moods."

The match flared up as he noisily sucked at the pipe bowl and tried to light up.

"You are -" He paused between inhalations - "Hawaii's Princess, that's all, - and you will - be - Hawaii's Princess - always and forever."

The pipe finally lit and the rich, potent smoke rose up around Kaiulani's face like a wreath.

"No matter what happens? In Hawaii?" The smoke cloud had an instant soporific effect on her nerves. It made her suddenly feel very tired, like a sleepwalker struggling to wake up from a dream.

A flicker of uncertainty shadowed her father's face.

"Well, yes, of course, Kaiulani." He sounded perplexed. "How could it be any other way?"

She looked so sad and worried, and a line of concern etched itself into a furrow between her eyes, a frown line he had never seen before. When he leaned in, as if to smooth her brow, she unconsciously pulled away from his touch.

"We belong wherever we are, my dear daughter, and must make the best of our situation," he sighed.

"'Put on a good face'?" She thought she was quoting him back to himself.

"'Put a good face on it,'" he corrected her, unthinking. "Yes, I suppose so."

There was a long silence as they looked out at the deceptively calm waters. Too far away for them to notice it yet, a rough ocean gale was stirring up, heading their way.

"I have never felt entirely - comfortable -" He spoke very quietly, - "not at all times, myself."

He seemed embarrassed by what he was saying and averted his eyes to avoid her beseeching gaze. He looked instead at the pale sun as it slowly sank lower and lower in the sky, coming closer and closer to the dark ocean waves.

He patted her hand again, as if to humor or quiet her, as if she was a child asking a foolish question or making an unreasonable demand of him. Barely audible, his voice again broke the silence.

"Your mother always seemed to know who she was, what she was doing," he mused softly, really to himself. "Though I never did understand what happened, there at the end…"

His words hung suspended in the air between them. There was only the sound of the ocean waves and the rustle of the breeze turning toward them now, taking sharp swipes at their hair, brushing and ruffling their clothes as it increased and began to whip up the sea foam.

The sun had almost set. The temperature of the air was dropping rapidly and soon they would be in darkness.

"Well!" he said, breaking their reverie as he rose and turned to offer his stiff arm to his daughter. "Shall we head in now, my dear?"

* * * * * * * * * * * * * * * * * * * *

By November, a few weeks after a quiet celebration of Kaiulani's twentieth birthday at the Davies, they returned to London, staying at a hotel and organizing their time to spend the winter together on the Riviera.

At the *Villa Dimure au Cap pres de Menton* Kaiulani was no longer incognito, recognized and greeted there as Hawaii's Princess. There were several expatriate royals among the wealthy, international set at the Riviera and it was a relief for her to feel her situation was not unusual. A series of social events and new friends as well as old kept them busy throughout the season.

At the villa of the Kennedys, a very rich older couple from America who loved to entertain and associate with other wealthy or famous people, there were parties and dances and musical occasions every Thursday. The Kennedys were delighted to count Princess Kaiulani and her father among their regular guests.

One Thursday at their villa, a renowned pianist from Paris was brought in to perform several pieces by Claude Debussy. This event drew a larger crowd than usual, including the rare appearance of Empress Elizabeth of Austria.

The Empress was residing that winter at the *Cap Martin* Hotel along with an extensive retinue of servants. A petite, wiry woman who had once been extremely beautiful, the Empress Elizabeth was obsessed with maintaining an attractive appearance by keeping herself slim and active. She had come to the Riviera to take very long walks, up to four or five hours each day; and often exhausted her younger companions and attendants with her uncanny stamina and endurance, for she was a driven, determined woman.

Although her figure was almost exactly the same as it had been on the day that she married Franz Josef, the Emperor, her face, hands and neck revealed her age. She was very old, perhaps more than sixty, Kaiulani thought. Her face was a carefully arranged mask with a fixed, neutral expression to discourage further wrinkles and preserve the status quo of her parchment-like skin. Her hair was a meticulously coifed helmet of soft, pearl gray curls that moved just a little when she spoke. Her green eyes sparkled like emeralds when they were focused, but otherwise became dim, as if she was seeing something far away.

When the Princess was presented to the Empress at the Kennedys' *soiree*, the older woman took Kaiulani's hands in her own bejeweled fingers and pulled her in close to look at her face as if she was trying to memorize every detail. She was clearly quite taken with the lovely young Princess.

"My dear," the stern faced Empress intoned, never releasing her vise-like grip on Kaiulani's hands, "I have decided to cultivate you."

Kaiulani was flattered by the attention from this grand and powerful woman, although she was not at all sure what the Empress meant by 'cultivate.'

Over many afternoon teas that winter the Empress told Kaiulani stories of her life with the Emperor Franz Josef, a small, slight man who always wore his military uniform, even at home, and worked from long before the sun came up every day until late into the night. He adhered to a strict schedule and made no deviations from his orderly routine, none. Why, he even slept in an iron army bed, most of the time! Only imagine! Of course, she admired him immensely and he was a very fine Emperor, but at the beginning of their marriage she had sorely missed the excitement of her homeland, her native Bavaria. She had, in fact, been rather lonely, at first.

And then her son, her darling Rudolph, came along and everything changed, just like that! Oh, they had a fine time, then, she and Rudolph! Her husband accused her of spoiling him and complained that the boy had no discipline, but who could resist that angelic, sweet face, those wonderful little hands?! He was her only child, there were no more after, and she adored him. Was there any harm in that, a mother's devotion to her son?

She would only hint at the mysterious nature of the tragic, unnecessary death of her only son Rudolph, just thirty-one years old when he died, only a few years ago. She sighed and shook out her elegant curls, and said half to Kaiulani, half to herself, "No one ever said it would be easy, this life. No one ever said it was going to be fair."

Kaiulani wondered what it would be like to be Empress Elizabeth. More than sixty years old, she walked and walked for hours every day, and always wore, even when she slept, the golden locket with the picture of her dear, dead son on one side and a tiny curl of his red-gold hair on the other.

One time Kaiulani asked Papa if he knew anything about the death of the Empress' son.

Papa had to think about it for a long moment before he replied. When he remembered the incident his face clouded up and he frowned.

"Oh, yes. Messy situation, that one. At a hunting lodge, I believe, in Mayerling." He looked intently at his daughter's face before he suggested, "Perhaps it is better not to talk about such things."

"Papa!" Kaiulani was wounded by his reticence. "You always said to me, growing up, that knowledge is power and power is truth! And that you would always answer my questions, no matter what!" she scolded him sharply.

"You are right, Kaiulani," he admitted with some reluctance, as he struggled with himself about what to do. "If you insist upon hearing it," he looked at his daughter pleadingly but her demeanor had not changed, "Well, then, I shall tell you," he acquiesced.

Archibald Cleghorn looked away from her and out the window of their apartment as he spoke. "It was murder and suicide, I am sorry to say. He killed his young mistress, a German girl, a commoner, I remember she was only 17, - and then turned the gun on himself. Franz Josef was left without an heir. Quite a scandal and a shame, too, really."

Kaiulani hated to think of the Empress Elizabeth's face when she heard the dreadful news. There were rumors that Franz Josef was so distraught he could not afterwards bear to be reminded of his son in any way. After the lurid and untimely death of their only child, the Emperor could no longer even stand the sight of his formerly dear wife's grieving face.

So the Empress had gone away to live on the Riviera where she walked and walked and walked, always with someone carrying a parasol to shield and protect her white face from the sun. She had lived in many places since then and had traveled all over Europe several times. But the wind and weather and time, even though it had not been so many years since Rudolph died, had etched lines on her neck and her hands, and her vivid green eyes seemed often a little vague.

She was glad she confessed to Kaiulani more than once, that Franz Josef could not see her now. Better for him to have the memories of how they had all been, before Rudolph died. Anyway, the Emperor never lacked for companionship, when he made time for such things. She had even helped encourage one relationship herself; had picked out a young woman she thought he might like, an actress, as a matter of fact. She had no cause to be ungrateful. The only thing she ever held against him was that he had always refused to have Strauss' waltzes played at their court balls, and she did so love to waltz to Strauss!

No, she was certainly not ungrateful. The Emperor had provided for her more than adequately. After all, it was not as if he had banished her, not at all. It had been her own choice to travel, her decision to go. And they had cared for each other for a very long time, before the death of their son. He had been a good husband, in his way. He was, after all, the father of her child. She was more than content with her solitude and her walks and her prayers.

She was so glad to have met Kaiulani. She told her many, many stories about her son Rudolph's childhood and his and her own youth. Sometimes she held the young Princess' hands and even kissed them as her sparkling green eyes glistened with tears that never fell.

Kaiulani felt there was perhaps some lesson she might learn from the Empress Elizabeth. That the elderly royal and the compromised circumstances of her life had some lesson to teach her; some clue about how to behave in life, or how not to, and what was important. What philosophy could she glean from this anxious woman, so hectic and restless, and yet so strangely immobilized at the same time? Never allowing herself to smile or frown; always that same fixed, static expression on her mask of a face…

But perhaps there was no lesson, after all. Try as she might Kaiulani could only understand that the Empress Elizabeth had connection to her own grief, and to mourning for her son, and for her own past pleasures. And that she had come to believe that life was not fair and never easy.

Although Kaiulani felt a strong sympathy for Elizabeth, she was glad when the season was over and it was time for her and Papa to move on. For, no matter how much the Empress talked to her, she never listened, not really, when Kaiulani spoke, which was seldom. So consumed was she by her own grief that it had blinded her to everything but her own suffering. She was entombed in a vast, dark tunnel which she would never leave, for this had become her reason for living. Kaiulani thought it a harsh choice, and was never able to reconcile the Empress' professed indifference with her endless, private, unwept tears. Kaiulani reckoned that she herself, faced with such dire circumstances, would act in a very different way.

So the time drifted away, one day like the next, but with different locations and faces, as she and Papa continued to wander.

They followed the Riviera crowd north for the summer to spend time on the Jersey shore at Rozel. In Paris they visited Miranda, who was more radiant than ever. Kaiulani met Maurice and was glad to find him pleasant and bright. She enjoyed the way he watched over Miranda. The couple seemed genuinely happy and devoted, and Kaiulani's earlier jealousy gave way to the welcome warmth of their love.

In Jersey, she and Papa became bird watchers. Living among the hard laboring farmers and their blunt, fierce wives on that tiny island, they took long walks around the wild, small bay areas. Papa often lectured her about the long royalist history of the area, which for hundreds of years had been a bastion of loyalty to kings and queens. Mostly, though, they watched the birds - starlings, magpies and cormorants in the daytime; and listened to the songs of the fat, melodious frogs at night.

Kaiulani felt a strange kind of peace, being with Papa again. There were times, of course, when she longed to go dancing again, or find some people her own age so she could flirt and be reckless and gay. But mostly she was content with her father's constant company. She had someone to look out for now, besides herself, and it helped her.

Aunt Liliu wrote to say she was finally being released from her parole, as were Koa and Kuhio. They were all going to Waialua to rest and recuperate. Mr. Davies had visited Honolulu on business and it was lovely to see him again, except that he seemed to have aged so! She supposed they all had, really. Kaiulani must promise not to be shocked at how stout she had grown when they finally were able to meet again.

At summer's end they crossed back over the Channel and visited for a time with friends and family in Scotland and England. Just before her next birthday, - Kaiulani found it hard to believe she was already turning twenty-one!- she received another letter from Aunt Liliu.

"Dearest Niece,
Aloha! You will be thrilled to know that you have recently acquired a 'new' cousin. I think you will like her very much. Elizabeth Kahanu Kaauwai has just married your cousin! Prince -"
Kaiulani's eyes blurred and for an instant she lost her focus.
"Kuhio," the letter said! It was Kuhio, not Koa, who was married! With sharp relief she read through the rest of it and then immediately sat down to write a letter of congratulations to her cousin and his new bride.

Soon after this announcement Mr. Davies' letter followed with the news that the PG government had officially appropriated "the sum of two thousand dollars per annum for the Princess Kaiulani's private use." The money, of course, would be a help to her and Papa since the funds from Mama's estate and her jewelry had been dwindling at an alarming rate. But how sad that she was to be given an allotment by the intruders. And wasn't it odd that even the PGs must still call her "Princess?"

In London again she sat for a formal portrait in pastels, wearing a low cut, royal yellow ball gown and holding a bouquet of marguerites that occasionally made her sneeze. Papa was pleased with the results but when Toby saw the picture he was troubled and said her expression seemed "rather sad." Kaiulani laughed and said perhaps that was because she sneezed so many times as a result of the bouquet. But she wondered to herself if she had looked like that because the modeling sessions had reminded her of Gustav Klimt.

Papa and Kaiulani decided to spend their second winter abroad at *Menton* on the Riviera. They stayed at the *Hotel du Louvre,* and

Kaiulani was secretly relieved that Empress Elizabeth had relocated to Italy for the present. Aunt Liliu, too, had at last been released to travel.

"Dole himself made out my passport, and wrote it for 'Liliuokalani of Hawaii.' I suppose one can presume that old habits die hard. I should have liked it even more, of course, had he made it out properly to "Her Majesty, the Queen." But I am grateful to be on my way to America. I hope we may find help there, in Washington.

O'ni pa'a, my brave Niece. Fond regards to your father and my love to you both.

Aunt Liliu."

* * * * * * * * * * * * * * * * * * *

Their second winter at Menton proved more difficult than the first. Funds had dipped dangerously low and Papa was constantly worried about how they would manage. Kaiulani's health was compromised, too, with bouts of colds and exhaustion offset by brief, manic bursts of energy.

She wrote to Miranda to ask her to please set aside a suitable gown she could borrow to wear at the Charity Ball, as she could not even think about spending right now. Miranda wrote back to reassure her that she had found "just the thing" and was already having some minor alterations done to adjust the length.

In January '97 a letter from Aunt Liliu informed them that she had arrived in Washington and settled at the Shoreham Hotel. Koa, who had traveled with her, was, as ever, a great comfort. She hoped there might be good news for them soon, although at the moment there still was none.

Winter passed and spring came again. Now it was Papa's turn to be sick with a cold, so by early April they decided that Kaiulani should go on alone, accompanied by a chaperone, for the Paris trip.

It was wonderful to be in Paris again, and the Princess' spirits lifted. With only a few weeks to go until the long-awaited Deb Ball she settled into a charming, furnished apartment at a hotel on the *Champs Elysees*. The April air was soft and mild and Kaiulani felt a sense of buoyancy and lightness she had not known in a while. She passed long, happy hours with Miranda, bustling about the city to find accessories for the ball and hunting down treasures for the bride-to-be's trousseau. They looked at scores of silver sets and china and linens, and assessed home furnishings of every style. With her mother's grudging approval, Miranda and Maurice had decided to at last announce their engagement.

"Not, of course," Miranda said to Kaiulani as she tried on kidskin gloves at *Le Bon Marche*, "until after the ball. But *Maman* agreed to our betrothal soon enough -"

Her eyes sparkled as she stroked an exceptionally expensive glove over her friend's cheek. "After all, Maurice is very rich, you know! But she will not allow her years of planning for the Ball to be 'cast aside,' I think she said, like, well, - "She teased Kaiulani and made her laugh when she coyly held the glove up against her own face, "Like an old glove!"

The streets of Paris those last days of April were like a carnival. Every sidewalk cafe and flower stall had a festive, playful air. The intensely colored posters that Kaiulani and Miranda had admired a few years ago seemed to have multiplied many times over. The striking paintings of Toulouse-Lautrec were well represented again. Their bold graphics advertised theatre, musicals, dance troupes, cafes and restaurants. Now, in addition, there were hundreds of other bright, startling advertisements in the streets. On store walls, buildings and bus kiosks, posted from the rooftops and in underground cafes, their enticing images promoted everything from bread and chocolate to milk and medications, champagne and cigarettes, fine wines, brandy and even books.

Suspended in the air like a whirling dervish was the wild figure of "Olympia," Jules Cheret's golden haired beauty who danced in thin air, her hair flying, cymbals crashing together as she announced the opening of the "Music Hall Extraordinaire!"

There were sylph-like creatures in tuxedoes wearing pencil-thin mustaches but showing off curiously feminine faces and limbs. Prowling black and white cats hunted, and mysterious women wore shawls or hid their faces behind extravagant arrangements of feathers or fans. Some were bare breasted, like the statuesque, larger-than-life Amazons in the studies of Alphonse Mucha. These were women to be contended with, majestic and imposing and eloquent with their unwavering gazes and lush, unsmiling, bee-stung lips. Mucha's women were fairy tale creatures of mythical proportions; they towered over the city streets and held giant paintbrushes or goblets or dragonflies in their oversized yet delicate hands. Even the great Sarah Bernhardt had posed to be immortalized by Mucha.

It was a relief to be back in Paris. Miranda's good humor was like a tonic and the giddy, never-ending excitement of the streets, with musicians and mimes and artists on nearly every corner, made Kaiulani feel young and carefree again. When Papa wrote to tell her his cold was improving and he expected to join her a day or two before the ball, she realized with a start that she had not thought of him for days.

Feeling guilty, she admitted this lapse to Miranda who hugged her close and gently suggested that Kaiulani's father had looked after himself for quite a long time without her help.

"You must not worry so, darling," Miranda smoothed out the furrowed wrinkle on Kaiulani's brow. "Really, you mustn't. It does no one any good. And, besides, it's bad for your complexion."

Kaiulani laughed, glad for her friend who made jokes about worrying. The ball was just a few days away and she was so excited; she looked forward to dancing and flirting for hours every night. Miranda had chosen a perfect gown for her, a dusky rose that set off her eyes and curls to wonderful advantage.

Since her return to Paris she had positively basked in the attention of admiring eyes. A certain confidence had returned to her, and she moved with a new purpose and assurance.

Had she become so superficial, she wondered? No, that was not it. This admiration had returned to her a sense of power and connection that had been missing in her life for some time now. It was lovely to see Papa again, and she appreciated the relatively peaceful life they had shared together of late. But being looked at with approval, just for herself and even, at times, with naked, undisguised lust, restored to her a sense of feeling desirable and attractive. It gave back to her an energy and strength she could find nowhere else just now.

And, who knew, after all; it was possible that she might meet someone suitable…

Yes, but then what? An image of Gustav Klimt's wide, open face and his capable, caressing hands shot through her like a flash of electricity but she willed it away.

* * * * * * * * * * * * * * * * * *

On the day before the Charity Bazaar Ball, Miranda took Kaiulani to see the transformation that had taken place at the *Rue Jean Goujon*. Row after row of closely packed stalls had been constructed to represent the shops and streets of Old Paris. The light wooden roof, which covered the entire bazaar, was hung with Turkish cloths and hundreds of bright, fragile decorations. The tar weatherproofing which covered the roof gave off a sharp accent that mixed with the odors of food, fragrances, paint and sweat. There were merry-go-rounds with painted wooden horses; and table after table of things to eat and drink, and still others piled high with fashions, novelties and toys.

There was a makeshift feeling to the entire arrangement; something theatrical in the close, mingled scents of fresh paint, new cut wood and spring flowers. Carpenters, workmen and painters added final touches while an army of caterers and florists dashed about like bees buzzing madly from one flower to the next.

Kaiulani, delighted with the stage-like setting, clapped her hands together like a child.

"Oh, Miranda, it's like a fairy tale come to life!" Visions of the enchanted night followed by more days and nights of revelry danced in her head.

The morning of the Ball Kaiulani woke up refreshed, vibrating with excitement in every cell. As the morning wore on, though, she began to feel the dull throb at the back of her neck that warned her of a threatening headache. For an entire hour in the afternoon she rested, tended by Miranda's cold compresses, soothing words and hot tea. But by mid-afternoon the dreaded headache was full blown and Kaiulani's head throbbed so she could hardly see. She wanted desperately to go to the Ball, Kaiulani whispered in tears to the terribly disappointed Miranda and her disapproving mother; more than anything. She had even put on the rose silk gown, which had been altered to fit her perfectly. And she wore the pearl earrings

Mama had given to her, with a pale-pink coral necklace that looked like tiny, jagged, rose-colored pearls.

But there was no way to escape the truth: she was unable to tolerate any light or motion at all. The slightest sound, even just the rustle of wind in the trees made her cringe, and the brush of silk against her skin felt like an assault.

Devastated, Madame de Courcy insisted on bringing in her own private physician to see if there was anything he could do to revive the Princess and salvage the occasion. The old man took a long time with his examination and checked her pulse and listened to her heartbeat several different times. At last, though, he slowly shook his head and announced that the young lady must not, under any circumstances, he was afraid, really could not, be permitted to visit the crowded Bazaar that evening. He was very sorry, but absolutely not. Then he administered a mild sedative and took his leave.

After many regrets a subdued Miranda and her sullen mother, who was one of the chaperones, left Kaiulani to her solitude. Afraid to even weep for fear of exacerbating her condition, the Princess lay silent and still, counting the roses on the wallpaper in the dim half-light and praying for the blessed release of sleep. It was the long awaited night of the grand Charity Ball that she had looked forward to for almost two years and here she was, trapped alone in a rented room with only an attending nurse for company.

Her hotel rooms were so close to the *Rue Jean Goujon* that she could hear in the distance the sounds of the great party beginning. The horses and carriages and laughter were like a rebuke from another land, out of reach and impossibly far away.

She must have fallen asleep for when she awoke she had a vague, confused impression of thunder or a storm. There was a pungent smell in the air - what was it like? She struggled to come to consciousness but the pain kept her eyes shut tight. Something worrisome flickered inside her head, but then the attentive nurse was by her side to soothe her. The nurse drew the bed curtains closed around her and smoothed out the sheets with her cool, professional hands and then shut out the world beyond the enveloping darkness.

The next morning when Kaiulani woke sunlight was filtering in through the lacy curtains. There was a strange, acrid taste in her mouth and nose, which she thought might perhaps be an after effect from the medicine that the doctor had given her to help her sleep. Tentatively, the Princess raised herself up on her elbows. The nurse rushed over at once but Kaiulani motioned her off, wanting to find out for herself what kind of condition she was in. She moved her head carefully and discovered, to her great relief, that the horrible headache was gone. It had left her rather stiff in the shoulders and neck but she was otherwise renewed and refreshed. With the nurse's assistance she slowly dressed, with some of the self-protective caution of an invalid, for the intense pain of the day before had left her a more than a little wobbly and weak.

She picked out a linen vest that was delicately embroidered with butterflies, flowers and bees, to wear over her gauzy lawn dress and admired the dozen or so irregularly shaped pearl buttons, which she and the nurse fastened together, one at a time. Garnet and gold filigree earrings completed her ensemble; and she tucked a small, fragrant rose into a lace handkerchief at her wrist and another in the front of her bodice, hoping to sweeten up the peculiar smell which still lingered in the air.

At the mirror on her way out she was grateful to observe that no visible trace remained of her ordeal. Then she headed downstairs to the lobby of the hotel, surprised and pleased to realize she was hungry for breakfast. She wanted to be strong and have stamina to catch up on all the news about the opening night she had missed.

When she got downstairs she could see at once that something was horribly wrong. People were huddled in small groups, talking in low, anxious tones and even whispering. Some clung to each other, fearful and shaken, while others looked as if they had seen a ghost or something equally disturbing. When the concierge saw the royal guest he rushed over and begged her to come away from the crowd and all the dreadful news. Someone walked in from the street and the acrid smell swept in with him like an unwelcome guest.

Soon, much too soon, Kaiulani and all of Paris knew the facts of the disaster. A few hours into the festivities a fire had broken out. When one of the gas-powered cinematographs exploded, it ignited dozens of Turkish hangings and embroideries everywhere, both above and below. Panic swept through the crowded Bazaar faster than the first small licks of flame spread onto the flimsy drapes.

The first desperate cries of *"Feu, Mesdames! Sortez!"* were quickly drowned out by shrieks of agony and terror as smoke and fire engulfed tier after tier of the frail, elaborate decorations. Delicate layer upon layer of silk, satin and velvet gowns flared up; capes and headdresses were transformed into burning shrouds. In less than five minutes the tarred wooden roof roared up like a bonfire and then collapsed, falling in huge chunks and pieces on the screaming men, women and children beneath.

The narrow exits had been completely jammed long before the roof lit on fire and the high walls bordering the three out of four sides of the Bazaar had turned it into a deadly *cul-de-sac*. All the streets bordering the Bazaar - *le Rue Francois*, *le Place Almon* and *L'Avenue Montaigne* - had swiftly become impassable. They were packed with relatives and lovers and firemen and friends, all locked in together, belly to shoulder, panicked, trying to find some way to rescue their loved ones from the inferno of vicious flames. People had gone insane from horror and the helplessness of it all. Another half dozen or so died in the stampede to get into the fairgrounds to save their children, comrades and daughters who already lay dying or dead.

Kaiulani knew at once with horrible certainty that Miranda had been a victim of the blaze. In less than half an hour one hundred and fifty had perished, most of them women and children. When the smoke began to clear enough for the fire fighters to start to recover the bodies, the pitiful shrieks of grieving mourners filled the streets a second time with cries of wretched pain.

Among the dead was Maurice, who could not bear to be apart from Miranda, even for one night, and so had signed himself up to volunteer at one of the booths. All of the people selling at the *Bazaar de Charité* were of or connected to the highest aristocracy of France. Madame de Courcy's charred, almost unrecognizable body was found at the bottom of the first pile up in front of the blocked main gate.

By the next morning, at the *Palais d'Industrie*, there were three very long rows of motionless figures laid out on wooden planks and covered with sheets. Daughters of ambassadors and noblemen lay side by side with the children of cooks and entertainers and shop girls, all of them lost forever. Like ghosts the relatives and friends, themselves as ashen and pale as death, moved slowly, like ghastly sleepwalkers searching among the corpses and remains. A huge pile of coffins was stacked at the center of this makeshift morgue, ready for their heavy freight.

At Notre Dame Cathedral a mass funeral was held, the tolling of the bells only briefly eclipsing the heart wrenching sobs of the bereaved. All theaters and restaurants were closed, all social events canceled. Special masses were given and businesses shut down, putting up their signs of mourning. All the formerly lively cafes of the city were shuttered and silent.

Papa arrived three days after the tragedy. In her enormous grief, Kaiulani had neither eaten nor slept since the horrid news of the fire. Archibald Cleghorn was so shocked by his daughter's haggard appearance that at first he thought she herself had somehow been trapped in and then escaped from the fire. He called in the doctors at once and was given strict orders not to move or disturb the patient for two weeks, after which she must be removed from the scene altogether for an open-ended time.

* * * * * * * * * * * * * * * * * * * *

Poor Toby! Kaiulani thought. How devastated he would be! She tried a few times to write to him but her hand was never steady enough.

At the end of the prescribed two weeks Papa took her back to England, to Ravensdale at Tunbridge Wells, where the Davies had recently set up another new home. From there she was able at last to send Toby a note of sympathy and commiseration. She also wrote to Aunt Liliu.

"I have never heard of anything so dreadful in my life. I have never seen anyplace so overcast as the once gay city of Paris."

In the privacy of her own thoughts, she could not keep from wondering why she had been spared. It was as if a hole had been ripped in her heart and she was afraid to even think about it, afraid she would never stop bleeding. She refused to allow herself to cry, thinking that once she started she might not ever stop.

Miranda, gone?! How could that be? How would she bear it? Never to see her kind, sweet face again! For seven years they had been friends and companions; sisters, really, true sisters to each other.

She should not have to bear another loss, she thought, as angry and bereft as a child who has been grievously harmed. It was not fair, and that was the truth!

Then she thought of all the families in Paris and France who had lost their wives, lovers, children and sisters in the fire, and her rage abated a little. There was a comfort - only a small one, but a comfort nevertheless, - that came to her when her heart reached out to those others who had also suffered such a loss.

For weeks she struggled with her thoughts, trying to keep her mind from returning again and again to the dreadful scene of the fire. Finally, she had been able to close that door. With a great effort of will she had shut that tragedy away from her daily life. The fear, at last, was gone. But the feelings of being deserted and abandoned did not leave her, not for one second. She went through the motions of smiling and talking and moving about, but locked away deep inside her was a fierce and fiery wound.

Papa was very concerned. He had never seen Kaiulani so listless and melancholy. Who could he call on to help her? The doctors advised only rest and more rest. But he could see how his daughter's despair was depleting and damaging her vital energies, and he worried about his child. The idea came to him that Koa might possibly cheer her up, at least a little, and anything was better than nothing at this point. Of course, he had never entirely approved of the young man, a shade too flamboyant for his taste, but, - well, he had to do something, anything! His daughter seemed to be wasting away before his very eyes. He could not stand to see her in such pain. So he sent a telegram to Liliuokalani in Washington, requesting that she send Koa over for a short visit, please, along with money for his fare, if possible.

Poor Papa, Kaiulani thought. He doesn't know what to do. There wasn't anything to do, really. No cure for her hurting heart. Perhaps it would have been better for everyone if she had taken her place by Miranda's side that night...

She stifled these thoughts. She felt ashamed, almost embarrassed in some odd way, by the breadth and depth of her sorrow.

Still, unbidden, her mind kept returning to the nightmare of flames which had cut short so many young lives; to the children who would never be born; to the weddings that would never take place.

In an effort to connect again with the present, immediate world, she gave in to Papa's pleadings and began to accompany him out to concerts and cafes and dinners and lunches with strangers and friends. At his and the Davies' insistence she made herself go through the motions of eating and sleeping and socializing; and slowly, slowly regained the possibilities of conversation and going around, discussing the arts and the weather.

Toby came to see her. He looked terrible, much older and thin as a skeleton, with red-rimmed, bloodshot eyes. Occasionally he gave in to a ragged sigh, but only when they were quite alone. She saw Miranda in his face and eyes and movements, and this comforted her but also injured her again, both at the same time. After only a few days he explained that he must return to London where his work kept him busy and prevented him from giving over entirely to his grief. He loved her, he said, and she knew it was true. The great good of his visit was that, once he was gone, she was able to write to him again, with the image of his face restored to her at last, rising like a phoenix above the ashes of their sadness.

Not long after Toby left Koa came to visit. Kaiulani thought it odd that he had come all the way from Washington just to see her, but Papa was quick to assure her that her cousin was in London on important business for the Queen and had been sent by Liliuokalani herself. And, indeed, Prince David Kawananakoa had arrived at the Davies with a sealed letter for her eyes only from Aunt Liliu, who said how sorry she was to hear of her loss and that she hoped Kaiulani would feel like herself again soon.

Koa seemed more subdued than before. He had gained a few pounds since they had seen each other in Washington. His face was fuller, his shape a little stockier than before. There was a certain sense of - what? - Resignation, perhaps? Furtiveness?- about him now. She could not quite put her finger on it, but he seemed to be missing the steadfast energy she was accustomed to in him. Could it be two years ago, already, that they had last met?

Koa was more cautious now, constantly worrying about things like whether it would rain each day, fretting over if he needed to carry an umbrella or not. He was handsome as ever, with his rich brown walnut color, but now his eyes darted about at times, as if he was checking to see if he was being watched. Her heart went out to him when she realized this must be a result of his long months in jail. He spoke more softly, too, and was hesitant, as if he did not want to be noticed by anyone except her.

But his very presence, the touch and familiar warmth of him, made her improve. She ate with a better appetite, and they even went out dancing once or twice, and again on his last night in town.

She had chosen an intimate cafe restaurant that had a tiny stage, almost swallowed up by a small piano, where poets read or musicians, solo or in duets, played late into the night. She had heard a peculiar French composer at this place a few weeks ago with Papa and hoped he would be there again.

The food was excellent and they complimented their supper with sparkling wine. For the first time Koa seemed at ease, almost his old self again. He had been telling her about the complicated and confusing political scene in Washington these days, where Auntie was still called "Queen" by her supporters, when the French piano player quietly stole up onto the stage, unannounced, and unceremoniously sat down at the piano.

Thrilled to see him, Kaiulani lightly touched Koa's hand and motioned him to look over at the man on the tiny platform stage.

"His name is Eric Satie," Kaiulani whispered. "He plays - his music is - I can't explain it very well. You must hear for yourself."

She leaned in closer to Koa and breathed in the dusky sandalwood scent of his skin as she held on to his hand.

"Claude Debussy orchestrated his music in Paris." She spoke softly into Koa's ear, delighting in the sensation of his dark curls brushing against her cheek. "I heard it there," she whispered as if telling him a lover's secret.

Koa returned the soft pressure of her hand.

The man at the piano had a fastidious look, every hair carefully arranged. His trim, full mustache curled in at precisely the same angle on each side of his Cupid's bow mouth. About thirty years old, he wore round pince-nez glasses and had a tidy, goatee-style beard and sideburns. His high white collar reached up to his jaw line and skimmed the clean sweep of his long, Bohemian hairstyle, which was brushed back and away from his face and temples. His jacket, loose and flowing, was made of an unusual, moss-like velvet. His hair was reddish brown, like a fox, and a strong, aristocratic nose balanced the otherwise pretty features of his face.

He began to play a light, lilting tune that had a dark undertone of sadness.

Kaiulani was thrilled by his music. It was so unearthly, so beautiful; so unutterably tender. It spoke to her of real life, of fierce, immediate joys and pleasures, even as it seemed to stain the air with its weeping, sob-like refrains. The lighter sounds kept trying to rise up and out of the shadows, but every time they fell back again. Dropping out and under, then surfacing again, the darker notes pulled at her like a hand reaching up from the grave to drag her down. She felt faint, as if the air in the room had suddenly become stifling and hot.

When she looked over at Koa a dense fog seemed to have floated up between them, though they were so close that their hands touched. He looked blurred and out of focus to her, as if he was hidden behind a thick layer of smoke.

He was talking to her, she suddenly realized. What had he said?

"Are you all right?" he repeated with some concern.

"I feel a little faint," She smiled wanly. "The heat, I suppose."

"But it is not warm in here," he said.

She shrugged.

"'*Troix Gymnopedies*,'" He read from the program, pleased with himself for being able to pronounce the French.

"'Three Gymnastic Pieces,'" she translated, wondering at the curious title.

Koa abruptly tossed the program down.

"What good is this useless music!?" He whispered in her ear. "It repeats and repeats and goes nowhere at all!"

His frustration and annoyance surprised her. Without thinking about it she had presumed that Koa was wrapped up in the same cocoon or web that the plaintive music had woven around her. She felt hurt, as if Koa had physically pushed her away, but she was also intrigued by his unexpected passion.

"But, Koa!" There was a slight edge of provocation in her tone. "You said that you love all music!"

"Pah!" he said to her. "This is not real music!" Casually, deliberately, he twined her fingers in his own. "I'll bet you cannot even dance to it."

It was a clear dare and she took it.

"You told me once you could dance to anything." The challenge in her voice was equal to his. "Don't you remember?"

"If I said so," his lips brushed across the tip of her ear, "then it is so."

He rose stiffly and held out his hand.

There were only a few people in the cafe so there was plenty of room to move. The room seemed to sway, then fade away as they danced.

In the dim, smoky light they might have been anywhere, even home. For the first time since he had come she looked directly into his eyes, so dark and sad, so much like her own. It was like looking into a mirror or falling down a well. In that moment she realized that Koa could not save or help her anymore than she could him. For all their connection and sympathy they were too much alike, both too vulnerable, to stop the tide of misfortune that threatened to drown them, and the Hawaiians.

All they could do was love each other, helplessly, hopelessly in the storm, clinging to each other on the sinking ship as it went down.

The world they had expected to grow old in was already torn apart and the lives they had rehearsed for so long ago at Mama Nui's house, when they pretended to be king and queen, - well, there was really no hope for that anymore. It had slid out from underneath them, washed away like sand in the tide.

She would have given anything to restore that world to Koa. It was his birthright, and hers! They had been promised it, born into it! But that world had all but disappeared, like quicksand, like a dream that had slipped away from them and been erased.

Koa! She longed to shout out his name, to call out to him and release herself, everything, all of it, into his strong arms. But she could do nothing but continue to dance. A wide, invisible chasm or valley had sprung up between them; it kept them separate from each another, alone and silent, afraid of what the next day might bring.

She felt like she was disappearing, losing substance. Like a Javanese shadow puppet show she had seen in the streets with Miranda in Paris just a few weeks ago...

"Oh, Koa. My dear Koa." She had to stop moving. She clung to his arm to stay steady. "I love you so much."

Even he was out of breath from their mad, whirling dance. "Of course you do. We have always loved each other, Kaiulani."

"Yes," she said. A shiver of bell-like laughter shimmered forth from her in a nervous rush. "I suppose we have."

"And always will," he said, unwavering in his respect and his never-ending loyalty.

"And always shall," she echoed. His hands were already growing cold in her own.

Chapter Twenty-Five

Kaiulani had traveled with her father for more than two years. In that time she had become a sophisticated woman of the world. She had also become a part of the great flow of the disenfranchised, rich and poor alike, who wander, homeless, haunting the world from one generation to the next.

Mr. Davies' son, Clive, had grown up during this time, too. Unlike Kaiulani, though, Clive had settled down, making his home on the island of Oahu where he looked after some of his father's expanding interests. In particular, Clive had been quite successful at managing the thriving Honolulu Iron Works, founded by his father when Kaiulani was just a child.

Clive Davies had been transformed from a slim, tentative youth into a confident man of business, carrying as visible proof of his prosperity the substantial girth and ruddy complexion that, in those times, often accompanied success. Since their first meeting at his college in Boston, Clive had remained a great admirer of the Princess, sending gifts and cards for her birthday and the holidays. Clive had become "a respectable citizen of the world," as his father loved to call him. Married and the proud father of an infant son, Clive had continued to write to Kaiulani, keeping her up to date with news of her homeland.

Clive's most recent letter had deeply distressed the wandering princess, although it did not, unfortunately, come as a surprise. She was well aware that, since Cleveland had been voted out of office in 1896, the incumbent President, McKinley, had put in long hours trying to push through a new version of the less complicated but still very controversial Hawaiian Annexation Treaty.

Recently, McKinley had appointed another new minister to Honolulu. Although Harold Sewall was respected by all, his appointment seemed to precipitate the long-dreaded possibility of the end of the Hawaiian monarchy. On June 16, 1897, McKinley presented another revamped annexation bill to the U.S. Senate. Protested by Liliuokalani and vehemently attacked by the majority of the English and American newspapers, the bill remained under scrutiny nevertheless.

Kaiulani and her father talked for a long time about what might happen if the annexation bill was passed; and what effect that could have on the Hawaiians. If the bill was squelched, on the one hand, the people would be in desperate need of someone to guide and support them. On the other hand, there was no doubt that passage of the bill would constitute a national disaster. For the Princess, exile from her homeland had now become senseless. Papa conceded that the time had come at last for Kaiulani to stand beside her people in their hour of need. On the way home, they would stop in Washington to see Aunt Liliu.

She wanted to rejoice and celebrate the end of her exile, but she could barely manage a smile. What a sad homecoming it would be, unless some miracle saved Hawaii. So many people were gone; so much had changed, forever. But she could not afford to dwell on such things now. The hard work of packing and preparing for the seven thousand mile trip kept her so busy that she had little time to brood.

In the few moments she did stop to think she found it hard to endure the terrible combination of hope and fear! The thought of being on Hawaiian soil again made her feel light-headed, giddy. She laughed and cried over nothing at all, and the photographs, clothing and articles she packed away triggered a thousand memories.

There was a beautiful silk and cashmere shawl, the cool blue color of English rain, embroidered with pale green and gold *fleurs-de-lis*. It had been a birthday present from Miranda. A wealth of feeling stirred as she held it against her cheek and seemed, for just a moment, to breathe in the familiar scent of her dearest friend's lilac perfume. Tears clouded her vision, so that she had to stop her work. She ended up spending the rest of the morning writing a long, rambling letter to

Toby, so full of emotion it was almost incoherent. Repeatedly, she tried to find a way to tell him how much she loved him, how grateful she was to have known him, and how she valued the anchor of family and stability she had always felt from him and Miranda. She wanted to let him know how much he had meant to her, and how they had both strengthened and helped her, every step of the way.

She hoped he would not mind too terribly, but she did not think she could bear to see him and then have to say good-by again, not just now, so soon after their other loss. She would look forward to his coming to see her, finally, back home in Hawaii! And she would give him a wonderful birthday *luau* for his very next birthday, or at least the one after that; she promised, as soon as everything had been settled. There were, after all, many who continued to voice the opinion that this shameful travesty of a republic must be brought down, and Hawaii restored to its own.

It was impossible to say what might happen. Some days things seemed to be in a bad way over there, to tell the truth. Then, she felt certain that the Hawaiians would never get their own back again, never. She would be quite sorry if the whole thing were to finish up that way, for it would be better to have to bear up under that greedy, so-called republic than to lose their nationality altogether. She felt very sorry for her people, as they would hate being taken over by another nation.

Her health was adequate these days, though not stellar. After playing croquet the other day, when she had not had much exercise in a while, she had one of her ridiculous fainting fits again.

She blessed him for his cheerful letters, and prayed he would always remain her dear, faithful Father Confessor.

She ended with, "With All my Love, Kaiulani."

On a sudden impulse she decided to send along the shawl. Perhaps, it might sometime pleasantly remind him of his dear, lost sister. And Kaiulani would seldom, if ever, have a use for anything so heavy in the warm Honolulu sunshine.

As for herself, she needed no mementos. She knew that Miranda lived on deep inside her and always would. Not a day went by that she did not think of friend. Every time she felt humor and hope pitting themselves against the shadows of darkness, her sister's spirit was there.

* * * * * * * * * * * * * * * * * * *

For two months they packed and said their good-bys. Then, before they set off from London for the states, Papa went alone to Scotland, Jersey and Menton to say their farewells; while Kaiulani remained at the Davies to pack and receive well wishers there.

Mrs. Sharp and Mrs. Rook came together to see her, full of advice on the most efficient ways to pack, and what should be shipped and what could be sent in the mails. The two eventually became embroiled in a brief but lively argument about what kind of weather Kaiulani might anticipate at this time of year "overseas" in America, where neither had ever been; but they wept when they had to leave her.

"Don't forget to write, darling," Mrs. Rook sobbed. "And remember, if the" - she shuddered slightly - "the - cultural differences -" - Mrs. Rook caught herself up short, suddenly remembering that the princess was, after all, originally from Hawaii. "Well, if the climate, you know," she amended, "is too much of an adjustment, you will always have a home with me."

"And me," Mrs. Sharp said briskly, as she heartily embraced her former student.

"You are a brave girl and a bright one," she said softly enough for Kaiulani's ears alone, "and I know you will be strong."

"Thank you, Mrs. Sharp," Kaiulani returned her hug. "I have had excellent teachers after whom to model myself."

Maddie became extremely interested in the route of their journey from New York to Washington and suggested several alternate plans of travel that might help them make a faster time of it. When Kaiulani gently explained that her father had already made all the arrangements, Maddie seemed crushed, but only for a moment. She rallied herself to come up with an intricate, elaborate plan for what they should do and whom they must see and meet once they arrived in the nation's capital city. Maddie loaded her down with list after list of names and addresses of society people, dress shops and new restaurants that both Mrs. Davies and the Princess knew she would never have time to visit.

Toby came, unexpectedly, at the last. One dreary Sunday morning Kaiulani was recovering from the emergency removal of a badly abscessed tooth. Papa had just returned from Scotland with a dreadful cold and the entirely irrational notion that this would somehow kill him off and Kaiulani would have to go on to America without him. Maddie and Theo were away for a few days and Papa was keeping to his bed, trying to sleep off his cold. Kaiulani's nerves were jangled and, as a result, she was not holding up very well against the pain.

She took one look at Toby, standing at the door in the pouring rain, looking stricken, with her cashmere shawl tucked carefully under his arm, and burst into tears.

He sat with her all day long, holding her hand and coming up with every ridiculous riddle and silly children's song he could think of to get her to laugh. He insisted on making the tea himself and spoon-fed her *blancmange* pudding, which was the only thing she could manage to eat. When night fell he built a cheerful fire in the parlor grate where they snuggled together, safe and close and warm.

They had been sitting silent and content for a long time when a log in the fire suddenly shifted and made a sharp, cracking sound, then scattered a few fragments of embers near the rug.

Toby got up to toss them back and when he sat down beside her again he looked into her sleepy face, cupped her chin in his hand for a moment and then stroked her wild, unfettered hair. He had never touched her like this before but it felt as right and natural as rain.

"I shall have to take the train back to London tonight," he said after another while, his voice heavy with regret.

"I know, I know," she said as softly as a mother soothing her babe. Slowly, almost unconsciously, she kissed the fingertips of his right hand, lazily, one at a time, one after another, taking all the time in the world.

"The papers say you are engaged."

He had spoken so quietly she thought she must have misheard him.

"Hmmm?" she murmured, and opened her sleepy eyes. The fading fire had again crackled loudly, startling them and making them both tremble.

"The San Francisco Chronicle - a friend read there that you are engaged." He sounded embarrassed although his voice was a little louder now and an edge of urgency had crept in.

Kaiulani shifted back so she could look into his eyes.

"Engaged? In what? With what? To be married??" Her own voice sounded dull and stupid to her as it echoed in the room.

Toby nodded mutely, unable or unwilling to speak.

Kaiulani shook her head, trying to clear away the lovely, relaxed mood that had overcome her for some time now.

"To whom? For what? No one has told me. It is certainly the first I've heard of it. You'd think they would bother to tell me!" She struggled to sound flippant but her voice was miserable and weary.

The San Francisco Chronicle society column had identified as probable a rumor that Princess Kaiulani of Hawaii, who would soon be on her way back home to the Pacific Islands, was betrothed to her first cousin, Prince David Kawananakoa.

Kaiulani's face flushed hotly, although the fire had fallen away almost into ashes.

"Won't Papa be sorry to hear that." Her attempt at sarcasm fell flat and she only sounded forlorn.

"Then it's not true?" The pleading passion in Toby's voice made her shudder. Or perhaps the room had turned cold, with only the barely smoldering embers to warm it.

Kaiulani shook her head and tears began to fall again for the first time in hours.

The billows of Toby's starched and copious linen handkerchief made her sneeze and then laugh as he wiped the salty wetness from her cheeks.

When she tried to speak he held his finger to her lips and then kissed her, releasing another flood of tears.

Finally, crushed in snugly against his waistcoat, Kaiulani was able to stop crying.

"Only listen now, dearest, for a moment." His voice was very low but she was pressed in so tightly against his chest she could hear every word.

"I know you must go home. Otherwise, I would ask you to marry me. Today. Tonight and tomorrow, too. All of those times, and then next week and the week after that again. Forever and always."

Her laughter freed his spirit and he slid down to kneel in front of her.

"I will wait for you, Kaiulani, as long as you will let me, for however long it takes, until you are free."

She held his large head in her hands and kissed him again and again. Yes, she said, over and over, all the time never knowing whether or not it was right; praying all along that she might somehow find the power to make it so by wishing and hoping.

He kept the cashmere shawl cradled in his arms like precious cargo, as if it was a sacred trust. The last thing he said to her, leaving, was that he would keep it close to his heart as her promise.

For a second she began to protest, desperately wanting to be honest with him, to tell him the truth, which was that she did not know what would happen and was therefore unable to make any promises at all.

For the second time that night he touched his finger to her lips to stay her words.

"Do you know what that promise is?" he asked with infinite tenderness.

Mute, miserable, she shook her head no, wanting so much to be clear and direct and straightforward with him.

Toby smiled sweetly.

"Only that you will do the right thing, which is whatever it takes to make you happy."

They sealed their pact with a kiss.

* * * * * * * * * * * * * * * * * * *

Papa got better, as everyone - except him - knew he would. The last minute preparations were finally all completed. The last box had been packed, sealed and shipped, and there was no one else to bid farewell.

On October 9, 1897, Theo and Maddie came to the dock to wave to them and call out good-by until they were hoarse as Kaiulani and her father sailed away from Southampton, headed for New York and then on to Washington, D.C.

Most of the trip was uneventful. October 16th came and went while they were at sea, and Kaiulani found it ironically appropriate to observe her twenty-second birthday when she was in transit on a boat, entirely uncertain of her future and so quite literally "out to sea" in every way. She was sorry Miranda was not around to enjoy the joke.

Toward the end of the trip, an autumn squall blew up and the waters turned very choppy. Both Kaiulani and Papa were laid low in their cabins for several days until they finally docked in New York.

By the time they arrived in Manhattan they were feeling rather delicate and needed some extended rest in a non-moving environment. Papa managed to keep the reporters who came to meet them at bay with a few brusque, "No comments." When he was briefly detained by customs, though, an especially aggressive newspaperman finagled Kaiulani's reluctant attention and attempted to interrogate her.

"So, ah, Princess -" He drawled as he glanced at his notes, "Kah-ee-ooo-lah-nee, does this mean yer gonna try to upstage your aunt, 'Queen Lil,' in D.C.?"

The reporter gave a derisive, quick snort, proud of himself for getting in the current derogatory nickname for Auntie, which Kaiulani at once deemed unfortunate and manifestly disrespectful.

"On the contrary, sir," she said, cool and collected with her best Mona Lisa smile. "I have come to give Queen Liliuokalani all my support in every possible way."

"So, ah," The reporter ostentatiously tapped his pen against his jaw and pretended to be thoughtful as he showed off for his cohorts. "Can ya tell us if there's any political significance attached to your return to Hawaii?"

"None at all. I am going to see old friends, and visit my horse."

The reporter sheepishly ducked away from the laughter that followed the Princess' pleasant but clearly sarcastic response. Then Papa showed up and took her away, again quashing the reporters' hopes with another brisk, "No comment."

During the next few days they fulfilled their obligations to meet the mayor of the city, and received a handful of friends and supporters. Both tried to marshal their energies for the long trip still ahead.

They took a carriage to meet Aunt Liliu's private secretary for lunch at the Plaza Hotel but were held up in traffic for almost an hour. They had just begun to remark upon all the flags and bunting hanging from several buildings when a parade of people, carrying signs and marching to protest Cuba's right to remain independent, blocked the roads for more than half a mile of Fifth Avenue.

Cries of "Cuba!" "Viva Cuba!" and "Free Cuba!" rang out from the milling crowd. The Cuban flag was held high on poles everywhere and the clusters of chanting demonstrators paused often to applaud and salute the flag.

Then a young woman in a carriage, protected by a stocky young man, moved through the crowd. Thin as a wraith, she had an unhealthy pallor to her cocoa brown skin, but she was beautifully dressed in a white satin gown with a fur collar wrapped around her slender neck. Her voice, as she intoned "Viva Cuba!" over and over, was weak and thin but her eyes glowed with satisfaction as she received the tremendous sympathy and support that flowed to her from the crowd.

When they arrived at the Plaza an hour late, an anxious Captain Julius Palmer was very relieved to see them. A tall, light-haired, worried-looking man, Captain Palmer was apparently of Norwegian or Swedish descent. His eyebrows were so pale he seemed not to have any, which gave him a perpetually startled look. A former Boston Globe reporter who had become friends with the Queen many years ago, he now served as Liliu's private secretary and had been sent on her behalf to welcome them to New York. Captain Palmer told them that the young refugee they had just seen in the streets was Señorita Evangelina Cosalo y Cisneros. She had been imprisoned in her own country after her daring attempt to assassinate one of the most notorious of the many overlords who were then oppressing Cuba. With the aid of a young American reporter, she escaped from the jail in Havana; and had then been smuggled into New York under armed guard. The newspapers were lavish in their praise of this young woman's fierce courage.

Kaiulani was fascinated by the story of this uncompromising patriot, a woman in circumstances similar to her own. But everything in the situation of Señorita Cisneros and Cuba seemed simple and clear.

Why, she wondered, weren't Hawaii's troubles perceived like that, with such simplicity? Who, and where, were the 'overlords' of Hawaii? Those who had profited so handsomely and for so long from the despair of the Hawaiians never showed their faces; they could not easily be named and fought against. They never really revealed themselves at all; instead, they paid off their thugs and lackeys to lobby the American Congress. They gave money and favors to the newspapers that were willing to insult her Aunt's character and slur her good name.

It was all so underhanded, so unfair. There was no one person or persons who, should she, like Cisneros, attempt to kill them, would shift the tide or begin to heal the Hawaiian kingdom's fatal wound.

She would show them, at least, that their wrongdoing had not gone unnoticed. She would do everything in her power to bear witness to the wanton destruction of her people, and proudly, too. They could hurt and even kill them, but they could not take away their pride.

How she wished her own life was simple. Here was the problem, there the solution. Follow this path, or take such-and-such a particular action and you would be sure to end up with the desired result. End of story. On to something else. When the next problem came up, you would know how to fix that one, too.

* * * * * * * * * * * * * * * * * * *

On their travels toward Washington the vast expanses of American land were a great comfort to her. The mountainous regions of the east took on the aspect of old friends, or friendly acquaintances, at least. She giggled when she realized she was giving them, in her mind, Hawaiian nicknames, such as those that were given to the *kanakas*. Papa asked her rather sharply what she was smiling at, and did not seem to understand the humor in the situation after she explained.

The prairies and flatlands made Kaiulani's imagination reach out to limitless concepts of eternity and infinity. Her imagination traveled sweeping internal landscapes of unbordered space and time. She pondered the measures and ways we use to judge and assess our own - and others - lives.

Why shouldn't things be made simple again? For instance, say that it was true that Koa loved her and she him. In that case, it only made sense for them to marry when they returned to Hawaii. And then—and then what? Would they rule over the seashore at Mama Nui's, pretending again as they had when they were children?

Or what if Hawaii was annexed to the United States? She shuddered at an abrupt, grim vision of dangerous surgery being performed under dirty, improvised conditions, as it had often been done on the battlefields of the American Civil War.

If Hawaii was no longer a monarchy and so would not need its Princes or Princesses or Queens any more, perhaps Kaiulani might return to England. She could marry Toby and have a family. She would paint pictures, and help her husband with his work. Then she could read whatever she liked whenever she wanted to, with no further thought given ever again to politics or propriety or preparing herself for some vague, unknowable future. Or perhaps she could become a teacher and scholar, like Mrs. Sharp.

Fervently, she wished that her life would be made simple again, so she could know with confidence how to behave and what to do next. The only thing she felt sure of at the moment was that she had to return to Hawaii, and be strong in whatever way she could. This was her duty, her sacred trust as the Princess. As long as her people needed her she would stand by them. If she could not, or was not meant to lead them, then she would comfort them and commiserate with them instead.

* * * * * * * * * * * * * * * * * *

Kaiulani was unmoved by the sights of the nation's capital this second time around. A biting wind seemed to blow through the city, and the people seemed menaced and anxious. Everyone was as brisk, efficient and polite as before, but to her the eyes of the people in the city now projected a different message than their smiling faces and cordial tones. The eyes of the Washingtonians seemed calculating and cold to her, as if they were always assigning a value and dollar amount to every transaction. Kaiulani was constantly reminded of the desperate economic scrambling for even the bare necessities that characterized these troubled times.

Not until she saw Aunt Liliu did she relax and let down her guard.

The Queen had recently moved from the older Shoreham Hotel to "The Cairo," a new, 13-story residence on Q. Street, N.W., not far from the Center Market that Kaiulani had visited with the Davies. Liliuokalani was put off, at first, by the city scenes that beleaguered her sight from every angle of the spacious tenth floor apartments. But she soon came to love her bird's eye view of the sprawling vistas of the Potomac River, and the country and cityscapes that seemed, from her elevated perspective, to exist side by side.

Kaiulani had anticipated their reunion for so long that she felt an eerie, *deja vu* quality about it, as if they had already gone through all their greetings and kisses and exclamations of "How you've changed!" before.

When Aunt Liliu held her in a close grasp Kaiulani realized with a rush of feeling how much she had missed the company of her steady, stoic aunt. It had been almost nine years since they had last met! Aunt Liliu was older and had put on some weight, but she looked wonderful to her niece.

Liliuokalani had visited the President, she explained to Kaiulani and Archibald, as soon as she arrived in town. She had presented to him the many, many letters she had received from Hawaiian natives and supporters of the monarchy all over the world, and had asked him to restore at once the Hawaiians' right to choose their own government. Some of these letters were addressed to President McKinley, others to President Cleveland, as they had been written and collected over a period of several years.

Kaiulani soaked up the sight and sound of her aunt as if she was a sponge, or a dry plant taking in water. She had forgotten how impressive and graceful and dignified she was.

"'Queen Lil', indeed!" Kaiulani thought to herself, recalling the shameful, derogatory nickname.

No wonder they felt compelled to try to diminish her. There was nothing little or small about Liliuokalani at all. The additional pounds only gave her, if anything, more of a feeling of substance and gravity. She was as unequivocal as any force of nature. The PGs and others had even spread lies that Liliuokalani was in ill health, suffering from one disease after another. The Queen, who was not yet sixty years old, looked healthy and vital. Her physical presence made Kaiulani feel a tremendous sense of relief. At her aunt's side the Princess felt grounded, brought back down to earth and away from the confusing jumble of her own thoughts, released and reassured by the older woman's company.

While they sat and sipped their tea Kaiulani was surprised to observe traces of her Mother in her Aunt's strong face. A certain occasional softness around the mouth, a playful, almost teasing sideways glance she did not remember from Aunt Liliu. She had never thought of her mother and aunt as being alike in any way, but of course they were. After all, they were sisters. Kaiulani was moved to recognize traits of her Mother in her Aunt. She could not get close enough to her and after a while rose from her chair to go and sit beside her aunt on the couch.

Liliuokalani was surprised by her action. She seemed amused but also was secretly touched that the lovely woman her niece had turned into, so poised and elegant, was becoming almost kittenish with her. Kaiulani appeared to be so sure of herself that she seemed to have nothing in common with the worried, fearful girl who had said good-by almost ten years ago.

"Archie," Hawaii's former Queen turned toward her brother-in-law, who had been sitting silent for a long time listening to the women talk. "You should be very proud of your accomplished daughter. What will you do with her, now that she has become such a sophisticated young woman?"

Archibald Cleghorn immediately shrugged, and assumed the mildly ironic, slightly bemused tone he had always taken with his sister-in-law.

"Since when have I ever had any influence or control over any royal Hawaiian women? I am here to serve you, not to command."

Kaiulani laughed and Liliu was enchanted to hear echoes of Likelike's silvery, wild laughter fill the air.

Kaiulani pretended to scold her father. "Oh, now, Papa, you know that isn't true! I always do exactly what you tell me to do, don't I, most of the time…?"

She caught her aunt's eye and a flash of recognition and mischief ignited them both.

"Except when you have ideas of your own?" Liliu suggested fondly.

They were infinitely curious about the world around them, these two women, and each responded fiercely to a challenge. They shared an unruly spirit and a passion for a good joke, even on the brink of despair.

"Pah," Archibald Cleghorn said, half-annoyed but enjoying their attention. "You ladies are all the same. Anything for a joke. Always a joke."

"'Friends must laugh when the sand looks dark in the moonlight.'" Aunt Liliu responded.

"'Na hoa 'aka o ke one hauli o ka malama.'" Kaiulani translated, her eyes flashing as she remembered the saying.

"You have not forgotten your Hawaiian. You will make us all proud, Princess."

Liliu's praise was music to her ears.

Later, when they were alone, Liliuokalani showed her the letters. There were three very large boxes full of them, hundreds, perhaps even thousands of letters. The first box was marked, "To - Or Forwarded By - The Honorable Grover Cleveland." The second carton was labeled "Under the Auspices of President McKinley." The third one had written on the side "For the Queen and the Princess of Hawaii."

The letters had been collected and sent to Liliuokalani from the U.S. government and several different patriotic leagues of native Hawaiians. Some were addressed to "The Queen of Hawaii" or other variations of "Queen Lili" or "Lily", etc. Others said only "The Royal Hawaiians" and many were sent to "The Princess and the Queen" or "Princess Kaiulani" or just "P.V.K".

There were statements of concern and support from organizations offering their services "in any way possible" to help restore the Queen and the sovereignty of the Hawaiian nation. They included, from all over the world, kind thoughts and prayers of those who had heard about and sympathized with the plight of the Hawaiians.

There were reminiscences and fond recollections of Princess Kaiulani's earlier visit when she came to speak in America and England. Newspaper clippings and photographs were folded into them; and there were even some drawings and sketches of her from private collections, sending best wishes and their hopes for good luck.

They came from The Organization of Texas Women, and the Arkansas School Teachers for Justice; the Citizens of the Cherokee

Nation, and the tribes people of the Navajos, the Shoshoni, the Dakotas and the Paiute.

There were small slips and scraps with messages carefully printed that said *"Aloha"* and "God Bless," and there were many notes written in the scrawled lettering of children, or painstakingly constructed one word or even a single letter at a time by hands not used to holding pen or pencil. On newspapers and torn-out pages of catalogs they had written to send their generous thoughts. Kaiulani's eyes were bright with tears as she read again and again, "We love you" and *"Mahalo nui loa* for your courage."

Some of the letters had been written only a month ago and some were from a year or two or three, even four years ago.

"I could not send you everything, dear," Liliu said softly. "You can see why." She spoke low, her voice moving slowly past the knot in her chest.

The women held each other close and, for the first and only time in their lives, together they cried. They sat in the parlor of the Queen's Washington apartment, with the city and patches of countryside spread out on every side, all around them, and read and read and read.

Two hours passed like it was a minute. Kaiulani was reading a letter from an American Indian princess who was living in Arizona with what was left of her tribe. She had written to say that the Princess and Queen and the people of Hawaii were in their daily prayers to the spirits of peace and protection. When Kaiulani looked up from the letter she saw that Liliuokalani's head was bowed in silent prayer.

After a while, as if some unspoken signal had directed them, the women rose again, to gather the letters together.

"We are in many people's hearts," Liliuokalani struggled to keep her composure.

"I know, Auntie." Kaiulani tucked herself in beside her stern Aunt and embraced her. "I know."

"When they came to arrest me at Washington Place, at my home, our people were there. They surged in close to me and blocked the path of the PGs and their guards." Liliuokalani's voice shook with passion and rage.

"They watched over me, ready to attack, and they looked to me for a sign. I could see that some were weeping but, even so, there was complete silence as they watched me."

Liliuokalani grasped Kaiulani's hand with an iron grip so charged it felt electric.

The Queen's eyes burned as hot as stars in her strong face, which was etched with the lines of many years.

"I raised my hand to them, and then I bowed my head to honor their loyalty."

She released her powerful grip and smiled as she patted Kaiulani's hand.

"They moved back then and I passed among them and got into the carriage. As it drove away I could no longer see the kanakas' faces, but their wailing filled the air like the cries of wild birds."

The older woman's voice was full of wonder and her face shined with such hope that for a moment she looked like a young girl.

Kaiulani's grasp was as strong as her aunt's had been before and her face glowed with the same lovely light.

"I understand, Auntie. I understand."

* * * * * * * * * * * * * * * * * * *

This time the reporters in Washington were relentless because the question of annexation had again become one of great national interest. The arrival of the darkly interesting Queen of Hawaii and now the return of her willowy, striking niece from Europe, only served to whet the country's appetite for news about Hawaii's predicament.

Reporters followed them to church on Sundays and appeared out of nowhere, at any hour of the day or night, every time that Kaiulani, Liliu and Archibald Cleghorn left the Queen's apartments.

Everyone wanted to discuss "The Hawaii Question." The Senate held secret hearings about the annexation treaty. The House of Representatives, though it had no power to approve or reject the controversial issue, was not about to be left out, and held highly publicized meetings to express their opinions. America had conquered its own internal boundaries, so the question of expansion "overseas," and how far to take it, was on everyone's mind. It was, in essence, a question of whether or not - and how - America could become more and more powerful.

Kaiulani wrote to Toby.

"Dear Father Confessor,

(Where did that name come from, anyway? I can't remember anymore!)

We have arrived in Washington again. Everything is very different from before. Or perhaps it is me. Many of the reporters seem like wolves, always ready or waiting to pounce on us.

Aunt Liliu is cheerful and optimistic, which is extraordinary, under the circumstances. She seems frailer and older now; at times I wonder if she may have shrunk a half-inch or so. Don't worry, though - she still commands attention! Her icy glare of disapproval made a surly *maitre'd* at our hotel turn positively lamb-like on the spot.

I must admit, dear friend, there are times I do not feel very young myself anymore.

We are all trying our best to keep a positive outlook. I trust and pray that our return to Hawaii, and my chance to be home again, at last, will help revive us.

All my Love,
Your Shepherdess
(Well, at least I remember the Tennyson!),
Kaiulani"

Before Kaiulani and Papa left for San Francisco, Liliuokalani privately showed her the almost-completed manuscript of her book, which was to be called "Hawaii's Story by Hawaii's Queen." Captain Julius Palmer had strongly encouraged her to record her experiences and thoughts from this difficult time, respectfully reminding her that "the pen is mightier than the sword."

Liliuokalani had filled up page after page with her precise, meticulous script. Kaiulani was impressed and very proud. She joked that Liliu must not make it very much longer, lest it turn out to be too long to read.

As they left Washington Archie showed his daughter yet another critical newspaper article. "No Official Action Taking During Meeting of Queen and Princess."

"What on earth did they expect?!" he snorted.

"Perhaps a lively round of gun volleys would have done," Kaiulani responded coolly.

The closer that they got to going home to Hawaii the less she cared what others might think of them, or how the rest of the world might speculate about their politics.

* * * * * * * * * * * * * * * * * * *

They arrived in San Francisco on October 29, and quietly checked in to the Occidental Hotel. They had managed to sneak past the crowd of reporters, as Kaiulani disguised herself by wearing an old, raggedy, gypsy-style shawl she had picked up in Washington just for that purpose.

By the second afternoon, though, the reporters were again lined up in droves, and lay in wait for them everywhere, begging and dunning them for interviews.

San Francisco! The last time she had seen this charming, colorful city she was a thirteen-year old schoolgirl! After all of her experiences in London, Vienna, Paris, New York, Boston and Washington, the Bay City now seemed almost cozy and rustic.

When she had come to San Francisco from Hawaii so many years ago, the place had seemed like an exciting metropolis. Now, though, the leisurely clip of the trolley cars, and all the houses and apartments, which seemed to have sprung up like mushrooms after rain, made the city seem rather quaint to her, more western and temperate than any place she had been in a long while.

The press followed her around like detectives or shadows, but their intrusion upon her privacy did not bother her any more. She was so close to going home; finally about to be actually on her way! The rumors of her alleged engagement to Koa were rampant here. She found herself being a little flirtatious with some of the reporters as she dropped playful, teasing hints about another beau back in London. She even told a few of them that she had modeled for a well-known artist in Europe and that he and she might very well be "staying in touch."

There were numerous distressing references in the papers regarding the "marital" aspects of Hawaii's possible union with the states. One local paper coyly opined, "Under such circumstances annexation is not, and will not, be a change. It is a consummation."

The Hawaiian Star declared, "Hawaii may be regarded as a bride whose marriage day is not yet definitely fixed, but who is prepared to go through with the ceremony whenever the signal is given."

Kaiulani felt her back get stiff and her jaw grow tight as she resolved never to give in. There would be no "marriage." Never. Not in so far as she could help it.

She and Papa visited Chinatown where the many mixed features of Oriental, Mexican, Spanish and Indian faces melted into a wealth of variations that made her long all the more for Hawaii. She insisted on taking Papa into a Chinese herbal medicine shop, steeped in exotic, earthy smells.

After lots of pantomime and smiles and laughter over their mutual confusion, Kaiulani managed to convey to the wizened proprietress that she wanted some kind of tonic for "sickness upon the sea." They left with several brown paper packets of candied ginger root, thickly sliced and heavily coated with cane syrup and sugar.

Kaiulani was so content to be on her way back home that she took to calling the coterie of reporters her "official escort." Sometimes she would politely wait for them if they began to lag behind when she and Papa traipsed about the rolling hills of the city to find last minute gifts to take home.

Most of the reporters were full of praise for the thoughtful, charming Princess.

One journalist with a taste for poetry wrote, "Her clothes say Paris, her accent says London, but her heart says Hawaii."

The harsh rumors promoted by the Provisional Government and its supporters, which represented Kaiulani as an uncivilized barbarian, were quickly dispelled by her encounters with the press.

"A Barbarian Princess?" A reporter for the *San Francisco Examiner* had fallen a little in love with her. "Not a bit of it!" he wrote. "Not even a hemi-semi-demi Barbarian! She is an exotic flower of civilization. The Princess is fascinating, individual, with the taste and style of a French woman, and the admirable poise and soft voice of an English lady. She is tall, erect, slender and graceful, with a pale face, full red lips, soft expression, dark eyes, a very good nose, and a cloud of crimpy black hair knotted high."

When she read this lyrical description Kaiulani smiled to herself, thinking what fun she and Miranda would have had with it. There was excellent potential here for making jokes, especially, she thought, in the part about her "very good nose." For the thousandth time, she missed her friend.

Another reporter, with whom she had, in fact, flirted just a little, enthused: "She is beautiful. No portrait could do justice to her proud, expressive face. But she is more than a beautiful pretender to an abdicated throne. She has been made a woman of the world by the life she has led. She says "our people" with a pretty pride as she shows off the many bouquets and gifts from her "friends in Hawaii" that decorate her suite everywhere."

* * * * * * * * * * * * * * * * * * *

The S.S. *Australia* set sail for Hawaii on November 5, 1897. The candied ginger cure for seasickness was such a great success that Kaiulani was able, for once, to spend the entire journey on deck. Papa took one taste of the concoction and immediately decided he could not abide the sharp, sweet, hot taste; he often stayed below.

338

Chapter Twenty-Six

Just before the break of dawn on November 9 murmurs of anticipation raced through the handful of passengers gathered on board the S.S. *Australia* to greet the new day. The rumor that land had been sighted brought only the most hardy or restless out of their beds and on deck to see.

Kaiulani had slept fitfully the night before. At half past three in the morning she got up and dressed in a full, flowing black skirt and a blouse of rich yellow silk she had bought in San Francisco just for this occasion. Her face was flushed and when she saw the distant shores of Molokai at last, her heart leaped into her throat.

Rays of morning light began to replace the pale shadows of dawn, and Molokai Island soon sparkled like emerald and sapphire jewels. Sea breezes undulated through the palm treetops and the graceful grasses of the rice fields. It was easy to forget that all who lived on that island were sick and in conditions of decay, or else tending to those who were ill at certain and inescapable personal risk.

Kaiulani sighed. Even at its most complicated and difficult, she thought, life was very precious.

By the time they reached Diamond Head she could see that thousands were waiting at the Oceanic Wharf to welcome her home. She had imagined this moment of homecoming for more than nine years. Even as the S.S. *Umatilla* had sailed away from that same dock at Honolulu Harbor, all those years ago, carrying the anxious thirteen-year-old Princess away; even in leaving then, Kaiulani had longed to return to Hawaii.

The desire for home had never left her, not for a moment. She had dreamed of this return for almost half her young life. And now that the time had come, she could not even say how or what she felt. She knew only that her heart was torn, ripped asunder between more than one world.

The smells and sounds and sights of Hawaiian earth and air and birds and flowers and trees greeted her like old friends. Her lovely Hawaii was like a proud, powerful, loyal chiefess dispensing bounty and beauty with her every movement, with each motion of sunlight and fragrance and wind in the trees.

But the sad faces and defeated postures of the people in the restless crowds, especially the poverty-stricken *kanakas*, made the Hawaiians look to their Princess like wounded, damaged creatures. Their despair was palpable, wrapped around them like shrouds. And their wan demeanors, with so many of them sick, ragged, discouraged or old, made them seem already like ghosts.

They looked like battered, beaten children to her, suspicious and hurt. And they all seemed to be turning their eyes and spirits toward her, entreating her to bring them some ray, however tiny or fragile, of brightness and hope.

A sound, that was somewhere between a chilling wail and a fierce cry, rose up from the people when they saw her. It echoed strangely and rang in Kaiulani's ears like a warning bell. And even as she rejoiced at returning to her beloved Hawaii, she felt a foreboding and dread, though she knew not why or what the cause.

With a tremendous effort of will, Kaiulani shook off these dark thoughts and raised her head high. Again and again, she lifted her hands in salute to the Hawaiians.

Koa came on board to greet her, more handsome than ever. The ashen pallor that had diminished him in Europe and America was gone now, replaced by the glow of the tropical sun that warmed his ruddy cheeks and glinted off his black-brown hair. He seemed to gleam, as burnished as a polished *kukui* nut. Truly, Koa looked like a Prince that day. Eva Parker, whose honey-blonde curls were tipped gold by the sun, had come with him. They had traveled all the way down from Parker Ranch on the Big Island to welcome the Princess. Eva's brusque embrace caught Kaiulani by surprise and took her breath away for a moment, for Eva, who had become a little stout, had the grasp and strength of a young bear cub. Kaiulani felt suddenly rather puny and insubstantial sandwiched in between her robust cousin and this sturdy, second generation, *hapa-haole* woman.

After he had politely greeted Mr. Cleghorn, Koa startled Kaiulani by enfolding her in an embrace, and gave her a kiss that was not at all like the tentative, offhand pecks they had shared in America and Europe. Excitement coursed through her blood as she was set on fire by his touch. With a shock she remembered him: this was her own, true Koa; not the aloof stranger she had been so puzzled by abroad. All at once she felt so disoriented that she wondered if she would fall.

Koa laughed at his delicate cousin and murmured tenderly in her ear. "Steady on, my Princess. We are counting on you to set an example for us to be strong."

His remark was like a bracing sea breeze to her, and made her light-headedness evaporate like morning dew. She remembered abruptly that all the reporters and PGs and their political spies would be everywhere from now on, all the time, waiting and hoping for a crack in her armor, watching for her to give up or fall apart, lose her dignity or falter.

She locked onto Koa's eyes as if they were the only safe place on earth. She thought how he had always been her protector, a true brother to her, and her friend. Never mind Papa's approval, or disapproval, anymore - for she was aware of her father's eyes upon them, just as she felt rather than saw him purse his thin lips. She was tired of being restricted, controlled and judged! She was home, and with Koa; she was Hawaii's hope and nothing else mattered.

"Well, then, cousin," she flashed him a smile, "I must be careful to stay steady, mustn't I?"

Half an hour passed as Kaiulani and her companions received her welcomers on board the ship.

Finally, Kaiulani, Koa, Eva Parker and Papa descended onto the pier, all of them covered with multiple flower *leis* of ginger, gardenias, carnations and *pikakae*. As she walked on to her native soil again, she felt like she was floating in air. Then they piled into the carriage, also filled with flowers, which waited to take them to Ainahau.

Along the four-mile drive from the wharf to the estate, the roads were lined with the Hawaiians and their relatives and friends. Many of them had put up camps the night before to wait for the Princess' arrival. Kaiulani was overwhelmed by the outpouring of *aloha*, and thrilled to see again the familiar faces of her people.

After what seemed like hours in the steadily rising heat, they finally turned onto the long, curved road that lead into Ainahau. The air began to change and shift as cool breezes wafted a softer note out into the bright autumn sun.

When they moved onto the shaded path road, the gates of Ainahau rose up before her misty eyes.

In accordance with Mama Nui's instructions when she gave the estate to her infant goddaughter, the words "*Kapu*" and "Princess Kaiulani" had been carved into the scrollwork at intervals on the high and massive wooden entranceway gates.

She looked at these gates and wondered what Mama Nui would have to say about their circumstances today. After all that had happened in the years since this land had been hers, what, anymore, was forbidden? Was it "*kapu*" now for Kaiulani and the Hawaiians to ever leave Ainahau again? Or was it perhaps becoming *kapu* for them even to go in? Would they become exiles in their own country? Perhaps it would soon be *kapu* for them to enter their own homes. Or was it *kapu* for them to be so unjustly forced out?

Kaiulani's banyan tree had blossomed out to a magnificent fullness and height. She was stunned to realize that the sprawling, two-story house behind her tree was Papa's new creation. This elegant, stately building had taken the place of the dark, comfortable old house she had known.

The new house was impressive, with great, sweeping wings that spread out on both sides of the broad, spacious *lanai*. The sun, which was much higher now, glinted off the tall glass windows so that she had to shield her eyes to protect them from the brilliant reflections.

Inside were wide, airy hallways with long, tall windows all around, everything paneled in highly polished woods, and accented with sparkling Italian marble tiles, porcelain and touches of gold leaf. The lush, green lawns of the estate spilled over each other like velvet carpets, shaped by an intricate variety of shrubs, flowers and trees. This was a house built for a Princess, a future Queen. The more the bitter irony of it tore at her, the more Kaiulani hid her sorrow and smiled.

The upstairs was even grander. Venetian blinds shaded the windows, and a personal suite for Kaiulani had high, vaulted ceilings with a motif of coronets and *kahilis* in the bedchamber. These proud symbols of royalty seemed only to further mock her sad heart.

From the flat expanse of roof at the top of the house the view was breathtaking. Koa and Eva, who had never been there before either, stood silent and still with Kaiulani, taking in the rice fields and the sprawling lawns and hills. The distant mountains were veiled in mists, and clouds drifted slowly over their high, sharp peaks; farther beyond that, they could see the ships and the ocean. Papa beamed with pride as Kaiulani drank in the sweet, clean air and smiled through her tears.

What struck her most of all was the smell, that powerful smell of Hawaii that was like nowhere else in the world. She was intoxicated, drunk with it; and breathed in so deeply that Papa was afraid she might hyperventilate. Plumeria, jasmine, sandalwood, honeysuckle! She would never get enough of that fragrance. She couldn't get close enough to it, even as she felt it wrapped all around her like a cloak or a shroud.

"Welcome home," Papa said in a husky voice as he touched her trembling shoulder. "Welcome home, daughter."

If not for Papa on one side and Koa on the other, Kaiulani thought she surely must fall. Eva, concerned at how pale she had become, moved in close beside them.

"Kaiulani, are you all right?" Eva asked.

For a moment, Kaiulani could only nod. Then she caught her breath again.

"May I -" She cleared her throat to release the ache and to raise her voice above the tremulous whisper it had become. "Oh, Papa! Please, will you take me to see Fairy!?"

Koa and Eva said their good-bys in the parlor, explaining that they had business to attend to in Honolulu.

Eva kissed the Princess' cheek and said rather gaily, with a mischievous look at her companion, "And not all of it politics, either!"

Kaiulani felt a surprising twinge of jealousy. But when she looked at Koa he was smiling as warmly as ever. It occurred to her that she had never seen him as an adult in Hawaii. She wondered if her good-looking cousin might be what the Americans would call "a ladies man."

Observing Eva glance at him adoringly as she tucked her arm into his, Kaiulani realized this was probably so. And why not? Why shouldn't he be? Cultured and attractive, he was the perfect gentleman. An ideal escort; as Miranda used to say, "A great catch." Wasn't it strange, though, for her to recognize it only now, after all the interminable rumors that he and she might be engaged? Any thoughts she had had of marriage, or a different connection than they already had, were suddenly gone, burned away in the hot light of reality. They would never marry. She was absolutely sure of that now.

The old, familiar stable had not changed. It was dark and gloomy, just as she remembered, with only a few motes of sunlight that filtered in through the slats of the shuttered wooden stalls. For a moment she could see nothing in the shadows, but then she heard a faint whinny and a neigh and then Fairy was beside her, nuzzling her nose into her mistress' face and neck.

Fairy's flowing, silky mane had turned pale silver, showing only faint traces where the white gold had been; and her muzzle and ears were also highlighted with silver. When she stroked her old friend, Kaiulani felt how the pony's back now swayed and noticed a certain stiffness in her joints.

"Ah, Fairy, my sweetheart, my good, sweet girl."

The pony sighed with intense pleasure at the touch of her mistress' gentle, tender hands.

Kaiulani buried her face in the horse's soft mane. "Time works its way with us all, my dear friend."

* * * * * * * * * * * * * * * * * * * *

Like her, like everyone, Fairy was older and slower now. Kaiulani rode her only a few times and was very careful. But on their third time out they came across some *kanakas* who had lingered at the gate in hopes of catching another glimpse of the Princess, and Fairy attempted to perform the bow that Kaiulani had taught her so long ago. The elderly horse stumbled badly and nearly fell, and the look of regret and apology in her eyes made Kaiulani burst into tears. She vowed never to subject Fairy to being ridden by anyone, not even herself, ever again.

After that, she continued to take her out but always walked beside her. She found another horse to ride, a placid mare with a mild personality who liked to canter along at an easy pace. Kaiulani always lead the mare the long way out of the stables, not riding her until they were out of sight of Fairy and the pasture where she stayed. She went to see her old horse every day, without fail, and brought her apples and bits of sugar.

The peacocks still patrolled the lawns in troops, strutting like loud, flashy soldiers. Many of them were the same birds Kaiulani had left behind, for peacocks live long lives. A few even seemed to recognize her. They rushed over and crowded in to be petted whenever she was around. But, being peacocks, they all seemed just the same, bossy and full of themselves with complaining, all eager to get close to Kaiulani in their perpetual hope that she carried grain or treats to feed them.

Visitors came every day and Kaiulani graciously received them all, *haoles* and natives alike. Many of the *haoles* were only curious to view the long-awaited Princess. But some, Hawaiians and non-Hawaiians, too, came to share memories with her, - of their days with Mama Nui and Papa Moi, their experiences at the coronation, or at parties and other events with Mama and the other *ali'i*. Some spoke to her of Tusitala, or told about a *luau* or other celebration they had attended with people Kaiulani had known and loved.

A few days after they had settled in at Ainahau—in so far as that was possible, with all the changes there, and the fact that Kaiulani could never quite get used to the elegant, formal new house, - Papa and Kaiulani drove up to Nuuanu to visit the Royal Mausoleum.

The day was unusually gray and overcast for Hawaii. But when they arrived at the crypts where King Kalakaua and Princesses Ruth and Likelike were entombed, a thin sliver of sunlight broke through the haze. And, although the mausoleum was still chilly and foreboding, a few birds began to chirp softly, welcoming the morsel of wan sunlight. Kaiulani was at peace here, where it was so wonderfully quiet and where she could feel the presence of those she loved. She came back several times after that alone to bring flowers and sit with her thoughts.

The next several weeks required her involvement with many social affairs and welcoming home parties. She performed her duties as a figurehead for the Hawaiians with as much energy and spirit as she could muster.

There were some undeniably difficult moments, though, such as the night at the opera. During the second intermission, she had found herself in the lobby side by side with Mr. Harold Sewall, the new American Minister to Hawaii. Sewall was accompanied by two United States Senators, one current and one former; both of them rumored to be on the Islands to discuss the possibilities of annexation. With them was the ever-dour Mr. Thurston, looking even more cranky than usual.

Kaiulani felt the eyes upon them, and registered the hushed tones or nervous silences as she became aware of who stood beside her. True to her breeding and self-control, however, she merely smiled politely at the men, and murmured a soft hello to all as she brushed past them and returned to her box with Koa, talking with easy animation the rest of the way. Whenever she was in public, she hid her pain from the world, and smiled and smiled. It was the least and, in a strange way, also the best she could do now for the Hawaiians.

When Koa and Kaiulani sat back in their box to watch the last act of the opera, Kaiulani was so restless she could barely keep her focus on the stage; or even stay in one position for long. Her black satin dress, brocade with brown velvet, felt very heavy, all wrong for Hawaii. She had received many compliments on the sophisticated design when she had worn it in Paris and London, but here it seemed constricting and much too warm. She began to feel self-conscious and worried that she must look ridiculous.

Well, she was actually glad she had seen them tonight, especially Mr. Thurston. She knew he could only have come as Mr. Sewall's guest, for she was willing to wager whatever little she had left in the world that Mr. Thurston had certainly never attended any opera before this evening! She was, in fact, happy to see him for it gave her the deep satisfaction of being sure that someone else in the audience was enjoying this opera even less than she was; possibly even less than poor Koa! Kaiulani had managed to tune out the performances during the earlier acts by escaping into her own thoughts and fantasies, but now she was unable to keep her distance.

She could not abide this wretched piece, and it had gotten worse and worse as it had gone along. The music was all right, though rather lightweight and repetitive. But the story was intolerable to her! "*La Boheme*," it was called, the latest thing out of Italy, performed there in Turin just a year or so ago.

"The Bohemians," indeed! A sullen group, if ever there was one, these immature and selfish students who were sure that their only obligation in life was to chase after some flimsy dream of "making art." They had all the responsibility and moral purpose of a school of sharks! For hours now all they had done was whimper and whine about their terrible hardships and how unappreciated they were by the cold, cruel world.

The performers weren't singing very well tonight, either. Oh, she knew that the music was supposed to be lyrical and lovely. But the singers were either too fast, or too slow. And why did they have to stare so, and behave so artificially, so unnaturally? Thank heaven it was the final act. She couldn't stand it much longer, especially this contrived and allegedly "tragic" conclusion! So little Mimi has consumption and must die. Struck down by poverty and loneliness.

"She declines every day," the callow and annoying Rodolpho intoned, singing, at least half the time anyway, off-key. "The poor girl is doomed." Well, then, why not get it over with? Why make the audience suffer, too?

"In winter," Rodolpho shrilly croaked, "one can die of loneliness." As if this was a seasonal problem! "Loneliness is too unbearable," he moaned. This wretched opera was what was unbearable to her!

She had no patience at all with these self-centered characters. They seemed useless to her, all wrapped up in their own petty problems, and so willfully ignorant of the rest of the world! Even their pathetic attempts at romance seemed stupid and small. What fools they were! In the first act, they had started out burning paper to make a fire, and then cheated their elderly landlord for sport! And now, here at the end, how shamelessly they wept, so sorry for themselves! Where was their pride?!

Koa was tapping her hand. She must have been sighing out loud again. Koa mistook her response for appreciation of the performance and smiled indulgently, in an almost fatherly way. He himself did not at all like the shrill, high-pitched music or the dramatic, overwrought plots of the opera. He had come to escort her, as he did more often than not these days, out of loyalty and devotion.

Standing by her side, she thought, holding her hand, or patting it, at least, as the ship of state faltered and rocked on rough seas.

It made perfect sense to her now that her handsome, dashing cousin was so obviously sought after by women. He was charming, after all, and quite malleable, really. Though he never did seem to have a very keen sense of humor, as he often missed her jokes, or asked for explanations of witty or ironic remarks; and was seldom what one might call 'playful.'

All these years, she thought with a pang of regret, she had imagined that they wanted each other, and would eventually become lovers, even betrothed. But she had been completely wrong. They loved one another, yes, but as brothers and sisters do. Had they ever married, he would probably have been at home only rarely, and she could not have counted on him to behave like a husband to no one but her. It would have been, she reasoned, feeling a gnawing sensation start up in her belly, rather like Papa Moi and Mama Moi. For years she had suspected, from stories here and hints there, that the patient Queen had long turned a blind eye to her husband's many flirtations, and possibly even affairs.

Kaiulani could not have endured such a situation, certainly not for long. She would have taken lovers of her own, she was almost sure of it; or lived alone as the Queen, like Aunt Liliu was doing now, her strongest connection to her people and the land.

Oh, she could not wait for this dreary performance to end! Here in Hawaii the spectacle of it felt only silly and contrived to her. When you lived in a paradise, with nature's power and beauty all around you, it seemed foolish to watch the made-up dramas of humans.

She longed to shed her uncomfortable dress, especially the sheath-like bodice that had begun to feel so suffocating and clinging, like a second skin; like a snake's skin, almost! At Ainahau she had taken to wearing *holoku* dresses, the long, concealing, "granny-style" gowns preferred by most of the poor native women. They were easy to wear, so unencumbering, and they hid the fact that she was becoming too thin. For while she had resumed eating *poi* and raw fish, she was surprised to discover that many of the native fruits she had grown up on - coconuts, bananas, pineapple, - no longer agreed with her system. She kept a tin of English toffees tucked in her drawer, for often that was all she felt like eating. Along with the flowing *holoku* dresses she liked to wear big, wide-rimmed hats, too, since the sun seemed to bother her these days.

Of course, she was careful to dress up for going out, and for the long hours when she received visitors at Ainahau. Otherwise, she had begun not to care. Abruptly, she was struck by the image of Mama in her dark, shrouded room those last few weeks, so emaciated; and it made her even more uncomfortable.

Koa was taping at her wrist again. With a start she saw that the curtain was going down. Finally, the opera was over! The lights came up on stage and the actors filed out to take their bows, so Kaiulani mechanically arranged a pleasant, fixed smile on her face and began to applaud.

She could not wait to be home again, far away from everyone, quiet and safe under the shade of her banyan tree in the company of her peacocks and the wind.

* * * * * * * * * * * * * * * * * * *

Another unpleasant incident occurred one afternoon at home when an old woman, one of her mother's servants from years ago, came to Ainahau to pay her respects. When she was ready to leave, the frail woman suddenly turned back to Kaiulani with a sly smile and began to softly laugh at her, as if they were sharing a secret joke.

She called Kaiulani, "Princess Likelike" and said over and over how she was "Clever, very clever, to have come back again so soon." The woman was quite elderly and almost blind, so that she could make out only the shapes of things and shadows. Obviously, much of her memory had faded and the thoughts that were left seemed jumbled and unreliable. Still, she insisted on patting Kaiulani's arm, rejoicing at how clever she was to have made it back again, "and so quickly, too!"

What could the old woman have been thinking, Kaiulani pondered that night. Could she have imagined that Mama had somehow returned from "the other side," as Mama Nui used to say, after all these years? It was cruel and sad if her feeble mind played such tricks on her, but it distressed Kaiulani terribly, giving her 'chicken skin' or 'goose bumps' at the very thought of it. Oh, she really must try to find someone she could discuss all these things with, and soon! Perhaps she could go see Mama Moi at Washington Place, where she lived now with Koa, Kuhio and Elizabeth.

An unexpected pleasure for Kaiulani in her first weeks of being home was getting to know Kuhio's new wife, the stunning Princess Elizabeth. Princess Elizabeth was a statuesque beauty, dark and graceful, and she exuded a strong aura of personal *mana* or power. Her tawny-gold skin and the bronze mane of her hair, like a wild halo framing her face, made her look like a proud, indifferent tigress. Elizabeth was educated and cultured, always dressed in rich colors and elegant jewelry, but she kept an air of wildness about her, of reckless, monumental abandon. There was an untamed glint in her sleepy, black-brown eyes.

They did not exactly strike up a close friendship, for Elizabeth, already pregnant with the couple's first child, was not inclined to talk unnecessarily, in any case. And Kaiulani, even if she had felt like confiding in the other Princess, which she did not, was too overwhelmed at the moment to even attempt getting to know someone new. Nevertheless, Kaiulani felt admiration and an affinity with this calm, centered woman who was so unaffected by the world outside herself.

Only two years younger than Kaiulani, Elizabeth had a completely opposite perspective on life. She had grown up on the Big Island in an easy-going, extended family of cousins, uncles and aunts. She had always been insulated by this large family, which kept apart from the shifts of politics and power.

One day when they sat together on the sequestered *lanai* at the back of the house at Ainahau, Kaiulani asked her new cousin if she would mind losing her title, should Hawaii be annexed. Elizabeth gazed at her from under her heavy lidded, half-asleep sloe-eyes.

"Why?" she said with guileless simplicity. "I was not born a Princess. It has nothing to do with who I am now."

Lazily, unconsciously, Elizabeth caressed her own belly, which was beginning to swell with her child. "It makes no difference to me in my life, what I am called."

Kuhio, who was close by, could not keep his eyes off his beautiful wife. The heat between them was palpable, like a constantly smoldering fire.

Kaiulani admired and at times even envied Elizabeth who was so supremely confident. She wished she herself could say such a thing and mean it. She smiled gratefully at the sensuous creature basking in the sun, and took great comfort in her silent company.

Later that afternoon she wrote a long overdue letter to her Aunt. She had put off writing to her, hoping to have some good news to tell about or at least to be in a more positive frame of mind. But now seemed as good a time as any.

"Dear Aunt Liliu,

It is wonderful to be back home and wake up every day to my "real life" all around me again.

My beautiful Ainahau makes my heart glad every morning and mostly seems just the same to me as before. The new house is gorgeous, of course, but takes a little getting used to. It does sometimes seem a bit troublesome, having cost so much to build, with Papa and I scrounging so hard every day just to scrape by.

I see the people almost every day. They bring food, flowers, carvings, hand-made mats and baskets, etc. I shall have to open a gift shop soon, to take care of the overflow! For now, I make a present twice weekly at minimum, delivering these gifts to St. Andrew's School and the Children's Hospital Home by the cart load. I try to have this done quietly, at night, so no one will see and mind that we must share their hard-come-by gifts to us, which of course are a great sacrifice for all the people, and for the threadbare, exhausted natives most of all.

Last Sunday I had hundreds of visitors. By six o'clock I was so tired I didn't know what to do with myself. I try my best to be gracious and listen to everyone, even including the few "opposition" *haoles*, who seem embarrassed but come nevertheless, and all the curiosity seekers. I do wish you were here; we all miss you so very much.

It makes me feel sad to see the Hawaiians looking so poor. In the old days I am sure there were not so many people so utterly destitute.

I keep my spirits up as best I can. When will you come home? We long for your return; at the same time, we hope your staying in Washington longer will bring us good news.

I try to exercise daily, as I know how much better I always feel when I do. But the weather here has been rather warm so that, at present, I stay inside a great deal as I seem to feel the heat so much more now.

Kuhio's new wife, Princess Elizabeth, has been a delight. She helps me not get too moody. Kuhio adores her, of course, and I am sure they will have a beautiful baby. The idea of a new life around here makes us all glad.

Papa sends his best. He is very busy, as usual, though I am never quite sure with what. Don't tell him I said so; he is such a sensitive dear.

> All my love,
> Your Niece,
> Kaiulani"

Chapter Twenty-Seven

When Kaiulani returned to Hawaii in early November 1897, there were only three years left of the century. For citizens, subjects and comrades everywhere, "*Le Fin de Siecle*" had an ominous, disturbing tone. Many believed that there had never before in history been such upheaval. People around the globe were convinced that the end of human society, of all structure and reason, - indeed, of the known world, - were close at hand. They were terrified at the prospect of impending chaos. But the end of the known world is always close at hand, forever in progress, constantly shifting and changing as life contracts and expands every second, with each breath of every creature that lives.

The beginning of the holiday season of 1897, when Kaiulani had been home for two months, brought more troubles for Hawaii.

In the papers Kaiulani read rumors that she and Papa would probably soon move from Ainahau and Waikiki to stay indefinitely at Aunt Liliu's home in Washington Place. One article delicately suggested this would be "a thoughtful convenience on the Princess' part, to accommodate all the people who could not go as far as Ainahau to call on her." Chilled by the ominous implications, Kaiulani went at once to find Papa and demanded his interpretation.

"Well, I'm sure that seems extremely unlikely and improbable, to me. But even if such was to be the case, for reasons unknown," he said, "I'm sure it would only be a temporary measure."

Kaiulani looked at him sharply for a moment, but Papa continued to shuffle through a pile of papers on his desk with great concentration. When it became obvious that he had no intention of discussing the matter further, or even of meeting her eyes, she snatched back the paper and left in a white heat.

Alone on the *lanai*, she took deep breaths, gulping in the sweet, familiar scents of *pikake*, gardenia and roses. Had she been able to magically send her sight back to Archibald Cleghorn's study, her heart might have melted, or perhaps frozen like ice. For her brave, strong father sat there, helpless, and cradled his head in his hands as he wept.

But Kaiulani could not see her father's tears. So she paced the long, spacious porch back and forth, again and again, like a tiger prowling in a cage.

She refused to give in or give up, no matter what! She felt like that little Dutch boy at the dam, who had kept the dangerous hole patched with nothing but his finger, desperately trying to ward off disaster. She would not let that dam flow, to ruin everything she had known and hoped for and expected in life. She would not allow that to happen to the Hawaiians. She was not going to let them down.

Later that same week of the terrible 'relocation' rumors, the Provisional Government held an auction to sell off the personal belongings of King Kalakaua. PG President Sanford Dole was away again, out of the country, in Washington, D.C., so it was not known who had authorized the auction. All of the wine glasses, plates and cups, saucers, candlesticks and decorative objects from Papa Moi's Iolani Palace home - all were sold, most of them grabbed up by *haoles* to be displayed in their offices and homes as curiosities, souvenirs of the Champagne Monarch's reign.

The afternoon of the sale Clive Davies sent Kaiulani a note. He wanted to explain to her that he had bid on and purchased two of Papa Moi's silver candelabras at the request of his father, who was still detained on business in California.

While Kaiulani felt it was not entirely inappropriate for Clive to let her know this; still, it seemed a rather sad, tainted sort of way for Theo and his son to choose to take mementos; and a strange way for her former guardian to commemorate his friendship with the King.

The longer she thought about the cruel sale of Papa and Mama Moi's personal things, the more Kaiulani's rage grew. Early the next morning she rode over to visit the Dowager Queen herself, the former

Queen Kapiolani, at her villa in Waikiki. The usually placid mare that the Princess rode on was so distressed from her rider's tense mood that the horse was panting and exhausted by the time they arrived, even though the weather was unusually mild and Kaiulani had forced herself to keep an even, steady pace.

Koa, Kuhio and Princess Elizabeth, who became more voluptuous and stunning every day, were all living there with Mama Moi. They had just been finishing a leisurely breakfast in the drawing room. But when Kaiulani stormed in and everyone saw the look of unguarded desperation on her face, Mama Moi beckoned to the others to leave her alone with the miserable Princess.

Mama Moi was a kind, considerate woman, and had become only more gracious with age. Rising with a measured grace that caused her black silk *holoku* to flutter a little in the wind that had swept in with Kaiulani, Mama Moi embraced the agitated Princess with a hold surprisingly firm for one so old.

The rich, familiar redolence of the old woman's gingery, rose perfume made Kaiulani collapse and weep with abandon in the former Queen's generous arms. Each time she would begin to pull herself together and raise her head, Kaiulani would be struck again by the sight of Papa Moi's serious, sympathetic face, which peered out at her from busts and portraits displayed all over the room. His compassionate eyes made her sob anew each time she saw them.

Mama Moi comforted her, sitting close by on the sofa, until at last the old Queen had managed to soothe away some of the tears.

"There, now. Now, now," Kapiolani cooed, speaking in Hawaiian as she always did now, having long ago forgotten the few words of English she once knew. Above the *lei* of golden yellow *o'o* feathers nestled around her neck, she wore a large golden brooch with a miniature portrait of her dead husband in blue and pink fire opal mosaic. On an ebony pedestal in front of the two women, a strikingly lifelike clay bust of Kalakaua smiled over at them, flanked on each side by two of the tallest *kahilis* Kaiulani had ever seen. Their towering plumes almost brushed the high ceiling.

Kaiulani had planned to ask Mama Moi how the PGs could do such a thing to them, and if there was no legal recourse to stop them. But when she had calmed down enough to speak, all the pent up feelings she had been holding in for so long - her sadness and fear, her uncertainty about what to do, - rushed out in a great flood. She asked Kapiolani the questions she had not been able to say out loud to anyone else, not because she did not dare but because she was afraid she already knew the answers.

Did Mama Moi think there was any chance that Hawaii might be saved?

The old Queen at once shook her head. "No. Hawaii will not be able to sustain independence, or even survive as a republic, not for long, anyway. The Kingdom has ended."

"Is there no hope?" Kaiulani pleaded. "None at all?"

Kapiolani shrugged and then sadly shook her head again. "When Cleveland was still in office, maybe there was a chance. But with McKinley, - no."

The Princess' voice was so muted it was almost inaudible, and the old woman had to lean in very close to hear. Did she think - would it happen soon?

Kapiolani was gentle as she held Kaiulani's hand in her own.

"When is soon?" Kapiolani asked. "Tomorrow? Sometime this year?"

The former Queen lightly, delicately held the unhappy Princess in another embrace. When she spoke again, her voice was as soft as a balmy summer breeze. "It makes no difference when. Soon is soon."

"And there is nothing," Kaiulani murmured, "Nothing left that I or Aunt Liliu can do." This time the Princess' voice was stronger and clear. She was no longer asking questions, only stating a fact.

"There is nothing that anyone can do," Kapiolani said firmly. "The Moi saw all this coming, years ago," Kapiolani sighed. "But there was nothing he could do, either."

She held herself a little apart from Kaiulani so that she could look into her eyes as she held the Princess' face close to her own.

"You have been very good to all of us, Kaiulani, and for Hawaii. Your godfather would be proud."

The light in Kaiulani's eyes showed more gratitude than any words could have. She grasped Kapiolani's moth-soft, wrinkled hand in her own and brought it to her lips to kiss.

Wordlessly, for there was nothing more to say, the Queen and the Princess rose together and stood side by side. Kaiulani was shocked by how slowly and carefully Kapiolani moved. For the first time, she took in how frail Mama Moi had become. The old woman's hands and legs shook with arthritic trembling brought on by the effort she had made to stand.

Although she struggled to catch her breath, Kapiolani never let go of Kaiulani's hand, or her eyes.

"*'Kulia I ka nu'u.*' Strive to reach the highest good. This has always been our motto, our family's way." She paused, bending forward a little to swallow air before she spoke again. "It is hard for you now, I know. But you will find it in your heart to do what is right, whatever is best for Hawaii."

Kaiulani felt a sharp, sudden chill and wondered if the temperature had dropped, or if another storm was brewing up.

Kapiolani reached up to touch the soft halo of Kaiulani's hair, which had mostly come undone. The musty, comforting smell of the old Queen's perfume triggered a jumbled rush of memories. Kaiulani thought of the coronation ceremony so long ago, and remembered how she had worried when the Queen's crown would not fit.

"Your mother was a good woman, and she meant well. Though, like any of us, she could not always be kind. She loved you as well as she could, in her way, although she was often very unhappy. Your father, too, has tried to take care of you, in his fashion. But they had much to struggle with, my dear, as we all do, in different ways, at various times."

She patted Kaiulani's cheek and smiled. "We can all of us only do the best we can, with the strength we have, in each moment."

She brushed the wild, dark cloud of hair out of Kaiulani's face, away from her teary eyes, and became a little dreamy and thoughtful as she stroked the Princess' silky, tightly curled hair.

Kaiulani surrendered to exhaustion and to the soothing touch of the old woman's fingers on her face, and allowed her eyes to close for a moment. She was about to drift off to sleep when the muted sound of Mama Moi's quiet voice brought her back. Kapiolani seemed, really, to be talking to herself. But Kaiulani took in every word.

"You were a *hanai* child, I think. Not officially. But your mother and father gave you away, though they probably did not even know it," she mused. "They gave you away to the world, so you were on your own at a very early age."

The old woman kept touching the young woman's face as if she was blind and trying to memorize the shape of it forever. *"Hanai* does not work that way, though. A child cannot belong to the world. Not everyone can be so independent, alone. You have had to raise yourself, for most of it. Hard on someone so tender. You have been wounded. Like Hawaii, like our people."

Kaiulani opened her eyes and saw the bright reflection that shined back at her from Kapiolani's eyes.

"You have given us comfort and hope, Princess." Her voice was like a blessing. "But it has become too difficult. We must wait for it to finish, and then we must let go."

The chill Kaiulani had felt a moment ago, and earlier, at Honolulu Harbor when she saw all the Hawaiians waiting for her, flooded over her again. But this time there was no warning or alarm, only a sense of release and acceptance. She was so tired. There was, after all, only so much she could do.

Kapiolani's murmuring voice floated and drifted above Kaiulani's bowed head like a gentle wind.

"A *hanai* child, especially, must have a proper mother or father. Preferably, both. The world cannot raise a child. The world has no heart, no memory. The world can only continue on its unsteady course, like a storm or a volcano or any other part of nature."

They stood in stillness for a long time, and then Kapiolani spoke tremulously, lost in another memory. With a last embrace, the old woman whispered in her ear as she held her close.

"When I went to Queen Victoria's fiftieth Jubilee - more than ten years ago now," - she shook her head in disbelief at the relentless passing of time. "When I went to Victoria's celebration, your Aunt Liliu came as my companion. She was my interpreter, too. It is strange to me, when I think of it now. One Queen served by another soon-to-be-queen."

Kapiolani's fingers lifted up to her breast to touch the mosaic pin that held Kalakaua's portrait.

"I wore a beautiful gown, designed for the occasion, made from velvets and silks, - silver, blue and black, - and decorated with real peacock feathers. It was the most elegant thing I had ever worn. People everywhere stopped us to ask questions about it. But I never wore it again, never. I always felt sorry for those peacocks who had given up their feathers only for the sake of fashion and display."

She smiled at Kaiulani. "Strange what one remembers, isn't it?"

They kissed one more time and then the Princess left to go home.

As Kaiulani rode back to Ainahau she felt, for the first time since she had come home, at peace. Whatever would come would come.

When she got back to the new house at Ainahau she went directly to bed and slept for several hours, quietly and without dreaming, even though it was the middle of the day.

* * * * * * * * * * * * * * * * * * * *

The holiday season had begun when news came from Aunt Liliu that the commission of native Hawaiians at last had arrived in Washington. They brought with them an enormous petition, signed by more than half of the islands' natives that asked the Senate and all members of the United States government to refuse to ratify the Annexation Treaty.

Thus far, Aunt Liliu reported, it seemed certain that the necessary two-thirds majority of the Senate vote, which was required to approve annexation, would not pass. But there was also, she warned, a new resolution to push through a bill to the House and the Senate, in which case only a 50% majority would be needed to pass the dreaded Treaty that would steal Hawaii from its people.

That holiday season Kaiulani forced herself to attend most of the parties, dances and balls. She smiled and acted the part of the gracious Princess of Hawaii.

She went to luncheons in her honor; and the term ending ceremonies for a prestigious local seminary school; and even to the United States Consul General Ball sponsored by Mr. Sewall. She did everything in her power to reassure the Hawaiians that their homeland was still intact.

New Year's Eve she danced with Papa at a gala ball given by U.S. Admiral Miller. At midnight the admiral's band struck up "The Star Spangled Banner." Kaiulani was appalled that they did not have the grace or tact to play the traditional *"Hawaii Ponoi"* afterwards, when it really should have been played, as always, first; but still, she only smiled and smiled.

In early January Mama Moi became ill with a dangerous cold, made all the more threatening by her frail condition. Kaiulani moved to the villa at Waikiki to care for her and stayed for three weeks, sitting up all night to hold the Queen Dowager's hand or touch a damp cloth to her cracked lips.

Koa came often and sat with them, too. At times the cousins together sang the old, traditional songs to the fragile Queen, who wept with gratitude when she knew they were there, and slept fitfully, sometimes with her eyes wide open, half-way between this world and the next. Kaiulani and Koa seldom spoke to each other as they watched over the dying woman and waited for the end. They were beyond words, but as close to each other in their spirits and shared sorrow as they ever had been.

One afternoon Kapiolani rallied so strongly that she tried to join Kaiulani and Koa, briefly attempting to sing a few notes of Papa Moi's "*Hawaii Ponoi*" with them. Then the royal widow sighed peacefully, fell into a deep sleep, and was gone. Princess Kaiulani closed the old Queen's eyes for the last time.

Kaiulani wrote to Aunt Liliu to tell her that Kapiolani had been released, and that she and Koa were fortunate enough to be there with her at the end.

Nothing else was going on, Kaiulani wrote, except that they were eager for her return. They were all glad that annexation was not a fact, and continued to try their best to keep up their hopes. She had to admit, however, that the people were not "half so happy as when I first came back" and ended with "I find everything so much changed."

On February 15, 1898, at Havana Harbor in Cuba, the U.S. battleship *Maine* was destroyed; all 264 crewmen on board were killed. The cause of the explosion was never settled. Most Americans believed it was a Spanish mine, while most Spaniards claimed it was an internal explosion in the ship, or else a malfunction of the engine. There was, however, no longer any question about the relations between the two countries. American and Spain would soon be at war. And this news could only mean the worst for the Kingdom of Hawaii.

Devastated by this certain knell of doom for Hawaii's independent state, Kaiulani rallied her strength by a steely act of will. She decided to make a public statement of her hope and faith by honoring Prince Koa's 30th birthday with a Saturday afternoon *luau* at Ainahau; she invited about 100 friends. She also wanted to thank Koa with the *luau* for all his support and affection over the years. What a fine prince consort he would have been! But that was all from another time and place, as distant from her now as the day of her own birth.

With some wistfulness she remembered that she had hoped to give a birthday *luau* for Toby in Hawaii. Wouldn't he laugh now over his former concern that she and Koa might be engaged! Koa had become a brother to her, no more, no less. But, she realized with some distraction, in the old days they might have married, as brother and sister. That had been the highest coupling, the most sacred marriage of all. How odd to think of that now...

Not long after the *luau*, during the first week of March, President Dole returned to Hawaii from Washington, D.C. The treaty, he explained to the press, was once again on hold. Congress had more pressing emergencies to deal with regarding the impending War with Spain.

That same week the first copies of Aunt Liliu's book, "Hawaii's Story by Hawaii's Queen," arrived in Honolulu. The PGS and their *haole* supporters were enraged, though most of them had read only the title. Commentaries in the PG press were vitriolic. And the newly published report of the Native Hawaiian Commissioners, who had recently returned from Washington, was even more obnoxious, making the members sound like savage illiterates.

Quotes that were supposed to be from the report were printed in all the PG, anti-royalist papers. Ludicrous lies were widely manufactured and then repeated ad nauseam. The commission and the Queen were both slandered, with the erudite Hawaiian commissioners supposed to have complained, "Queen Liliuokalani, she only want money. Print big book to sell for money for herself. She believe the United States annex us and then she have claim. She want one hundred million dollars. We do not want her. We want our young Princess."

How terrible, Kaiulani thought, that even as the PG Republicans mercilessly looted and plundered her country, they continued to try to disrupt and destroy the loyalty of the people to the *ali'i*, and the love of the *ali'i* for the people, with their gross lies!

Well, probably it did not matter anymore; Kaiulani struggled in vain to console herself with the thought.

But something had changed inside her, in her most secret self, since the conversation with Queen Kapiolani and, most especially, after the awesome experience of staying by the old Queen's side to comfort her as she left life. Ever since, there had been a shift in Kaiulani's emotions and soul, subtle but strong and powerful as a sea change.

It was not that she had given up. She would never give up. But she had begun to come to terms with reality. She had accepted that there was nothing she could do, at least for now, to save Hawaii. She could only bide her time and stay on course in the face of almost certain defeat.

There was an unexpected relief for her in this acceptance of that which seemed inevitable. She was no longer at all concerned anymore, for instance, over what Dole or Thurston or any of the PGs might think of her. She was indifferent to whatever they might be plotting. The damage, as far as she could tell, had already been done. She had heard the claims, too, even from some of the Hawaiians, that Liliu had stayed in Washington for so long with the intention of preventing Kaiulani from gathering support and coming into power. She did not care about any of this anymore.

Sometime, when she hadn't even noticed it, the shape of her life had changed. She struggled to understand what this might mean.

Apparently, her life been going forward in a more or less normal way; progressing, it seemed to her, toward something. But now it was as if time had somehow looped back on itself, so that the past and the future were, in some mysterious way, coming together.

It made her tired, really, to think about it. But she also felt a strange sense of release. As if she no longer needed to worry anymore or puzzle everything out all the time, or try to change anything but had only to accept the inevitable. She did not know what it might mean. She only knew that, no matter what came to pass, nothing would ever be the same.

Chapter Twenty-Eight

At the beginning of April Kaiulani made an appearance at a concert at the Opera House. The performance was a benefit for two of Hawaii's oldest churches, *Moanalua* and *Kahili*, so the house was packed with supporters of Hawaiian culture.

The elderly Kawaihau Brothers, an acapella trio of Hawaiian singers, were the featured performers that night. The first number on their program was a tribute to the Princess that had been written in her honor by composer Charles King. The song told the story of a *lei* made for Kaiulani from the flowers of a favorite native tree, the *lehua* tree, which had long been a symbol of the islands of Hawaii in all their glory and pride. The bright red *lehua* flowers also served as an emblem of the loyalty of the Hawaiian people to their *ali'i*, and of the *ali'i* to the people.

The singers announced the title of their song in a single voice as they bowed low to the Princess.

"A Wreath for Kaiulani."

In tones so smoothly blended that the three voices sounded like one, the Kawaihau Brothers began to sing.

> "Bring forth the wreath of *lehua*,
> The wreath for our beloved Princess.
> Loving hands didst weave
> A beautiful crown for Kaiulani."

Their ethereal voices and the sweet lyrics of the song made Kaiulani want to weep. Instead, she smiled radiantly out at the Brothers and the audience. The old men's voices wove together into the seamless harmony they had developed after decades together, full of the echoing rhythms of the ancient *meles* and chants.

The oldest of the brothers gazed up at Kaiulani, clutching a wreath in his arms as if it was a child that he was offering to her from the stage. She sensed rather than clearly saw what was happening, for her eyesight had become very bad. Even the tiny *lorgnette* that she had used for several years no longer helped. But she could still make out shapes and colors at a distance, and she could feel the *aloha* that flowed to her from the singers and the audience.

With effort, squeezing her eyes half-shut to gain focus, she could just make out when the three men bowed in unison again. She flashed another smile down at them from her place of honor in the upper mezzanine, and the crowd murmured with delight.

> "Upon thy head we place it,
> How lovely and charming to behold there.
> Royal and queenly thou art,
> Our loving Kaiulani."

How blessed she was, Kaiulani thought. Truly, she had loved and been loved in her life.

The brothers bowed low a third time and then began their final verse.

> "This token of love for thee we bring,
> Oh, receive it, Kaiulani!
> Wear your *lei* of yellow *lehua*
> Entwined with the fragrant *maile* leaves."

When several members of the audience stood and began to applaud her, Kaiulani felt like her private box had become a cloud, lifting her higher and higher until she thought she must catch on fire from the sun, or else float up into heaven. For the first time since she had come back, she was sure that at last she was home.

That night, her *lehua* wreath resting beside her head and the flower petals scattered on and under her pillows, she slept as peacefully as a baby.

* * * * * * * * * * * * * * * * * * *

On May 1, American troops under the command of Commodore George Dewey sank a Spanish fleet in the harbor at Manila in the Philippines. By the middle of the month the United States officially declared war on Spain. Ten thousand American troops would soon descend upon Hawaii, passing through Honolulu on their way to fight the war.

Mr. Thurston had jumped on the situation right away, taking advantage of the great surge of American patriotism and nationalism to publish his latest piece of work, the "Handbook On The Annexation Of Hawaii." In it, he had examined each point of the potential vulnerability of America in the Pacific, and used his conclusions to encourage immediate annexation.

According to Thurston's logic, taking over the Hawaiian Islands would be the swiftest and most effective way to curb the impending threat of Japanese aggression. This action would inevitably benefit American commerce, he explained, thus consequently strengthening America's "rightful position of dominance overseas."

Conversely, Thurston argued, he knew of no United States' constitutional law that had ever ruled against the annexation of territory. Neither, of course, was it possible to consider incorporating the Hawaiians as American citizens, since there was not even a remote possibility of overlooking the enormous differences in terms of race, culture and native character. All of which, though well meaning and agreeably compliant, at times, to a degree, were naturally quite inferior.

Annexation, Mr. Thurston assured his readers, was no plot of self-interested businessmen! It was instead the only sensible and reasonable action that would move everyone that essential next step forward toward continuing the practice of good government and promoting lasting peace.

* * * * * * * * * * * * * * * * * * *

Papa had been reading excerpts from Thurston's "Handbook," which was serialized in most of the pro-Annexationist newspapers, to Kaiulani at the breakfast and dinner table for nearly two weeks. Kaiulani had stopped reading the papers soon after the news of America's intentions to go to war with Spain. Why should she get worked up about any one version of what was going on, when the information and "facts" were sure to change by the very next minute, anyway? She had no patience for these half-truths and the so-called 'white lies' anymore. Her tolerance for equivocation was at an end.

She had been incensed, at first, furious over the injustice of Thurston's blatant lies. But she found herself rapidly becoming detached to the point of indifference and then, to her own surprise, boredom. What more could these stupid people do to them, anyway? Things would either get better, or they would get worse. The damage was already done. She was tired of reacting to lies and stories, getting upset time and again for nothing, over nothing, when there was nothing she could do.

So when Papa complained, again, about how Thurston was showing his true colors and had become a complete traitor to the Hawaiian's cause, Kaiulani reminded him that the surly lawyer was, after all, a missionary's son, and therefore had always been against the real Hawaiians and their cause. Furthermore, he would always, she was quite sure, remain so. It was naive for Papa to expect him to behave otherwise.

Papa seemed startled by her response, and apparently received it as a rebuke, for soon after he left the room with a transparent excuse. But that was the last time he read to her from the papers.

She was sorry if she had hurt his feelings; honestly, she was. That had never been her intention. But she couldn't always be protecting Papa now, either; or constantly worrying about how he would cope. She did not have a lot of strength at the moment and she would need whatever she did have to try to manage on her own. Things were far from over or resolved.

* * * * * * * * * * * * * * * * * * *

The mad scramble of making plans to entertain the oncoming American troops was very distasteful to Kaiulani. What a shame, she thought, that all that energy and enthusiasm could not be channeled into a more worthy cause.

This new, rising generation, many of them *hapa-haole*, half-Hawaiian, like herself, was eager, it seemed to her, to prove their pro-American intentions. They tried to imitate American fashions, for example, although their outfits were usually at least a year or two or even three behind the California styles, never mind anywhere near the New York or Parisian trends. She thought it rather ironic, really, that so many people here insisted on "aping" American and European taste. Especially when she herself, who had lived in those places, now preferred to return to the loose, flowing, traditional Hawaiian look. Besides, it really made little difference to her anymore what she looked like, unless she was putting herself on show for some public event.

It was easy to see how all this near hysterical activity about the Americans coming was such a devastating blow to the older generation of Hawaiians. They wandered about looking stunned, melancholy and dazed, almost as if they felt they were somehow in the way. Kaiulani hated to see them like that.

Fundraisers had been organized by the *haoles* and other PGs to purchase the massive amounts of food and drink that would be needed, and to schedule entertainments in honor of the American soldiers. It was said that 10,000 "boys in blue" would pass through Hawaii!

Kaiulani was revolted to see sprouting up all over the red, white and blue banners that announced, "Welcome Troops!" and "We Support America!" To Aunt Liliu she wrote, "Honolulu is making a fool of itself and I only hope we won't all be ridiculed."

Even she and Papa were forced to participate, though, so as not to appear sullen or ungracious. Papa sent a letter to the head of the Committee for Entertaining The Troops to say that he and Princess Kaiulani would be pleased to receive visits from the Americans at Ainahau. Reluctantly, but with full awareness of her responsibilities in the matter, Kaiulani had acquiesced to this plan. She dreaded the locust-like invasion of soldiers in Honolulu; it would feel so much like a military occupation. But she knew she must be pleasant to all, for the sake of Hawaii.

Even Koa and Kuhio had grudgingly agreed to take part, presenting a hand-sewn Hawaiian flag made by a committee of native women to Captain Glass on board the American ship, the *U.S.S. Charleston.* At least Princess Elizabeth, whose pregnancy was quite advanced, was allowed to stay home.

Some sad news came to the Cleghorn family during this busy time. In early June they learned that Theo Davies had died of a sudden heart attack on May 25. He had been on his way back to Hawaii, staying in San Francisco at, ironically, the same hotel where Papa Moi had passed away.

She would never see those stern, thoughtful eyes again; never hear Mr. Davies' sober, measured tones. She shut herself off from this loss, though, for she really could not bear much more right at the moment. She would miss him terribly, of course, but for now she must force herself to imagine that he was only away on business, or taking an extended holiday.

What would Maddie do, she wondered? Well, Maddie had always been clever and charming, and she was still young. She would manage all right, she was sure.

Mr. Davies, gone. So many things changed, again and again, in her world. It made her tired. She was disinclined to even want to keep track of it all anymore, except when she absolutely had to. There was too much to remember and try to figure out.

Two events brightened up the month for the Princess and gave her some distraction from the interminable visits of the American troops. Three steamers had landed in Honolulu the first week of June, jammed with loud, eager young soldiers. Within a few days, two thousand and four hundred troops, the beginning of the onslaught, crammed the city's streets. Iolani Palace, now called either "The Executive Building" or "The Capitol Building" by the PGs, was thrown open to serve as a kind of social club and giant mess hall. There was the constant bustle of hauling literally tons of sandwiches, potato salads, fruits and cakes and pies; and the comings and going of hundreds of gallons of milk, lemonade, coffee and cookies, all trucked through the palace gates to feed the ravenous hordes of soldiers and sailors.

Then, in mid-month on the 16th, Kuhio and Elizabeth's baby daughter was born. With her alert, sparkling eyes and endearing tendency to make happy cooing sounds when she nursed or as she lay about half-asleep in her bassinet, the baby was like a healthy, lively bird. They named her Liliu Victoria Bernice, after Aunt Liliu and Kaiulani and Princess Elizabeth's mother, but everyone called her "Lili." Kaiulani loved to hold her in her arms whenever she could, and even pretended once or twice that the little darling was her own.

The other pleasant and exciting event came at the end of the month when a Mr. Burton Holmes, a young American with no connection whatsoever to the war or the military, arrived in Honolulu.

When the second fleet of American soldiers heading for Manila docked in Hawaii the last week of June, the "occupied" feeling that Kaiulani had dreaded became inescapable. There were soldiers in the streets, parks and on the beaches. They packed every sporting and cultural event to overflowing and swarmed in mobs onto the grounds of Ainahau every day. That eerie, insect-like quality Kaiulani had observed at the armory in Washington haunted her again. But this time her feeling of being suffocated by the endless, milling crowds was even more stifling. For now all these noisy, aggressive young men in their identical blue uniforms had descended on her home.

Burton Holmes and his assistant, the gangly, awkward Oscar Bennett de Pue, had managed to catch a ride with the second fleet of American soldiers, and had traveled with them all the way from San Francisco. By the time they reached Hawaii they were grateful and relieved to be at the end of the trip, finally "cut loose," as Holmes put it, from the unruly mob. For Kaiulani, the arrival of Holmes and de Pue and their intriguing activities were a welcome distraction from the military uproar.

Burton Holmes had just recently celebrated his thirtieth birthday. His dark, curly hair flowed down to his shoulders and he usually wore a scarf or two tied loosely around his neck. His bright eyes lit up with laughter at the slightest provocation, and the energy that surged forth from his compact, kinetic body was contagious to all around him. He had an excess of vitality, so that the mere presence of Burton Holmes was enough to cheer Kaiulani up.

Holmes had a reputation as both a successful artist and an up-and-coming entrepreneur. He had developed and marketed a series of travel lectures with a unique, contemporary twist. For he illustrated these lectures with moving, photographic images of the actual people and places he visited, to give them the thrilling illusion of real life. With his partner, Bennett de Pue, managing the so-called "magic lantern" and all of the other electrical appurtenances necessary to create the phenomenon of these "moving pictures," Holmes was free to "gold dig" and direct de Pue in "shooting" the highlights of each local culture.

A tall, slow-moving fellow, de Pue seemed to be all arms, legs, elbows and feet. He had a permanent expression of bewilderment on his angular face.

The two men were a contrast in temperaments, and the sight of this offbeat pair as they wove in and out of each other's way, entangled in cameras and lights, always amused Kaiulani immensely. The obvious excitement they derived from each other's company and collaboration made them a pleasure to be around.

Koa and Kuhio had met Holmes and de Pue when they went on board the second troop ship to present the Hawaiian flag for the second time to the latest batch of soldiers and their captain.

Holmes had made a heartfelt remark about the sailors under his breath, saying how he hoped to God he would never have to see so much blue again as long as he lived since, between the sailors' uniforms and the ocean, he had been overloaded for eternity. De Pue gloomily agreed that he, too, had seen enough blue to last a lifetime, thank you very much.

When Koa and Kuhio overheard this exchange, they laughed out loud at the outspoken pair. This only encouraged the two filmmakers to egg each other on with more extravagant exaggerations and jokes at the sailors' expense, trying to get the Hawaiian Princes to laugh again. From that moment on, Koa and Kuhio were hard pressed to keep straight faces throughout the rest of the ceremony.

After the presentation they insisted that the filmmakers come home with them for supper. Kaiulani and Princess Elizabeth found them to be excellent company as well. Even baby Lili seemed to light up more when "the American film boys" came around.

Within a short time Holmes had managed to persuade them all to perform as his "stars," as he phrased it, to be the "talent" when he filmed several "scenes" of surfing and outrigger canoe races in the next few weeks.

So, one morning just before five, when it was still the end of the night sky, six boatloads of surfers and canoe racers gathered at the beach for a "shoot." Kaiulani, Eva Parker, Koa and even Kuhio came to be in the "motion pictures" and to cheer on the racers and surfers.

For hours they rode the waves and sailed the boats while de Pue set and reset cameras and lights and Burton Holmes shouted praise and directions to the *ali'i* and the other performers over his outsized megaphone.

Kaiulani's laughter and shouts echoed throughout the races, which were immensely spurred on by her presence and participation. The fact that "filming" was taking place, with the "eye" of the camera watching everything like a benevolent goddess or god, and the awareness that they were all being magically recorded for posterity, added yet another element of excitement.

Kaiulani felt more alive than she had in months. It was as if she was a child again and the world was new.

The weather those few days was perfect, balmy, breezy and mild, so Kaiulani was able to stay outside in the soft sunlight the entire time without a care. She glowed, lit up from inside with happiness, and from outside by the Hawaiian sun and the artful lighting of Bennet de Pue. In all of the "still" photographs she stood out, radiant and exotic as a rare flower.

Kaiulani was so happy to be released, even temporarily, from her obligations and duties as Princess that she was reckless with joy. At the canoe races her passion knew no bounds. She yelled and cheered until she was hoarse and exhausted, so that even Koa looked at her out of the corners of his eyes to make sure she was all right.

Papa came by one day for a few hours and cautioned her to "calm down a little" and "not be so wild." But she was so excited to be free that she startled him even more by kissing the tip of his nose. Quite gaily, she called him "a stick-in-the-mud," a bit of slang they had just learned from the American filmmakers, that everyone had been throwing around "on the shoot" all day long. She had no idea what it meant, but she loved to say it out loud, along with the others. It had such a cheerful, lively sound. She had used it on everyone, as often as possible, at every opportunity.

"Don't worry so, Papa! I'm fine, really!" She reassured him. "I'm only having a little fun, for a change!"

But Papa continued to look uncomfortable and soon found a reason to leave.

De Pue and Holmes both fell madly in love with Kaiulani, thrilled by her spirit and passion. They were struck by how eerily photogenic she was and by her incredible poise and beauty. At night, long after they had finished their plans for the filming the next day and should have been trying to catch a few hours of sleep before they began again, their conversation always focused on Kaiulani. Both agreed she might have had a fine career as a performer, were she not already enmeshed in her role as a royal.

They talked about her late into the night, and played a game of imagining which of them she might pick if she had to choose between them because some terrible disaster had left the three of them the last people on earth.

The day came when, regretfully, de Pue and Holmes had at last to bid *aloha* to Honolulu and head on to New Guinea. They left on the first of July. Three days later Kaiulani had to suffer through the local celebrations of America's Independence Day, complete with volleys of gunfire and barrages of exploding fireworks. There were near-rioting crowds in the streets that reminded the Hawaiians over and over again of the U.S.' military occupation, which felt so like an invasion of their land.

Kaiulani confessed to Koa that she found the Americans' enthusiastic reenactment of battles and war-like conditions rather repulsive. She could not understand why anyone would wish to remain outside in it to be threatened by such violent behavior. Koa admitted that he and Kuhio had speculated about what it might have been like if the American colonies had remained under British rule.

Most of the Hawaiians, including the *ali'i*, stayed indoors that day and the next to express their contempt for the usurpers' displays of aggression.

The next time Kaiulani and Koa came out together for a public event, they attended a magic show performed by "The Great Dante" who billed himself as "The World's Greatest Living Magician." He had come all the way from Connecticut to entertain the American troops. Unfortunately, his performance was lackluster and boring, executed with much less skill and daring than almost any of the acts that the cousins had seen abroad in Europe and even in America.

But the soldiers, browned by the Hawaiian sun and heated up with thoughts of the impending dangers they would face in the Philippines, applauded everything with wild, throaty shouts for more, while the Hawaiians stayed politely neutral. One *kananka* remarked dryly to another that he had seen better magic in the daily changes of the weather. Midway through the performance Koa made Kaiulani laugh when he spoke softly into her ear to ask if she thought that the Great Dante might be capable of making the American troops disappear. She whispered back that it would be almost as lovely if the Great Dante would make himself disappear.

On July 13th the long-dreaded news reached Hawaii that the S.S. *Coptic* had sailed into Diamond Head Harbor bringing its "glad tidings." On June 15th two-thirds of the House of Representatives had voted in favor of the annexation resolution. By July 6th the Senate had followed with a 50/50 division of yeas and nays. And on the 7th of July President McKinley had signed the bill.

Within minutes of the *Coptic's* landing the shrill whistles of firehouses, factories and power stations were screeching out the news. Fireworks explosions incited the crowds that had rushed down to meet the ship and its crew, who were in frenzies of raucous shouting and cheers. Then a tremendous volley of gunfire exploded from the "Executive Building." It sounded like menacing thunder as it rumbled through Honolulu and echoed out into the surrounding valleys and hills.

Thousands of *haoles*, many of them waving American flags, descended on the docks to add to the deafening noise and confusion. Soldiers, Americans and PGs choked the streets, and the grounds of the former palace were glutted with people drinking and carrying on.

Some of the Hawaiians were at first under the impression that the Americans had somehow already won their war with Spain. When they heard the actual news they were stunned. Some were speechless, crestfallen or crushed, while others swore angrily under their breath.

A special edition of the PG newspaper that afternoon had huge headlines that read: "ANNEXATION! HERE TO STAY! AND THE STAR-SPANGLED BANNER IN TRIUMPH SHALL WAVE O'ER THE ISLES OF HAWAII AND THE HOMES OF THE BRAVE!"

And which "brave" might those be, Kaiulani wondered. The paper described the mood of the city as "jubilant." Jubilant. Papa and Mama Moi's coronation had been majestic, stately, impressive. Both her homecoming and her exile had been painful and overwhelming.

But those damn PGs and their kind would 'skew' everything they could, even making out this last, lethal blow to the independent Hawaiian nation to be something "jubilant." A cause for celebration. More like a triumph of true greed. Another gorging of the greedy and the monstrous, those insatiable, giant powers that grew and continued to grow at the expense and, often, at the demise of entire other cultures and races.

Like the natives who had been slaughtered in Africa. Wholesale, like animals, for the transgression of daring to live on their own land. Were their deaths also justified by the notion that they, too, had somehow been hindering the *haoles'* wonderful, so-called "progress?"

And the Indian tribes in America - she supposed they had been an obstacle, too, an imminent danger to be 'righteously,' murderously overcome by the white race, which was so eager to fulfill its "Manifest Destiny." Was it all right, then, she presumed, to spill any amount of native people's blood, as long as it paved the way for this precious "civilization?" And who was it, again, that was supposed to be "barbaric?"

The blaring noise of the crowds went on for hours, and Kaiulani was struck again and again by the intensely militaristic nature of the Americans. All those gun volleys, as if they were continuously declaring war, or in a constant state of emergency or crisis. Why couldn't they just dance once in a while, when they got excited? Or celebrate by singing something pleasant and attractive? But, no, it was always that wretched "Star-Spangled Banner." Which, unfortunately, she could hear the Royal Hawaiian Band playing right now, rather reluctantly, she thought, and more than a little off-key, for the umpteenth time that afternoon. That shrill, high melody and all that praise of "Perilous nights" and "rockets red glare" and "bombs bursting," indeed! Really, it began to seem to her that unless the Americans were actively involved in violence, they were never really happy.

Well. At least the awful waiting was over. It was official: Hawaii was to be made part of the United States. And Aunt Liliu, at last, with no more reason to wait, would soon be on her way home.

In the "Executive Building," which was really Iolani Palace, Minister Harold Sewall received the captain of the S.S. *Coptic*, who presented him with a specially designed, completely unofficial flag of the "new" United States. Instead of forty-five stars, there were forty-six. The extra one represented Hawaii.

Rumors that Kaiulani would soon leave Hawaii to live in England were rampant, even after Papa had issued a formal denial. The Princess was in delicate health, he explained, due to an abrupt, relapse occurrence of a bad cold. Consequently, she would soon go for an extended rest to the country ranch home of her good friends, the Parkers, in Mana, for a few months. But she would first wait for the return, of course, of her Aunt Liliuokalani, the ex-Queen.

Kaiulani thought how sad it was that it had all come to this. She and Liliu would again be in exile, but this time it was in their own country.

Chapter Twenty-Nine

In Kaiulani's dream the peacocks surrounded her in a wide circle. Everywhere she looked she saw them, their feathers fanned out, crests shuddering and wings trembling as if they were struggling to keep balance in a harsh wind. Their beaks continually opened and closed. There were hundreds, perhaps thousands of them - every peacock she had ever seen in her entire life, and all of them crying and wailing with the sad voices of disappointed children.

She woke in a cold sweat. What a horrid nightmare, all that yelling and screaming! And so many birds! Thank God she had only been dreaming; she struggled to reassure herself, trying to break free of the vivid, distressing images of fluttering, rustling wings and the echoes of those shrill, screeching cries. She was home, at Ainahau, she was safe. The sun was coming up and a light breeze teased the curtains at her bedroom window.

But everything was not all right. Liliu would be home soon, because Hawaii was going to be annexed to America and so there was no longer any reason for her to stay away. A dull pain gnawed at Kaiulani inside. Her headaches had returned, full force and almost daily. She was hanging on, willing herself to go through the motions while she waited for her Aunt to return.

The Hawaiians seemed stricken, which they were, by the terrible news, while the *haoles* and PGs went around grinning like cats that had eaten canaries. Kaiulani could relax a little only during the rare times when she was able to sit quietly and hold baby Lili in her arms.

She was horribly restless, yet could do nothing but continue to wait, not even knowing any more what for.

* * * * * * * * * * * * * * * * * * *

Liliu's ship was to land around midnight on August 1st. Though she had all the energy of a sleepwalker, Kaiulani marshaled enough strength to go out among her people so she could comfort them in their grief. The Hawaiians were stunned and subdued, which was just how Kaiulani felt. Everything was suspended, on hold until Liliu's return.

The Princess' carriage had raced over from Ainahau to the harbor around eleven. Kaiulani's hair, tousled by the night breezes, shined in the bright moonlight like a blue-black wing. Panting a little, she spotted Koa, who stood near the water's edge carrying a *lei* for the Queen made of ginger, carnations and *lehua* leaves. When he saw Kaiulani wave, he solemnly nodded and waved back.

The S.S. *Gaelic*, Liliuokalani's ship, had been sighted off Koko Head shortly before midnight. The full moon lit up the beaches and ocean as brightly as if it was day. Delicate cloud banks drifted by, causing the moonlight to filter in and out and bounce off the blue-green waves onto the dark green hills, then rebound to reflect off the ocean in hypnotic, irregular patterns.

By the time the Queen's ship headed in to harbor, the roads had filled up. Hundreds of people lined the paths and streamed down to the shore to meet her boat. The news of Liliuokalani's arrival had spread like fire in a dry, dusty field. Within minutes the waterfront was packed with natives and royalists, silent and solemn, waiting to see their Queen.

The stillness as everyone waited for Liliuokalani made Kaiulani remember the deep, peaceful quiet that always settled in during the first moments after a heavy snowfall, when nothing at all seems to move, as if the world was holding its breath.

And then the S.S. *Gaelic* glided onto shore. The heavy sound of the boat settling in to anchor seemed to break the spell of silence and many of the Hawaiians began to weep.

Koa hurried on board to escort the Queen. Ramrod straight and dressed all in black, Liliuokalani wore a large, plumed hat that cast shadows over her face. She walked with her head high and her hand on Koa's arm as she looked out onto the faces of her own people again, at last.   Her eyes were shining with grief and pride. Liliuokalani took off her hat and handed it to Koa before she placed the fragrant *lei* he had brought around her neck and then turned out to the mass of faces that surrounded her.

"*Aloha,*" the Queen said. Her deep, rich voice poured out like honey, like a sweet benediction on the Hawaiians. The sight of her was like an intimate blessing to thousand of eyes. Liliu's dulcet tones resonated in the night air like an embrace.

"*Aloha.*" The people replied to their Queen who was no longer supposed to be Queen, but who was still and would always be their Queen. "*Aloha.*" "*Aloha.*" "*Aloha.*"

A handful of American and English royalists attempted to start a cheer, but their brash shouts fell away almost at once, engulfed by the profound silence in which only the cries of "*Aloha*" continued to echo.

Kaiulani had come down from her carriage to stand at attention to greet her Aunt. She thought her heart would break at the sight of the slow-moving, infinitely proud woman who held tightly to Koa's arm, yet moved with such grace and deliberation. Liliuokalani nodded her head at the people as they wept and reached out to her, as if she was a fire that could warm them. When she arrived at the place where her niece stood waiting, the two women kissed each other and held on close for a moment. The perfumed scent of the flowers of her Aunt's *lei* clung to Kaiulani like a veil.

The Queen allowed Koa and Kaiulani to help her into the carriage. The only sounds after that were the steady rhythm of the horses' hooves and the sighs and sobs of the Hawaiians.

* * * * * * * * * * * * * * * * * * *

Liliu's Washington Place home was lit up like a palace, transformed by candles, *lehua* branches, flowers and wreaths. *Kukui* nut torches flamed in the hands of old native men who had waited hours for her arrival, wanting to be there to light every step of the Queen's way home.

Within a few minutes Liliu had changed from her dark traveling costume into a gown of royal yellow silk edged in black velvet. A diamond brooch sparkled on her bosom and an emerald and coral tiara rested like a delicate halo on top of her silver and black hair.

Liliuokalani sat on the front *lanai* of her home in a brocade chair of lavender silk. She stayed there in her doorway for hours, holding out her open arms to receive the people with a kind word and an *aloha* for all. They came by all night, one after another, and fell on their knees before her to kiss her age-spotted hands and to cry and commiserate with their Queen.

All night long the ancient chants and *meles* lingered in the air. Not until the sun came up did Liliuokalani retire into her house, and then only for a little while. Everyone who had been there remembered the sad magic of that night for the rest of their lives. Many who were not there, some not even born yet, continued for years to hear stories of the night the Queen returned home.

* * * * * * * * * * * * * * * * * * *

A few days later hateful invitations came to the royals. Kaiulani's letter "cordially" invited the Princess to be part of the Annexation Ceremonies, which would take place at half past eleven on Friday, August 12th at the Executive Building. The "final transfer of sovereignty," which included a flag changing ceremony, would be the conclusion of the event.

What kind of grim joke was this? Kaiulani felt her jaw getting tight. How dare they even dream of requesting the presence of the *ali'i* to dignify their travesty?

No. Kaiulani made her face become rigid, so she would not give in to the pain. They were lying again, the PGs, as they had so many times before. This "Executive Building" of theirs did not even exist. The evil transfer would take place at Iolani Palace, which had been built by her godfather, King David Kalakaua, for the *ali'i* and to honor the people of her land. From the bottom of her heart she hoped that all the goddesses and gods of Hawaii, and all of the ancestors, and all of the lost generations of Hawaiians would be there in spirit to watch it, every second, with the sharp, unforgiving, all-seeing eyes of royal hawks.

She remembered something Mama Nui used to say when she was sad, and whispered the words out loud. *"Ua ohi pakahi a aku nei e ka pu.* The night has taken them, one by one."

Kaiulani swore it to herself - the tragedy of the Hawaiians would not go unwitnessed. The injustice being done to them would not be forgotten. Not if she could help it.

Kaiulani could not bring herself to respond, so Papa declined the invitation for both of them. Everyone agreed that they would all gather at Liliu's Washington Place home on that wretched day.

For the next several days Kaiulani, Koa and Aunt Liliu stayed together at Washington Place to receive the Hawaiians and other well wishers. The handful of *haole* royalists who came to visit were so ashamed of what the PGs had finally done that they could barely meet the *ali'is'* eyes. But Liliuokalani was gracious and kind, and soon put them at their ease. Kaiulani was amazed, at first, by her Aunt's equanimity. But then she realized that it was the American government, after all, the politicians and the businessmen, who had done these things, and not the American people.

Koa and Kaiulani stood reserved, polite but mostly silent in the presence of the *haoles.* For the first time in her life, Kaiulani felt acutely conscious of being half-*haole* herself. She was embarrassed to realize she was grateful that Papa had decided to stay away from Washington Place at this time, preferring to wander about in town to "gather information" about the annexation plans.

The impoverished Hawaiians, many of them with nothing more than the sun and sky to sustain them, had managed somehow, nevertheless, to bring presents to honor the return of their Queen. Even the poorest *kanakas* came with fruit or *poi* wrapped in *ti* leaves, homely handmade carvings, simple woven baskets or crude *tapa* cloth designs to give to Liliuokalani.

The mood of those days before annexation reminded Kaiulani of Mama Nui's funeral and of the services for her mother. She stayed close by Koa's side. Although they rarely spoke to each another, the cousins talked with the Hawaiians at length, sharing memories, listening to them, or even just chatting about the weather. A few of the older people wept and at times the *ali'i* wept with them.

Koa and Kaiulani gave each other silent strength and support. They barely looked at each other or touched, but only stood beside one another, as they had so many other times before in their lives.

The heat was unusually intense at the beginning of August that year. Even so, Kaiulani was surprised by how much it affected her. At Washington Place, it was not quite so warm, but Ainahau was like a steam bath. The cool breezes seemed to have evaporated so that the place was like a sweatbox, sometimes even at night. She thought it strange that she had lived through terrible bouts of cold and snow in England, only to have the climate of her own country make her more exhausted than she ever dreamed she could be. At home she took to wearing *holokus* and sandals whenever she could, and almost never went anywhere without one of her large hats, although she still only dressed formally when she was receiving at Washington Place.

Papa continued to report the news. He had seen people downtown wearing large badges with an ugly political satire cartoon depicting the despicable "marriage" of Hawaii and America. The United States was a leering, old Uncle Sam who knelt at the altar with a dark skinned, scowling young woman. The woman appeared to be from Africa but pasted across her back was the name "Polly Nesia." The caption read, "This is Our Wedding Day."

Papa had also seen, several times, a carriage, which was decorated in red, white and blue streamers and American flags, which raced through the city streets blowing a very loud horn.

Kaiulani was indifferent to all of this. It had nothing at all, really, to do with her troubles. But she commiserated with Papa and shook her head over the vulgar and inappropriate activities going on in Honolulu's streets these days.

Toby, like the angel that he was, had kept up his letters to her even though her own correspondence had flagged. He had recently reminded her of his promise to come to Hawaii. She felt compelled to respond soon, to prevent him from beginning to make plans. Although she loved Toby dearly, she could not imagine seeing him in Hawaii, not at this time.

"Dearest Toby,

Thank you for all your wonderful letters, when I have been so terrible and lazy about keeping up with you! Everything is a mess just now. The plan for annexation is like that sword of Damocles; it hangs by a mere thread above our heads and threatens to drop on us at any second!

I would so love to see you, but it is not possible right now. I hope you will find it in your heart to forgive me, again, and will not take back my "rain check" for a visit from you sometime soon, in the very near future, but not just yet.

I must say I am rather crushed by what has happened. I struggle mightily every day not to take a gloomy outlook. *"Noblesse oblige,"* - Isn't that what they say?

I must have been born under an unlucky star. No matter what I try to do, I seem to have my life planned out for me in such a way that I cannot alter it.

My health is questionable again. Even here in Hawaii with no English snow or American cold weather to blame it on! Please do not give up on me, dear friend, and continue to send your cheerful letters. They do my heart more good than you can possibly imagine.

Papa sends his regards. I send you all my love, as always, My Dearest Toby.

> Yours Ever Sincerely,
> Kaiulani of Hawaii"

When she read over the letter she thought it strange that she had signed it so formally. After all, Toby knew, if anyone did, who she was and where, for heaven's sake! But the work of rewriting the entire page only to change her signature was too much of an effort, so she left it alone.

The days slipped by much too soon and it was August 9th already, and then the10th and 11th, and then the dreaded annexation was the next day.

Late at night on the 11th, out of nowhere, the skies darkened and it began to rain, a great, drenching, pouring rain, which was very unusual for that time of year, especially given the recent drought-like heat. For years after many of the Hawaiian people swore that a small, secret group of only the most powerful *kahunas* had chanted for several days and nights, praying for rain to ruin the ceremonies. A powerful eruption from Pele would have been even better but there were, unfortunately, no active, exploding volcanoes just then.

* * * * * * * * * * * * * * * * * * * *

By the morning of the 12th the torrents of rain had died down to a light drizzle. The skies were still gray, though, sullen and overcast, to match the Hawaiians' dark mood.

Another two thousand four hundred American soldiers, from the Marines Corps this time, had landed their warships in Honolulu Harbor and the blue of their uniforms flashed from every city street. A makeshift platform erected in front of Iolani Palace for the annexation looked like a gallows that had been patched together for a hasty execution.

Kaiulani woke early that morning from a fitful night. A throb in her right temple signaled the beginning of a crippling headache. The pressure made her feel like a giant was holding her face between his huge, vice-like hands as he tried to squeeze her eyes together. Even so, she was grateful to be awake and released from her foreboding dreams, until she remembered what day it was.

She dressed quickly in something somber and saw reflected back in the mirror a thin, ghostly-pale woman with shadows under her eyes so dark they looked like bruises. The hollowed-out space beneath her cheekbones made her appear haggard and old.

At the last minute she had decided that she would rather stay home, alone at Ainahau on this painful day. When she had gently suggested the possibility to Aunt Liliu the night before, to ask if she would mind, Liliu had immediately agreed. There was no reason, after all, to multiply their sorrows further by sharing them. Liliu would have more than enough company at Washington Place and, besides, she respected Kaiulani's desire to be alone.

Like all of the Hawaiians that day, Kaiulani would keep her house at Ainahau shuttered and dark, hoping more than anything for some privacy in her grief.

Papa decided he should go to the annexation, or at least be in the neighborhood to report back what went on. He was rather apologetic about his interest but insisted it was "proper" that someone be there "to represent our side of the matter." And, that way, he would be able to see with his own eyes what transpired.

Kaiulani kissed her father good-by that morning, secretly relieved to be left alone. They had clung to each other for a moment and Archibald Cleghorn's voice shook as he whispered in her ear, "I love you."

Kaiulani smiled sadly at her father. "I love you, too, Papa, of course."

Then he disappeared into the misty morning.

Kaiulani could not get comfortable that day, no matter what she tried to do. Unable to relax or distract herself from brooding, she remained miserable all day long. Everywhere she went - in her house or out on the grounds or in the gardens, she felt ill at ease and unhappy. She changed from her stiff dress into the loose comfort of a *holoku*, but still she was uncomfortable and wretchedly tired. She could not read or eat or even sleep.

At last she gave up trying to do anything and just sat outside under her banyan tree, wearing the biggest hat she could find to shield her from the muggy air and faltering bouts of pale sunlight interspersed with drizzling rain. Her peacocks wandered around aimlessly and were just as anxious and discontent.

By late morning she could stand it no longer. Never in her life before had she ever felt so lonely and alone. She called one of the house attendants to arrange for a carriage, changed back again into the dark, high-necked dress and left for Washington Place.

Liliu received her niece with wordless grief and a gentle embrace. For the rest of that long day Kaiulani stood beside Koa, subdued and full of misery. Even so, the warmth of her cousin's close body and the solace of his sandalwood smell reminded her that perhaps there was some wisdom in sharing sorrow, after all.

Many Hawaiians were miserable that day, and not only those who stayed inside their dark houses and tried to think of other things or nothing at all. Some wept, some prayed, while others cursed and raged, or tried to escape into busyness or drink or sleep or work. But everyone knew there was nothing they could do to change a single second.

While the Hawaiians, sheltered and shut away, mourned, those who were at the ceremonies saw and heard strange things. All

Honolulu businesses were closed that day, and many of the downtown houses were decorated with red, white and blue streamers and American flags of every size.

The annexation began on time at ten am. What was left of the Royal Hawaiian Band was there, reduced to about one third of its original number.

Captain Henri Berger stood in his usual place to conduct them, though he himself was in a barely contained state of rage. The veins on his forehead were swollen and his normally ruddy skin had an alarming purple tinge. He unconsciously clenched his teeth and looked so formidable that no one dared to come near. None of the band members wanted to be there, nor did Captain Berger. But, like all the Hawaiians, they had fallen on hard times, and that day they were being paid, for a change, a small amount to perform. Berger had made a short, clipped speech to remind them to "keep up a stiff upper lip." He advised sternly that they must remember that there was honor, too, in "the crew going down with the ship."

* * * * * * * * * * * * * * * * * * *

Minister Harold Sewall began with a dry and rather antiseptic speech that announced the details of the United States' official resolution and the government's decision to annex Hawaii. Sewall droned on and on about procedures and protocols, and what it meant to transfer sovereignty from Hawaii to America, which he called its "great protector." His reedy voice echoed hollowly throughout the half-empty pavilion for a long time. Then President Dole rose and made a few terse remarks about the honor and glory of the momentous occasion while Thurston, at his side, smirked. Then the United States Commissioner, a dour-faced man with frown lines permanently etched into his forehead and mouth, formally accepted the transfer of the islands on behalf of a grateful President McKinley.

At a sharp signal from Captain Berger, the Royal Hawaiian Band began to play *"Hawaii Ponoi,"* King Kalakaua's song, for the last time as the anthem of an independent nation. The band sounded mournful and struggled to keep the beat. When a few feeble rays of sunshine broke through the clouds and briefly lit up the platform on which they stood, the shabby condition of their frayed, threadbare uniforms was more obvious than ever. Their wretched appearance matched the defeated expressions in their eyes.

Captain Berger pumped his conductor's baton furiously and his arms flailed about in the air as he tried to get them to attack the song with more concentration and focus. But even Captain Berger's competent hands shook and his lips, which had been pursed tightly together, began to tremble. In vain he tried to lift up the pace and spirit of the piece. Then he, too, seemed suddenly to give up, as if all his energy and vitality had been drained away by the effort.

Halfway through the song, a few of the musicians in the winds section lost their breath entirely from an excess of emotion. Unable to go on, they fled from the bandstand clutching their instruments. The remaining players began to falter and stumble on the notes they had played so many times before and knew so well. After a few more bars, most of the other band members choked up, too, leaving only a few stray musicians to pathetically finish up the tune.

By the time the last, plaintive note was sounded, another gloomy, unstable bank of clouds had drifted over to blot out the dull sun, leaving the bandstand and what was left of the band and the other participants in hazy shadows.

Just before the Hawaiian flag was brought down from the central flagpole high at the top of Iolani Palace, in the final act of transfer, a great barrage of shots rang out. The American field soldiers of the National Guard were paying tribute, volleying with a near-deafening, twenty-one gun salute as the last honor paid to the independent nation of Hawaii. When the echoes of the gunshots had died out, a lone soldier moved into position at the flagpole and grabbed the cords to pull down forever the flag of Hawaii.

Although the plan was to bring it down swiftly, the flag descended at an erratic, uneven pace. It hesitated and fluttered as it was buffeted about by fresh, gusting winds. The old flag lifted and then fell time and again on its agonizing way down and looked like a fatally wounded bird making an uneven trajectory as it struggled to cling to life. When it had finally descended all the way to the bottom, a soldier dumped it into a small wooden crate where it crumpled into a heap.

The gun volleys of the marines and the horns of the American military ships docked nearby blared out a jarring salute, as the ships' band of the *U.S.S. Philadelphia* stomped into view. Even in the dim light, which fitfully came and went, the band was dazzling in their bright, new uniforms of crisp white and blue. They struck up a rousing version of "The Star Spangled Banner," pounding out the rhythms with their feet as they marched. In the uneven sunlight that flickered in and out of the scene, the shiny brass buttons of their uniforms winked like little blind eyes.

At the stroke of noon precisely a thirty-six foot American flag, especially designed for the occasion, was hoisted up onto Iolani Palace's main flagpole. It whipped around in a sudden, strong wind like a mad, whirling dervish. Just as the flag reached the top of the pole the sun faded out again, this time for good.

Before the band had finished, while the gun volleys and ships' horns still crackled in the air, a thin, sharp rain began to fall and the spectators rushed off to their carriages and waiting horses.

Some of the Americans and even a few of the PG officials were seen furtively dabbing at their eyes. The lifeless flag of Hawaii was already gone, presumably snatched up for souvenirs by some enterprising capitalist; and the huge, new American flag was starting to hang heavy and limp in the ever-increasing rain.

Later that night, in the Throne Room where Liliuokalani had been tried and convicted of treason, the new government held their first reception and ball. Later still, there were fireworks.

No Hawaiians came that night. Even the pro-PG handful, who had attended the annexation ceremonies, stayed away. And all present, even the ones who had pushed and lobbied for years, hardest of all, for annexation, felt the pallor that lay heavy over everything and everyone that day and far into the dark night.

Chapter Thirty

Not long after annexation Aunt Liliu decided to return to Washington. There was nothing she could do there anymore, she told Kaiulani; she knew that. But perhaps her presence might be helpful in some way, or at least contribute toward keeping the hope of restoration alive. Now it was Kaiulani's turn to understand her Aunt's restlessness, and be sympathetic to the Queen's reluctance to remain in their former homeland, now occupied by soldiers and mined by foreign interests, where every new day brought them despair.

Kaiulani wanted to believe that Aunt Liliu might somehow do some good for them all back in America. But in her heart she knew there wasn't anything more to be done. What was that ugly and painfully accurate phrase she had heard in New York and again in Boston? It would be like "kicking a dead horse." Theirs was a lost cause, she was afraid. Even so, Liliu's decision to leave made Kaiulani feel abandoned. She could not shake off the feeling that she was being deserted. Left alone, essentially, to hold down the fort, or what was left of it, anyway.

Perhaps she too should leave Hawaii? In England or America, she might be able to break free of the pervasive sense of uselessness and immobility that grew more oppressive every day. But her heart was not in it. She had no desire to leave again, none. She had just gotten back, after all those years away. For better or for worse, she was home to stay.

The day that Liliu left, Kaiulani broke down and bitterly wept. She refused to leave her Aunt's side even for a minute, although the ship's departure was delayed for hours. During that time the two women spoke together softly, far into the long hours, of Likelike, Mama Nui, Papa Moi and Queen Kapiolani. They talked passionately about their country's powerful traditions and its rich culture, which they both must struggle to keep alive, now more than ever. Even with all that had happened to change their lives and their ways, even though they themselves, along with their people, had been displaced within their own world.

And then it was finally time for Liliu's ship to go. Kaiulani watched through tears as the S.S. *Coptic* sailed away from Honolulu Harbor. She waved and waved until her arm and shoulder ached and her hand began to go numb, but still she could not give up waving good-by to her Aunt, not even when the ship had disappeared out to sea and was engulfed in the moonless night.

A prickly sense of *deja vu* made Kaiulani shiver as she remembered her own departure so many years ago. For an instant, she imagined that it was she herself, the child Kaiulani, who was sailing away again. As if she could stand there and watch herself, a much younger Kaiulani, vulnerable and only partly formed, leave her sorrows - most of them, anyway, - behind her, and say good-by to sadness and despair as she set out on a momentous adventure.

* * * * * * * * * * * * * * * * * * *

After Aunt Liliu left, Kaiulani became lethargic and bored. She rarely ventured from the grounds and house at Ainahau. Most of the time she wore *holokus* and wide brimmed hats, protected and shaded like a delicate, old lady. On her better days she would wear a *lei* or two around her neck, enjoying the heady scents of the "*pikakae*," her jasmine flowers, and the soft perfume of ginger flowers and carnations.

One afternoon on the *lanai* she had seen Koa and Eva whisper together when they thought she was upstairs taking a nap. She heard her own name several times, and realized they were worried about her from the way they kept their voices low and frequently shook their heads. She longed to reassure them that there was no need to worry; that she only needed some time to rest and figure out what to do next, now that everything had changed so. But she had eavesdropped on their conversation secretly and so could not say anything without letting them know that she had listened when they did not know she was there.

There were few visitors at Ainahau those days following the annexation. Feeling very tender themselves, the Hawaiians had no desire to intrude upon or in any way add their own grief to further burden their Princess. And most of the *haoles* and soldiers had quickly lost interest in the former royals of the former nation of Hawaii.

But one day several American soldiers came onto Kaiulani's estate. They had barged in, she supposed, through the front gates, which were now often left carelessly unlocked. The soldiers pounded rather violently on the front door of the main house, making a terrible racket. Although it was only mid-afternoon, some of the young men smelled like whiskey or beer. Only a few of the dozen or so were in uniform, and it took a couple of minutes for them to calm down enough to state the purpose of their visit. They had hoped, they explained to a tight-lipped Cleghorn, that the Ex-Princess would consent to have her picture taken with them. They wanted their pictures taken, they told him, "with a real Princess." Papa looked very dubious, but finally agreed to go inside and ask her.

When Kaiulani herself came out to see them the soldiers were startled by her fragile, gaunt appearance and the wounded expression on her face made them quiet down at once. Two of the youngest, who had been joking and rough housing together, hung their heads at the sight of her and looked ashamed.

"Please," Kaiulani said to them in a firm but gentle tone, "This really is not the time or place. Please," she repeated, her voice very low, "Go home."

No longer playful or boisterous at all, the Americans cast down their eyes and left quietly without another word.

Papa saw how much the soldiers' visit had distressed her, and tried to cheer her up by reminding her that the American government respected her position.

"Officially, at any rate," he added, unnerved by the woeful look she gave him.

"And there is no question that they will provide an income for you and your Aunt. And the people - your people, here - will continue to look to you as ... a leader...," he trailed off rather lamely.

"Yes," Kaiulani's voice was very soft, "but I won't be much of a real Princess anymore, will I?" When she raised her eyes again, she saw that Papa looked so hurt that she rushed over to hold his hand.

"Oh, now, Papa, I'm sorry. It's all right; don't worry so; it will all be all right. We can make it all right, somehow."

Papa looked like he desperately wanted to believe her but remained uncertain and concerned.

Kaiulani smiled at him wanly. Still, she could not overcome her dark sorrow and murmured, almost in a whisper. "Sometimes, though, I think my heart is broken."

Later that week Kaiulani wrote to Liliu in Washington and told her about the soldiers' visit.

"Will they never leave us alone? They have taken everything from us and the little that is left is our very life itself. We live now in such a semi-retired way that people wonder if we even exist anymore. I, too, wonder, dear Aunt, and cannot help but ask myself to what purpose?"

* * * * * * * * * * * * * * * * * * *

Eva Parker was getting married at last, to Frank Woods, a cousin she had known since childhood. The wedding would be held at Parker Ranch on the Big Island, and was the first real social event for the Hawaiians in quite a while. Kaiulani delighted in the idea of getting away from Honolulu.

On December 7, 1898, with a small group of friends, Kaiulani left on the steamer boat *Kinau* headed for the Big Island to go to Parker Ranch and Eva Parker's wedding.

The lush, gorgeous expanse of the Parkers' Mana Ranch was somehow, impossibly, even more breathtaking than she remembered. Her spirits soared at the sight of it, and throughout the rest of her time there it was as if a small, delicate bird fluttered its wings inside her chest. She had forgotten how achingly, incredibly, amazingly beautiful Hawaii could be. A sigh welled up from deep inside her as she realized the truth. She loved Hawaii so much that she would rather die here than live a half-life anywhere else.

For seventy-five years Parker Ranch had thrived. The original house, built of local *koa* wood, right down to the wooden nails that held it together, still stood from the first days that John Palmer Parker and Kipikane, his Hawaiian bride, had settled there. They had made their fortune in the cattle business, and the dairy barns, sheds and pastures provided a lively background of sounds, smells and constant activity at Mana Ranch. The gardens were wonderfully kept, and admired by all who had ever seen them, even Papa Cleghorn, who was inclined to be critical because of his own background and expertise.

But it was the wild areas of the estate that captivated Kaiulani's soul. There were vast, majestic arbors of towering, statuesque trees that had grown up over generations; and groves of deep, mysterious woods alternating with great, open tracts of land. There were wide, expansive plains to ride on and explore and get lost in. There were steep, mountainous paths and ridges that twisted sharply in and out of sunlight amid shadows and streams.

And the horses - the fresh, spirited, healthy horses, eager and excited to gallop over the lush, varied terrain of rolling green hills and misty valleys. There was Waipio Valley and beautiful Waimea Canyon, with their waterfalls, fern grottoes and cliffs that appeared out of nowhere; and their dark, rich, fragrant, beautiful glades that were like sanctuaries and tombs all at once. The greens and blues of the landscape stood out like electric shocks against the dusty reds and browns of exposed volcanic rock.

When Kaiulani walked or rode her horse past the arching cliffs that abruptly sheered off into dense, wooded acres, there were times she had the breathless feeling that she was moving through acres of wet, crushed velvet while being held and protected by huge, sheltering hands. In those moments she felt like a tiny, temporary creature suspended and hanging for just a moment in a vast, never-ending universe.

Eva and Helen Parker were very glad to see her again, and Koa was there, too, of course, and she made many new friends. The wedding was extravagant and enormous and Kaiulani enjoyed herself more than she had in a very long time, even flirting a little again for the first time since she had come home.

The events and festivities that surrounded the wedding went on for weeks. Then it was time for Christmas celebrations that flowed swiftly into New Year's and her life, for those few, brief weeks, was filled with dancing and champagne and wild, reckless rides on the horses.

Several cousins of the Parkers were more than happy to escort the Princess day and night, squiring her about to all the picnics and late night swimming parties and *luaus* and banquets and dances. There was also canoeing and fishing and hunting and hiking for those who were so inclined. For the first time in a long while Kaiulani felt quick stirrings and flashes of happiness.

There was even the hint of a possible romance with one of the Parkers' handsome cousins, Sam Woods. An adoring companion, Sam was a successful bank manager who was a few years younger than Kaiulani. He spoke little but had a rare, sweet smile and seemed determined to set her on fire with his intense, soulful glances. When he left shortly after Christmas, he solemnly promised to write to her and she acquiesced, though privately she wondered what correspondence could possibly survive with a man of so few words.

When Kaiulani could not sleep she went out in the middle of the night, in secret, to ride her favorite horse, a half-wild stallion called Sunset. He had a shock of fiery red-gold hair that always seemed to be falling in his eyes and flashing out around his face when he shook his full mane; and a brilliant, high-gloss sheen to his gold and rust colored coat. She knew there was some danger, riding alone like that in the dark, but that was undeniably part of the thrill. There was an intoxicating freedom about those night rides that soothed her spirit and stirred her soul. Oh, she knew that Papa, for one, would worry dreadfully if he knew what she was doing, and certainly she did not mean to hurt or upset anyone. But she felt compelled to ride! So many things raced through her mind on those late night adventures. What if something should happen to her, then? What if Sunset, who galloped with such careless abandon, tripped somewhere, or fell? Who would find them; or would they ever find them, if they were to fall down one of those steep cliffs or into the dense, thick forests?

She found herself wondering if she had done a good job for her people, hoping that she had been strong for them as their last Princess. She had, for the most part, tried her best. She knew they had counted on and depended on her, to an extent, and she wanted to do right by them. Mama would understand, she thought, why this was so important to her. And Koa, too, she imagined. She hoped no one would misunderstand her intentions.

By January 8th the majority of the guests had left the ranch to journey back to their home islands. The Parkers were still there, of course, and a small group of stragglers who were loathe to leave remained behind, including Kaiulani, hanging on to the good times they had enjoyed there, although even Eva and her new husband had left for their honeymoon trip by then.

The weather began to change for the worse with a slow, steady increase of overcast, often glowering skies and the constant threat of rain. A cold, bitter wind began to snake through the mountains and valleys, biting with the razor sharpness of sharks' teeth.

Koa politely offered himself as an escort for perhaps the third or fourth time, saying that he would be happy to take her home. But Kaiulani just smiled at him and he immediately returned the smile. It had become a game between them, his coaxing. For they both knew, now that they were back in Hawaii, she would do exactly what she wanted to do, in her own time and when she was ready. There had always been an understanding between them.

Kaiulani wrote to Papa and asked him please to send her some warmer clothes and more *holokus*, as well as some headache powders, which she had almost run out of, and more money and a few Quinine pills.

One morning during the second week of January the sun suddenly broke out full and radiant again, beaming down like an old friend. The wind had shifted and the air was light and balmy as late spring. A small group of the stragglers were inspired to take advantage of the fine weather and made up a spur-of-the-moment picnic. They decided to ride from the ranch to a lovely wooded area close by, which could be reached by traveling across a short but narrow mountain path. The sun shined down on them like a blessing and their spirits were high as they rode.

But about halfway up the trail a few clouds started to gather and then slowly clustered up, beginning to blot out the sun. The raincoats which, at this time of year, were always kept rolled up in each saddle, were brought out by most of the riders. But Kaiulani, feeling daring and free, only laughed when her friends urged her to put hers on. Suddenly, it turned almost as dark as night and then a light rain began to fall, just a fine drizzle at first.

That morning Kaiulani had put on the Pele's Tears earrings that Mama had given her so long ago. But they soon felt rather heavy - she had not worn them in quite a while - and began to hurt her every time she moved or turned her head. She decided to take them off, and motioned for the others to go ahead as she stopped her horse by the side of the road to undo them.

And then the rain came - that harsh, horizontal, unrelenting Waimea rain. There was a very old song, a chant, really, about the Waimea rain that came back to her in that moment. Something about how the wind was like a spear that would pierce you, and how the bitter cold would blight the trees.

Mama Nui had told her that there were rainbows all over Hawaii on the day she was born. Well, there were no rainbows now. But never mind, she would ride in the rain, and imagine those rainbows all around her. Perhaps there would be rainbows when the rain cleared, after the rain.

She was so tired, she realized, even as she pushed herself to spur on Sunset. She had never been this tired before in her entire life. The crisp, sharp wind felt good on her face and cheeks, waking her up, replenishing her energy. Perhaps if she rode in the wind and rain for a little while it would change things. Revitalize her blood.

She was surprised to feel that the rain really was like a spear, this slanting, slashing rain that cut through her like a knife. She was so startled by the ferocity of it that she accidentally dropped the earrings she had been holding in her hand. Pulling up her horse abruptly, she hesitated in the road, getting drenched and soaked as she wondered whether it was worth it to try and find them. Just as she decided against it, a gale of icy wind blew up, chilling her to the bone.

But still she would ride, as if in defiance of all the laws of nature that warned her against it. She pushed herself ahead of her small group and then beyond, deaf to the faint cries and warnings of her friends, who she saw only dimly through the cascading torrents of rain.

Then she thought she saw something flash out at her in the road just ahead. Was it a tree, bending in the strong wind? Or a figure, some hapless soul caught out here on foot? She remembered a tale of *kahunas* who would show up and then disappear in the Waimea rain, and wondered if it was some kind of message. But almost at once she decided she did not care. She threw off her light shawl, which was now soaking wet, and reached up to undo her hair clasp, releasing her long, wild mane as she rode on and on and on until the ending of the trail forced her to stop.

When her friends caught up with Kaiulani they admonished her strongly, urging her to stop and change, or at least dry out her clothes and saddle blanket a bit. But she laughed at them, feeling exhilarated and renewed by her wild adventure, and paid no attention to being soaked until they had gotten all the way back to Mana. And even then, she still laughed, protesting that she was actually quite hot the whole time as she was scolded and bathed and finally put to bed.

By the next morning she was very sick. Papa was contacted at once and came up as quickly as he could, bringing with him Dr. Walters, the old family physician. With great patience and care, they nursed her back enough to at last set out on the journey to the steamer dock to get back home.

* * * * * * * * * * * * * * * * * * *

Kaiulani was quite subdued and contrite for all the trouble she had caused and begged Papa, when she had enough strength to talk, to accept her apology. They carried her down on a litter from Mana Ranch to the steamer, which waited for her at Kawaihae. The doctor treated her for rheumatism, then exophthalmic goiter. By the time they arrived at Ainahau, she seemed to be well on the mend, with only mild symptoms remaining, and a cold.

Papa read to her from the paper about a petition in process in Washington, which was being drawn up to commend her efforts and the dignified way she had accepted the inevitable overthrow. She smiled for him and he held her hand, but still her symptoms would not subside and she lay immobilized in her bed. Doctor Walters called in another physician. Elizabeth and Kuhio came to visit several times, but Kaiulani always insisted that they leave baby Lili at home, terrified by the remote chance that she might have something the child could catch. The month of February somehow passed, and still the Princess was not well, nor could she leave her darkened room or even her bed.

At the start of March she seemed to weaken, and the doctors became concerned that the rheumatism might have damaged her lungs or heart. Then she rallied a little and seemed to improve, even making a weak joke with Koa about being sure she would be all right if only she could make it through the dreaded ides of March.

For a few days she drifted in and out of consciousness and a deep, dreamless sleep. It was just a few minutes after midnight on March 6th when Kaiulani's breathing started to become ragged and labored. Koa and Papa and the rest of the family were called in and she sensed rather than felt the circle of love that surrounded her.

At exactly two o'clock Kaiulani shifted slightly and then cried out a single word. Some believed she had said her cousin Koa's name. Others thought they heard her say "Mama!" or "Papa!" There were those who said it was not a word at all, but only a cried out sound.

The newspapers carried the terrible news that morning. But all those within a five-mile radius of Ainahau already knew. They had been awakened just after two by the shrill, chilling screams of Princess Kaiulani's peacocks. It was as if her *pikakaes* knew they had lost their Princess and wanted the rest of the world to know and mourn her, too.

Chapter Thirty-One

No one could believe she was really gone. She had been back among them, their Princess, living as one of them, with them for such a short time. Before, she had lived in their hearts and thoughts and prayers, when she was so far away from them, in exile. And now she would have to live again only in their memories, but this time forever, their kind, lovely young Princess, their sweet Kaiulani.

Even those closest to her could hardly believe they would never see her gentle face again. Even those who had been there with her at the end - Papa and Koa, Princess Elizabeth and Kuhio, - struggled to come to terms with the reality that, this time, she would never return to them. It was so sad. It was almost unbearable. And yet it was true, and it must be borne and suffered.

The light that had been the life of Princess Victoria Lunalilo Kaiulani had flickered and faltered like the flame of a dying candle, and then had gone out. Extinguished, that light would never shine again. Hawaii's Hope - "The Royal Sacred One" - was no more.

The first to arrive to pay their respects were a hundred or so Hawaiians who had set out on foot in the early morning hours as soon as they heard the terrible news.

The second wave of mourners included hundreds more, people of every age, class and background - *kanakas, haoles*, solid citizens and politicians. Even before dawn carriages began to arrive at Ainahau; all day long people kept coming and going.

So many flowers were left at the front gates that, long before noon, the *leis*, bouquets and single flowers had piled up on top of each other. The first crowds milled aimlessly around outside the gates and grounds of Ainahau. Some wept or bowed their heads, others fell to the ground and rocked and moaned, as stricken as if they had lost a member of their own family.

When Archibald Cleghorn saw what was happening, he directed that the gates of Ainahau be opened to the grieving people. Even in his own distraction and sorrow, he recognized that all the others who had loved her, too, had their rights to mourn her and say farewell. No one was turned away. Within a little while the number of mourners had multiplied, then multiplied again. People spilled out into the gardens and the surrounding land. Many of them seemed to be looking for something, almost as if in hopes that, by some miracle or magic, if they watched very carefully, they might be able to catch one last glimpse of her. Or breathe in the lingering scent of her perfume, or see something she once had touched.

President Dole had called an early morning meeting of his Cabinet. A substantial sum was agreed upon, along with the offer of numerous government resources to be put at the disposal of Archibald Cleghorn to provide for an appropriate state funeral. Mr. Dole also suggested that the Throne Room of Iolani Palace could be made available for the Princess' lying-in-state. Papa declined immediately when he heard, sending Koa and Kuhio to tell them no.

Cleghorn insisted that Kaiulani should lie in state at her own home first, in the house he had built for her to live in, until she was carried to Kawaiahao Church for a service that would include all who wished to come. Or perhaps Old St. Andrews, the church where she had been christened as an infant, would be the place where her life and death would be honored and grieved for the last time. The government could provide as it wanted for the rest of her services and the procession, but he would have this time first, these few days, to say good-by to his daughter and to allow her people to bid farewell to their Princess.

By Wednesday morning she had been laid out in a white robe in a white casket, her beautiful face silent and still. Kaiulani looked peaceful, the tiny lines of worry between her brows now smoothed away for all time. She seemed serene and almost happy, as if at any moment she might open her eyes and smile again, or sit up and look around, amused, searching for the source of all the strange commotion.

The bier she lay upon was on the back veranda facing out to the sea. Raised about three feet above the shining wood floor, it was draped with a velvet pall of deep purple embroidered all over in gleaming gold and yellow silk strands with Kaiulani's own coat of arms.

Four retainers stood at attention on each side of the casket at all times throughout, trading off in four hour shifts, to wave the tall, royal *kahilis* over the still Princess. Another twelve *kahilis* surrounded the bier. The only flowers in the room where she lay were delicate orchids and white orange blossoms tinged with pale shades of yellow and gold.

The darkened rooms of the rest of the house were filled with the potent, almost overwhelmingly sweet scent of every kind of flower and the smoke of many candles.

Representatives came from the churches and hospitals, the Hawaiian League and the military. Government people paid their respects: President and Mrs. Dole came around midday, while Thurston and several other cabinet members arrived a little later. Delegations were sent from the Red Cross and the Maternity Home, where Kaiulani had often visited and shared her time. There were hundreds of her friends and admirers, including many who had never met her personally but cared about her or even loved her, just the same. They filed in and out of Ainahau for days.

Ushers escorted small groups into the room where her bier lay and later guided them out. The flowers, cards, poems and letters grew, spilled over in great heaps everywhere, some mounds reaching as high as the tall front gates on which Kaiulani's name had been so carefully carved when she was first officially presented to the world.

The papers were full of the news though there was little, really, to say, except that she was gone. Some reporters wrote about her all too brief life, or told the story of her ill-fated journey to Parker's Ranch and the reckless Waimea ride. Other wrote of how gracious the sweet Princess had always been, to everyone, even in the face of great adversity. All agreed that she had been universally loved by her people, and even respected and honored by those who must be called her foes, who had stood against the monarchy and everything that had meant to Hawaii. And to the gentle Princess, who was no more.

A strange spell hung over Honolulu. Most businesses were closed; many voices were hushed. Few cried out loud, although tears flowed freely everywhere, especially among the natives. An unspoken vow of near silence held the Hawaiians in its grip. Flags flew at half-mast at Iolani and the Opera House, in public gardens and parks and the hospitals, as well as on all the government buildings, military barracks and foreign consulates.

The Princess' peacocks remained edgy and sullen, very annoyed by the ceaseless activity. The usually mild-tempered birds were irritable and the most aggressive of them picked fights over nothing. Fairy lay low in her stable, sulking and mournful, and refused to come out from the dark corners of her stall.

Under Kaiulani's own towering banyan tree at the front of the house the Government Band played dirges all day. Koa, Kuhio and Elizabeth received condolences in the front parlor. Archibald Cleghorn stayed shut away alone in his upstairs room.

On the last day the doors were finally closed at six pm, and then the servants from the house were taken in to say good-by. Some of the older ones had held Kaiulani in their arms when she was a baby, and then watched her grow into a lively girl, and later had welcomed her back, a thoughtful and dignified young woman. With some privacy, now, in their grief, they at last allowed themselves to keen and sob and cry out loud.

A half hour before midnight on Friday, which was the time when the pallbearers—Koa, Kuhio and several of the Parker cousins - would quietly lift up the body of their Princess and carry her from Ainahau into the city, Papa Cleghorn finally came down.

Even the attendants with the *kahilis* left the room so the father could be alone with his child. Shaking with grief, Archibald Cleghorn moved like a very old man. He leaned in to the casket to touch his daughter's cold hand and hold it once again in his own. Then he bowed his head and knelt beside her for the last time.

* * * * * * * * * * * * * * * * * * * *

Thousands of Hawaiians followed Kaiulani's bier and its bearers on the long walk to Kawaiahao Church. Torches lit the way and an honor guard rode their horses in a wide circle surrounding her. All the dogs and chickens had been shut away indoors to keep the deep silence; even the horses' hooves had been tied up in soft cloths or blankets to muffle all sound.

It was almost two hours later when the funeral procession reached the church where the Bishop of Honolulu and the clergy waited with hundreds more mourners to greet the honor guard and the pallbearers as they laid their burden down.

Then Koa and Kuhio and the other pallbearers slowly lifted the slim white coffin and carried it up the stairs into the church.

The interior was draped with cloths of pure white and golden-yellow. The altar bore the royal standards of both Princess Likelike and Princess Kaiulani. Jasmine, white orchids and yellow-gold flowers were everywhere. Those fortunate enough to be in the front of the procession quietly filed into the church. Hundreds more stood or knelt outside. When everyone had settled in and the silence fell again, the Bishop read a short prayer and a blessing. Then he read a part of the 39th Psalm in a low, constricted voice.

"Lord, make me to know my end, and what is the measure of my days, that I may know how frail I am.

Indeed, You have made my days as handbreadths, and my age is as nothing before You; certainly every man at his best state is as vapor.

Surely every man walks about like a shadow; surely they busy themselves in vain; he heaps up riches, and does not know who will gather them.

And now, my Lord, what do I wait for? My hope is in You.

Hear my prayer, O Lord, and give ear to my cry; do not be silent at my tears; for I am a stranger with You, a sojourner, as all my fathers were."

Then the Bishop knelt down and was quiet, too. Minutes passed, full of the deep, dark silence.

* * * * * * * * * * * * * * * * * * *

Like the cry of a wounded bird, the tremulous voice of an old woman tore at the air as she began to chant the plaintive notes of the ancient death wail for the *ali'i*. Her voice echoed and shivered, crying out Princess Kaiulani's name again and again, tearing at the air like a knife piercing and ripping through the veil of silence. When her anguished voice began to falter and fade, another old woman took up the death chant. When her voice gave out, another followed her, and then another.

The second day of Kaiulani's lying-in-state, a Saturday, it rained all day. But the crowds, now in the thousands, remained steady and strong. The wailing women's' voices paused for brief intervals only, weaving a dark tapestry of mournful sound around the sad event. Many of the Hawaiians had stayed all night, catching a few minutes of sleep on the floors or in the pews or just outside the church.

On Sunday the sun came out again. The official service was an afternoon funeral at Kawaiahao. Crowds were packed in and around the church and lined the streets where the procession would be. Thousands more kept coming, on foot or in carriages and cabs, choking the entire area with mostly unmoving masses of traffic. The nearby Opera House was so jammed that the police had to order the crowds to come down from the roof, which had begun to creak ominously under their weight.

Inside Kawaiahao the pews were packed with judges and public officers and soldiers and Dole and his cabinet and even with all manner of Hawaiians as well. Cleghorn was brought in during the organ prelude and seated at the front of the main aisle with Koa, Kuhio and Elizabeth. The prelude was the "In Memoriam" that had been written for Princess Likelike and played only once before at her funeral.

The choirs sang and the Bishop and the church's pastor spoke. When the last hymn was over Kaiulani's white coffin was carried out to the hearse. Bugles were sounded and church bells tolled just as they had twenty-three years ago to announce the Princess' birth.

For two days her casket remained at Kawaiahao Church. On the last day another honor guard, this time with everyone on foot, rolled her caisson, which had been so generously provided by the Provisional Government, along King Street and up Nuuanu Avenue to the Royal Mausoleum.

In the days that Kaiulani lay in state, the flowers and tokens had continued to grow like mushrooms in rain. Great mounds of them had been heaped up, along with letters, poetry and other tributes. They were not only all over and around Ainahau and the church, but also at the Iolani Palace grounds, and Liliu's home in Washington Place, at Parker Ranch, and even at the beginning and end of the Waimea Trail where she had ridden in the relentless rain. Where her horse had carried her into the beginning of slow oblivion, into those shadows from which no one returns.

Two hundred and thirty native men carried the hearse and pulled the cart with long, black and white ropes. Two hundred and thirty cords had been tied to the Princess' casket, tugging her out of the world into which she had come attached by only one. More than twenty thousand people lined the streets to say farewell and see her go.

Archibald Cleghorn was in the first of the mourners' carriages. The second, an empty coach, represented the absent, former Queen. The third carried Koa, Kuhio, Elizabeth and baby Lili. In the fourth rode President and Mrs. Dole.

The caisson rolled along King Street, then up Nuuanu Valley to the Royal Mausoleum. By the time the entourage arrived outside the flower-strewn gates of the Mausoleum, all but a few had fallen behind. Massive blankets and hedges of flowers sheltered the royal crypts from view. The men who had been pulling the caisson stepped aside to stand behind the hearse.

The old caretaker unlocked the creaking metal doors of the tomb and the pallbearers carried Kaiulani's coffin inside. Koa's face crumpled when he lay the casket down but, with tremendous determination, he stopped himself from sobbing. Cleghorn stood trembling by his daughter's side, but only for a moment and then he, too, left her, along with the others, in her final place of rest. Kaiulani was laid beside her mother in the Royal Mausoleum.

The guns shouted out one last time to tell the world that Princess Kaiulani was gone forever. As the old caretaker locked the gates a light wind blew up and lifted a few flowers from a bouquet and then dropped them down by the heavy doors of the tomb.

* * * * * * * * * * * * * * * * * * * *

For a long time after his daughter's death Archibald Cleghorn received letters from all over the world.

At first, there were even a few letters addressed to Kaiulani herself, several from a Count de Courcy in England; but then they abruptly stopped. Archibald Cleghorn sent them back. He hoped it was not cruel but he did not know what else to do. He did not wish to read them. He did not even want to read the letters that had been sent to him, not for a while. He was afraid that these messages, whether from strangers or friends, would only increase his sorrow.

But late one night he decided to risk it. His Scottish conscience tweaked him. He knew he should acknowledge or, at the very least, receive these communications. He knew it was his duty to respond.

The first was a short, concise note written in an educated, careful hand by a Mrs. Sharp. She had been Kaiulani's headmistress, teacher and friend at Great Harrowden Hall School in England. She was extremely sorry to hear of Kaiulani's demise. His daughter had been an excellent student, as well as a wonderful and dear friend of hers. She would never forget their time together, and felt the deepest sympathy for Mr. Cleghorn's terrible loss. Such a fine young woman had surely deserved better from her all too short, sweet life.

The letter made Cleghorn cry. He sobbed like a child with a great outpouring of grief. Not long after he realized that he felt, for the first time since her death, a sense of comfort and relief.

Many wrote to him to bear witness to her life with remembrances of her kindness or humor or wit. Many regretted her untimely death and invoked God or Heaven for a better reward.

The letters came from California and London, Boston and Chicago and New York and Washington, D.C. There were postmarks from the Cap d'Antibe in the Riviera and from Paris and from sleepy villages in the English countryside. People wrote to him from the barely settled American territories and from the most elegant addresses in the world.

An elder from a tribe in South Dakota told him how closely he and his people had followed the course of events in the lives of Princess Kaiulani and the former Queen, Liliuokalani, and what a great inspiration they had been to them all.

Cherished memories of her generosity and charm and hospitality were spoken of again and again. Her spirit and passion had inspired countless numbers of people who sent their prayers and best wishes in hopes that these might bring him solace in his grief.

Some decried the cowardly acts and wicked crimes which had been perpetrated upon Hawaii. One woman wrote to tell him that her son had danced with Kaiulani once at a party for the mayor of Boston, and how he had remembered ever after "the way she lit up the entire room." Her son had been killed at the brave siege on San Juan Hill, but even in his last letter home he mentioned how often he dreamed of Princess Kaiulani and how he was always comforted by the kindness of her nature.

Some had heard her when she was a shy teenager, giving her heartfelt speeches about Hawaii's plight, and they would never forget that brave young girl.

Most of the letters were from people he had never met, who had nevertheless made some psychic or spiritual or emotional connection with Kaiulani, at home or in her travels around Europe and America. Their daughters had gone to school with her, or they had ridden horses together once, or their sons had played with her when they were babies. Some had only seen her picture in the papers, or read in the news about the troubled monarchy, or the tragedy of the Princess who lost her chance to be Queen.

The people who wrote these letters hoped he would never forget the joy and delight his daughter had brought into the world. He should take great pride, they told him, in her many accomplishments. They were faithfully and sincerely and truly his, and they joined him in his heartache and in his deep, deep sorrow. Many asked for pictures of the Princess, which Cleghorn had made up and sent out himself over a long, long while.

And then it was all over.

But nothing is ever really over or done, forever.

There are still rainbows and sudden, terrible rainstorms in Hawaii. And sometimes there are even both, more than once, in the very same day.

* * * * * * * * * * * * * * * * * * *

About the Author

Pamela Jameson has written plays (including "Geneva" and "Blue Days Bright") short stories, newspaper articles and a screenplay ("Perfect Set Up").

As an actress, voice over performer and broadcast announcer, she has worked in Chicago, San Francisco, New York City and Minneapolis.

CPSIA information can be obtained at www.ICGtesting.com
Printed in the USA
LVOW081541180112

264477LV00005B/82/A

9 781414 023908